Hostile Witness

William Lashner is a Philadelphia-based lawyer. A graduate of New York University Law School and the University of Iowa Writers Program, he has served as a trial attorney in the criminal division of the United States Justice Department. He is currently working on a sequel to *Hostile Witness*.

WILLIAM LASHNER

HOSTILE WITNESS

HarperCollins*Publishers*

HarperCollins*Publishers*
77–85 Fulham Palace Road,
Hammersmith, London W6 8JB

Special overseas edition 1996
This paperback edition 1996
3 5 7 9 8 6 4 2

First published in Great Britain by
HarperCollins*Publishers* 1995

ISBN 0 00 649633 4

Set in Meridien

Printed and bound in Great Britain by
Mackays of Chatham plc, Chatham, Kent

For Pam Ellen,
whose love makes everything possible

Acknowledgments

For their generous help with this manuscript I wish to thank Dr Barry Fabius, Richard Goldberg, Pete 'The Tick' Hendley, David Howard, Alan Stern, Matt Roshkow, Marilyn Auerbach and Lewis Goodrich, who spoke Yiddish at home with his parents, my great-grandparents. I also wish to thank Jim Salter for teaching me much and my agent, Ray Lincoln, and editor, Judith Regan, for turning me into a professional. My mother and father have been my most ardent advocates since I crawled out of my playpen, and I continue to thank them greatly for their love and support, grammatical and otherwise. Finally, all my gratitude and love to Pam, Nora and Jack for filling my life.

Perhaps the only true dignity of man
is his capacity to despise himself.

GEORGE SANTAYANA

PART ONE

Indictment

1

What I have learned through my short and disastrous legal career is that in law, as in life, the only rational expectation is calamity. Take my first case as a lawyer.

There were three of us at the start, fresh out of law school, hanging up our shingles together because none of the large and prosperous firms in Philadelphia would have us. We were still young then, still wildly optimistic, still determined to crack it on our own. Guthrie, Derringer and Carl. I'm Carl. All it would take, we figured, was one case, one accidental paraplegia, one outrageous sexual harassment, one slip of the surgeon's knife, one slam-bam-in-your-face case to make our reputations, not to mention our fortunes. We were only one case away from becoming figures of note in the legal community that had so far left us out in the cold. But before that grand and munificent case came walking through our door, we were sitting with our feet on our desks, reading the newspapers, waiting for anything.

'I've got something right here for you, Victor,' said Samuel R. Sussman, dropping a document on my desk. He was a bellicose little man who leaned forward when he talked and did annoying things like jab his finger into my chest for emphasis. But he was family.

The document was a demand note, personally guaranteed by a Winston Osbourne, representing a debt of one million dollars. Seven figures was two figures more than anything I had ever seen before.

'I picked up this baby at a discount,' said my Uncle Sammy.

'What exactly do you want me to do with it?'

3

'Collect it,' he said with a finger jab. 'Osbourne says he's broke and not going to pay me a cent. Get what you can off this society *schmuck*, and whatever you find keep a quarter for yourself. You're getting married in the spring, right?'

'That's the plan,' I said.

He winked. 'Consider this my wedding gift.'

That was how my first case out of law school came to be a collection. I had not intended to use my degree to collect debts, I had not gone to law school so I could most effectively foreclose on the houses of the poor, but at the start I was desperate for anything. And besides, Winston Osbourne was not your usual deadbeat.

He was the scion of an old Protestant family, born to wealth, to society, given every advantage withheld from me, and through talent, luck, and sheer perseverance he became bankrupt. Tall, finely manicured, with a prosperous round face and sincere thin lips, he was of the Bryn Mawr Osbournes, an old and revered family, blue of blood, properly Mayflowered through a line of cousins, listed with the Biddles and the Ambers and the Peppers in the *Social Register*. In every expression, in every gesture, Osbourne's breeding showed. He looked like a somebody, one wasn't sure exactly whom, but a somebody who was a something and I guess that was how he managed to borrow so much money on his personal guarantee, money he invested in a huge tract of undeveloped land in Whitpain Township, seeking to reap the miracle benefits of subdivision. 'Real estate is the only sure thing,' he used to say, jaw locked, chin up, 'because they simply can't make any more of it.' As he strode across his glorious acreage in Whitpain Township, planning the location of the fine luxury homes he would build there, he must not have noticed the strange foul liquid, pale and sulfurous, like the earth's own bile, seeping into each of his footprints. Within six months of buying the property Winston Osbourne faced environmental catastrophe, and within a year he was in utter default.

4

'So you're the grubby little shyster who's chasing my money,' Winston Osbourne said to me when I first hauled him into my office in search of his assets. He was wearing a perfect gray suit, Gucci loafers, his sandy hair was trimmed close and neat, a gold Rolex flashed from beneath his cuff, and he actually said that. Well, not in those exact words, maybe, but that's what he was thinking. It was as clear as the cleft in his chin. What he actually said was, 'I've lost almost everything I ever had, Victor, and what little I have left is judgment proof. But I'm willing to pay you ten thousand dollars to end this. Believe me, Victor, that is the most you'll ever get from me.'

I rejected his offer, and though I had a chip with which to bargain him higher, to Jew him up as it were, I thought the wiser play was to hold onto it, to flash it elsewhere in an effort to pry loose the entire million. I had no intention of letting him off the hook that was buried deep within his properly locked jaw. Winston Osbourne represented something to which I knew I could never ascend but my exclusion from which I could never quite accept. His old-line family name, the glorious prospects handed him at birth, his natural charm, even his bland sandy good looks, I resented it all, and for all of it he would pay. That was why that very day the process server was delivering a subpoena to Osbourne's house in exclusive Gladwyne, ordering his wife to appear in my offices for deposition. I had plans for Mrs Osbourne.

She was a handsome woman, elegant tweed suit, skin surgically tight around her blue eyes, pearls, hair that was done, I mean really done, a hundred and forty dollars' worth of done, and I had her just where I wanted her, in our conference room, across the table from me, required to answer all my questions and sworn to tell the truth. She had chosen to come without counsel, which pleased me.

'How many cars do you and your husband own, Mrs Osbourne?' I asked.

'Three,' she said in a reedy, masculine voice. 'There is the station wagon.'

'That's a Volvo, right?'

'Right,' she said. 'It is a Volvo. Then there is the blue sedan.'

'A BMW?'

'From your tone of voice it sounds like a crime, Mr Carl.'

'And the other?' I asked.

'A vintage car my husband maintains. His toy, really, but quite valuable. It was his father's.'

'A Duesenberg.'

'Yes, that's right. We have an old Lincoln, for transporting our dogs to the shows, but that's hardly worth anything anymore. It's almost four years old.'

'So that makes four cars total.'

'Yes, I suppose,' said Mrs Osbourne.

'And in whose names are the titles to these cars?'

'Mine and my husband's.'

'Even the Duesenberg?'

'Yes, Mr Carl,' she said, confidently stroking her pearls. 'Everything is in both of our names and, as you know, I've signed nothing.'

I knew that, yes I did. In Pennsylvania, property owned by a husband and wife together cannot be grabbed to satisfy the individual debts of either, so long as they remain married. Mrs Osbourne, as best as I could determine, owed nothing to no one, not even to American Express. She had not guaranteed the loan and therefore all property she owned jointly with her husband was safely hidden from my grasp, so long as they remained married. And everything Winston Osbourne owned, his house, his cars, his bank accounts, even his damn Rolex, everything he owned he owned jointly with his wife. Well, almost everything.

'You own a house in Gladwyne, Mrs Osbourne, is that right?'

'Yes. The title is in both of our names.'

'Has the house been appraised?'

'For insurance purposes, yes. It was appraised at two and a half million dollars. But that is our house, we live there, we raised our children there, we would never think of selling.'

'You're aware, aren't you, Mrs Osbourne, that your husband owes Mr Sussman a million dollars.'

'I am aware that Mr Sussman is a speculator who bought that note for an absurdly low amount and now wants to grab his handful of flesh. My husband is a wonderful man, Mr Carl, and I love him very much. But he is not the cleverest of businessmen, not as sharp, I am sure, as your Mr Sussman. Anyone who lends my husband money does so at his own risk.'

I actually admired Mrs Osbourne as she sat in our crummy little conference room and so bravely defended her husband's standard of living. If I was in less need of my twenty-five percent share of Winston Osbourne's cash I might have thought twice about what I was planning to do. But even after a second thought I would have continued. My investigation had uncovered information of which Mrs Osbourne might not have been aware and of which I assumed it was my duty to apprise her.

'You own a property in Aspen, is that right, Mrs Osbourne?'

'A condominium, yes. The children love to ski.'

'And that is in both of your names?'

'Of course.'

'And there is the property in Palm Beach.'

'Yes, but that is not ours. That is owned by Winston's mother. Winston's grandfather built it, it is a fabulous place, really. Have you been to Palm Beach, Mr Carl?'

'No.'

'Where do you winter?'

'In front of the television.'

'I see. Well, the house in Palm Beach is not ours. We are permitted to use it, but when we are there we are guests. My understanding is that Winston's mother has willed it to Winston's brother, Richard.'

'So my patience would not be rewarded.'

'No, I'm afraid not. The entire family is aware of Winston's current troubles. Whatever is to be left is being left to the children. Winston has made you an offer, has he not?'

'And there is the boat,' I continued, ignoring her comment about the offer. 'You own a boat.'

'Yes.' She sighed. 'He named it after me. We leave it in Florida.'

'How big is the boat?'

'Something like forty feet, I'm not sure. Winston is the sailor. He is quite dashing in his white ducks and blue blazer.'

'In whose name is the boat titled?'

'Isn't this getting repetitious, Mr Carl? It is in both of our names. Everything is in both of our names.'

'Including the condominium in Atlantic City?'

'We don't own a condominium in Atlantic City.'

'Are you sure?' I said. 'There is a condo in a building right on the Boardwalk titled to Winston Osbourne. Let me show you a copy of the deed. I'll mark this P12.'

'There must be some mistake, you must be thinking of another man. We don't own a condominium in Atlantic City.'

'The person living there identified your husband as the owner.'

'I'm not aware of a condominium in Atlantic City.'

'Well, this person living there now says she doesn't pay rent to Mr Osbourne, and I was wondering if she paid the rent to you. Any such rent would be attachable on behalf of Mr Sussman.'

'No, of course I am not receiving the rent.'

'Perhaps you know the person living in your husband's apartment, a Miss LeGrand?'

'No.'

8

'Let me show you a picture. I'll mark this P13.'

'What is this? This is a brochure of some sort.'

'Yes, for a gentlemen's club called the Pussy Willow. Why don't you look through it. I'm referring to the section about the exotic dancers. Let me show you. The woman right there.'

'Tiffany LeGrand?'

'Oh, so you do know her,' I said, even though the shaking of her head, her dazed eyes, opened brutally, unnaturally wide, the death grip with which she now held onto her pearls, all of it stated with total clarity that no, no, she did not know her, had never heard of her, no.

I ran into Winston Osbourne again the gray and tremulous fall of which now I speak, a full six years after I had begun my relentless search for his final dollar. Halfway up 21st Street from Chestnut, just before my small and decrepit office building, yawned an alleyway. There was a stink to that alley, it was where the dumpsters were stored for the buildings on either side; it smelled of fish bones from the seafood restaurant on 22nd Street, of rotting vegetables from the Korean grocery beneath my office. Two homeless men shared the alley as sure as if they had signed a lease. They pissed in the entranceways of all the surrounding buildings, like wolves marking their territory. They panhandled, drank out of brown paper bags, shouted obscenities when the mood struck, and sometimes actually worked by carrying a sandwich board for Condom Nation, a prophylactic store, back and forth in the neighborhood. Every time I walked up 21st Street, I accelerated as I approached the alley, keeping my eyes straight and my shoulders hunched, trying to avoid any contact with my neighbors. I had just passed the gap one night that fall when I heard my name being called and felt a grab at my arm.

I whirled away from the contact, expecting to see one of the homeless men, but who I saw instead was Winston

9

Osbourne. His raincoat was grimed, his hair long and stringy, his once prosperous face now drawn and sallow. His fingernails struck me particularly; where they had been manicured and glossy they were now long, yellow, opaque with ridges. They were the fingernails of a corpse.

'Victor,' he said, his voice still dripping with superiority. 'We've been discussing you, Victor.'

'You should have your lawyer contact me, Mr Osbourne,' I said, staring at his nails. 'I can only speak to your lawyer.'

He took a rolling step toward me. There was a limp now that hadn't been there before. 'Yes. But you see, I couldn't afford to pay him.' He took another step forward. 'Since the divorce I've gone through a difficult time, Victor. Much toil, much trouble. But I'm certain I can see my way clear of it now.'

'That's good, Mr Osbourne.'

'But I need to open a bank account, Victor, a local account for business purposes, and every time I try you end up attaching the funds. This has become very inconvenient for me.'

'With interest, Mr Osbourne, you still owe Mr Sussman almost nine hundred thousand dollars.' My gambit with his wife had not worked as well as I had intended. Osbourne, sheared in the divorce settlement, had been able to secrete most of what little his wife's lawyer had left him before I could file my attachments. Foreign bank accounts, straw-man holding companies. He was much better at hiding money than at making it.

'I'm aware of exactly all that I owe Sussman,' said Winston Osbourne. 'And I do wish I could pay him back for everything. You too, Victor. In fact, plans are being laid this very instant to pay you back. But I need to open a bank account. I can't revive my prospects without a bank account, now can I, Victor?'

'Have you talked to a lawyer about declaring bankruptcy?'

'Yes, of course. But I'm an Osbourne, Victor, something you can't begin to understand.' He shuffled his feet uncomfortably. 'And not all my debts are dischargeable, I've been told.'

'What do you want, Mr Osbourne?'

'I want you to leave me alone. All I'm asking is for you to behave reasonably. This is your last chance. I'm willing to pay you to leave me alone.'

'How much?'

'Ten thousand dollars, like before. But, unfortunately, nothing for at least a year.'

'Mr Osbourne, you still have a vintage Duesenberg hidden somewhere. I believe you have money stashed in the Cayman Islands, as well as in certain Swiss banks. I understand you recently traveled to Florida, out of season, yes, but still Florida. Frankly, I think you can do better, Mr Osbourne, than a slim promise of maybe ten thousand dollars to be paid in a year.'

'You can't know how difficult it's been for me since the divorce.'

'Florida. The Sunshine State.'

His head dropped slightly. 'My daughter insisted I go with her.'

'Where is your Duesenberg, Mr Osbourne?'

'It's not worth anything anymore. It's too old, I haven't been able to keep it in repair. For your own good, Victor, take my offer.'

'Turn your car over to the sheriff, Mr Osbourne, and we'll talk.'

I walked away from him, toward the door of the building, when I heard him shout, 'By God, man. I just want to be able to open a damn bank account like a human being.'

I couldn't erase the image of Winston Osbourne and his fingernails from my mind for the whole of that season. There was a time in his life when the wealthy, handsome, socially prominent, socially registered, socially social

11

Winston Osbourne was everything I ever wanted to be. Now, as I struggled with the frustrations in my life, he was everything I feared I would become. The case we had been waiting for, the slam-bam-in-your-face case, had never come, and we too now had bills we couldn't meet, dunning letters came by the bushelful, we couldn't pay our secretary week to week, not to mention the office rent. One of my partners had already bailed and I couldn't really blame him, though I did. Six years out of law school and I was flat-out broke, one step up from the grimed broken figure I saw outside my office. I had once bitterly resented Winston Osbourne for all he was born to, but now I feared falling to his depths and so I resented him all the more. If he wanted to open a bank account that meant there was money and if there was money, by God, I would get my hands on it. Every last dollar, you bastard, every last dollar until you die.

I see now that I was suffering a profound weariness that autumn. The disappointments of my life had worn me down, not to mention that I was alone and lonely and had been both for far too long. Whatever optimism I had once held had been supplanted by a deep and gnawing resentment of everyone and everything. Then in that sad gray fall there finally arrived the chance for which I had been waiting. It was an opportunity rooted in murder, premised on betrayal, an opportunity that required the suspension of all I once held sacrosanct, but still there it was. And the only question was whether I was man enough to pay its price.

When I think back upon that season I see its inauguration in the apparitional appearance of the ruined Winston Osbourne, but from there it spun furiously out of control. It was the season of my opportunity, yes, but also a season of corruption, of treachery, a calamitous season of self-delusion and abnegation. Most of all it was a season of love, a sweat-soaked love that still leaves me gasping when I awake with a start in the middle of the night and remember. It was a season that promised my most desperate dreams and stroked my deepest fears.

It was fall in Philadelphia.

2

One Liberty Place was a huge granite and glass rocket that blasted beyond the staid and squared-off Philadelphia skyline until it lost itself in smoky autumnal skies, the highest, grandest, most prestigious building in the reviving City of Brotherly Love. Which explained why the law firm of Talbott, Kittredge and Chase had leased the fifty-fourth, fifty-fifth, and fifty-sixth floors for its offices even before construction was completed. Talbott, Kittredge and Chase was the city's most entrenched law firm. It was the home of congressmen and mayors; it had yielded six judges to the Third Circuit Court of Appeals and one to the Supreme Court. It was the dream of every law student who sought the brightest of the golden rings the law had to offer. Only the best was good enough for Talbott, Kittredge and Chase.

I applied for a position at Talbott, Kittredge as a second-year law student. I wrote a spiffy letter and goosed my resume until I didn't recognize myself on its crisp ivory paper. I was not law review and my grade point average was merely mediocre, but still I sent my application off with a queer confidence, sure that my true quality would shine through the flat black type, and for all I know it did. But only the best was good enough for Talbott, Kittredge and Chase. I didn't even rate an interview.

I wasn't consciously thinking of this rejection as I walked through the great stone lobby of One Liberty Place and stepped onto the marble-walled elevator seven years after sending off that letter, but as I rose to the fifty-fourth floor my resentment rose with me, and not just a resentment of Talbott, Kittredge and Chase. There was Dechert Price

& Rhoads, there was Morgan, Lewis & Bockius, there was Rawle & Henderson, White & Williams, there was Drinker, Biddle, and Reath. There was even Wolf, Block, Schorr & Solis-Cohen. Out of law school I applied to the top twenty-five firms in the city and they all passed on my offer to slave in their libraries and work outrageous hours so their partners could become obscenely rich. Cut adrift, I was forced to stoop lower than I could ever have imagined and work for myself.

By the fall of my visit to Talbott, Kittredge and Chase there were only two of us left in our sad little firm, we were now merely Derringer and Carl. Our third partner, Guthrie, had fled. Seeing the inevitability of our failure, Guthrie had found himself a rich girl with family connections and had ridden her name to a job with Blaine, Cox, Amber & Cox, one of the fine old firms that had initially rejected us all. Where he found his young and prosperous wife, now Lauren Amber Guthrie, was in my bedroom, which made his leaving for the money and the prestige and the wood-paneled offices of his new employer particularly galling. The bastard left without a backward glance and he took our best cases with him. That left just Derringer and me and the bills we couldn't pay and the files Guthrie didn't think were worth stealing. One of those files was *Saltz v. Metropolitan Investors*, in the service of which my resentment and I were rising like a firecracker to the fifty-fourth floor of One Liberty Place.

The elevator opened on a broad and open lobby, tastefully floored with a rich wood parquet and furnished with antique couches. TALBOTT, KITTREDGE & CHASE read the glossy brass letters tacked above the receptionist's desk. Two of the walls were of glass, offering killer views of the city south and east into New Jersey, with the blue sweep of the Benjamin Franklin Bridge spanning the breadth of the Delaware. The other walls were paneled in cherry, waxed and buffed to a military shine. But it was not those walls that were most impressive, nor the huge oriental carpets nor the couches nor the fine wood cocktail tables nor the gorgeous blonde receptionist who smiled warmly at me the moment I stepped off the elevator. What was most impressive was the enormity of the space itself, a breathtaking expanse bigger than a basketball court, a tract with no purpose other than projecting an image of elegance and wealth and power at fifty bucks a square foot. I couldn't help myself from doing the math. With what they spent each year on that lobby alone they could buy me five times over.

'Victor Carl to see William Prescott,' I said to the receptionist.

'Fine, Mr Carl. Take a seat and I'll tell him you're here.'

I stepped toward one of the couches and then turned back to the receptionist, who was already on the phone. She was a strikingly beautiful woman, this receptionist. The kind of woman who should only exist in perfume ads or on car show platforms. Her hair was pale and windswept, as if even while I stood in the enormous calm of that lobby, she was perched on the deck of an ocean yacht.

'Do I know you?' I asked. That was my line at the time, though it has since been discarded, like all the others, due to continued and unmitigated failure.

She looked me over carefully and then gave a light toss to her oceanic hair. 'No, I don't think so,' she said.

'It was worth a try.'

'Not in this lifetime, Mr Carl,' she said with a look that exiled me to one of the couches at the far end of the lobby.

But she was right, of course. Women like that did not exist for guys like me, they existed for the wealthy, the witty, the thrillingly articulate, for ballplayers and movie stars and presidential aides. And, of course, they were for adorning the offices of those brilliant firms like Talbott, Kittredge and Chase that refused to let me join their ranks. Oh man, I hated this place, I hated it so bad I could taste it.

'Mr Carl,' said a pretty, sharp-suited woman who had crossed the broad expanse of lobby to the couch where I was sitting. I had been waiting for half an hour, pretending to be interested in a copy of the *Wall Street Journal* I picked off one of the cocktail tables in the pathetic hope that the receptionist might mistake me for a corporate client checking on the value of his stock options. 'Come with me, please,' the woman in the suit said. 'I'll take you to Mr Prescott's office.'

I followed her up a flight of stairs and through twists and turns of broad hallways. I passed desks of grim secretaries typing efficiently into their word processors and caught glimpses of well decorated rooms from which worried associates darted back and forth. There was a hum of activity in those offices, a melange of sound emanating from the fluorescent lights, from the computer fans, from the laser printers squeezing out page after page after page, from the incessant soft ring of the phones and quiet voices explaining that Mr Wilson or Ms Antonelli or Mr Schwartz was on another line but would get right back to you. To a lawyer the sound was of more than just run-of-the-mill office activity. It was the sound of billable hours, it was the sound of money. It was not a sound I heard too often. In our hallway what I heard instead was the hush of financial desperation.

She ushered me into a large corner office, an office bigger than my apartment. The view stretched south and west. Straight ahead Broad Street ran like a mighty river to Veterans Stadium in the distance, and to the right I could see old Franklin Field and the campus of the University of Pennsylvania, whose law school, along with Harvard's and Yale's and Stanford's and NYU's and all the other top ten's, had rejected my application. Prescott's office was wood clad, like a judge's chambers, furnished with an elegant living room set at one end, a long oak table piled with briefs and exhibits in the middle, and a large, gilded desk in the windowed corner, with two tapestry-covered chairs before it and a low wooden credenza behind it. Across one of the walls was a flurry of framed photographs, pictures of mayors and congressmen, senators and presidents, each smiling as they stood next to a tall, stern-faced patrician, the photographs inscribed across the bottoms. On the far wall, above the living room set, hung a large neorealist painting of two boxers circling each other against an angry yellow background. The boxers' bodies were clenched, they peered over their gloves, waiting for the moment to explode into violence. The painting was as tense as a coiled spring and the eyes of the fighters were filled with hate. It was a litigator's painting.

'Mr Prescott will be right in,' said my guide. 'Make yourself comfortable.' She gestured at one of the chairs before the desk and I sat like a trained puppy.

On the credenza was a picture of the perfect family, three smiling beef-fed kids, a pretty wife, the tall patrician once again. In another the children were older, the wife wider, they stood before a beautiful country home with a wide veranda surrounded by thickly leafed trees, the patrician now in a wicker chair with a newspaper and a pipe. In that sad fall of my life such teeming family bliss seemed the most remote of all the ambitions I had so far failed to achieve.

I had never met William Prescott III but I had heard of him, everyone had. He was a great man, this William Prescott, the pride of his old and revered family. Skull and Bones at Yale, the law review at Harvard, he was a former deputy attorney general, a former ambassador to some obscure country in South America, a former Chancellor of the Philadelphia Bar. He was a pillar of the Republican Party and served on the boards of the Art Museum, the Free Library, the Philadelphia Orchestra. And now he was the top trial lawyer, the prime rainmaker, the managing partner at Talbott, Kittredge and Chase. One had to wonder what price he had paid for such success. He had everything a lawyer could ever want, but was he happy? Well, to tell from the pictures, he was ecstatic. I had never met this William Prescott but already I despised him.

'Victor, thank you for coming up to see me,' said a grayer version of the man in all the photographs.

I stood quickly, like a thief caught in the act, when William Prescott swept into the room. He entered like an emissary from some great nation-state. Very tall, very thin, with narrow lips and high prominent cheekbones, he peered from beneath bushy black eyebrows with blue eyes of startling clarity. He was not a classically handsome man, his nose was too long and his lips too thin, but he was a compelling presence, the very image of integrity. He wore a navy blue pinstriped Brooks Brothers suit, a banker's suit, which he kept formally buttoned as he reached out in greeting. My hand was swallowed by his. Despite his slenderness, I had the unpleasant sensation that had he wanted to squeeze my hand until the bones crumbled he could have.

'You know Madeline Burroughs, Victor, I'm sure,' he said as he led me to the living room set beneath the painting of the boxers.

I hadn't seen her there, my attention drawn so completely to Prescott and his presence. 'Yes, of course.'

'Hello, Victor,' said Madeline. She was a round-faced, frumpish woman who dressed and acted like a spinster though still in her twenties. She smiled awkwardly for a moment; it was like a fist opening and closing.

'Sit down, please, both of you,' said Prescott. His voice was precise, graveled with age but still charmingly formal, like the wide unpaved driveways leading to Versailles. He came from the same world as Winston Osbourne and that was in his voice too, but where Osbourne's voice betrayed all his innate snideness, in Prescott's it was well hidden if it existed at all. I sat in one of the easy chairs, he sat directly across from me on the couch, leaning back and crossing his legs in a way that put me immediately at ease. Madeline sat tensely in the bend of the couch off to the side.

19

'I may call you Victor?' he asked.

'Yes, sir.'

'Normally I love the autumn, don't you? But the grayness of the skies this year takes all the pleasure out of it. It might be time to visit our Miami office.' His blue eyes smiled at me and then turned cold. '*Saltz v. Metropolitan Investors*, Victor. That's why we're here today. How long have we been tangling over this case?'

'Three years, sir,' I said. The 'sir' came instinctively, drawn out by his very demeanor and appearance. He seemed to accept my deference as his due.

'You've been hanging on all that time like a bulldog. Three years on a complaint not worth the filing fee. A bulldog. Good for you, Victor. Now Madeline here, one of our toughest litigators, has filed four motions to dismiss but the judge has kept it alive out of mercy.'

'Judge Tifaro is too timid to make a decision,' said Madeline, breaking into the discussion.

'What you're both trying to say,' I said, 'is that all your attempts to kill our case have failed.'

'Yes,' said Prescott, giving me an appraising look. 'That is it exactly.'

Saltz was the weakest of those cases my ex-partner Guthrie left behind when he fled our firm on his way to success. A real estate limited partnership had gone bad, as they all seemed to have gone bad, and Guthrie had convinced the investors to sue those who had syndicated and sold the deal. There was a lengthy complaint with wild allegations of fraud and conspiracy. We had the case on a one-third contingency. I had thrown away a pot of money investigating only to find that there was no real evidence of anything other than stupidity on the part of all involved. My investigation wasn't helped by the fact that a crucial witness, the accountant who prepared the prospectus, a weasel named Stocker, had disappeared, taking certain of his clients' trust funds with him. Without him we had nothing but a hope that we could bluff our way into a settlement. Which was why I was there, to take one last look at my hand, to press my lips together, to look around the table and back at my hand and then to raise, confidently, in the faint chance the bastards would fold. Not likely. I had been asking for half a million, hoping they'd give me a counteroffer in the mid-five figures, upon which I planned to leap.

'Would you like some coffee or a soft drink, Victor?' asked Prescott. He reached to a phone sitting on the coffee table between us and pressed a button. The pretty woman who had led me to the office immediately appeared. 'Janice, a coffee for me, please. And for you, Victor?'

'Coffee, black.' Janice left without taking a request from Madeline.

'We're not here to argue, Victor,' said Prescott, which was a lie, because that was precisely why we were there. 'The syndicators have asked that I take a more personal interest in this case as we approach the trial. Glancing through the file, I noticed your name wasn't on the complaint. It was filed by a Samuel Guthrie.'

'He was my partner, but he left the firm.'

'Yes. Joined Blaine, Cox, Amber and Cox, didn't he?'

'They gave him a very handsome offer.'

'Married an Amber, I understand. Their youngest, the pretty one. I was invited to the wedding but was overseas at the time.'

'I couldn't make it either,' I said, though I hadn't missed it because I was overseas. I think there was something on television I needed to see that night, *The World of Disney on Ice* maybe, or something.

'I suppose the marriage might have had something to do with the offer.'

'Something.'

'That leaves you with two lawyers now, is that right?'

'Yes, sir.' Prescott had done more than merely glance through the file.

'I assume Mr Guthrie took a number of his clients with

him,' he continued. 'But he didn't take this case. Tell us why not, Victor.'

'Because it barks,' said Madeline.

I glanced sideways at her and let out a soft growl under my breath.

'Do you know what the key to any successful law practice is, Victor?' asked Prescott.

I couldn't help my bitter smile. 'Obviously not, sir.'

'Objectivity,' he said, with a rich man's certainty. 'It's all too easy in this business to take positions that satisfy our emotions but that ultimately hurt our clients. It's all too easy to let our passions stir.'

I tried but failed to imagine passions stirring in the formal upright man before me.

'Now we've given you all our files and you've found nothing,' he continued. His graveled voice, still precise and formal, now gained a touch of anger, just a hint, but just a hint was enough to send me slinking back in my chair. 'Some minor discrepancies between the information we received and what went out in the prospectus, yes, but not enough to show a pattern. And you won't be able to prove reliance on the prospectus anyway. Nobody reads those things. You can be assured the jury will learn of the many charitable organizations our clients support, the many philanthropic boards they sit upon. And in the end the jurors will view your clients as fools with so much money they were willing to throw it away on any twisted tax shelter that promised they wouldn't have to pay their fair share. Frankly, Victor, if we go to trial we're going to bloody you, and you know it.'

He paused when the door opened. 'Ah, Janice.'

She came in with a large silver tray and laid it upon the low table. There was a silver coffeepot and two white china cups and a crystal creamer and a crystal sugar bowl with a fine silver spoon. On a doily set upon a china plate perched an array of fancy cookies. It looked as if the Queen were coming to join us. I was grateful for the respite as my eyes had begun watering. My eyes water whenever I am under attack, a condition that was hell in elementary school, and I was under attack now. In less than a minute Prescott had exposed every weakness in my case. As Janice poured for me, I tried to squeeze back the tears.

'The project never made a dime,' I said before taking a sip of coffee. It was so exquisite it startled me for a moment, rich and crisply bitter. I took another sip. 'As soon as you took our money it all went down the tubes. I'll make that very clear for the jury.'

'The real estate market died on us,' said Prescott. 'Everyone on the jury will know that. They can't sell their houses either.'

'Your projections weren't even close.'

'They were only projections. We never claimed we could predict the future.' He put a shrug into his voice. 'It was a business deal between businessmen that went bad. Business deals go bad every day without any fraud involved. We can go on all day like this, Victor, back and forth, but that's no way to find common ground. Our clients want to fight to the end.' Then he flashed the smile of a diplomat greeting an unworthy adversary whom protocol required him to flatter and said the words I had been waiting to hear. 'But I have convinced them that the economics are in favor of our working something out.'

I felt a thrill ripple through me just then, the thrill of a settlement on the horizon, of money in my bank. Without changing a card, my poker hand had grown brawny.

Keeping his eyes focused on mine, he said, 'Madeline, what were the most recent figures discussed?'

'Plaintiffs demanded half a million dollars,' she said through a smirk. 'We offered five thousand.'

'It hadn't seemed worth pursuing,' I said.

'Well, let's try, Victor,' said Prescott. 'Even if you won everything you'd win what? A million dollars?'

'We've asked for punitives.'

'Yes, and we've asked for sanctions for the filing of a

frivolous lawsuit. We'll say a million. You received tax benefits on the losses of about thirty percent, so let's put actual compensatory damages at seven hundred thousand. Now tell me honestly, Victor, since this is all off the record, at what do you put your chance of actually winning? Five percent? Ten percent?'

'Fifty-fifty?' I hadn't meant it to, but my answer ended up being phrased as a question.

'That's a joke, right?' said Madeline.

'Be reasonable, Victor?' said Prescott. 'We're trying to work together here. Let's put it at ten percent.'

'It's not worth seventy thousand dollars,' said Madeline.

'Ten percent, Victor? Seventy thousand dollars. What do you say?'

One third of seventy thousand dollars came to something like twenty-three grand, enough to pay off our firm's bills and make payroll and rent for the next month. I had to hold myself back from shouting yes, yes, yes, yes, yes. 'It's not enough,' I said. 'You couldn't try this case for less than a hundred thousand, and you still might lose. I'd go back to my clients with an offer of two hundred and fifty thousand.'

'Of course you would,' said Prescott.

'I told you it wasn't worth discussing,' said Madeline. 'Guthrie we could talk to, but Victor acts like he's on some crusade.'

'You're using my hourly rate against us, Victor,' said Prescott. 'That doesn't seem quite fair. Ninety thousand.'

'I don't set your fees, Mr Prescott,' I said, even as I figured. If we could pull in thirty thousand from this case, I thought, I could even take a draw, start to pay down my credit card bills. I put down the coffee cup so it wouldn't rattle as my nerves started to pop. 'For two hundred thousand we could settle this today.'

'One hundred thousand dollars, Victor. And we won't go higher.'

Madeline said, 'That's way too high for this frivolous piece of . . .'

'One-ninety,' I said, cutting her off.

Prescott laughed. It was a deep, genuine laugh, warm in its way. It was so authoritative a laugh that I had to struggle not to join in, even though he was laughing at me. 'No, we're not splitting the difference, Victor. One hundred thousand dollars, that's as high as we go.'

'That's not going to do it,' I said. But threes started to jiggle like belly dancers before my eyes. Thirty-three, three hundred, thirty-three. Thirty-three, three hundred, thirty-three. It had a golden sound to it, like bangles sweeping one against the other during a slow, seductive dance. Thirty-three, three hundred, thirty-three. And thirty-three cents. 'One hundred and eighty thousand,' I countered.

'You're disappointing me, Victor,' said Prescott. 'I thought we could reach an accommodation.' He leaned back again and looked away from me, toward the window and the view. 'I have instructed Madeline to begin trial preparations tomorrow. Once we start spending money on the trial, paying experts, compiling exhibits, organizing the documents, once we start all that, I can't offer the same amount. So this offer is only good until you leave this office.'

'I'll tell you what, Mr Prescott. For one hundred and eighty thousand dollars, we'll disappear. We won't say anything to the press, won't sully the perfect reputations of your clients. No nasty trial. Nothing. The end.'

He shrugged. 'That's all a necessary precondition in any event. One hundred thousand dollars.'

I stood. 'That's not enough.'

'I'll whip you in court, son.'

'You just might at that, sir.'

Prescott stared me down. I was supposed to turn to leave, that was the act, but the sound of those threes jangling bangling through my mind froze my feet in place and I stared back at him, waiting for him to save me.

'I'll tell you what I'm willing to do,' said Prescott. 'I hate doing this, I think I'm going too far, but you are a bulldog, Victor, and you don't leave me much choice. What I'm willing to do is give you one more number. This number is a blue light special, do you understand? I want to hear a quick yes or no. If it's yes we have a deal. If it's no we'll fight it out in court. Are you ready for the number, Victor?'

'Yes, sir,' I said.

'One hundred and twenty thousand dollars.'

The division was so easy it couldn't have been unintentional. Forty thousand dollars registered in my mind with the ringing clarity of a bell. In the blink of an eye I plotted my expenditures. Twenty thousand directly to the office, overdue salary to our secretary and receptionist, overdue rent, overdue use and occupancy tax, overdue dues due to the bar association. Blue Cross had been hounding us for money, as had West Publishing and Xerox, which had refused to service the machine because we were behind on our maintenance payments. All our copies came out badly streaked and gray, as if they were copies of copies of copies. We were short of stationery, manila folders, yellow pads; our postage meter hadn't been reset in months. Twenty thousand dollars disappearing like so much drifting paper into the abyss of our failing legal practice. We'd put five in the bank to take care of another month's nut, just in case, leaving fifteen grand to be split between Derringer and me, which, after paying overdue estimated taxes, would leave me with four thousand dollars. One of my credit cards was maxed, so I'd pay that down, and my student loans were deeply in default, maybe a payment or two would renew their patience, and I still owed my father the five thousand I had borrowed last year when things got very very tight.

'We have a deal, Mr Prescott,' I said.

He slapped his palms onto his thighs and stood, smiling warmly, pumping my hand like I was a new father. 'Splendid. Just splendid. Madeline,' he said without looking at her. 'Why don't you get to work right away drawing up the papers.' He said nothing more until she stood and, without saying farewell, left the office.

'I should get going too,' I said. 'Tell my clients the news.'

'Not just yet, Victor. You're tenacious, I'll give you that. A bulldog. Let's take a moment together. I might have a proposition for you, son.'

He put his arm around my shoulder. The gesture was so unexpected that I froze as if under attack.

'I might just have for you,' he said, 'the opportunity of a lifetime.'

Connie Mack, the ageless Philadelphia baseball magnate who coincidentally looked very much like William Prescott III, once said, 'Opportunity knocks at every man's door,' but I didn't believe it for a second. There were men and women who toiled all the days of their lives without getting a single chance. I knew them, I was related to them, I was one. I had been waiting for it all my life and still it had never come for me, never called my name, never knocked on my door, never slipped itself through my mail slot. Or then again, maybe the post office had simply misplaced it, along with that letter I'd been expecting from Ed McMahon. No, it was the great myth of America that this is the land of opportunity. For guys like me, I had learned painfully, there was no such thing as opportunity, only a grind to wear away our spirits as it stole the heart from our lives day by day. So I was naturally skeptical. When someone like Prescott whispered the word opportunity in my ear, it generally meant the opportunity for him to take advantage of me.

'A brilliant man,' said Prescott, gesturing toward a picture of himself standing beside a slouching President Nixon. 'It was an honor to work for him.'

'I'm sure it was,' I said. There were things I could say to him about Nixon the perjurer, the man who lied about his secret plan to end the war and then saturated Hanoi with his bombs, who resigned in disgrace and was saved from indictment only by presidential pardon, but this wasn't the moment.

'Oh, he made mistakes, of course,' said Prescott. 'But in my mind that gives him all the more stature. He is a tragic hero, a man brought to power and glory through his brilliant, slightly paranoid will and brought to ruin by the same. But while he was at the top of his ride, he was a damn good president.'

'I'm an admirer of Kennedy.'

'Oh, yes.' He stepped over to another picture of a very youthful William Prescott III shaking hands with a smiling Jack Kennedy. We were standing before his wall of photographs, a shrine, really, to himself, as Prescott introduced me to the greats and near greats who had known him. I listened politely, fighting all the while to restrain the giddy joy I felt about the settlement we had reached in *Saltz*.

'All charm and good looks, Kennedy,' continued Prescott. 'But a bumbler, really. He stumbled into the Bay of Pigs, almost fumbled us into a nuclear war over Cuba, and then put us into Vietnam. November 22, 1963, was a terrible day, but frankly I think the country was better off because of it.'

'Kennedy had vision,' I said.

'No, not really. What did he care about civil rights before King started grabbing headlines? Now Reagan had vision.' There was a large color photograph of Ronald Reagan with his arm around Prescott. 'He was a genuinely nice man, too. He wasn't the brightest, but he didn't have to be. There are a million smart bureaucrats in the federal government, that's not what we need at the top. But Reagan's vision was unrealistic. That's why of all the presidents I've known, the one I admire most is Bush.'

He guided me to a picture of himself with George and Barbara Bush. The Bushes were smiling warmly at Prescott, who was standing with a regal stiffness, staring straight into the camera.

'A fine man,' said Prescott. 'A great leader. A true pragmatist in a world of ideologues. He was betrayed by his own people. That's how the clown we have now slipped in.'

I voted for the clown, but this wasn't the moment to

bring that up either, though I did say, 'I'm not sure pure pragmatism is admirable in a politician.'

'Anything else is just diddling, Victor. If you don't concentrate on the practical consequences of your actions, what do you concentrate on, intent? Good intentions were not the problem with our presence in Vietnam, it was just that, practically, victory there was impossible. A quarter million French had been defeated by the Vietnamese, how did we think we could prevail? The only way to govern effectively is to look beyond the ideology, beyond the surface morality, right to the heart of the doing.'

'But what goals do you seek without an ideological framework?'

'Peace, prosperity, justice, equality. Life, liberty, and the pursuit of happiness. Goals are easy, everyone wants the same things, but a pragmatist won't be misled by a false ideology and won't let narrow restrictions on means get in his way. Lawyers are by their very nature pragmatists. Whether or not we're in ideological agreement with our clients, our job is to win for them within the rules, no matter how. Anything less is a violation of duty.'

'I like to think we're more than hired guns.'

'So, Victor, you show yourself to be a romantic. Very good.'

'I was wondering,' I said, trying to change the conversation to a safer subject. 'How soon do you think we can close on the *Saltz* settlement?'

Prescott laughed. 'Maybe I stand corrected. I'll have Madeline work the night on it. We can close as soon as your clients sign releases.'

'Terrific,' I said, trying to fight the smile. 'The sooner the better.'

'We'll do everything we can to accommodate you. Everything.'

Normally I hated Republicans, there was something oily and insincere about them. I didn't care much for weepy hearted Democrats, either, but it was Republicans who really set me off. Maybe it was that theirs was the party of big money and I had none. Maybe it was that their cure for every ill was a cut in the capital gains tax when I had never in my life had a capital gain. Or maybe it was just that when a Republican pulled you aside to explain that assault weapons were as wholesomely American as apple pie and DDT, or that ketchup really was a vegetable, the blather would all come out of a self-satisfied George Willian smirk that you would slug if you were on the fifth-grade playground. Normally I hated Republicans, but there was something about Prescott that I couldn't help but like: his formality, his honesty, the way he exuded integrity. There was about him and his portrait gallery an air of noblesse oblige that I admired. Most likely my newfound affection derived from the fact that he had just given me forty grand, but for whatever reason I felt the glow of good fellowship in his office, even as we disagreed on the political issues of the day.

'Come over here,' he said, leading me to his desk. 'Sit down for a minute, Victor.' He lowered himself into the deep maroon desk chair and leaned forward, hands clasped before him. I sat stiffly in one of the upholstered chairs.

'Now that your calendar has suddenly cleared for the next month,' he said, 'I might have an opportunity for you.' That ominous word again. 'I was impressed with the way you handled the *Saltz* case. Your tenacity. I read your briefs. Very solid. We pride ourselves on teaching our associates how to litigate here, but you can only teach so much. We can't teach how to spin gold from straw; it is either innate or it will never be learned.'

'Our case isn't mere straw.'

He waved away my comment. 'We've settled.' He clenched his fist and shook it at me with affection. 'Tenacity. Victor, I think you're a terrific lawyer, yes I do.' He looked at me as if he were deciding something about my face. 'Ever do any criminal work?'

31

'Some. DUI, a few drug cases that pleaded out. I tried one aggravated assault to verdict.'

'How did it go?'

'Fine, until the jury came back.'

'Juries can be like that. The only lawyers who never lose a case are the ones who won't try the tough ones. Do much federal work?'

'Yes, sir. It's the only way to get to a jury before the client expires from old age.'

'Ever appear before Judge Gimbel?'

'No, but I heard he's a tough old bird.'

'Yes, he is,' said Prescott. 'A little overdone for my liking, too.'

I rubbed my chin to wipe off whatever it was he was staring at. Then he leaned farther forward. His voice became conspiratorially soft. 'Jimmy Moore, the councilman.'

'I know of him.'

'He and his chief aide, Chester Concannon, are under indictment for extortion and racketeering.'

'Yes. I know that also.'

'Moore is accused of using his City Council post to try to extort a million and a half dollars from the owner of the nightclub Bissonette's.'

'That's a lot of dollars,' I said.

'Yes, it is. He's accused of actually getting five hundred thousand. He is also accused of brutally beating Zack Bissonette, the former baseball player who was also part owner of the club, because Bissonette had tried to interfere in the extortion plot. Finally, he is accused of burning down Bissonette's because the payments stopped. All very serious charges that, if true, would make Jimmy Moore a monster. I represent him.'

'Good luck,' I said, without really meaning it. From everything I had read about the case in the *Philadelphia Inquirer*, Moore was guilty as hell and going to spend many, many years in a federal prison. And the whole city knew that Bissonette, a retired second baseman who had been a darling of the Veterans Stadium crowd, was still in a coma from the beating.

'Frankly, Moore's politics are the exact opposite of mine,' said Prescott. 'But in court that doesn't matter. Now, Chester Concannon, the aide, was represented by my old friend Pete McCrae.'

'It's a shame what happened to him,' I said. McCrae was an obese Republican politico who had recently died in a Chinatown restaurant. They had thought it was a heart attack until they cut open his throat at the autopsy and found a large, fatty piece of duck lodged there. Dr Heimlich, I guess, was dining elsewhere that night.

'A tragedy,' agreed Prescott. 'But now Chester Concannon needs new counsel. I was impressed with the way you handled the *Saltz* case and I thought you might want the opportunity.'

'I'm flattered,' I said.

'You should be. Trial is in two weeks.'

'Wait a second,' I said. 'If trial's in two weeks I won't have time to prepare.'

'Everything you'll need we have here for you, the documents, copies of the government's tapes.' He gestured at the piles on his conference table. 'We've done all the discovery already and McCrae's files are readily available.'

'I'd be thrilled to handle it, Mr Prescott. But I would need more time. What's the chance of getting a continuance?'

'We don't want a continuance. For political reasons the government indicted too soon, hoping to affect this fall's election. Now they're stuck going to trial with an incomplete investigation. And Bissonette is still in the hospital, unable to testify. They're hoping he revives. We think, due to the weakness of their case, it's to our advantage to get to trial before he does. We've opposed every motion for a continuance and asserted our rights under the Speedy Trial Act. The government wants a delay but the judge is holding to the trial date so long as the defense agrees. We need someone who can get up to speed quickly and be ready to go in two weeks.'

'I can't be ready to try a major criminal case in two weeks.'

'Actually, you won't have to. McCrae, before his visit to Ying's Peking Duck House, was satisfied to let me present a joint defense on behalf of both defendants. He found, and I'm sure you will too, that if we stand together we can turn the government's case into cheesecloth. I believe we could be a very effective team, Victor. And if you're able to take this case, other work together could be arranged. I often used McCrae for outside counsel and gave him cases we couldn't handle ourselves because of a conflict. He built up quite a lucrative practice that way. You could, too.'

'I'm very interested in the other work, Mr Prescott, very, but I just don't think I can accept this case. The Rules of Professional Conduct won't allow me to take a case where I couldn't be adequately prepared.'

He pressed his lips together and then began writing on a pad. Without looking up at me he said, 'That's fine, Victor. We're not always ready to seize our opportunities, no matter how transient they may be. I understand completely. Janice will show you out.'

I waited for a moment, waited for him to look up and smile, waited for him to again tell me how good a lawyer I was and all that we could do together, but he didn't say another word, concentrating instead only on the pad upon which he wrote. After more than a few moments of waiting I rose and headed for his door.

'Did I mention the retainer,' he said as I turned the doorknob.

'No, you didn't.'

'Fifteen thousand dollars up front if you decide to take the case.'

'That sheds a new light on the offer,' I said, releasing

the knob from my grip.

'I thought it might.'

'Mostly, sir, it would be the honor of working with you.'

'Yes, I see. So I take it you're on board?'

I hesitated a moment, but not too long a moment. 'Yes, sir.'

'Terrific,' he said brightly and he smiled his charismatic smile that warmed me. 'The trial team is meeting Monday night, here, at six. You can meet your client then. Before the Monday meeting you can look at whatever evidence we have. I'll set up a room for you, say starting at ten.'

'Fine.'

'We have a status hearing before Judge Gimbel on Tuesday morning. I'll make sure your retainer is ready by then. By the way, Victor, what's your hourly fee?'

'One-fifty,' I said.

'You're going to make us look like chiselers by comparison. For this case your fee is two-fifty. Is that acceptable?'

'Perfectly.'

'It's great to have you on the team, Victor. This is a terrific opportunity for you, son,' he said, and I knew that it was. Prescott was offering me more than just a high publicity case in which my picture would make the papers and my name become known. He was offering to mentor me, to guide my career, to raise me to something more than second-rate. There was no telling what I could gain from his wise guidance and touching concern for my welfare.

'I understand,' I said, 'and I am very grateful for the chance.'

'Yes,' he replied, without a hint of credulity in his face. 'I believe that you are. And I have no doubts but that you'll come through for us.'

So maybe I had been wrong after all. Maybe this glorious land to which my great-grandfather had brought his family from Russia actually was the land of opportunity he sought and maybe this William Prescott III was the instrument

35

of that opportunity, along with whichever fate had lodged that chunk of roasted duck in fat Pete McCrae's throat. I still had my doubts, sure, but fifteen grand up front and two-fifty an hour did a lot of easing.

4

Beside a ragged door in a hallway atop a Korean grocery on 21st Street, south of Chestnut, hung a series of names spelled out in small chromed letters. There was VIMHOFF & COMPANY, ACCOUNTANTS, and beneath that PARALLEL DESIGN INC., and beneath that JOHN STEVENSON, ARCHITECT, and beneath that, oddly off-center from the rest, DERRINGER AND CARL, ATTORNEYS. The name of our firm was off-center because the first series of letters had been ripped off the wall, and hastily, too, if the presence of plastic nubs still imbedded in the drywall was any indication. A careful examination of the dirt shadows around the missing word revealed the name Guthrie. I won't deny that I had been the ripper and it had felt damn good, too, even as the sharp edges of that bastard's name bit into my flesh. When is betrayal not betrayal? When it is only business.

All the firms shared a receptionist, an older woman named Rita with a white streak in her blue-black hair and a blue streak in her voice. 'Any messages?' I asked her when I returned from my meeting with Prescott.

'Nothing worthwhile, Mr Carl. Surprise.' Her voice was pure New Jersey, like an annoying siren. 'Except that guy from the copier company called again. He started complaining to me, like I was the one who owed him the money. I told him to make a xerox of the invoice and send it in.'

I took the pink slips from my place in the message rack and shuffled through them. 'They don't want you to call it a xerox,' I said idly. 'It's a trade name.'

'Yeah, I know. But I love when they start explaining it over the telephone. He's sending you a warning letter and a xerox of their trademark policy. Vimhoff's looking for you,' she said.

'Is he here?'

'No, but he said he wants to talk with you Monday morning. How much rent do you owe?'

'I won't be in Monday morning.'

'That much?'

'A new case. Really.'

She didn't laugh, she gave off more of a snort.

I took my messages and followed the vinyl-papered hallway past Vimhoff's office, as neat and orderly as a row of numbers, past the large design office filled with the whirr of Macintosh computers, past the architect's office, door closed as always, until I reached the rear, where Ellie, our secretary, sat quietly at her desk, chewing gum, reading a magazine, guarding our three sad little offices. She was impossibly young, Ellie, very pretty in a Catholic school way, red hair, freckles, cute comic book nose, and always dressed inappropriately bright and sharp, as if each morning she was on her way to a christening. Guthrie had hired her right out of high school, had gotten her name from a nun, though when he left for his new firm he took with him Carolyn, our other secretary, the one who knew how to type. But Ellie had kept coming around even after her paychecks stopped, which was better than her knowing how to type. 'Where's Derringer?' I asked. 'I have news.'

'On the way back from Social Security.'

'How did it go?'

'It was the Cooperman case,' said Ellie in a tone that meant nothing else needed to be said. 'By the way, Mr Vimhoff's looking for you.'

'I know. I finally settled *Saltz*.'

'That dog?'

'Be polite.'

'Does that mean I get paid this month?'

'Just as soon as the check clears. By the way, Ellie, do me a favor. I ran into Winston Osbourne the other day and it got me thinking. Find out who Osbourne's daughter is, her name, I think she's married, and her address. Call Mrs Osbourne at the house. She'll know. Pretend you're an old friend.'

'Sure.'

'I've a hunch where we're going to find ourselves a Duesenberg.'

My office proper was a small dark place. I had once had plans for it. I was going to paint the walls an eggshell blue, lay down an oriental carpet, haul in a huge mahogany desk, hide the pale metal of the filing cabinets in a wood veneer. From the galleries on Walnut Street I was to pick a large landscape, Early American, epic and green, and hang it catercorner to the window. Plants, there would be tall leafy plants, and deep leather chairs for my clients to sit upon as I wove for them the sage legal advice for which I would become renowned. But the plans for my office, like the plans for my life, had dissolved before the relentless progression of my reality. My office now was a small dark place, cluttered with the detritus of a failing career – disorganized piles of meaningless paper, dusty stacks of long dead files. On the windowsill was the narrow brown spine of a wandering Jew who had settled down in death. There was desolation in my office that would not be eased by forty thousand dollars, only prolonged.

'Abington Cardiology.'

'Dr Saltz, please,' I said into the phone.

'Who's calling?' asked the receptionist.

'Victor Carl. He'll know what it's about.'

'One minute, please.'

There was a click, and then the soft sounds of Henry Mancini vibrating gently from a thousand strings, from a thousand and one, and then Saltz's slurry gangster voice.

'Hey Vic, hold on a minute, will you? I'm on the other line.'

'Sure.'

And once more the sweep of violins. I hated being placed

on hold. It was not the waste of time so much as the fact that my time was being wasted by someone else. The indignity of it. The not so subtle message that I was nowhere near as important as whoever was on the other line. I bet the President never got put on hold, nor football stars, nor billionaires, nor women with whippet bodies and deep blue eyes. Shady lawyers in failing firms with maxed credit lines got put on hold. And why did they pipe music through the hold line? *You're not important enough to deal with right now, but so your time won't totally be wasted* . . . I would have hung up then and there but I needed to talk to Saltz and I had nothing else pressing and, well, Saltz probably was talking to someone more important than me, a powerful and desperate patient in the middle of a heart attack receiving the vital information he needed to stay alive.

'Victor,' he said finally. 'Thanks for waiting. I was talking to my plumber. The money those guys charge, Jesus. What's up?'

'Good news,' I said. 'We got a settlement offer.'

'How much?'

'I met with a fellow named Prescott, the big hitter over at Talbott, Kittredge, who seems to have taken control of the case. We met for over an hour, yelling at each other, but I pushed him up to something great.'

'How much?'

'I got him to give us a hundred and twenty thousand.'

'And how much of that would I get?'

'There are eight of you with equal shares, so after our fee that would be ten thousand each.'

There was a pause where I waited for the congratulations to spill out my side of the receiver.

'Is that all?' he said in his rough, loose voice. 'What the fuck's that, that's nothing. I put a hundred and twenty-five grand into that piece-of-crap building and all I'm going to get out of it is a measly ten thou? They defrauded the hell out of me. I should be getting more than ten grand there,

Victor. I should be getting their balls on a plaque.'

'Lou,' I said quietly, 'if they wanted to stonewall and take us to trial, we'd lose.'

'A hundred and twenty-five grand I lost. Did you ever find that accountant who did the numbers in that bullshit prospectus? What's his name?'

'Stocker,' I said. 'Still missing. The FBI is looking for him, too.'

'I bet he's got stories to tell.'

'Not in time to help us. He's probably on the beach somewhere in Brazil, doing the samba with dark-skinned women and laughing at us.'

'I hate to think I'm getting taken again here, Victor. Maybe we should just throw the dice and let those bastards fade us, see what the jury comes up with. Did you talk to the other guys?'

'I wanted to talk to you first.'

'Set up a meeting next week,' he said. 'We'll talk about it together. Maybe it will look better to me then. I got to go, the electrician's on the line and I don't want to put him on hold.'

'What is it, home improvement week?'

'We bought a house in Radnor. Two point five mil and the thing still needs to be gutted. Go figure. But you know what that's like, what am I telling you for?'

'Right.'

'I'll talk to you at the meeting next week.'

'Sure.'

What I hated most about the rich was not their money. I envied them their money, I coveted their money, but I didn't hate their money. What I hated was the way they pretended it was no big deal.

I went about returning my messages, unfamiliar names and numbers on little pink sheets. They involved bills, each and every one. There was a call from a computer specialist who had fixed the blink in our word processor, one from Little, Brown & Co. about payment for a book Guthrie had ordered before he left, one about a transcript in the *Saltz* case, which I had ordered but didn't expect to need any longer. To each I said I would check our records and get back to them and then tossed the pink sheet into the over-flowing wastebasket. Vimhoff was supposed to get our offices cleaned twice a week and I realized with a flash of lawyerly insight that the overflowing wastebaskets were my defense to being late with the rent. Constructive eviction. 'Clean the damn offices and we'll pay our rent,' I would say with a bite of indignation. That might work, at least until I tidied up the *Saltz* settlement. Ellie poked her head into my office and said she was leaving. I played with my time sheets a bit, fluffing up my hours, and waited to tell Derringer the news of our new case. I didn't have to wait long.

'So how did it go with the snobs at Talbott?' she said when she strode into my office without knocking and sat on a wooden bridge chair across from my desk.

'They threw money at me,' I said.

'No, really.'

Elizabeth Derringer was short and slight, with glossy black hair cut like a helmet around her head. She wore round glasses that made her look very serious, even when she smiled, but if you could see past the glasses and the sharp features you could see the glint of a vicious humor. I had met her in law school, where she had been attending nights while she did social work for the city. Her final year she quit her job to get enough credits to gradu-ate a semester early and that's when I met her. She was smarter than me, she was smart as hell, and tougher than burned beef, but she ended up with a night school degree and the firms that turned me down didn't hire from the night schools. They must have figured that if a law student was smart enough to join their firms, she was smart enough to figure out how to find parents who could afford to pay her tuition. But they missed a prize.

42

'They're giving us a hundred and twenty thousand to settle *Saltz*,' I said.

'Golly, we're rich. And for that dog yet.'

'If it goes through. Saltz doesn't think it's enough.'

'Tell him we have bills to pay,' she said.

'I'm setting up a meeting next week to nail it down. What happened with Cooperman?'

'Don't ask.'

'There's no way they were going to find him disabled because of a little ringing in his ear,' I said.

'Please, Victor, have some respect for the ill. Tinnitus. And he can't work if it's driving him crazy.'

'He's in demolition.'

'I'll win the appeal,' she said. 'I've got those SSI bureaucrats right where I want them.'

Beth was mugged once, in broad daylight, by a crackhead whose courage was stoked by a five dollar hit. He walked up to her, smiled, and then in one quick motion grabbed her purse strap and started to run. Beth held on. Even as the crackhead dragged her down the sidewalk she held on. She was raised in Manayunk, before it was discovered and gentrified. It's a hilly place, Manayunk, uneven streets, tough kids. She broke her wrist in the fall and scraped her face on the sidewalk, but still she held on. Finally he was the one who let go and ran from this crazed little woman he had dragged half a block, ran straight into a beige Impala with Jesus headlights. The police scraped him off the street. At the preliminary hearing he glowered at her through his bandages, trying to intimidate her out of testifying. She smiled sweetly and buried him.

'I guess I'm not going to convince you to drop the case,' I said.

'Nope.'

'What say we talk about it over a beer and a burger at the Irish Pub.'

'I can't. I'm going out tonight.'

'On a Friday night?' I asked. 'You have a date?'

'It's not a date, not really. It's a blind date. A blind date is more an interview with a prospective date, an exchange of resumes, silly chatter designed to test social skills, nothing more.'

'I was going to tell you about the new case I picked up today,' I said, a little jealous that she had someplace, anyplace, to go that night.

She stood up. 'Tell me tomorrow, I'm going to be late.'

And then she was gone.

I readied to leave and turned out my office lights and then sat down again in my chair to watch the shifting city light play out across the garbage cans in the alley. I could feel it all about me. It was inescapable, falling cold and hard from stars in the sky, dripping from the leafless trees along the polluted city streets, surging down in waves, swirling like the sea about me. The air melted in thick, heavy drops and the spots on the walls danced maniacally and the order of all things was pointlessness and despair and finally death. Its scent lay fetid in the air, rotten, musked, overpoweringly seductive, like the juice of a strange woman. It played across the sallow face of Winston Osbourne in his calamity, it grew despite the X-rays pumped through my father's lungs, it lay crouched and silent within my heart and infected everything I touched, my practice, my dreams, my relationships. I wanted to get out so bad, out of this life and its manifest pointlessness. I would do anything to get out, anything at all, anything. I was sick to death with the wanting.

When I was in junior high I was picked to perform a genetics experiment with different forms of fruit flies called drosophilae. In the back of the classroom I mated the red-eyed variety with the white-eyed variety and then determined the characteristics of the offspring. Drosophilae were perfect for the experiment because their lives were so short and their reproductive cycle so swift that in a very few days I could follow their genetic adventures through a number of generations. For the length of my experiment

44

they were like pets, and when I was supposed to etherize the final batch of offspring to get a precise count of the red-eyed and white-eyed descendants, a procedure that would inevitably kill a majority, I decided instead to release them. 'Go, my friends,' I said as I opened the small vials in which they had been bred. 'Be free.' And I watched as successive rows of my classmates waved distractedly at the air. I thought about my friends the drosophilae in those moments when I felt overwhelmed by the evocations of despair swirling around me and envied them their short, sentienceless lives. To fly, to suck at fruit, to mate and reproduce, all with absolutely no consciousness of their inevitable fate.

So what I did that night after Beth left me was what I did most every night. I stopped off at a storefront grill and ordered a cheese steak with ketchup and onions to go and took it home and ate it in front of the television with half a six-pack beside me. Whatever the night, there was always one show almost worth watching and I was able to stretch a whole night of mindlessness around that one show, running from *Jeopardy!* through prime time through the late news and the talk shows and finally the late late movie on UHF, until I'd fallen asleep on the couch, drugged by all I had seen. That Friday night was like every other night of what my life had become, and for the few blessed moments that I was caught like a science fiction hero in the power of that electron beam I lost whatever sentience I held and became as connected to the now of my life as the simple but noble drosophila.

5

Though I had never met Jimmy Moore, I knew his name. I knew thousands of names, actors and criminals, sports heroes and politicians, authors, rock stars, the silly little guy who sells suits on South Street. It is the names who rule the world, the Tina Browns, the Jerry Browns, the Jim Browns. They are the aristocracy of America and whatever their rank, and there is a ranking, from the national to the local to the almost obscure, it is the names who attend the best parties, screw the prettiest people, drink the finest champagne, laugh loudest and longest. Jimmy Moore was a local name, a businessman turned politician, a city councilman with a populist, anti-drug agenda that bridged the lower and middle classes. He was a name with aspirations and a loyal following. A name who would be mayor.

I spent the better part of Monday in the offices of Talbott, Kittredge and Chase listening to Jimmy Moore on the telephone. He wasn't on the telephone with me, of course, as I was not a name and thus not worth talking to. Instead he was on the phone with Michael Ruffing, a restaurateur whose flashy enterprises in the city had made him a local name among the city's well-cultured and whose phone at his night-club, Bissonette's, named after his partner Zack Bissonette, the currently comatose former second baseman, happened to have been tapped by the FBI. I sat alone at the foot of a long marble table in a huge conference room. Fine antique prints of Old Philadelphia lined the walls: Independence Hall, Carpenters Hall, Christ Church, the Second Bank of the United States. The carpet was thick and blue. A tray of soft drinks lay on a credenza behind me and I didn't have to pay six bits to open one, they were just there, for me. I can't help but admit that sitting in that room like an invited guest, sitting there like a colleague, gave me a thrill. I was in the very heart of success, someone else's success maybe, but still the closest I had ever come to the real thing. And there was a dark joy in my heart the whole of my time there because I knew that if all went right this could be my success, too. So I couldn't help smiling every now and then as I sat in that conference room with earphones on and a yellow pad before me, listening to a score of cassettes holding Jimmy Moore's taped conversations with Michael Ruffing.

Moore: Your plan for the riverfront is brilliant. Prescient. But I see problems in council.

Ruffing: Uh, like, what kinds of . . .

Moore: Jesus, Mikey, you got problems.

Ruffing: I don't need no more problems.

Moore: Every damn councilman gets a take out of the water going a certain way. That's why it still looks like the Bronx down there. What you need is a champion. What you need is a Joe Frazier.

Ruffing: Okay. I see that. That's who I need then, what I'm looking for.

Moore: Take Fontelli. Part of the waterfront's in his district, so he thinks the whole damn river's his pisspot.

Ruffing: I don't want Fontelli, you know. I've heard things.

Moore: They're all true. What have you heard?

Ruffing: He's, you know. What I heard. Connected.

Moore: Of course he is, Mikey. You know who he's married to.

Ruffing: I don't want them.

Moore: Of course not. Of course not. In for an inch and they're screwing your sister. Now I like

	your place, you know that. I'm in there almost every week, you know that.
Ruffing:	And you don't stint on the Dom, either.
[laughter]	
Moore:	Fuck no, you're either class or you're shit. Now I could help with this. We could help each other, Mikey.
Ruffing:	Okay, yeah.
Moore:	But the kind of influence you're talking about here, well, you know.
Ruffing:	Of course. That's, uh, assumed.
Moore:	But I'll be your Joe Frazier.
Ruffing:	What exactly are we talking about here?
Moore:	I'll send my man Concannon over to discuss arrangements.
Ruffing:	Give me an idea.
Moore:	He'll call you. You'll deal with him on everything.
Ruffing:	Sure, then.
Moore:	This is going to work out for everybody, Mikey. For everybody. Trust me. This project's going to take off like a rocket ship.

It was these tapes and certain subsequent events that were the basis for the government's case against Moore and Concannon. Ruffing's waterfront development plan was budgeted at $140 million, and Moore wanted a full 1 percent to propose and ensure passage of the enabling legislation in City Council. The government's theory was that Moore and Concannon were shaking down Ruffing for the million point four and that when Ruffing stopped paying after the first half mil they turned violent, first beating the hell out of Bissonette, the club's minority owner who had convinced Ruffing to stop the payments, and then burning down the club. Moore and Concannon had been indicted for violations of the Hobbs Act, RICO, the federal conspiracy laws, and there was plenty of evidence to back it all up. Ruffing would testify at the trial to an arrangement that had gone very bad, and there were reams of records, which I had not yet been able to examine, that purported to follow the trail of money from Ruffing to Concannon to Moore's political action committee, Citizens for a United Philadelphia, or CUP, as well as physical evidence relating to the assault. But most significant of all were Moore's own words, captured with startling clarity on the ferric oxide of the tapes.

Moore:	I don't understand the problem.
Ruffing:	We're going a different way is all.
Moore:	But we had a deal. A deal, Mikey.
Ruffing:	I'm not happy about it but I don't got no fucking choice. Bissonette found out about us.
Moore:	And I should care about that. He hit two-twenty life-time, Mikey, two-twenty. We can walk all over him.
Ruffing:	There are things about him I didn't . . . I got a new investor with a new plan.
Moore:	Don't do this, Mikey. You back out now, your project's dead. Dead.
Ruffing:	My new investor don't think so.
Moore:	It's that cookie baker, isn't it?
Ruffing:	Shut up. You were taking too much anyway, you know? You were being greedy.
Moore:	So that's it, is it, Mikey? I'm sending my man Concannon down.
Ruffing:	I don't want Concannon.
Moore:	You listen, you shit. You talk to Concannon, right? I ain't no hack from Hackensack, we had a deal. A deal. This isn't just politics. We're on a mission here, Mikey, and I won't let you back down from your responsibilities. You catch what I'm telling you here? You catch it, Mikey?

49

I worked through lunch, eating a tuna salad sandwich as I listened to the tapes. I had not even touched the six boxes full of documents when I felt a tap on my shoulder. I whirled around and saw standing behind me Prescott, tall, stern faced, dressed in his severe navy blue pinstripes. I nearly jumped when I saw him. He looked like a mortician. I took off the headphones and was disoriented for a moment by the Dolby quiet of reality.

'What do you think?' asked Prescott.

'I haven't been able to look at everything yet,' I said.

'But from what you saw. Be honest now, Victor.'

'Well, sir, to be honest, the tapes make Jimmy Moore out to be the archetypal grasping politician.'

'I knew you'd catch on,' he said as his stern features eased into merriment. 'That's exactly our defense. Come, Chester Concannon is waiting for us and Jimmy's on his way. Chester especially is anxious to meet you.'

'Fine,' I said, grabbing hold of my pad and following Prescott out the door. He led me through a maze of hallways and up a flight of steps.

'It's very important,' he said as I followed, 'that Chester agrees to your representation and to maintain our current strategy.'

'I'll do what I can,' I said, masking my apprehension. This, I knew, was the first crucial moment of my opportunity. I had never met Chester Concannon, had no idea what he looked like, what his manner was, but somehow I had to convince this stranger with his life on the line to hire me as his lawyer and to allow me to follow Prescott blindly.

Prescott brought me through another hallway and into a different conference room, just as elegant and imposing as the one in which I had spent the day, but this one filled with a pack of lawyer types. In the middle, sporting a ragged corduroy jacket, sat a rather ugly man who didn't fit. His brown hair fell scraggly to his shoulders and he scrunched fat fish lips between forefinger and thumb as he watched me walk into the room. I assumed he was Chester Concannon. You can always tell the client among his lawyers because he looks like the one who's been forced to pay for everyone else's worsted wool.

'I'd like you all to meet Victor Carl,' said Prescott when we stood together before the table. Prescott's arm rested like a father's on my shoulder. 'Victor is a terrific litigator and going to be a big help to us all.'

I smiled the smile I was expected to smile.

'So you're the mannequin,' said the ugly man in corduroy, his voice loud and sharp, like the bark of a Pomeranian.

'Excuse me,' I said.

'They said they needed a mannequin with a pulse and a clean tie to take over for McCrae,' he said. 'So I guess that's you, Vic. Except I see you don't have the clean tie. You got a pulse at least, Vic?'

I fought the impulse to check my tie and turned my head just enough so I could look at him sideways without letting him see the tears involuntarily welling. If this indeed was my client-to-be I was in deep trouble. 'Last time I checked,' I said.

'Good for you,' he said. 'Just take a shower in your wash-and-wear so you'll be presentable when you pose for the judge.'

'Victor,' said Prescott. 'I'd like you to meet Chester Concannon.'

I hesitantly reached out my hand toward the man in the corduroy but he remained seated, his thick lips back to being pinched by his forefinger and thumb. Next to him an African-American man in a tight fitting, expensive suit stood and took hold of my hand.

'Pleased to meet you, Mr Carl,' he said in a strong voice. Chester Concannon was boyishly handsome, with thin shoulders and strong hands. While his smile was bright, his suit was subdued and his tie striped and simple. 'I appreciate you joining our team.'

'And this,' said Prescott, gesturing to the man in the corduroy who had called me a mannequin, 'is Chuckie Lamb, Councilman Moore's press secretary.'

Chuckie Lamb gave me a sort of snorting nod and then leaned back in his chair until the chair's front legs tilted off the carpet.

'I've told both Chet and Jimmy all about you, Victor, and the tenacious job you did on the *Saltz* case,' said Prescott. 'They were both enthusiastic about your coming on board. This is the rest of our crew,' he said and introduced me to the Talbott, Kittredge contingent seated around the table, whose names I forgot the instant they escaped from Prescott's lips. They were finely dressed, perfectly groomed men and women, showily multicultural, as if cast by a politically correct producer for a television series about litigators. There was an Asian-American man and an African-American woman, and there was a blond guy with a perpetual smirk on his face. And then at the end of the table was Madeline Burroughs, who eyed me suspiciously, arms crossed, the fist of her face closed. It was the very picture of the sharp legal team of which I had always dreamed of being a part and on which I had always suspected, somewhere deep down, I didn't belong.

'Now Victor has spent the day looking through Pete McCrae's files and the materials provided us by the US Attorney's office,' said Prescott, 'and he assures me that he can be ready for trial in two weeks.'

'What a stunning surprise,' barked Chuckie Lamb. 'The mannequin is ready to pose.'

'That's enough,' said Concannon softly, and Chuckie Lamb quieted immediately.

'Victor's readiness,' said Prescott, 'means we won't require the continuance the government so desperately wants us to have.'

'I haven't looked at everything yet,' I said, glancing at Chuckie Lamb for a moment. 'But it shouldn't take me too long to get up to speed.'

There were smiles from all the bright young successes and I smiled back. I was an actor playing the part of a competent and experienced lawyer and doing quite well, I thought. And if they all didn't believe in what I was presenting they were acting quite well themselves, all except for Chuckie.

'Terrific,' said Prescott. 'But maybe, before we proceed any further, Victor should spend a few minutes alone with Chester.' He raised his eyebrows at me, giving me my cue.

'I guess we should see if you really want to hire me,' I said to Concannon with my most ingratiating smile. Chuckie Lamb laughed in my face.

Concannon and I were escorted to an open office. On my way there, without letting anyone notice, I checked my tie. Chuckie had not been lying, a glob of tuna had crusted on the edge. I rubbed it off, leaving a dark oily patch, streaked larger by my thumb.

I closed the door behind us and gestured for Concannon to sit in one of the chairs arrayed expectantly before some Talbott partner's desk. I sat on the tabletop. Behind the desk was a collection of swords and sabers and battle-axes, the metal edges gleaming. Another litigator's office.

'Mr Concannon,' I started, 'I thought we should talk a bit before you agreed to hire me or I agreed to represent you.'

'That's fine, Mr Carl.'

'Call me Victor,' I said.

'Victor or Vic?'

'Victor. I never liked Vic. It makes me sound too disposable, like a throwaway lighter or a ballpoint pen.'

He laughed at my old joke, which was good. He seemed a charming enough man, Chet Concannon, quiet and very polite. I told him I was sorry about what happened to Pete McCrae. I told him a little about myself, my experience, the highlights of my career, just a little about myself because there was only a little to tell. Then it was time for the defense attorney's lecture, so I paused, took a breath, and began. I gave him the talk about lawyer-client confidentiality, about how my job was not to find the truth but to defend him, and how if I learned the truth I was duty-bound to stop him from saying anything other than the truth on the stand.

'You mean stop me from lying,' he said, obviously amused.

'I know you might want to confess, the urge is understandable,' I said. 'And whatever you say remains with me, but you have to be aware that any such confession could have consequences as to our defense.'

There was more to it than that, of course. I could have gone on speaking for a good ten minutes, but after talking about his undoubted need to confess and seeing him sitting there, calm, composed, his face lacking the slightest indicia of an urgency to tell me anything, I stopped.

'I guess you've heard all this before,' I said.

'I guess,' he replied.

'Good,' I said, though I started to sweat a little. There was something about his composure that was unnerving. 'Now just a few questions. Have you ever been arrested before?'

'Yes,' he said without a wince. 'Before I met Jimmy I was involved with drugs and drug sellers. I was arrested often.'

'Were you convicted of anything?'

'Once of possession with intent to distribute a banned substance, to wit, cocaine, and twice of forgery. I supported my habit by check,' he said with a smile. 'Except the checks weren't always mine. None of this is a secret. I'm one of Jimmy's success stories, one of his saved souls. He likes to be able to point at us to show what is possible with drug rehabilitation.'

'Still, you probably won't be testifying,' I said. 'Forgery is just the kind of prior conviction that a prosecutor would use to show your lack of honesty or trustworthiness.'

'That's what Mr McCrae said too.'

'Did you know Zack Bissonette?'

'Sure,' he said. 'Nice guy, lousy ballplayer.'

'Assuming you didn't do it, any idea who would have beaten that nice guy into a coma?'

'I heard it was the mob.'

'Is that what you heard?'

'That's what I heard.'

'Is that what he's going to say when he wakes up?'

'What I also heard, Victor,' he said, his hands laying still, one atop the other on his lap, 'is that he's on the edge of never waking up.'

'And then you'd only be up for murder.'

There was a crack in the calm facade at that moment, a lowering of the guard, and what I saw was not the confident insider but a child, scared and lonely, the kid at the edge of the playground, the kid never passed to in the basketball games, who only received two valentines while his classmates took home sacks full. The peek inside didn't last long, quick as a politician's lie the facade was back, but I had a glimpse of what he was feeling and how much he was hiding and it all touched me in a strangely personal way. And suddenly my playacting the role of a hard-boiled criminal defense attorney didn't seem quite so clever.

'Are you sure you don't want someone more experienced?' I asked.

'You'll do fine,' he said. 'Jimmy said you'll do fine.'

I thought about it for a moment. 'If we both agree that I will represent you,' I said, 'we also are going to have to agree on a strategy. What line of defense was Mr McCrae going to follow?'

'He was going to follow Prescott completely,' he said.

I tried to smile reassuringly. 'From what I've seen, that looks like your best bet,' I said. 'But that decision is up to you.'

'I know,' he said. 'And that's the way Jimmy still wants it to go.'

'You know, Chester,' I said, speaking very slowly, very

carefully, wanting to phrase what I was required to say just right. 'With co-defendants there is always a potential conflict between defenses. One defendant could always point the finger at the other and say I didn't do it, he did it.'

'There is no conflict here,' he said quickly, without hesitation.

'Do you trust the councilman with your life?'

'Absolutely.'

'Rushing to trial like we are, I might not be able to help you if things go wrong.'

'I appreciate you wanting to be in a position to help me, Victor,' he said, without putting even a touch of patronization in his voice, which was pretty impressive. 'I really do. But there's always been someone reaching out to help me, someone with a clipboard from the city or the state or the federal government, and all they've ever done is dig my hole a little deeper. Only one man ever reached out a hand and really, truly helped.'

'And who was that?'

'Jimmy Moore,' he said. 'Jimmy's been called a lot of things by a lot of people and he's everything they say. But he's been the best friend I ever had. He told me to hire you, so you're hired. He told me to follow Mr Prescott's lead, so that's what we're going to do.'

'Then your explicit instructions are not to interfere with Prescott.'

'Exactly.'

I looked at him carefully. He was a smart man, I could see that, and he trusted Jimmy Moore completely. Who was I to get in the way? This had been easier than ever I had thought. I slapped my knee and stood up. 'Good,' I said. 'Then that's settled.'

'So you'll represent me?' he asked.

'If you want me to, I will.'

'I do,' he said.

'I don't have the connections old Pete McCrae had.'

'You'll do fine,' he said. 'Don't worry, Victor. You'll make out just fine.'

And that's how we left it, Chet Concannon patting my arm to help brace my courage as I faced the coming ordeal, as if I were the defendant and he were the lawyer, instead of the other way around. He opened the door and gestured for me to precede him out of the office. I had just stepped through the opening when I heard a loud voice rasp through the hushed Talbott, Kittredge hallways.

'Hell, I'm hungry. Hungry.' It was a sharp, emphatic voice, the voice of an overzealous lieutenant colonel or a college basketball coach. 'I'm too hungry to work just yet. We have all night.' It was a voice of authority, an exuberant, demanding voice. 'Let's get out of this dump and find something to eat.'

I recognized the voice right off. I had been listening to it all day. It was the voice of Jimmy Moore.

6

'Let me tell you something,' said Jimmy Moore in his insistent voice, poking his cigarette right at me. 'Those fat goons in the mayor's office have no idea what is happening. No idea. They can't understand it. They see the numbers, same as I do. If the primary was right now, even with the indictment, I'd beat that bastard by a hundred thousand votes, easy. Easy. And he knows it, he knows it, but he doesn't know why. He doesn't know my secret. He doesn't know where my power lies. But I'll tell you where.'

He took a drag from his cigarette, held between the tips of his thumb and first three fingers.

'It's in my passion,' he said with a violent expulsion of smoke. 'Just like Samson's strength was in his hair. If ever I lose the passion, well then stick a fork in me, I'm done. I might as well retire to Palm Springs and play golf every day. Too bad for the mayor I never cared for the game, right, Chet?'

'That's right, Councilman,' said Chester Concannon.

We were at DiLullo Centro, a shining, famous bistro across the street from the Academy of Music, where a stylish crowd greeted each other warmly as they hopped from table to table. Everyone seemed to know at least someone there, and the one who everyone seemed to know was Jimmy Moore.

Moore was a thick-shouldered man of about fifty, short gray hair cut like Caesar's, clean-shaven, with a round, angry face. He wore a flash Italian suit, designed for men thinner and taller. It was too tight on him and, in it, he looked nothing like the draped, statuesque mannequins in magazine ads. He had transformed it from a suit of elegance to a suit of armor. Embroidered on the white cuff of his shirt were the initials JDM. He had the intense eyes of an athlete and sucked attention to himself as he spoke, grabbed it with those eyes and the vicious certainty in his voice. He moved quickly, aggressively, head turning in sudden jerks like a giant bird. When he looked at me, it was as though he was looking into me and there was a sudden and intense connection. For that instant there was no one else in the room but him and me. And then he looked away, at someone else, and the connection was broken. But, even so, his animalistic power lingered like an afterimage burned onto the cornea, leaving no doubt that here was a dangerous man.

There were seven of us at a large, round table in DiLullo's, having just finished a lavish meal. Next to Jimmy sat his wife, Leslie, grasping tightly to the stem of her champagne glass, the puffed shoulders of her bright red dress shining like huge apples. She was still a pretty woman, auburn hair done up in all kinds of wing things, smooth shiny skin tight over sharp cheekbones, a dramatic neck, but the years with Jimmy Moore's passion had clearly not been easy ones and her face showed the wear. Next to Leslie Moore was her sister, Renee, a heavier, more bitter version of Mrs Moore, whose mission in life, it appeared, was to keep Leslie's champagne glass filled. Then sat Chuckie Lamb, Concannon, myself, and Prescott, who had encouraged me to have the champagne but had taken none for himself. Jimmy Moore was holding court here, his voice loud and rich, his strong large hand warmly shaking those of his admirers as they came to the table paying respect.

'The mayor thinks he can destroy my reputation with this indictment, but he's dreaming. Dreaming. His stooges in the so-called Department of Justice can try to sully my name, they can drag me through their mud, hell let them. Let them. I got enough to kick their butts halfway to Jersey and still become mayor. They all think I'm doing this with mirrors, my numbers rising like a rocket ship, my fund-raising shooting through the roof. Over two million in the last year for CUP, my group, not to mention the fat stream of donations I have going for my youth treatment centers. And let me tell you something, I got some big guns giving, sure, but I get more ten dollar donations, twenty dollars, fifty dollars, more than anybody. Nobody understands it. Nobody. I was just a normal political hack like every other slob in City Hall when Nadine died, just another grubby councilman looking for his piece of the pie. But when she died, when they killed her with their poisons, murdered her, fuck. Fuck.'

He slammed his cigarette into an ashtray and lit another with his gold lighter. Leslie Moore drained her glass of champagne and reached for the bottle herself. There was a long silence. The Moores' daughter, Nadine, had died of an overdose of barbiturates, it was in all the papers five or six years back, a teenager still when she started playing around with a dangerous crowd, experimenting with whatever was available. And then one night at a party, after too much cocaine and too many of the wrong pills, she collapsed and died. Moore was on the evening news, crying first and then shouting about vengeance, railing at the drug dealers who were destroying the city's youth. A few weeks later he started his campaign to wipe them out, neighborhood by neighborhood, crack house by crack house. There were marches, there were raids, there were mysterious fires and unexplained deaths. He had started a war.

After a drag from his cigarette, Moore continued. 'I've been building my new coalition day by day. I speak in the neighborhoods, I do the good work, I open the athletic centers, the shelters, my youth treatment centers, but it's not the speeches, it's not the buildings, it's not the pro-grams that draw my support. These people, they look into my eyes and you know what they see?'

'Their taxes being raised,' said Prescott.

Jimmy Moore laughed, a genuine, head thrown back laugh. 'My lawyer the Republican wouldn't vote for me on a bet, I know that.'

'I can't vote for you,' Prescott said. 'I live in Merion.'

'Of course you do. But I didn't hire you for your vote. I hired you because you're going to kick the government's ass.'

'We'll do what we can.'

'No, you'll do what you have to. But let me tell you, Bill. What the people see in my eyes is real. It can't be faked. You won't find a white politician in the entire country with the following I have in the black community and that's because they know the pain I've felt, they know the hate I feel, they know I will rid them of their greatest threat or die trying. What they see is my passion.' He leaned over and draped one of his thick, tightly clothed arms over his wife's shoulders.

'It's no different than what I felt when I first saw Leslie, standing in that crowd outside the schoolyard, with her little Catholic school skirt and her saddle shoes. She was so shy, she was, hiding out at the back of the group, unable to meet my stare from the other side of the fence. I was in my football uniform when I first saw her, on the practice field, and my passion spoke and I knew. I wouldn't let anything get in the way. Not her mother, not her little private school boyfriend with the fancy sweaters. Nothing.'

'And nothing did,' said Leslie Moore without even the hint of a smile.

'That's right,' said Moore. 'Remember the flowers and jewelry and poems, those marvelous rich poems?'

'Cribbed,' said Mrs Moore's sister, Renee. 'You couldn't even write your own love poems to Leslie.'

'I was not as sharp with words in my youth as I have since become,' said Jimmy. 'And John Donne expressed what I was feeling far better than I could have then.' He gazed into his wife's eyes and recited, ' "Twice or thrice I

61

have loved thee, before I knew thy face or name." ' Mrs Moore took another drink from her glass.

'What happened to the boy with the sweaters?' I asked. Chuckie Lamb, who was in the middle of a champagne gulp, coughed the bubbles loudly out his nose and fumbled for a napkin.

'Richard Simpson,' said Mrs Moore. 'Sweet Richard Simpson. He was such a nice boy. Refined.'

'He stopped coming around after we started together,' said Moore, turning to greet a stooped, grayed man who passed by our table. 'Judge,' he said loudly to the man.

'You broke his jaw,' said Renee.

'Judge Westcock,' said Moore, reaching out to shake the old man's hand. 'You're looking better than ever, you fox.' The judge's palm pressed into the back of a pretty young woman as he spoke warmly with Moore, the conversation at our table stopping cold until Moore was free again to lead it. Every few minutes someone of import stopped by to shake the councilman's hand and whisper in his ear, and during these interludes we waited until Moore could once again turn his attention back to the table. I knew the names of many of the people who came, basketball players and politicians and local names from every stratum. It was as if this table at DiLullo's was the councilman's after-hours office, where he could always be reached and deals always be cut.

'Funny,' said Chuckie after the judge left. 'That didn't look like Mrs Westcock.'

'She's about fifty pounds lighter and fifty years younger than Mrs Westcock,' said Jimmy Moore, laughing.

'I'm tired,' said Mrs Moore.

Moore lifted the champagne bottle out of its silver bucket and poured what was left into Mrs Moore's glass. 'That will perk you up, it always does. Chuckie, get another bottle.'

Chuckie Lamb pressed his lips together and said, 'Yes, Councilman,' before ducking away from the table to find a waiter. This would be our fourth bottle, and though the plan had been to grab a quick dinner before heading back to join the Talbott, Kittredge team at work, the champagne had successfully numbed our desire to deal with the piles of paper waiting for us at Prescott's office.

'What kind of name is Carl?' asked Moore, turning his attention at me.

'My family is Jewish,' I said.

'So you're a Jew,' he said in a voice so loud I shrunk from it. He might as well have been a druggist asking for the whole store to hear whether I wanted ribbed or lubricated.

'I'm sort of nothing, but my family is Jewish.'

'It's good we have some diversity now. Prescott's a fine lawyer but WASPs have such thin blood. It's that northern heritage, all those millennia shivering atop Scandinavian glaciers. There's no passion bubbling through his veins, just cool calculation. But the Jews are a Semitic people, your blood was thickened in the heat of the Egyptian desert and the centuries settling beside the Mediterranean.'

'My grandfather came over from Russia,' I said.

'You'll provide the passion in our defense,' said Moore.

Chuckie Lamb slipped back into his seat and said, 'Just don't spill all that passion until after the trial.'

'Victor will do just fine,' said Chet Concannon.

'No doubt,' said Prescott.

'I'm tired,' said Mrs Moore, draining what was left of her champagne. 'Renee and I would like to go home.'

'Why are we leaving so soon?' asked Renee.

The waiter just then brought another bottle of champagne and loosed the cork at the table. It shot into the napkin he held with a festive smack and bright white lather streamed down the bottle's sides.

'The car will take you home,' said Moore. Concannon stood as the women readied to leave. Prescott and I joined him.

The waiter had poured a small amount of the champagne into Moore's glass and was waiting for a sign to pour it generally. Renee grabbed the bottle from his hand and poured it into her glass, taking a quick gulp.

'It was a pleasure meeting you, Victor,' said Leslie Moore.

'Thank you, Mrs Moore,' I said. 'But the pleasure was mine.'

'I'll walk you out,' said Moore.

'No need,' said Leslie.

'I insist,' said Jimmy.

'Something's wrong with that bottle,' said Renee, pouring another glass for herself.

'Let me see that,' said Jimmy. He pulled the bottle from her hand and examined the label. 'Who bought this crap?'

'It was our fourth bottle,' said Chuckie. 'I thought . . .'

'Don't think too much, okay, Chuckie? That's not why I pay you. You think too much, you'll end up back in that shithole I dug you out of. I don't care how much it costs, always get the best. I've told you that before.'

'But I just . . .'

'Shut up. I don't want to hear it. You buy another crappy bottle of champagne and I'll can your butt, understand?'

'I understand,' said Chuckie.

'Now give this California piss to some homeless voter and buy us another bottle of the real thing.'

'Yes, Councilman,' said Chuckie, his head down and his barking voice now pale and small.

As Jimmy and his wife walked to the restaurant's exit, Renee took another quick swallow before following the others.

'I guess Jimmy prefers the imports,' said Prescott.

'The councilman can't tell the difference after one bottle,' said Concannon, 'but Renee's got a taste for the best the councilman can buy. Sit down, Charles. I'll take care of it.' He called a waiter over. 'Dom Perignon, seventy-eight. And take this bottle away, please.'

The waiter bent a little lower and put on an expression. 'Is something unsatisfactory, sir?' he said.

'You mean other than your breath?' said Chuckie, slumped in his seat.

'The wine was a bit too insouciant,' said Concannon calmly. 'The sommelier knows our tastes. Tell him we were disappointed.'

'Of course, sir,' said the waiter, whisking the offending bottle from the table.

Concannon mussed Chuckie's hair. 'It's just the trial,' he said. 'Jimmy's on edge.'

'Too bad it's not a knife's edge,' said Chuckie.

'Leslie looked good tonight,' said Prescott, changing the subject.

'Therapy four times a week,' said Concannon.

'She seemed almost cheery.'

'For the amount of money that doctor costs,' said Chuckie Lamb, 'she should be damn joyful. She should be a fucking Santa Claus.'

'Well, it's working, then,' said Prescott.

'I don't know about you,' I said, 'but that is as sad a woman as I have ever seen.'

'And still,' said Prescott, 'the improvement is startling.' He pushed his length out of his chair. 'I see Senator Specter over there. Chester, why don't we give our regards before I head home. When Jimmy comes back,' he commanded me, 'tell him I'll talk to him in the morning.' Off he strode with Concannon to the other end of the dining room.

'Mrs Moore is upset about the indictment, I guess,' I said to Chuckie.

'Shit. Look at the bar,' he said. 'As soon as the councilman finishes escorting his wife out of the restaurant the councilman's girlfriend will step away from it and join us.'

I scanned the bar, crowded with couples waiting for tables and singles, dressed as if they were in New York, waiting for something else. On one of the stools at the end of the bar an aggressively curved woman sat alone, drinking. From the angle we could see the breadth of her cheekbones and the swell of her chest. She turned her head to look at us for a moment.

'She's been here the whole time?' I asked.

'Just waiting for Leslie to get lost.'

'Does Mrs Moore know?'

'She knows,' said Chuckie Lamb. 'She knows every last thing, that's her problem.' He stood. 'I'll be back,' he said. 'I got to pee.'

Chuckie Lamb left for the bathroom and I was left alone like a geek at that large, now empty table to concentrate on the woman at the bar, Moore's mistress. From the way she was turned I could see just enough. Where do these women come from, I wondered, thinking of Moore's mistress, thinking of the receptionist at Talbott, Kittredge and Chase, thinking of the new Miss Jersey Tomato, whose picture in the *Daily News* that morning I couldn't help but admire. How do their breasts grow so? Some sort of growth rub? Who does their hair and how do they get it to stay model-perfect, as if it had just been teased by a stylist before the photo shoot? How many cases of Aqua Net? Is there a finishing school for these women, a Barbizon trade school, do they have their own professional association? And if there are so damn many of them, spread across the country like overripe peaches on a tree, why do they always end the night in someone else's bed? Maybe I should move to Georgia, improve my chances.

As I stared at the curve of her back and my feeling of deprivation grew, I noticed another woman walking up the aisle that ran past our table. She was Audrey Hepburn to the Marilyn Monroe at the bar. She was beautiful too, but in a 180-degree different way. Tall, with shoulder-length, straight brown hair. Her thin hips shifted as she walked. Her shoulders were marine straight, but her head hung low, with pale blue eyes, big and just slightly limpid, subtle cheekbones, a soft, round nose. She wore a short black dress with thin shoulder straps and she was looking at me as she walked up that aisle. I wondered if everyone else saw the beauty lurking there, hoped they hadn't, hoped she had a mother who always told her how homely she was, hoped she was insecure about her slight breasts, hoped she had been a high school outcast. Guys like me know that things like that can help. She saw me looking at her, possibly read the hope in my eyes, and she smiled at me. Her smile was incandescent.

I smiled back, expecting her to nod and move on, lost to me for all time because that was the way it always was with girls I passed on the street with whom I fell instantly in love, but then she did something strange. She came right up to the table and sat down next to me.

'Hi,' she said.

'Do I know you?' I asked hopefully.

'Veronica,' she said, reaching out a slim, soft hand.

'Victor Carl.'

'Explain something to me, Victor Carl,' she said. 'Men with toupees.'

'What's to explain?'

'Explain to me why. Look over there by the bar, the man with the dead beaver on his head. Why would a man wear so obvious a rug? You're an initiate to those dark secrets of manhood. Explain toupees to me.'

'It's a calculation,' I said. 'Champagne?'

She smiled and let out a soft giggle that was sexy, not silly. 'Yes, please.'

I reached across the table for the new bottle the waiter had deposited in the wine bucket and turned over Prescott's unused goblet. I filled her glass and then mine. She tasted the wine and looked at me and gave me that smile again.

'That is so good,' she said.

'It is, isn't it. The French.' I couldn't understand why I had never before tried to pick up a woman with Dom Perignon.

'I don't remember seeing you here before,' she said.

'I'm here with City Councilman James Moore.'

'Is that so? What do you think of him?'

I shrugged. 'He's a politician.'

'Yes. So tell me about toupees.'

'I'm of the theory,' I said, 'derived from my misspent college career as an economist, that every choice in life is a calculation. Everything we do is the product of a cost-benefit analysis as to what is best for us.'

'Everything?'

'Everything. Now that fellow at the bar has calculated that he looks better with hair, even when that hair lays on his head like a dead rodent. And who's to say he's wrong?'

'Me.'

'You've never seen him bald. I'm sure he feels a lot peppier looking fifty with the hairpiece than sixty-five without it.'

'But couldn't he get a better looking one?' she asked.

'That's where calculation becomes miscalculation. He thinks it's snazzy.'

'Oh, it's snazzy all right. I don't believe everything is calculation, Victor Carl,' she said.

'Because you don't want to believe.'

'What about love?'

'The biggest calculation of them all. We each have lists of qualities we're looking for and love comes when enough of the boxes are checked, or at least we get as many checks as we think we're going to get.'

'How romantic.'

'Some fellow won a Nobel Prize for coming up with that.'

'He must be a charmer.'

'I'm sure his wife appreciates him.'

'Well, I'll tell you something, Victor Carl. I don't believe it, and you don't believe it either.'

'I don't?'

'I read eyes like some people read palms and I'll tell you what your eyes say.'

She brought her face close and put her soft fingers on my cheek and brow, peering into my eyes as if she were reading something writ in tiny letters on my retinae. Her breath smelled sweet and dry from the champagne and as she looked into my eyes I felt as if I were drowning in pale blue waters. Then she pulled back suddenly.

'See, I was right,' she said.

'What did you see?'

'I saw enough to know.'

'Tell me what you saw,' I said, only partly joking now.

I heard the scrape of a chair and Jimmy Moore sat down next to Veronica and all of a sudden I was embarrassed, as if this woman who had just been gazing into my eyes should be kept away from the likes of Jimmy Moore. Even so, I was about to introduce them when Jimmy said, 'I thought they'd never leave,' and Veronica stretched her long beautiful neck and turned away from me, resting her chin on the back of her hand, facing Jimmy. I looked at the bar and saw the aggressively curved woman there laughing with a man who had his arm around her neck, and with a sickening disappointment I realized that sitting next to me was not a woman mysteriously attracted to my smile and wit but instead was Jimmy Moore's mistress. It was enough to break my heart in two.

7

Even in the best of times I am not one of those people who leap out of bed in the morning ready to attack any challenge the day might bring. I wake like I enter a swimming pool, slowly, hesitantly, one step at a time as my body gradually becomes accustomed to the cold. The morning after the night before, with my head swollen from the councilman's champagne and my legs sore from I knew not what, I might have stayed comfortably unconscious until noon except for a shrieking pain in my bladder that demanded, DEMANDED, attention. Good thing, too, since as I was pissing relievedly at 9:05 I realized I had to be in Judge Gimbel's courtroom at 10:00 in *United States v. Moore and Concannon*.

I didn't remember all of what happened after the fourth bottle of champagne the night before. I remembered Veronica, who grew more beautiful by the drink until I would have sworn I had never seen anyone as perfect before, and Jimmy Moore, growing larger, louder, ever more powerful, ever more passionate, and Chuckie Lamb, his surliness expanding with the hour, and Chester Concannon, easing our transitions as we moved in a group from club to club. There was Henry, the councilman's driver, a handsome, silent Jamaican with purple-black skin and a high forehead, standing just over six feet tall and sporting evil looking sunglasses despite the darkness. And then of course the limousine, that great black cat of a car. It had a boomerang hovering over its trunk and a bar and television in back and it wasn't rented, it was owned by the councilman and cared for by Henry, so it was clean as soap and it shined in the city light and moved as smoothly

70

and as predatorily as a panther through the night. I remembered that car all right. My first limousine ride, looking out the darkened windows at those who could only wonder who we were to deserve such splendor. I had always hated limousines, their ostentation, their imposing bulk, the way they tied up traffic on tight streets, parked in front of restaurants too expensive for me, the way they proclaimed that the people inside were somebodies, names, and that the people outside were nobodies, the nameless. I had always hated limousines, but I had to admit that viewed from inside they were entirely more benign.

'Want a rose, Ronnie?' said Jimmy, lowering his window and snapping his fingers at an Asian girl carrying a basket of cellophane-wrapped flowers in the street. We had walked from DiLullo's to an open Art Deco club with swarms of hunters, where we had shared another bottle, and now we were in the limousine heading to some other of the councilman's haunts.

'I don't need anything,' said Veronica.

'Buy a rose for Veronica,' said Jimmy to Chuckie Lamb, who immediately fished into his pocket for dollar bills.

'Aren't they Moonies?' asked Veronica.

'Moonies have a right to eat too,' said Concannon.

'And we need a pin with it,' said Jimmy.

'Two dollar,' said the girl into the window. She was far too perky for that time of night.

'Help her on with it, Victor,' said Jimmy.

I took the flower and slipped my fingers beneath Veronica's shoulder strap so as not to jab her collarbone, fiddling the stem's pin into the thick cotton of the strap. I felt the softness of her skin on the back of my fingers. She looked down at my hands as I worked and I wished I'd had a manicure at least once in my life. There was something about Veronica that was so delicately beautiful it hurt. Her face had a sad cast about it, and the coltish way she moved was sad, and the way her head hung low was sad. But every now and then, like a gift, was that smile,

71

brilliant, promising. Though she watched closely as I fastened the flower to her strap, and though I was embarrassed at my peeling cuticles and cracked nails, I couldn't help but linger.

I was in an entourage, and the very idea of it was thrilling. At some point in the evening a few others joined up, a state senator, an afternoon disc jockey, a famous jazz musician, and we rode around in that car together, hitting place after place, first the waterfront, then South Philly, then an after-hours place above a storefront off Market. Each club was different in design but all had the same atmosphere of practiced decadence. I was tired, and I knew I had to be in court the next day, but there was something about being in an entourage, even the entourage of a luminary as small-time as Jimmy Moore. Whenever Jimmy Moore arrived, his group trailing behind him, doors opened, greetings were warmly given, corks popped like firecrackers off perfectly cooled bottles. He could have been Eddie Murphy, Leon Spinks, hell, he could have been Elvis. And as I was with him, part of the grandeur splashed off on me. It didn't seem to matter a whit what I actually thought of the man. Throughout the night I had tried to pull out, to get to bed, but always Jimmy would tell me one more place and Veronica would flash that smile and I would duck with the rest of them back into the limousine.

'Club Purgatory,' said Jimmy.

'Yaboss,' said Henry through the partition and we were on our way.

'Prescott says you do real estate law,' said Moore.

'Just this fraud case we've settled,' I said.

'We might need a real estate lawyer,' said Moore.

'I don't really do too much.'

'Ronnie's having trouble with her landlord,' said Moore.

'He is being quite unreasonable,' said Veronica.

'Give me your card, Victor,' said Moore.

I nervously patted my jacket. In the inside pocket I found a card, corners bent, the old, still optimistic name of our firm listed, but my name front and center in solid black printing. I handed it to him.

'Guthrie, Derringer and Carl,' said Moore.

'Guthrie left,' I said.

'Here, Ronnie,' said Moore. 'If that Greek bastard hands you any more trouble you give Victor here a call.'

'I will,' she said, and she tossed me that smile and then and there I hoped that the Greek bastard, whoever he was, gave her a peck of trouble soon.

'You'll do a fine job, Victor,' said Jimmy Moore. 'I know it. I wouldn't leave Chester with anyone but the best.'

'I appreciate your confidence,' I said. Concannon was looking out the window as we spoke.

'Be sure you do,' said Jimmy. 'I have a feeling you're going places, Victor. And I'll help you get there. Just be sure where you're going is where you want to be.'

'I don't understand.'

'Up or down, boy?' said Jimmy. 'It's your choice. Choose up.'

'He wants to make sure you stick with the program,' said Chuckie.

'Up or down, boy?'

'Victor will stay out of trouble,' said Chester softly.

'Keep your eye on this one, Ronnie,' said Jimmy with a loud and dangerous laugh as he wagged a finger at me. 'He is going places.'

That's what I remembered as I dressed for court, hurrying out of the shower and putting on my shirt while my skin was still wet, so that the cotton stuck to my back, and tying my tie frantically and sloppily. And I remembered also that as the limousine had dropped me off in front of my building and slid away into the night, leaving me alone on the deserted street, facing nothing but the emptiness of my apartment and the loneliness of my bed, and with the bud of nausea starting its gorgeous blossom in the pit of my champagne-sloshed stomach, I couldn't help but laugh, long and out loud, a laugh that had echoed like the howl of a hyena through the dark, empty street and had announced to the whole of the world that finally, dammit, I was on my way.

8

Judge Gimbel's courtroom was like all the courtrooms in the Federal Courthouse, two stories high, wood paneled, dark, designed with a ridged modern texture that was dated even as the workmen were slapping it onto the new building's steel girders. Scattered in the benches were twenty-five lawyers waiting for Judge Gimbel's status call, twenty-five lawyers at, let's say, a total of $5,000 an hour, waiting for His Honor, who was already half an hour late. He had probably stopped off at the ACME to pick up a sack of potatoes on special, saving himself forty-nine cents and costing all the litigants together $2,500. Thus the efficient engine of the law. Seated with the lawyers racking up their billable hours were the print and television reporters covering the Jimmy Moore case. Some were clustered around Chuckie Lamb, who was releasing the councilman's statement for the day. Moore, Concannon, and Prescott huddled together in the corner. I was sitting alone, merrily letting my meter run at my new and inflated rate of $250 an hour. Safely within my inside jacket pocket was a fifteen-thousand-dollar check drawn upon the account of 'Citizens for a United Philadelphia,' or CUP, Moore's political action committee. When I saw it was CUP that was paying my retainer for Concannon's defense I balked a bit, but not too much.

'I'd rather it come from a different source,' I said to Prescott after he had handed the check to me outside the courtroom. 'Like from Concannon himself.'

'I don't believe Chester could pay two hundred and fifty dollars an hour,' explained Prescott. 'By the way, there is a CUP fund-raiser for the councilman's new youth center tonight at the Art Museum. You should come. Definitely. I'll put you on the list. You do have a tuxedo, don't you?' asked Prescott, his voice suddenly as snide as Winston Osbourne's in its prime.

'Yes,' I said, conscious of the insult.

'There will be some people there you should know,' he said, his tone once again avuncular. 'It's never too early to start meeting the right people.'

'But about the check.'

'Don't worry, Victor. Concannon is on the board of directors of CUP and his indemnification is provided for by the committee's bylaws. It is all perfectly legal, I assure you. Take it.'

So I took it, and stuffed it in my pocket, and sat with it in the courtroom, thinking of the black-tie affair to which I had just been invited, wondering at all the important people there to whom Prescott would introduce me. I was imagining the scene, sparkling with tuxedos and gowns in a pure black and white, like a Fred Astaire and Ginger Rogers movie, when I was tapped on the shoulder by a tall, pale man.

'You Carl?' he asked.

I nodded.

'Let's talk,' he said, giving a toss to his head in the general direction of the hallway.

He wore a blue suit, a red tie, black, heavy police shoes, the generic uniform of a prosecutor. There was a weariness in his eye, a sense of having seen it all before. Prosecutors have two primary expressions, one of weary cynicism when they think they are being lied to, which is often, and one of weary self-righteousness when they believe themselves to be the last bastions of truth and justice in the world, which is always. These expressions are as much a part of the uniform as the red ties. When they hire on with the government they must be sent down to Washington to train with an army of mimes in a basement of the

76

Justice Department building, mastering their weary expressions.

'I'm Marshall Eggert,' he said, perfunctorily holding out his hand when we reached the hallway. It was like grabbing hold of an eel. 'I'm prosecuting the Moore case. I understand you'll be representing Concannon.'

'That's right.'

'We're glad as hell that McCrae's off the case,' he said. 'If we had known that's all it took we would have taken him out for some Peking duck months ago.'

'Your sympathy is heartwarming,' I said.

'We could never get McCrae to accept a deal for Concannon. Could never get him to even consider one.'

'What kind of deal?' I asked warily.

'We'll drop everything down to one felony and recommend a minimal term. And we won't object if the Bureau of Prisons gets soft and sends him to a Level 1 facility like Allenwood.'

'And what does he do?'

'Testify.'

'Against his boss.'

'Exactly.'

'And for that he gets jail time? It won't happen, Marshall, can I call you Marshall? Chet Concannon's a stand-up guy. He won't flip.'

Eggert sniffed at me. 'What would he want?'

Good question. Truthfully, I had no idea what Chester Concannon would want to testify against his boss, but I knew exactly what I wanted here. 'Complete immunity,' I said.

'You know better than that, Carl. We would never give immunity in a case like this.'

I shrugged.

'Your boy's in a tough spot,' said Eggert, who had dropped a hand into his navy blue pants pocket and was now jingling his loose change. 'With his priors he's looking at serious time. And he's liable to be caught in the crossfire

77

between the government and Moore. If I were you I'd be jumping out of my pants to make a deal. Look everything over, talk to Concannon. We'll keep our offer open for a week, but then it disappears. Now how much time will you need to get ready for trial? We're willing to be flexible.'

'Trial's in a week and a half,' I said. 'That should be enough.'

The jingling stopped suddenly and Eggert's expression shifted to weary incredulity. He sniffed twice, cracked a weary smile, and the jingling began again. 'Ever tried a racketeering case before, Carl?'

'No.'

'This is not your usual rear-ender. There are tapes, there are boxes of documents, there are reams of financial records, there are over a thousand pages of Jencks Act material from the grand jury. And there's a half a million dollars flowing from the good guys to the bad guys, a half million we can't all account for. This is complex stuff. There's no way you can be ready in a week and a half.'

'I'll work overtime,' I said.

'Listen, pal, if you don't ask for more time I'm going to demand it, and make you look like a fool in the process. I'm not going to have my conviction overturned upstairs because of your incompetence.'

My eyes were watering, so I turned aside and looked down the hall. 'You started the clock running when you indicted, Marshall. Time to step up to the line, ready or not.'

'Oh, we'll be ready,' he said, the jingling of his change growing furious. 'The government is always ready. But you'd be well advised to be careful here, Carl. These people you're palling around with now, they're not boy scouts. Bissonette would tell you so if he could talk out a skull still as soft as a ripe guava. And fat Pete McCrae, whom you replaced, that piece of duck might have done him a favor. He was two weeks from getting indicted himself.'

'I can look out for myself,' I said.

'I don't know how you fell into this case, Carl,' he said, 'but trust me when I tell you that you didn't fall in clover.'

Then Marshall Eggert, a knight in cheap navy blue wool and clunky black shoes, a weary prosecutor weighed down by all his grave and portentous righteousness, Marshall Eggert turned from me and stalked back into the court-room. Well, I could never say I hadn't been warned.

Judge Gimbel was a great prune of a man, his skull covered in a wrinkled bag of skin without even a pretense of hair, except for wiry sprouts erupting from his brows and ears. His mouth was dried and downturned. A set of reading glasses perched aggressively on the tip of his sharp nose, through which he peered with a marked disdain for those with the temerity to stand before him. He had been a federal judge longer than anyone could remember and acted as if he had been born to the job. His voice, turned grotesque by age and disease, was like a handsaw eating through a log.

'Did Mr Concannon get new counsel?' the judge asked. There was a slight echo in the courtroom that gave the proceedings an air of grave importance.

'Yes, Your Honor,' I said. 'Victor Carl on behalf of Chester Concannon. I filed an appearance of counsel this morning.'

There were four of us at the defense table. Prescott stood next to me, straight as a pole in his stock navy suit, his own pair of reading glasses perched on his nose, lending him the virtuous air of a scholar. Moore and Concannon sat on either side of us. Behind our table was the Talbott, Kittredge team, all in a row, waiting to hand off any document for which Prescott snapped his fingers. At the prosecution's table stood only Eggert.

'Are you satisfied with Mr Carl's representation, Mr Con-cannon?'

Concannon stood and said, 'Yes, sir.'

'I can attest,' said Prescott, 'that Mr Carl is a highly qualified attorney.'

'We'll see, won't we,' said the judge. 'When's our trial date?'

'October sixth,' said the judge's clerk, a young woman sitting at a table in front of the bench, ceaselessly working through piles of paper as she spoke.

'That's thirteen days from now,' said the judge. 'Are we going to be ready?'

'Yes, Your Honor,' said Prescott.

'The government will be ready, Your Honor,' said Eggert, 'but in light of the fact that Mr Carl filed his appearance only this morning, we believe a continuance is in order.'

'I've discussed the case with Mr Carl,' said Prescott. 'He's had access to all our discovery and to Mr McCrae's files and he has informed me that no delay of the trial date will be necessary.'

'Your Honor,' said Eggert, 'Mr Prescott does not speak on behalf of Mr Concannon and, with all respect due Mr Carl,' he glanced at me and his face clearly indicated exactly how little he thought that amounted to, 'we don't want to go through the expense of a trial only to have a conviction overturned somewhere down the line for ineffectiveness of counsel.'

'That's enough carping, both of you,' said Judge Gimbel. 'Mr Carl, can you be ready in thirteen days?'

'I think so,' I said.

'You only think so?' said the judge. 'Mr Concannon.' Concannon stood again. 'Your counsel has just told me he only thinks he'll be ready for trial in thirteen days but wants to go ahead anyway. What is your opinion of that?'

'We'll be ready, Your Honor,' said Concannon.

'Why don't you have a little talk with your attorney before you decide.' The judge waved us to the back of the courtroom. We sat next to each other on the last bench and spoke softly while everyone else waited.

'The judge wants me to explain to you what's going on,' I said.

'I understand what's going on,' he said. 'They think because I'm black they have to say it twice, like English is my second language. Just do whatever Prescott says.'

'The truth is, Chet,' I said quietly, 'Eggert's right. There's no way I can go over everything before the trial. There's too much material.'

'Whatever Prescott says.'

I saw something move to our side and I turned my head quickly. One of the reporters was sneaking up the bench, trying to listen in on our conversation. 'Do you mind?' I said loud enough for the entire courtroom to hear. The judge stared hard at her as she smiled awkwardly and backed away from us.

'Vultures,' said Concannon, his head hanging low. He didn't look so assured just then, he looked young and scared and sick of it all.

I looked away, scanned the courtroom, saw the gaggle of Talbott, Kittredge lawyers conversing easily. I swallowed once and said, 'The government offered me a deal for you.'

'Let me guess,' he said. 'They want me to testify.'

'That's right. You'd end up with a minimal term. I could probably work out a recommendation for no jail time if I push.'

'They want me to testify against the councilman?'

'Yes.'

'And then what happens to me?'

'Maybe probation for a few years.'

'And then what?'

'And then nothing. You're off the hook.'

'And then what?' he said. 'Don't you understand, Victor? There is no choice for me here. Before working for the councilman I was sitting on the stoop in my under-shirt, buying malt liquor with my mother's check. For the guys I grew up with that was the ultimate career goal.

Occasionally, for a little extra beer money, I would cook up cheese steaks at a place my uncle owns, sweating into the chipped beef as I mixed it with the onions and Cheez Whiz. Two years of Temple University but that was still all the work I could find. I have a record, no worse than anyone else I grew up with, but enough to kill my future. Then comes the councilman, seeking guys with records who had cleaned up their acts, role models for his crusade. And so there I was looking for something and there he was looking for me. He saved me, absolutely. Now I drive around in his limousine and drink champagne every other night and make good money and do good work. And when he becomes mayor I'm going to be his chief of staff. Now what happens if I testify against him?'

'Chet, do you want to go to prison?'

'I've been there already and let me tell you, I'd rather sit in prison than on that stoop. You do whatever Prescott tells you to do. I'll take my chances with the councilman.'

Another lawyer might have decided to withdraw, might have told the judge that despite his client's wishes he could not be ready, forcing a continuance so that new counsel would have sufficient time to prepare. Another lawyer might have walked away knowing he was acting in the best interests of his client. That is what another lawyer might have done. But it wasn't another lawyer standing there before prune-faced Judge Gimbel, it was me, with a $15,000 retainer check in my inside jacket pocket and my name on a guest list to a black-tie fund-raiser where I would meet the important people it was so very important for me to know. And somewhere in the uncertain future were newspapers with my picture featured prominently on the front page, adorning articles about this case, and deals in which Prescott had promised to include me, and cases he had promised to refer to me, and gobs of money he had all but guaranteed would be mine. And, yes, somewhere out there in that gray and ugly city was the mysterious Veronica, on whose dress strap I had pinned a single

82

rose and who now had my number on a bent and spindled card.

'We'll be ready,' I told the judge when Concannon and I had returned from the back of the courtroom.

'Now, Mr Concannon,' said the judge. 'I'm willing to give you a continuance if you ask, but your counsel tells me you don't want one. Is that correct?'

Concannon stood. 'That's correct, Your Honor.'

'So I don't want to hear from you that your counsel didn't have enough time to prepare if the verdict goes against you,' said the judge. 'You are waiving your right to that claim in any future proceedings, and your right to any other insufficiency of counsel claim. Do you understand what that means?'

'Yes, sir,' said Concannon.

'Explain it to him anyway, Mr Carl,' said the judge.

I leaned over and explained it to him as if English was indeed his second language.

'That's fine with me,' said Concannon.

'You satisfied with that, Mr Eggert?'

'Yes, Your Honor,' said Eggert.

'Do us all a favor, Mr Carl,' said Judge Gimbel, 'and stay away from Chinatown until this case is over. October sixth, ten o'clock. Come prepared to pick a jury.'

9

The Philadelphia Museum of Art sits aristocratic and brown atop a rise at a bend in the Schuylkill River, spreading its wings to embrace the whole of the city before it. Long flights of stairs rise from a great statue of Washington on horseback to a courtyard fountain, surrounded by columns supporting colorful Greek pediments. It is a grand entrance, made famous by the movies, and the courtyard affords a spectacular view of Philadelphia. At night, with a full moon and the city lights twinkling, if you squint you can imagine yourself someplace exquisite and full of hope, someplace elegant and magical. For me that had always meant someplace else until that evening. That evening the city truly did seem to sparkle like a jewel of promise in the night, a jewel ready to be plucked.

I didn't have an invitation and so, while gay, formally dressed men and women with haircuts and gleaming teeth flashed their invitations and breezed on by, laughing, I had to wait as the guard at the rear lobby checked for my name on the list.

'Oh, yeah, here you are, Mr Carl,' said the guard. 'But it only says one.'

'There must have been a mistake,' I said in my best Winston Osbourne impression.

'I guess so, Mr Carl. Go on in and enjoy yourself. You too, ma'am.'

'I suppose men in tuxedos do get more respect,' I said once we got inside.

'Unless they're mistaken for busboys,' said Beth.

I had brought Beth because I needed company as I brushed shoulders with a crowd two or three classes above me. She would rather have spent the night at Chaucer's Pub, where the draft beer is Rolling Rock and T-shirts are acceptable, but as a favor to me she had put on her red dress, the tight one, about which she was forever fretting as to whether or not it still fit. It fit tonight. Its smooth curves softened the normal sharpness of her face and she looked almost beautiful. I had always been a little bit in love with Beth. It was never a sexual attraction, really, but there was a power in Beth that I could sense, a sharp integrity. In some strange way I needed her to think I was worthy of her and, to my astonishment, she always had. Beth was my best friend, it was as simple as that. And that night I thought my best friend looked pretty damn good.

I looked pretty damn good myself. It was the first time I had ever worn my tuxedo. I bought it when I was still full of optimism and beneficence, six years before, in anticipation of my wedding. It is a long story, but suffice it to say that on the eve of the ceremony my bride-to-be took a long hard look at me and decided she was too young to be married. The tuxedo didn't fit like it had when I bought it, but I guess that's why they invented cummerbunds.

We handed our coats off to the coat check guy and climbed the stairs alongside the huge yellow Chagall mural of a sun and a field of wheat and a man stuck out alone in a boat. We passed statues of fat naked women, turgid bronze breasts thrust forward, and stepped into the Great Hall, where a huge formal staircase rose to a bronze of the naked Evelyn Nesbit as Venus. Underneath a soaring Calder mobile we snatched champagne glasses from a passing silver tray. The place was teeming with tuxedos and formal gowns; they leaned against the walls and huddled in cliques and glided like spirits in and out of the open galleries. A small jazz band played at the foot of the stairs. A tray of cheese sticks passed by and I swiped three.

'What's this benefit for again?' asked Beth as she sipped her champagne and looked around.

'Drugs, I think, or maybe AIDS,' I said. 'I'm not sure.'

'Misery is such a clever excuse for a party.'

'I've never been to one of these before,' I said. 'Are those little shish kebabs over there?'

'It's amazing how far you've come in just a few days, Victor. Our finances are on the edge of solvency, your face was on the television this evening, standing behind Moore as he gave his speech on the courtroom steps, and if you don't watch out your name will be in bold print in the society column. "Who was that partying into the wee hours last night for AIDS? Why, our own Victor Carl, looking very chic in his black tie."'

'I was beginning to wonder if I would ever wear this thing.'

'You look good in it.'

'Yes, I do,' I said. I did look good in it, and I felt good in it, too. For a moment as I stood among that crowd of the wealthy, the sophisticated, the elite, who had done all they could to keep me out, as I stood there and surveyed the scene something hard and cold in my gut began to ease and the bitterness seemed to melt away. I was finally where I was always meant to be. I looked around and sipped champagne and decided I would stay.

'I should wear my tuxedo more often,' I said.

'Julie doesn't know what she missed.'

'Let's find Prescott,' I said, suddenly scanning the crowd. 'You should meet him.'

'Look at that face on you, my God. Oh, I'm sorry, Victor.'

'There he is, now,' I said and I led her to a stern looking Prescott and two sober-faced round men in the corner. Together they looked like mourners at a wake. They were standing before a Diego Rivera mural, three soldiers swathed in bandoliers cutting down a whipped and hogtied man and wrapping him in blankets. As we approached Prescott I slowed down, warned off by the demeanor of the men and the somberness of the mural, but then Prescott saw me and his face cracked into a smile that drew me to him.

'Ah, Victor,' he said over the band, shaking my hand. 'Terrific that you could come.'

'Thank you for having me, Mr Prescott. This is Elizabeth Derringer, my partner.'

'Pleased to meet you, Elizabeth. It's a shame my partners don't look so good in their evening wear.'

'Richard DeLasko is one of your partners, isn't he?' asked Beth. DeLasko was the current Chancellor of the Philadelphia Bar Association.

'Yes, he is,' said Prescott, proudly.

'Well, you know,' said Beth in a confiding whisper, 'I heard the Chancellor looks just marvelous in his black pumps and red sequined gown.'

Prescott was taken aback for a moment and then he smiled tightly, saying, 'Yes, well,' before turning to me. 'Victor, these are two men I'd like you to meet, Jack and Simon Bishop.' I knew of them, they were names for sure, the most successful real estate developers in the area. Each month a new Bishop Brothers development was opening somewhere in the far suburbs.

'Good to see you, Victor,' said one of them, Jack or Simon, I couldn't tell yet which. His accent was British, his voice smooth and melodious. 'Bill has told us all about you. Said you might fancy working with us on a new project we're developing. He speaks quite highly of you.'

'Valley Hunt Estates,' said the other brother, with a harsher voice and a harsher accent. 'We bought ourselves an old mansion not too far from the Schuylkill. Hit upon the notion of a neighborhood of manor homes around it. Huge front lawns, six bedrooms and whatnot. For those with upscale dreams, if you gather what we're proposing.'

'Luxury throughout,' said the first brother.

'But very traditional too, mind you,' said the second. 'And the options are gorgeous. Optional stable. Optional carriage house. Optional stained-glass window running up three stories, makes you think you're living in Westminster

87

Abbey. Valley Hunt Estates . . . Simon's the genius came up with the name.'

'Yes, well, but it does have a certain ring, doesn't it,' said Simon Bishop.

'I'm taking a more active role in this limited partnership than I normally do,' said Prescott. 'Recently I've begun to take an interest in the business side of things and so we were talking about the need for outside counsel. For opinion letters and the like. Your name came up.'

'Take my card, Victor,' said Simon, reaching into his inside pocket. 'Ring us up tomorrow.'

'I will,' I said.

'Have you received the documents?' asked Prescott.

'Yes, sir,' I said. He had sent me over six boxes of documents released by the government and copied for me by Talbott, Kittredge and Chase, six boxes at twenty-five cents a page, all billed to CUP. I was overwhelmed by the quantity of it. 'Thank you.'

'If you need anything else, let me know. Anything at all.'

'I will, sir.'

'So that is how it's done,' said Beth after we had swung away from the trio. The jazz band was playing 'Begin the Beguine,' an older couple started dancing in the open area in front of the stairs. They must have been names because, as if on cue, other couples crowded past us to start dancing alongside them. A tray of tiny egg roll squares swept through, but as I reached for them I was stymied by a broad tuxedo back and then the tray was gone.

'That's how what is done?' I asked.

'Networking. I had heard about it but I never saw the real thing until tonight. You're surprisingly good at it.'

'Just trying to build up the practice. You see any more of those egg roll things?'

'Yes, sir, no, sir, anything you want, sir. But you shouldn't kiss Prescott's butt so intently, Victor. It can leave stains on your ears.'

'It doesn't help,' I said, 'when you start accusing his partners of cross-dressing.'

'Your friend Prescott's a snake. I wouldn't trust him for a second. I looked him up in *Martindale-Hubbell*. Did you know he worked for Nixon?'

'A lot of fine people worked for Nixon.'

'Ehrlichman,' she said. 'Haldeman, Mitchell, Dean, Kissinger.'

'Kissinger never went to jail. Oh, Nixon wasn't so bad. Take away Watergate and Vietnam and he was a pretty good president. Pretty damn good.'

'Victor,' she shouted loud enough to get the attention of a group nearby.

I tried to shush her quiet.

'Listen to yourself,' she said. 'Don't turn into a whore, Victor, just because some Republican gave you a case.'

'At fifty bucks an hour you're a whore,' I said. 'At two-fifty an hour you're a success.'

From out of one of the galleries and into the foyer came first a clatter of noise and shouts and then the surge of a crowd of tuxedos and gowns and sprayed hair. At the front, marching forward with his back arched and head high, was Jimmy Moore. Behind him was an entourage, grown larger by the event, a gaggle of followers following gladly. Jimmy's tuxedo was tight around his barrel chest and thick shoulders. He was laughing, eyes bright, shaking hands as he passed the partyers, talking a bit here, talking a bit there, shaking hands with the vigor of a politician on the campaign trail, which I guess is what he was.

'Victor Carl, Victor Carl,' he said when he reached me, grabbing my hand and shaking it with the enthusiasm of a Kennedy. 'Terrific of you to join us. Terrific.'

'I wouldn't have missed it, sir.'

The crowd behind him seemed to flow around us until we were in the center of a very large group.

'Quite the turnout, wouldn't you say, Victor. Funding for our youth home on Lehigh Avenue is just about completed. We'll be able to start construction as planned, thanks to these good people. You'll be generous, I'm sure, Victor. Lawyers are always so generous when it comes to the needy,' he said with a wink.

'It's good to see you again, Mrs Moore,' I said.

Leslie Moore was by her husband's side, clutching a small purse in one hand and a glass of champagne in the other. The tendons in her long neck were as taut as suspension wires. Her sister, Renee, held tightly to her arm as if to keep her standing. 'Thank you, Victor,' said Leslie in her soft voice, barely discernible above the blatting of the crowd. 'We're both so grateful you could come.'

'This is my partner, Elizabeth Derringer,' I said.

'Good to see you, young lady,' said the councilman. 'Yes. Always grand to see another lawyer for the cause.'

'And what cause is that?' asked Beth.

'Why, giving kids a second chance,' said Jimmy with a huge smile. 'Raising up the disadvantaged, healing the sick. Righteousness.'

'Since when did City Council ever care about righteousness,' said Beth, taking a sip of her drink. 'I thought all it cared about was parking spaces.'

As Jimmy and Beth were talking I saw Chester Concannon walk by the group, looking unusually sharp in his evening clothes. He held onto the arm of a tall young woman whom I didn't recognize until she turned her head to look at me. It was Veronica. I raised a finger to say hello, but she acted as if she didn't remember me. They were a handsome couple, Chester and Veronica. After they passed I looked back at Jimmy and Leslie. Jimmy was concentrating on Beth, his eyes never wavering, but Leslie followed the handsome couple as they walked the length of the wide hall. There was something fierce and strained in her face as she watched them, something serpentine.

'But if you'll excuse me, Victor,' said Jimmy, interrupting my spying. 'It's time for the obligatory speech. It was a distinct pleasure, Ms Derringer.'

'Good luck, Councilman,' she said.

'Where would I be if I depended on luck?' he said. 'Keep up the good work, Victor.'

And then the crowd surged past us, like we were two stones in the middle of a mighty river. The band stopped playing. Jimmy climbed four of the steps, hopped onto one of the great granite blocks that rose on either side of the stairway, and turned around. Magically the foyer quieted. Jimmy gave his speech.

I had heard it all before.

I was at the bar, waiting on a Sea Breeze for me and a beer for Beth, when I heard a familiar voice behind me. 'You're missing the speech, Vic.' I turned around. Chuckie Lamb was grinning at me with those fish lips, his scraggly hair brushing the shoulders of a rather ragged tuxedo.

'It's the same old crap,' I said.

'Yes, I know,' said Chuckie. 'I wrote it. Bourbon,' he barked at the bartender and then turned back to me. 'You got yourself a nice gig here, Vic, lawyering for Chester. Big bucks, invitations to the nicest parties, a chance to wear a rented tux.'

'Yes, it is nice,' I said.

'Who'd you blow for all this? Prescott?'

'Did we go to school together, Chuckie?' I asked him. 'Did I beat you up at recess or something and you still hold the grudge, is that it? Because otherwise I don't understand why you despise me so.'

'Don't tell me you're one of those jellyfish who just want to be liked.'

'Isn't everyone?'

'Not everyone. But you want to know why, Vic? All right. Because my instinct tells me you'd sell your mother for a hundred bucks. Is my instinct right?'

'Actually, yes,' I said, turning back to the bar to pick up my drinks. 'But then you don't know my mother. In any event, what's any of it to you? I don't see your name on an indictment.'

91

'Yeah, well, I got lucky.' He reached over my shoulder for his drink. 'And so did you. But I'm naturally lucky. Are you naturally lucky, Vic?' He raised the bourbon up as if he were toasting me and then swallowed half the drink in one swallow. 'You better hope so.'

I blinked twice as I watched him go.

I handed Beth her beer and together we wandered through the open galleries. It was a treat to have the museum to ourselves, and even though there were plenty of people, that it was a private party made it feel like we had the museum to ourselves. We were drifting in the museum's Impressionist gallery, paintings by Renoir, Degas, paintings by Mary Cassatt, who had been born in Pennsylvania but had been clever enough to leave. Then we passed from the nineteenth to the twentieth century. Shadowy figures from Jasper Johns, a collage in flames by Rauschenberg. I paused at a stark painting of a grand and empty courtyard, slashing shadows, a bare statue, repetitive arches, and in the background just the top of a train belching smoke into the empty air. There was a terrifying emptiness about the painting, a palpable sense of loss.

'Giorgio de Chirico,' said Beth, reading from the little plaque on the wall.

'It should be called "My Life," '. I said.

'Now what do you know about de Chirico's life?' asked Beth.

'Who's talking about de Chirico?'

'Well, look who's over there,' said Beth.

I turned to see a tall thin woman in silk pants, leaning back, hips thrust forward like a model's. She was strikingly beautiful, blue eyes, straight narrow nose. Her black hair swept out with the unnatural wings of a television anchorwoman. She was with a tall, gray-haired man who looked perfectly natural in his expensive tuxedo and who was not her husband. I knew that because I knew her husband, I hated her husband terribly, and never before had I seen the gray-haired man who now put his arm over her shoulders and brushed the top of her head with his lips.

'Let's get out of here,' I said softly.

'Don't you think we should say hello?'

'Let's go. Please.'

'Oh, Lauren,' said Beth in a high-pitched call, loud enough for the woman to hear. She turned, and her eyes brightened into a smile. With her adulterous friend in tow she came to us, leading with her hips, walking across the room as if it were a runway at a Paris opening. She reached out her arm to me, wrist cocked down. Two thick gold bracelets, stamped with runes and encrusted with diamonds, slid bangling down on her thin forearm. 'Why, Victor,' said Lauren Amber Guthrie, wife of my ex-partner Guthrie. 'I'm surprised to see you here. You don't usually come to these sorts of affairs.'

'Hello, Lauren,' I said.

'Beth dear,' said Lauren in her soft breathy voice. 'What a cute little dress.'

'You know, Lauren,' said Beth, 'I've been looking but I haven't seen Guthrie here tonight.'

'I don't think he's coming,' said Lauren. 'I'm here with Rodolpho. Rodolpho dear, meet two dear friends, Victor and Elizabeth.'

'Charmed,' said the gray-haired man in a voice twisted by a strong Italian accent. 'I justa love this . . .' He gestured to all the paintings, struggled to find the right word, and then shrugged. 'This,' he said.

'Don't give up on the tapes,' said Beth. 'They take time.'

'Rodolpho is in silk,' said Lauren. 'He comes from Como.'

'Como, Texas?' asked Beth.

'Italia. I'm from Italia.'

'She knows, dear,' said Lauren. 'She is just being funny.'

'Ah, yes. Now I see.' He laughed deeply and falsely.

'Where's Guthrie tonight, Lauren?' I asked.

'I really don't know.'

'Don't you think you should know where your husband is?'

'Unwatched husbands sometimes stray,' said Beth.

'How would you know, dear?' said Lauren.

'Husband?' said Rodolpho.

'He's hardly ever violent,' I said. 'Except when he becomes jealous.'

'Husband? Do I know about this husband?'

'I could use another champagne, Rodolpho,' said Lauren. 'Be a dear?'

'Of course. But we musta talk about this husband, yes?'

'Tonight, yes. Now hurry,' she said, her breathy voice turning breathless. 'I'm so very thirsty.'

We watched Rodolpho as he walked with mincing European steps out of the gallery on his way to the bar.

'I met him at a reception at the Italian consulate,' said Lauren. 'You'd be surprised how many Italians are in Philadelphia, it's like a glorious, sophisticated subculture in the midst of the Philistines.'

'That you have made it your mission to entertain,' said Beth.

'Be nice, dear, and I'll introduce you to it.'

'Don't you think you should be more discreet in your infidelity?' I asked.

'I have been, Victor. I've been the soul of discretion. But things have changed.'

'You'll introduce me?' asked Beth.

Lauren looked Beth up and down, examining her closely. I expected her to stick a finger in Beth's mouth to check her teeth. 'There's a serious young man, Alberto.' She rolled the 'r' in Alberto. 'An architect working with Venturi. Dirt poor but very handsome. Give me your number, dear, and I'll pass it on.'

'How have things changed?' I asked.

'We're separated, Victor. I moved out. Well, really Sam moved out, but I would have been the one to leave if my father hadn't bought the house for us.'

'I'm sorry to hear that,' I lied. 'How's Guthrie taking it?'

'Not well, I'm afraid.'

'That's too bad,' I said, fighting the smile.

Beth was rifling through her small red handbag.

'And Victor,' said Lauren. 'You know that crack about the jealous husband, it was not so far off.'

'Guthrie?'

'He can be brutal. Violent. An absolute beast. I should have known from the first. Anyone who sweats as much as he.'

'You married him,' I said accusingly.

'I thought it was charmingly masculine at the start, those subtle beads of perspiration. He is very athletic, you know. But it kept on coming. Like Niagara Falls. Finally I had him go to the doctor about it, but there was nothing to be done.'

'And so Rodolpho,' I said.

'For tonight, at least. Have you smelled him? He wears the most marvelous scent.'

'Turn around, Victor,' said Beth. I did as she ordered and, using my back as an easel, she scratched out something on a business card. 'My home number's on the back,' said Beth as she handed the card to Lauren.

'You should have two different cards, dear,' said Lauren. 'One professional, one personal. That's what I do.'

'But you don't work, Lauren,' I said.

'Now that I'm suddenly single, I've gone into fashion.'

'Ah, yes,' I said. 'The destitute divorced woman, abandoned by her husband, forced to scratch out a desperate living on her own.'

'Close enough,' said Lauren. 'Oh, here comes Rodolpho. If you'll both excuse me, you've worried him so. I need to calm him.'

'You won't forget,' said Beth.

'Alberto,' said Lauren, again rolling the 'r,' her eyes widening with the excitement of it all. 'Victor, now that things have changed, give me a call. I've missed you.'

'I don't think so,' I said.

'Oh, do, Victor. We had such fun. *Ciao*.' And off she

swept, hips forward, right arm raised, her gold runic bracelets jangling together on her arm, off to intercept the
worried Rodolpho and lead him on to another gallery.

'Alberto,' said Beth, rolling the 'r.'

'Poor old Guthrie,' I said.

'Yes, Guthrie the beast. All that money,' mused Beth.
'That wonderful old name. Gone.'

'But at least he had everything for a time.'

'What about you? You were with her first. What
happened?'

I shrugged. 'She was slumming when she met me, looking for fun. She said she found me too serious. It was his
basic insincerity that first attracted her to Guthrie. And she
liked the way he hit on her all the while she was sleeping
with me.'

'What else are partners for?'

'Well, at least it's working out all right in the end.'

We strolled through the rest of the twentieth-century
wing, ending in a room dominated by the work of Marcel
Duchamp. There were tiny surreal sculptures, a wall of
cubist paintings, visual jokes on paper, a glass vial of 50 cc
of Parisian air in a case by a window looking out over the
front courtyard. In the rear of the room, in its own alcove,
was a wooden door with a peephole. I looked. Through a
hole in a brick wall I saw a faceless woman, lying on her
back, naked in the straw, her vagina jagged as a wound.
The woman was holding a lantern that illuminated the
scene brightly. It was a wildly disconcerting view through
that little hole and I was slightly off balance when I left
the alcove and bumped into Veronica. Chester Concannon
was with her, still playing the beard.

Veronica was wearing a short silk dress, her head purposefully facing away from us, scanning the walls, showing
off her long neck and gentle gentile profile, as I made
the introductions. When I mentioned her name her head
slowly turned until she stared me straight in the eye.
'Hello, Mr Carl.'

'Pleased to meet you, Veronica,' said Beth with an amused voice that Veronica ignored.

'How's that landlord of yours?' I asked.

'Still a problem,' she said. 'So tell me, Mr Carl, what do you think of this painting?'

She gestured to a large canvas on the wall. It was painted in different shades of red and brown and tan, a flurry of abstract shapes. I walked over to it and bent down to read the label. 'Duchamp: *Nude Descending a Staircase, No. 2. 1912.*' I stood back and could just make out the figure on the stairs and track her movement downward and to the right.

'Interesting,' I said.

'I had a boyfriend once who told me I looked like that,' said Veronica.

I stared into her eyes for an instant and then turned back to the painting. 'It's sort of abstract,' I said. 'Which makes it hard to tell.'

'It's easier if you see me with my clothes off.'

She was smiling at me, I could tell, even with my back to her. When I faced her again I smiled back and so we smiled at each other.

'Do you want to join us after the fund-raiser, Victor?' asked Chester, interrupting our smiling. 'You too, Elizabeth. We're meeting at Marabella's.'

'Thank you, Chester,' I said. 'But I should get some sleep this week, don't you think? Can I have a word, though?' I motioned him away from the two women so we could talk confidentially. 'Tell me a little about your friend Chuckie Lamb,' I said quietly.

'Oh, Charles is all right,' he said. 'He's smart as hell, but peculiar, too. Very loyal to the councilman, very loyal to his friends, devoted to his mother. But if you catch him wrong he can be difficult to take.'

'I must have caught him wrong.'

'Then you're in pretty good company.'

'Why wasn't he indicted with you and Jimmy?' I asked.

That was the question I was really interested in. Chuckie said it was luck that kept him out of it, but federal prisons are full of guys who thought luck would keep them out of it.

'They didn't have any direct evidence about him at the time.'

'I don't understand.'

'Well, you see, he never met with Ruffing or talked to him on the phone. It turned out Charles had only one meeting.'

'And let me guess,' I said. 'That meeting was with Bissonette.'

'That's right. And with Bissonette unable to testify they didn't have anything about Charles they could put before the grand jury.'

'Quite the convenient little coma for Chuckie,' I said.

'You could say that,' said Chester, slowly, like an idea was starting to form. He looked at me for a moment. 'Don't get into any trouble, Victor.'

I shrugged.

Then he called out to Veronica, 'Look, Ronnie, we have to go. He wants us there first.'

'Good-bye, Mr Carl,' said Veronica as she turned to follow Chet.

'Nice meeting you too,' said Beth to her back.

I watched them go, well, actually watched her go, watched the way she shifted inside her shift, and then turned back to the Duchamp painting. I studied its lines and angles ever more closely, and found them suddenly very sensual.

'That's a sweet little girl,' said Beth.

'The councilman's mistress,' I said.

'Aaah,' she said. 'And dangerous to boot. When's that trial of yours scheduled?'

'A week from Monday.'

'What are you doing to prepare?'

'I have some documents to look at, but other than that,

nothing, which is exactly what my client wants me to do.'

'But that would leave the whole trial to Prescott.'

'Do you think she looks like this?' I asked, still looking at the canvas, feeling an erection stir. 'I'm beginning to see the resemblance.'

'Have you ever thought, Victor,' said Beth with an audible sigh, 'that the reason Prescott gave you the hundred-and-twenty-thousand-dollar settlement in *Saltz* was so that you would take this case and then stay out of his way as he screwed your client? Did you ever consider that?'

That brought me away from the painting. 'You're saying he bought me off?'

'I was just bringing up a possibility. I mean, of all the lawyers in all the firms in this overlawyered city, why did he pick you to step in to represent Concannon?'

'He hired me because he thinks I'm a good lawyer and a smart enough guy to stay out of his way and he's right. They gave me a fifteen-thousand-dollar retainer, they're paying me two-fifty an hour, and there has been the promise of more good things to come. Whatever he wants me to do, I'm going to do.'

'You just don't get it, do you, Victor,' said Beth. 'They're never going to let you join their little club.'

I didn't get a chance to respond because just then a flash of red shot through the window onto the wall, and then blue and then red again. There was a police car now outside in the front courtyard, and then two more, their lights all spinning. Five cops and a man in a tan raincoat stepped out of the cars and headed up the stairs to the entrance of the museum.

10

By the time I got to the Great Hall, the five uniformed officers and the man in the tan raincoat were already there, surrounded by a mob of tuxedos and gowns. The man in the raincoat was an African-American. He wore thick round glasses, a navy suit, a red tie, and his shoes were black and clunky. I recognized the uniform, if not the man. He stepped right through the crowd until he reached Jimmy Moore at its center.

'What is the meaning of this?' bellowed Moore.

Two officers immediately moved to either side of Jimmy. The man in the raincoat waved a document and said in a weary but precise voice, 'James Douglas Moore and Chester Concannon, I am here on behalf of the Commonwealth of Pennsylvania with warrants for your arrests.'

That brought a shocked little babble from the crowd.

One of the officers, a broad-shouldered woman, said to Moore, 'Put your hands behind your back, sir.' She had the voice of a gym teacher urging her girls up the hanging ropes.

'This is a travesty,' shouted Moore. 'I am being persecuted.'

'Hands behind your back, sir,' said the woman.

Concannon, who was standing at the rear of the crowd with Veronica, tried to back away but a young blond officer grabbed his arm and another officer, older, with a serious face, put a hand on Chet's shoulder. 'Hands behind your back, please, Mr Concannon,' said the older officer. His serious face squeezed itself in embarrassment as he brought out his handcuffs. 'I'm sorry, sir, but I have to cuff you. I have orders.'

'I'm Mr Concannon's lawyer,' I said after I had made my way to my client through the crowd. 'By whose orders is he being cuffed?'

The officer nodded at the African-American man in the raincoat. 'Assistant District Attorney K. Lawrence Slocum.'

Prescott cut through the crowd and took hold of Slocum's arm. 'What is this about, Larry?' he said, his voice sharpened to a fine edge.

Slocum looked down at his arm until Prescott let go. 'We're making an arrest.'

'I'm acting as Councilman Moore's attorney. You tell me what is happening, immediately, or I'll slap a civil suit against the state and city before you leave the Parkway.'

'Stay out of our way, Bill,' said Slocum calmly, 'until the suspects are taken into custody.'

'Hands behind your back,' said the woman officer as she took hold of Moore's arm, turned him to the side, and leaned him forward.

'James Moore and Chester Concannon,' said Slocum as soon as the men were cuffed. 'You are both under arrest for the murder of Zachariah Bissonette.'

I looked at Concannon, whose head was down and whose arms were pinned behind his back. His eyes darted to and fro like minnows as the young blond officer frisked him.

'Bissonette?' I said to Concannon. 'I thought he was in a coma.'

'Not anymore, sir,' said the officer with the embarrassed, serious face. 'He died at eight-o-two this evening at Pennsylvania Hospital. Too bad, too. He seemed like a nice enough guy.'

'But a butcher in the field,' said the young officer.

'I didn't do anything,' said an angry Concannon. 'I didn't do a damn thing.'

'Shut up, Chester,' I said sharply. 'Don't say a word to anyone. Give your name, your address, your Social

101

Security number, and nothing else. We will get you out of jail and we will take it from there, but you keep your mouth shut.'

His lips twitched, but he managed to calm himself. 'What are you going to do?'

'Do you understand what I told you?'

'Yes.'

'You just hang on,' I said. 'We'll get you out.'

Flashes popped as the society photographers clicked away, thrilled at something more exciting than a spilled glass of Pinot Chardonnay to photograph on their beat. 'Look this way Councilman,' one shouted as Moore and Concannon were led to the museum doors, 'and be sure to give us a smile.' Old habits, I guess, die hard.

'Enjoy yourselves,' shouted Moore to the throng of gawking swells. 'Continue the festivities. My lawyer will clear up this little misunderstanding.' He started to say something else, but before he could get it out he and Concannon were whisked out the doors and down the front steps to the waiting police cars. They were barely out the door when the band started up and the whirl of conversation turned gay again. No reason to let a silly little thing like a murder arrest get in the way of a party.

I followed Slocum out the doors to learn what exactly would be happening to my client. Assistant District Attorney K. Lawrence Slocum stopped between two columns right outside the entrance and watched with Prescott as the suspects were led down the steps and around the fountain to the cars. He was bobbing up and down on the balls of his feet.

'I'm surprised at you, Larry,' said Prescott as we watched the woman officer put her hand on Moore's head and press it down so it wouldn't hit the roof as she placed him into the back seat of one of the cars. 'I would have expected you to find a more public place for the arrest.'

'You know how it is, Bill. The Eagles were out of town this week.'

'I'm Victor Carl,' I said. 'I'm representing Chester Con-cannon.'

'What can I do for you, Carl?'

'Tell us when we can bail out our clients.'

'We'll arraign them at the Roundhouse right away.'

'Who's the judge there this evening?' asked Prescott.

'Does it matter?' said Slocum. 'We'll ask to hold them without bail but whatever judge we get probably owes his seat to Moore and will set a half a million at ten percent. For Concannon too.'

'And where do you think they are going?' asked Prescott.

'This is a homicide here,' said Slocum in all his weary righteousness, the jaw muscles beneath his smooth dark skin working. 'A death penalty case. They shouldn't walk with just fifty thousand down.'

'Do you have anything more on them than the US Attorney?' I asked.

'They got everything but the tapes from us in the first place,' said Slocum. He turned his head and spat onto the step below Prescott. 'But Eggert's not one to wait his turn.'

'I assume you notified the press at the Roundhouse,' said Prescott.

'They'll be waiting.'

'You've always been a hound, Larry,' said Prescott.

'A city councilman being arraigned in night court. Front page of the *Daily News*, don't you think?' said Slocum. 'That's why I had them cuffed. Looks better on page one.'

'You missed your calling,' said Prescott.

'Maybe so,' said Slocum, taking off his thick glasses to wipe the lenses with his tie. 'But I'd rather make news than report it.'

The cop with the serious face climbed up the steps to Slocum. 'We're all set.'

'You read them their rights?'

'Word for word.'

'Well, gentlemen, it was a pleasure,' said Slocum. 'Want a ride to the Roundhouse?'

'We'll take the limo,' said Prescott. 'Better scotch in the back seat.'

'Oh man,' said Slocum, shaking his head as he walked slowly down the steps to the police cars waiting for him, their engines running, their lights still flashing. 'I can't wait for private practice.'

'Is he any good?' I asked Prescott as Slocum ducked into one of the cars and all three pulled back around the museum.

'The best they have,' he said. 'Let's get our clients out of jail. Chuckie will prepare a statement for the press.'

'Concannon was a little unraveled,' I said.

'He'll get over it. I'll tell you what's really unraveling. The federal case. Eggert had always hoped that Bissonette would revive and finger Jimmy. That's one of the reasons he wanted to delay everything. Now there's one less witness to worry about.'

'So who do you think actually did kill Bissonette?' I asked offhandedly.

He looked at me with his cold blue eyes squinted sternly for a moment and then eased his face into a paternal smile. 'It doesn't really matter, does it?' he said.

PART TWO

Pretrial Emotions

11

The District Attorney's office was in a narrow, dirty building sandwiched between two glass skyscrapers. Lawyers with offices in the skyscrapers bustled in and out of the revolving doors, the tassels on their loafers swishing, their Rolexes flashing as they hailed the cabs lined up on the street, the drivers all hoping for that apocryphal fare to the airport. Lawyers from the DA's office passed out of their filthy lobby in weary navy blue waves, pushing shopping carts full of their day's files, girded for battle in the city's grimed and undermanned courtrooms. There was about this throng of city attorneys the air of a soon-to-be-defeated army pushing forward only because any avenue of retreat had been cut off.

'ADA Slocum,' I said to the receptionist in the lobby, a flabby-faced woman with wrinkles around her eyes and the tan stains of a smoker between the first two fingers of her right hand. She was ensconced behind a thick wall of Plexiglas with only a circle of airholes for her to speak through. 'He's expecting me. Victor Carl.'

'Have a seat,' she said, gesturing to a dirty row of ruined plastic chairs out of some high school auditorium. I chose to stand. With the lobby's dim light and its general filthiness, I felt like I was in a subway station. That receptionist, that lobby, it was all quite a leap down from Talbott, Kittredge and Chase.

A few minutes later the elevator opened and a thin young woman stepped out while still holding the door.

'Mr Carl?' she said.

We stopped at the fifth floor. On the way to Slocum's office the woman led me past a maze of secretarial desks and cubicles, through the frenzied sounds of drastically overworked assistant district attorneys. What could have possessed them to take such a job, I wondered. They started at less than thirty grand, they worked killer hours pleading with cops and yelling at witnesses on the phone late into the evening, sending out subpoenas that were ignored, glancing at piles of files the night before the day they had to try them. And when it was time to leave the office for private practice it was tough to find a job other than hustling for cases in the city's criminal courts. With my spirits buoyed by the grand possibilities that Prescott was promising, I could only feel pity.

Slocum was in his shirtsleeves, leaning back in his chair, his feet resting on his desk as he talked on the phone. His shirt cuffs were rolled up, revealing dark and powerful forearms. Behind his desk were two flags on posts, one the Stars and Stripes, one sky blue and mustard with gold markings, which was the city's flag. Slocum's office was cramped with boxes and file cabinets and large posterboard exhibits leaning against the walls, a map of one of the city's parks, a diagram of an apartment with the outline of a sprawled body in the living room, a photograph of a woman with bruising around her face. The walls were covered with a cheap and fraying paneling. One of Slocum's shoes had a hole in the sole. Slocum was talking to his car repair guy, arguing over what was required for his car to pass inspection.

'That's got to be the biggest racket going,' said Slocum after hanging up the phone. 'I bring in my car for a thirty-dollar inspection and end up paying five hundred dollars for a new exhaust system in order to pass. Isn't there a law?'

'You tell me,' I said. 'You're the expert.'

'I told my mechanic once I was going to put an undercover unit on his tail. He laughed at me. Said it didn't matter how many plainclothes cops came into his shop, it was still going to cost me three-fifty for a brake job. He told me what I really needed was a new car. That was four years ago.'

'Maybe your mechanic's right,' I said. 'Judging by the sole of your shoe you do too much walking.'

He laughed. 'The real trick is sitting at the counsel table so the jury can see the bottom of my shoes. Jurors like their public prosecutors a little ragged around the edges. It adds to our sincerity. And they don't want to think they're paying us too much. If I hadn't worn it through naturally I'd have filed a hole in there by now. So what do you need, Carl?'

'You know I represent Chester Concannon.'

'Sure,' he said, webbing his hands behind his head. 'You took Pete McCrae's spot. Too bad about him, huh?' A broad smile hid his evident grief.

'On Concannon's behalf,' I said, 'I'm looking into the Bissonette murder.' Prescott had said it didn't really matter who killed Zack Bissonette, but I couldn't agree. My client had been accused of killing that man and it was my job to do what I could to defend him. Investigating Bissonette's murder might not have been in strict accordance with my client's orders, sure, but I didn't figure I was risking much by snooping around. If it turned up nothing, no one would ever need to know, and if it turned up something, well, maybe I'd be a hero. So the night before, standing in my tuxedo in the Roundhouse courtroom, with derelicts staring down at me from the glass-enclosed bleachers up above, I had pulled Slocum aside for a few seconds while the defendants were in the lockup and Prescott was out raising bail and I had set up this meeting.

'Your federal trial starts in a week and a half,' said Slocum. 'My advice, Carl? Go back to your office and finish preparing for that trial. This will keep.'

'My team's working on the federal case,' I said.

'How many people in your office?'

'Two.'

'I thought so,' he said with a scornful laugh. 'Make a

discovery request and I'll consider it in due time.'

'I don't have due time. I was hoping I could get something right now.'

He dropped his feet from the desk and leaned forward, his hands now clasped angelically before him. He smiled a broad smile and his eyes, even through his thick round glasses, were glistening. 'It's a sad thing how often in this life our hopes go unfulfilled.'

My eyes started watering as he continued to flash that broad, dashing smile and for an instant I didn't know what to do so I did what I sometimes do when I don't know what to do, I laughed, and he laughed with me and we both laughed together, laughed loud and long, laughed hysterically at how he had all the power over me at this meeting and could send me home with nothing if he chose and it looked like he was choosing exactly that. We laughed so hard that he had to take off his glasses to wipe tears from his eyes and I pressed the palms of my hands into my own eyes as if I could squeeze back the water and we laughed some more at how wildly we were laughing. We let our laughter gear down into guffaws and into chuckles until finally we were only shaking our heads in amazement at how hard we had laughed before. And then I stopped even chuckling when I realized there was nothing funny about it.

'So,' I said. 'What about it? Am I going to get some help?'

'File your motions,' he said. 'The discovery judge should get to them maybe sometime next month.' He started laughing again, but this time I didn't join in. Polite requests obviously weren't going to work. I could think of only one gambit, weak though it was, that might.

'If I have to file the motions,' I said, 'I'll file the motions, but that will take a lot of time.'

'Which you don't have. You agreed to the trial date, didn't you?'

'I agreed, but I'll tell the judge I'm not getting the

cooperation I expected and I need more time. He'll chew the hell out of me.'

'That he will.'

'But then he'll give it to me.'

'Prescott will love that,' said Slocum.

'No, Prescott won't be happy,' I said with a shrug. 'But you know who will be thrilled?'

'Who?'

'Your buddy Marshall Eggert, who's anxious as hell for some sort of delay because he needs more time to prepare for the biggest trial of his career as a federal prosecutor and he's terrified of blowing it.'

As soon as I said Eggert's name any remnant of Slocum's smile fled from his face. 'That skinny little bastard,' said Slocum. 'I was good to go on the attempted murder charges when he got the Attorney General herself to convince the DA to let the feds try Moore first on his racketeering crap. Except for that your clients are scumballs, I'd like nothing better than to see him shoot a blank.' He stopped talking for a moment and gave me a strange look. It was a strange look coming from him because I sensed it was almost a look of respect. 'But you knew that, didn't you?'

'I suspected,' I said. 'He seems to be concerned that there's a lot of money he can't account for, money that seems to have disappeared.'

'Only a quarter million,' said Slocum. 'But Eggert's concerned about more than just that. The murder evidence is pretty tight but there are other holes that he hasn't yet filled and he knows it. They overreached in their indictment.' He rubbed his mouth for a moment and then said, 'I assume, Carl, that you are now making a formal discovery request.'

'That's right,' I said.

'And in view of extenuating circumstances you are seeking to receive the information immediately or the prosecution of a major racketeering case will be delayed, inconveniencing the court and all parties, including the

Assistant United States Attorney, and delaying the swift and sure execution of justice.'

'Exactly,' I said.

'And these extenuating circumstances will be detailed in a letter that will be hand-delivered to this office first thing tomorrow morning along with a formal petition.'

'My secretary is typing it up this very instant,' I said.

'I'll check upstairs and let you know by early tomorrow if I can free up a detective to sign out the evidence.' He rubbed his palm across his mouth again. 'You know, Carl, my guess is you're in way over your head.'

'Most likely,' I said.

'We are not lifeguards in this office,' he said. 'Whatever trouble you get into, don't be looking to us for help. My only goal here is to make sure that Jimmy Moore and Chet Concannon pay the steepest possible price for killing that man.'

'I understand,' I said.

'That's good, Carl. You see, if I have to use you for a stepping stone as you flail about in the water, I don't want you thinking you'll get anything more from me than the bottom of my shoe on your face.'

12

I was in my office, on the phone to Dr Louis Saltz, when she called. It was after hours, and Ellie was strictly nine to five, so I had to put Saltz on hold to answer the other line. When I realized who it was I felt the briefest moment of panic. 'Hold on a moment,' I told her and then switched back to Saltz.

'Listen, Lou, something has come up. I have to run.'

'We're set for tomorrow then, right?'

'Four-thirty in my offices,' I said.

'I got hold of the others and most will be there. I still have my doubts. You're going to have to do some convincing to get me to agree, but I'll wait for the others.'

'Lou,' I said. 'Believe me when I tell you, this offer's a gift. We should take it and be giddy.'

'Be good, pal,' he said and then he was off.

I sat at my desk for a moment, the light on my phone blinking to indicate a caller on hold, and thought about how much trouble that call could be, how disastrous it could turn out if I took it, but then, smack in the middle of my sensible thoughts, I punched her line. 'Ho,' I said. 'I'm back.'

'Mr Carl? Jimmy told me to call you if I had any more troubles with my landlord,' said Veronica Ashland.

'I really don't do much real estate work, Miss Ashland,' I said. 'Maybe you should find someone else who knows what he's doing. I could refer you.'

'I'm sure this isn't too complicated for you,' she said. 'It's just that my landlord wants to evict me.'

'Have you been paying your rent?'

'Sort of.'

'Well, that's sort of the problem, I guess,' I said. 'Land-lords generally want their rent paid on time.'

'I've noticed that. They get very picky if you miss a payment.'

'They learn that in landlord school,' I said.

'That must also be where they learn to turn the heat on in the summer.'

'And that sixty-two degrees is plenty comfortable in the winter,' I said. 'And how much money they save by turn-ing off the water periodically for mysterious repairs.'

'Maybe you should come over and see what you can do,' she said.

'Now?'

'I told you,' she said. 'My landlord is trying to evict me.'

'Did he leave an eviction notice on your door?'

'No, that's not what he left. He's an old Greek, he doesn't know about eviction notices.'

'So what did he leave?' I asked.

'A dead cat,' she said.

13

Olde City Philadelphia is one of those strange, hybrid places that could only have been conceived in the fevered imagination of some Senate subcommittee charged with finding tax loopholes for the financially deranged. It started out two hundred years ago as a residential district, where our founding fathers worshipped at Christ Church during their deliberations over the Constitution, but swiftly devolved into a manufacturing and distribution area where the sugar shipped to Philadelphia from the Caribbean was refined and the iron ore shipped down the Delaware River was smelted and the wood shipped from the South was turned on a lathe into fine and not so fine furniture. Fifteen years ago it was a tidy little area of small factories and wholesalers and restaurant supply warehouses filling the whole of the suburban restaurant market with bar stools and formica tables and huge copper pots. But then some senator slipped a loophole into the tax code allowing tax breaks for renovations of historically significant buildings, and a whole new real estate scam was born.

The clever guys bought up all the old and rotting industrial buildings in Olde City and syndicated them in a series of limited partnerships in which the limited partners badly overpaid for the opportunity to get a piece of the tax break. With the limited partners' money in hand, leveraged with high-interest mortgages, the clever guys converted all these decrepit buildings into fancy condo units, setting high enough prices for the units so that the limiteds could get a decent return. It all would have worked just fine except that no one wanted to live in an industrially zoned corner of the city with no restaurants or stores or nightclubs and the clever guys couldn't unload their high-priced condos at a high enough price to pay the mortgages. One by one the partnerships collapsed into insolvency, including the partnership owned by Dr Saltz and his fellow investors, and with insolvency came tax recapture and sheriff sales of the buildings. After the clever guys had run off with their commissions and fees, what was left were the lawsuits and hundreds of luxury units interspersed among seedy wholesale outlets, serenaded daily by the rumbling of factory machines coming through filthy block windows.

I found a spot outside a shoe store with a hand-lettered sign, wholesale only, in its sooted window and parallel parked my little Mazda between a van and a pickup truck. Like all men, I believed I was the world's greatest parallel parker, and I banged the pickup only once as I squeezed into my space. Veronica had said she lived in one of the rehabbed Olde City buildings on the same street as Christ Church, so I followed the tall white spire to Church Street and continued on through the narrow cobblestone alley to her building. It had been a sugar refinery in its more authentic days, but now windows had been knocked into its high brick walls and an elevator rose up and down a large steel and Plexiglas tube appended to the side. There was a parking lot and a courtyard in front and stores had been planned for the lower level, but the plate-glass windows were papered over. The whole look of that empty plaza and its vacant stores was one of desolation. I found her number on the security board and she buzzed me up.

The cat lay on the carpet in front of her door, its head sodden with blood.

I kneeled down beside the corpse like a homicide detective in a bad movie and dipped two fingers in the puddle of blood around the cat's head. I don't know why I did that, it is just something that homicide detectives who lean over corpses in bad movies always seem to do, and I regretted it immediately. The blood was still damp. I was just

116

about to wipe my fingers clean on the cat's fur when she opened the door.

'It's still dead, I suppose,' said Veronica.

She was leaning face forward against the partly open door, her thin pelvis resting against the edge of the door so that I could only see half of her. Her brown hair spilled forward, lightly, like a veil, giving her simple, pretty face an air of mystery. She was wearing blue jeans and a gray ribbed sleeveless T-shirt. Her feet were bare. Wearing jeans, with her hair loose and flowing forward like it was, she looked more the artist than the mistress. There was something sharp and bohemian about her that was very different from the finely dressed society woman she had seemed that night in the limousine with Jimmy Moore and at the museum.

I looked at her longer than I had intended to before I turned back to the cat.

'It looks like its throat was slit,' I said. 'Did you know this cat?'

'Can anyone ever know a cat?' she said and then opened the door wide and turned to go back into her apartment.

Quickly I wiped my still wet fingers on the dead cat and rose to follow her, closing her door behind me.

Her apartment was a huge brown duplex with heavy splintering beams overhead and a varnished floor of thick, uneven slabs of wood. There was one wall of brick, the rest were white, and there were huge, sliding-door windows on the far wall. The main area was furnished with a wrap-around couch and a projection TV, and there was a long dining room table covered with piles of papers and unopened envelopes. The kitchen was filthy, dishes stacked haphazardly in the sink, and the living room furniture was covered with pants and shirts scattered here and there. A sweatshirt leaned back comfortably over the edge of a chair. To the side of the entrance was a flight of heavy stairs that reached a wide loft open to the living area. It was a large, masculine space, that apartment, even the mess that covered it was masculine, and when Veronica sat down on the sofa and curled her legs beneath her she seemed small and foreign there.

'Nice place,' I said, looking around.

'What about the cat?'

'The cat, the dead cat,' I said, trying to figure out exactly what I was doing there. 'Have you called the police?'

'About a cat?' she said. 'I don't think so.'

'This is not just any dead cat,' I said. 'This cat was murdered.'

'I'm not going to call the police about a cat,' she said. 'What I think we should do is get rid of it and then figure out how to get my landlord off my neck.'

'How do you know it's your landlord?' I asked.

'Who else would it be?' she said.

'All right,' I said. 'Let's first get rid of the cat.'

'There are some bags in the closet,' she said. 'And paper towels somewhere around in the kitchen.'

'You're not going to help?'

'Do I look like the kind of girl who messes with dead cats?'

There was a bright yellow Strawbridge & Clothier bag in the closet and a roll of paper towels on a cluttered kitchen counter. I wadded up one of the paper towels and used the wad as a mitt as I grabbed the cat's tail and lifted. It was surprisingly light. While placing it in the bag I kept it as far from me as possible, as if the damn cat could suddenly come to life and swat at my face with its claws. When the cat was in the bag I did what I could to wipe the excess blood from the carpet. It was a pale red carpet, which helped hide the blood, but when I was through there was still an ominous stain. Strangely, the stain didn't look like a cat's head; it looked like a fish. Maybe the final wish of a dying cat directed the flow of blood from its incised throat. Maybe not. When I was finished wiping I dumped all the bloodied towels in the Strawbridge bag and rolled it up tight and dropped it down the trash chute in the hallway.

Then I bundled all the resentment that had spilled upon the floor as I cleaned up the dead cat and headed back to the apartment. What is it about me, I wondered. Is there a kick me sign on my forehead that can be seen only by women? Do they have a club and pass around my name as a dependable sucker who can be counted on to clean up dead cats in emergencies? I mean, if I was sleeping with the woman, then, sure, it would be okay to be on my knees with paper towels, cleaning up the blood from some dead feline on her doorstep, but when it's someone else's girl, why am I the one doing the cleaning? I went back to the apartment angry as hell and fully prepared to tell Veronica that I was a lawyer, dammit, not a janitor and that I was leaving and that the next time she had a problem with a dead cat she should call her friend Jimmy Moore.

She hadn't moved from the couch but in the short time I had been gone she had grown more beautiful. 'It's taken care of,' I said, my anger balling up like a wet paper towel in my throat.

'What did you do with it?' she asked.

'Down the garbage chute.'

'That's cold.'

'What was I going to do, bury it in the hallway? Look, I have to go.'

'What about my Greek landlord?' she asked.

I shrugged. 'Pay your rent.'

'He wants to kick me out anyway. I have a special deal because of Jimmy, but now with Jimmy in trouble he figures he can kick me out and rent it for twice as much.'

'How much do you pay for this?' I asked.

'A hundred a month.'

'Jesus,' I said. The apartment was worth ten times that. I wondered what Jimmy had done for the old Greek to get such a deal for his girlfriend.

'What should I do? He wants me out. He killed a damn cat to get me out.'

'And you're sure it's him?'

'He's crazy. He slit the cat's throat.'

'Look. I'm a lawyer, not the SPCA. I don't know what I can do for you. I have to go. I have a lot of work tomorrow.'

She stood up and walked toward me, her hands clasped and to her side. 'Can you at least look at my lease?'

'Why isn't Jimmy here?' I asked. 'Isn't this cat thing and this landlord thing his problem?'

'Jimmy doesn't want to know my problems. He has a wife with enough problems to keep him busy till Memorial Day. He's at some political dinner with her tonight, so I'm on my own.'

I stared at her, trying to keep hold of my anger, but she smiled nervously. She looked very young for a moment and I wondered how old she was. She looked like a college kid, a sweet pretty college kid, suddenly very needy and soft. Why wasn't she in college? I lifted my hands and said, 'Where can I wash up?' She pointed me to a bathroom up the stairs.

I was washing my hands in the sink, scrubbing violently with a thick lather of soap, trying my best to get the cat off my fingers, when I noticed, between the toilet and the bath-tub, a litter box. It was filled with clay pellets. The ends of neat little cat turds poked above the surface.

I agreed to look at her lease. I cleared a space at the dining table and examined what she gave me while she went upstairs for a moment. It was not the standard form filled with paragraph after paragraph of tiny print giving the landlord all the power to screw the tenant that the law allowed. Instead, she had given me a two-page, double-spaced document, signed by Veronica Ashland, lessee, and Spiros Giamoticos, lessor, that provided she could stay there as long as she wanted for $100 a month and that the landlord could never raise her rent or kick her out. The only rule was that she couldn't sublease without

Giamoticos's consent. Noticeably absent were provisions about late payment or eviction. From the face of the lease it was apparent that Jimmy Moore had done a whopper of a favor for Spiros Giamoticos, in return for which Spiros had given the apartment to Moore's girlfriend for next to nothing. It was little wonder that Spiros wanted out of the lease.

While sitting at the dining room table I noticed her mail arranged in rough piles. While she was still upstairs, I took the liberty of looking through it. There was a final notice from the electric company, an overdue notice from the water company, a letter from the American Record Club threatening her with a lawsuit if she didn't pay for the compact disks she had ordered, a MasterCard bill showing a balance owed of over three thousand dollars. Her mail looked much like my mail. I searched through other piles until I found a letter from her bank. It had already been ripped open. I glanced around to make sure she hadn't quietly come back down into the room or was looking from the balcony, and then took out the statement. It was a checking account, in her name and in Chester Concannon's name, with a grand total of $187.92, down from $1349.92 the month before. She had written a $62 check to her credit card company to pay the minimum balance. The rest of the entries were cash withdrawals from different ATMs around the city. I stuffed the statement back into the envelope.

'Your landlord here can huff and puff all he wants,' I told her when she came back down, 'but there is nothing he can legally do to kick you out as long as you pay your rent.'

'What about the cat?'

'Call the police or file for a restraining order. I could file a motion for you, but other than that I don't know. Getting Jimmy to talk to him would be your best bet. What did Jimmy give this Giamoticos, anyway, to get you this lease?'

'A street,' she said.

'A street,' I said, shaking my head. 'He gave away a public street just like that?'

'It wasn't a big street,' she said with a shrug. 'More like an alley. I needed a place, so Jimmy introduced a bill or something.' She stood before me with her arms crossed, shifting her weight from one leg to the other. She wanted something, but she didn't know how to ask.

'Listen, Veronica,' I said. 'I don't mean to pry, but I couldn't help noticing all your overdue bills. Are you going to be able to pay them off?'

She laughed nervously and leaned over me at the table, turning her papers facedown. She smelled terrific and fresh, like a cherry tree in full blossom. 'No,' she said. 'Who can pay all their bills now, really? Bad times all over, right?'

'What are you going to do?'

'I'll do what I always do. When I get a big enough pile I give them to Jimmy who gives them to Chet who takes care of them.' That was why Concannon's name was on her account, I figured, to make it easier for him to supply her with the councilman's cash when her money got low.

'Don't you work?'

'I'm thirsty,' she said, looking down at me as I sat by the dining room table. Her breath was minty, as if she had just been upstairs gargling. 'Are you thirsty? Finding a dead cat in the hallway always makes me thirsty. Let's get a drink.'

I was tired and I had work to do tomorrow and there were a lot of things I needed to be doing, but the mintyness of her breath, her long slender arms, the way she leaned over me at the table, it all sent my stomach afluttering. My throat tightened on me, so that when I said, 'Sure,' it came out in a raspy whisper.

Outside her building, as she held onto my arm and led me off to a bar she knew near Independence Hall, I glanced behind us on Church Street. I caught the glint of the street-light off the cobblestones and then, farther back, the shine of a boomerang hovering over the tail end of a black limousine. The car's lights were off, and I couldn't see inside, but whatever sexual charge had been within me dissipated immediately, grounded by the sight of that car. It was too dark to make out the license plate, but I had no doubt at all as to who the owner was. That was Jimmy Moore's limousine and whoever was inside was staking out the councilman's girlfriend. And there I was, my arm linked in hers, stepping out with her into the night. It was a warmish fall evening, the air thick and humid like in springtime, but by the time we had turned from Church Street onto 3rd I was shivering.

14

From the other side of the door I could hear the muffled sound of a busy office, typewriters clacketing, phones ringing, voices shouting from one desk to another. Inside the small, battleship-gray room it was just me and Detective Griffin.

Detective Griffin was a pasty-faced, donut-shaped man with deep dark swaths beneath his eyes. He grunted as he paged through the *Daily News*, occasionally throwing out bits of gossip he seemed to take great delight in. 'Hey, can you believe this stuff?' he would say before he'd read to me from the lurid middle pages of the tabloid. Then he would let out a great, noisy groan of weariness. I was in that small, stuffy room in the DA's office to examine a stack of files and two large cardboard boxes of physical evidence, the whole of the basis for Slocum's indictment in *Commonwealth v. Moore and Concannon*. The evidence had been signed out from Room 800 in the attic of City Hall by Detective Griffin, personally, and he was there to make sure I didn't walk away with any of it.

'Hey, can you believe this stuff? Listen,' said Detective Griffin. 'That guy Bobbitt, whose wife sliced off his peter, right, he's stripping now in some gay strip joint. His new girlfriend, some Penthouse Pet, is ripping off his G-string with her teeth while the guys all cheer. He says he's getting sensation back a millimeter a month. It's like he's proud it got wacked. Can you believe that guy?'

I could, yes.

The detective stretched his arms out wide and yawned. 'Geez, I'm tired.'

This is what the evidence I was looking at showed. On

the night of Bissonette's final beating a young homeless man, only slightly psychotic, while digging in a dumpster for a late-night snack, had seen a black limousine pull up to the back of Bissonette's. He didn't see who got out of the car, but Michael Ruffing did. Ruffing and Bissonette were alone, closing the club, when, through a window, he saw the limo pull up and Concannon and Moore get out. This had all happened on Henry's night off, and Henry's alibi had checked out, so it was apparently Concannon who had been driving. Before the two could come in the club Ruffing left through the front door, hoping to avoid a confrontation. Inside there had been some sort of discussion, a few drinks had been poured, and then a fight broke out. Bissonette had gone behind the bar, supposedly to reach for a gun taped beneath the counter. His fingerprints were on it. One of the two visitors had grabbed a Mike Schmidt autographed bat from off the wall and knocked Bissonette down with it before Bissonette could grab the gun. He had proceeded to beat Bissonette with the bat all across his body, fracturing bones in both his arms, his fibula, his patella, his coxae, five ribs, and his skull, leaving a five-inch dent in the side of his head. The medical records were voluminous and ugly. Even through the technical jargon, the savagery of the beating was clear. When the paramedics found Bissonette he was covered with blood and vomit. They intubated him immediately and put him on a respirator the moment he arrived at the emergency room. He never regained consciousness.

A tough way to go for such a nice guy, I thought. Even if he couldn't hit a slider.

The assailants had apparently not rushed to leave after the beating. The bat had been cleaned of fingerprints, the glasses from the drinks had been rinsed. Everything had been sanitized while Bissonette was undoubtedly moaning and breathing with difficulty through the blood and vomit. In my mind I saw Chester Concannon casually wiping the bar with a rag as Bissonette struggled to stay alive behind the bar, his breath rising and falling in a horrific slurp. That would be just like Chester, I thought, not wanting to leave a mess, such a polite young man.

The two men had left no fingerprints, not even on the doorknobs, all wiped clean, but one of them had stepped in the blood and vomit by accident and so the freshly mopped floor had revealed his stride from the bar to the back door. Forensics hadn't been able to get a shoe size from the partial markings, but the stride was consistent with a man the height of Chester Concannon. A security guard in a nearby store had noticed a long black limousine pulling out from Bissonette's about twenty-five minutes after Ruffing had reported Moore and Concannon arriving. It had been a brutal twenty-five minutes.

Along with the evidence of the murder were the same reams of financial documents that the feds had given Prescott and Prescott had given me, records supposedly showing the flow of money from Ruffing to Concannon to Moore to CUP, half a million dollars passed around like pastries. And then the flow abruptly stopping. This was motive evidence, to show why Moore and Concannon had deigned to beat Bissonette into his fatal coma, and the pattern was damning. There was money, then the money stopped, then there was the murder. Only about half the $500,000 supposedly delivered was accounted for in the documents, but that didn't seem to matter much, really. Especially with those phone conversations between Moore and Ruffing, all on tape, all recorded in high fidelity, the most damning carefully transcribed by the DA's office.

Moore: You listen, you shit. You talk to Concannon, right? I ain't no hack from Hackensack, we had a deal. A deal. This isn't just politics. We're on a mission here, Mikey, and I won't let you back down from your responsibilities. You catch what I'm telling you here? You catch it, Mikey?

Slocum thought he had caught it perfectly.

The boxes filled with the physical evidence were most interesting to me because they weren't in the materials given me by Prescott. The Mike Schmidt autographed bat, an Adirondack Big Stick with the sharp red band just above the handle, was safe in a large plastic sack. I gripped it through the plastic, stood, and took a swing. Detective Griffin looked to be drowsing to sleep into his paper, as if he wasn't watching me, but when I swung he ducked. It was a little heavy but perfectly balanced: a Hall of Fame bat.

'What's a Mike Schmidt autographed bat worth these days?' I asked Detective Griffin. 'Three, four hundred dollars?'

'Don't even,' he said as he turned the page of his paper and yawned.

In the label, where Schmidt's name was burned into the wood, there were still flecks of blood. The laboratory had confirmed that the blood was Bissonette's. The rinsed glasses were also there, as well as the rag that had been used to clean the bar. It was stained the dull maroon of dried blood. Bissonette's bloodied clothes, sliced to shreds when removed in the ER, were in one bag; his Gucci loafers, stained with blood and vomit, were in another. His wallet had $230 in ten dollar bills. His key ring was heavy with keys of all shapes. There were four empty crack vials found in his pocket.

So the second baseman was no boy scout after all. I immediately checked back with the medical records but found that there was no cocaine in his blood when he came into the hospital.

And then there were the photographs. The first looked like a pizza where the cheese and sauce had kind of slid off to the side. With a quiet shock I realized it wasn't a pizza at all, it was Bissonette's face after the beating. The rest weren't any more pleasant.

I was starting to open the second box when Slocum came

into the room. He swung a chair around and straddled it so that his powerful forearms rested on the chair back. 'Don't go racking your brain over who did it, Carl,' he said. 'We already know and we got them nailed.'

'Hey, Larry, can you believe this stuff?' said Detective Griffin. 'Listen. These idiots were screwing on a subway track in New York and like, what do you expect, but the train runs over them. Now their lawyer's suing the Transit Authority. Can you believe that? Lawyers are such pigs.'

'How you doing, Doug?' Slocum asked the detective. 'You look beat.'

'I'm fresh off last out,' said Griffin. 'All night at a crime scene. Nothing new. The perp's wife was squawking at him about his drug use, so he shoots her, takes her upstairs, and shoots her again just to be sure. Sells the gun for a hundred bucks, buys more crack, and sets himself up downstairs, smoking, watching TV, eating takeout Chinese while the wife is up there bleeding. Took her three days to die.'

'Jesus,' I said. 'That's brutal.'

Detective Griffin stood, hiked up his pants, and groaned. 'Shit like that happens every day. Look, I got to take a dump.'

'I'll watch him,' said Slocum.

'What about those crack vials they found on Bissonette?' I asked after Griffin had left.

'Ruffing says they found them every night in the bathrooms.'

'At a high-class joint like Bissonette's?'

'The drug doesn't care how much money you got,' he said. 'But Bissonette wasn't using or selling. His blood was clean and the vials were empty, but had traces of the drug in them. Sellers don't keep the vials, they go with the drug.'

'What's this second box?' I asked.

'Stuff from Bissonette's apartment. Check it out, you'll love it.'

I opened the box and suddenly understood why Bissonette was such a favorite of the fans. At least some of the fans. What I pulled out of that box was enough to make Hugh Hefner blush. There were all manner of sex toys, appropriately bagged and numbered. There were shackles and ropes and dildos of varied lengths and widths and surfaces, there were vibrators, there were belts of leather and underpants of leather, there were strange harnesses, there were sadistic metal instruments that looked like something out of an alien dentist's office. Not bagged were the videos and sex magazines and photographs from a Polaroid camera.

'Our Mr Bissonette got around,' I said.

'Anyone you recognize?' asked Slocum.

'Not likely,' I said, though I did review the photographs one by one. They were blurred and the shots were off center; the camera had been set above and behind the bed and obviously operated by remote control. They were all of a well-built man, ponytailed, with the familiar ballplayer's face, having sex with women, sometimes just one, sometimes more than one. In many the heads of the women were obscured, showing only long legs, thin arms, bustiers, a tangle of swollen body parts. And in some there were other men.

'Didn't know he was a switch hitter, did you,' said Slocum.

'It wasn't on his baseball card,' I said, still looking through the photographs. One caught my eye, a long pale woman with dark hair stretching her body across his, her back arched, her thin butt riding high as Bissonette worked from below. She was reaching back with her arm and squeezing his balls. There was something familiar, tasty about the woman.

'Maybe it was a jealous husband who did him in,' I suggested.

'Give it up, Carl,' said Slocum. 'No jealous husband here. The murderer was too careful for a crime of passion. Besides, we have the IDs.'

Quickly I shuffled the photos so it wouldn't look like I

was concentrating too long on any one. In my shuffling I brought back the picture of the long pale woman. This time I saw it clearly, what I had missed before. I shuffled the pictures again and put them back.

'If you take away Ruffing's testimony,' I said, 'all you got is a black limousine and some guy about Concannon's height.'

'And if you take away the Atlantic we could walk to London. We have motive, we have opportunity, we have eyewitness identifications, we have two convictions here.'

'What's this?' I said as I pulled out the final object in the carton, a wooden box the size of a head, painted black with Chinese designs inlaid with mother-of-pearl.

'That's his love chest,' said Slocum. 'Open with care.'

Slowly I lifted the lid.

'Jesus,' I said. 'He might not have been a boy scout, but he was sure as hell prepared.'

Inside the box were hundreds of loose condoms in different colors and shapes, lubricated, unlubricated, some of genuine goatskin. The little packets glistened in their foil wrappers and looking at them was a little like looking at a display window of a candy store. Beneath the layers of condoms were stacks of casino chips, heavy, in black and gold colors. There were hundred-dollar chips from Bally's and Trump Plaza and Resorts, over a thousand dollars' worth, and a series of heavy gold and green chips without a casino's name printed on them, just the head of a wild boar embossed in gold. There was a small pot of ointment that smelled of sweet and spice, like liniment, with pictures of tigers on the outside. And there were little pipes with screens and a glass tube and, most interesting of all, a goldenrod colored paper slip with the words 'Property Receipt' on top and a date stamp. It was signed by our Detective Griffin and indicated that the lab had been given one glassine bag of a chunky, off-white substance.

I lifted up the property receipt. 'Now why didn't the feds tell us about this?'

'It's not relevant,' said Slocum.

'It's not *Brady*?' *Brady v. Maryland* was a Supreme Court case that required the prosecution to turn over any evidence that would tend to exculpate a defendant. 'It seems to me that knowing the victim was a drug user could show that the crime was drug related.'

'His blood was clean and he had no drug priors or drug history. You know what that little bag was?' said Slocum, gesturing to the property receipt. 'That was his last chance aphrodisiac. Any hunter in this town knows enough to pack some coke if he's really looking. If all else fails, you'll always pull in something with free jam.'

'What about these casino chips without a name, just a wild boar's head?'

Slocum shrugged. 'Maybe some casino out of the area.'

'Seems to me there are a lot of maybes about this guy.'

'What's not a maybe,' he said, 'is that he's dead.'

Detective Griffin waddled back in and dropped into his chair.

'I got to get to court,' said Slocum. 'But hurry it up, Carl, so we can get the detective some sleep.'

'Just a few more minutes,' I said.

I started going through the documents as quickly as I could, checking for anything I didn't already have, when I caught Griffin dozing off into his paper. His neck drooped, his head dropped lower, then lower still, until he snapped it up and looked at me with surprise on his face.

'Tough shift?'

'Up all night and then Slocum drags me in for this,' said the detective.

'Want me to get you some coffee?' I asked sweetly.

'No, just hurry it up, all right?'

I continued going through the papers, all the time keeping an eye on Detective Griffin as he kept a tired eye on me. He blinked a couple of times and then opened his eyes wide. His neck again began to droop and slowly his head fell off to the side until his cheek rested on his shoulder.

Out of the love chest I quickly grabbed one of the boar's head casino chips and one of the condoms for good measure, stuffing both into my inside suit pocket. Then I took hold of the pictures and shuffled back to the photograph of the long pale woman. It wasn't only the body that I recognized. On her arm, the same arm that was reaching back to get a solid hold on Zack Bissonette's testicles, were two thick gold bracelets, stamped with runes and encrusted with diamonds. I considered taking that picture, too, taking it to protect her, but thought I might need it in Slocum's possession if things turned out like I now suspected they might.

The photographs were back in the box and I was looking through one of the file folders when Detective Griffin snapped awake with a gasp. He blinked at me and grunted and turned back again to his paper.

'Hey,' he said after a few moments. 'Can you believe this new stuff about Roseanne? Jesus. Listen to this.'

I listened. I figured I owed him that.

15

'Maybe I'm not a lawyer,' said Dr Louis Saltz. 'But it seems to me that until we find that crooked accountant, Stocker, we can't really know the value of our case.' Saltz was a tall, gangly man with a long face and hairy arms who had a way of seeming to have figured out everything, which I guess is good in a doctor but which just then I was finding annoying.

'That's true to a point,' I said. 'Stocker collated the figures and made the projections that we claim were fraudulent. If we could put him on the stand and if he testified that the defendants told him to cook the books, we'd win for sure. We'd get punitive damages, too.'

'Exactly,' said Saltz, with a rich smile directed around the room. 'We'd wipe the bastards out.'

We were in the conference room shared by all of Vimhoff's tenants, the same ratty little place in which I had deposed Mrs Osbourne and ruined Winston Osbourne's life. In the room was a narrow formica table and walls of cheap particleboard bookshelves stocked with accounting journals and tax codes and sets of law books now out of date. Ellie used to spend hours each week updating our sets from West Publishing, from Collier, from BNA, replacing the pocket parts, slipping in the new pages, lining up the most recent volumes, making sure our *Shepard's Citations* were absolutely current. But after Guthrie left and invoices went unpaid, one by one our contracts were cancelled and the updates stopped coming. A legal library falls out of date with a startling quickness. The fear of having our crucial arguments trumped by a recent case not in our now dated law books sent us scurrying to the Bar

Association library, where for five dollars a day we could wander like ghosts around the association's volumes with the rest of those second-rate lawyers too poor to own their own books. We could have sold what books we had for a small amount, but we kept them out of vanity – to the untrained eye these volumes gave the conference room a lawyerly sheen. Of course, when we met with other lawyers we always arranged to meet in their offices because to another lawyer, familiar with the volumes, our incomplete sets proclaimed with utter clarity our financial despair. But it wasn't other lawyers I was meeting with that afternoon, it was Saltz and five of his fellow limited partners, there to discuss the settlement offer bestowed upon us by the good graces of William Prescott III.

'The problem, Lou,' I said, 'is that we aren't going to find Stocker before the trial. We're not the only ones looking for him, there's also the FBI and the IRS. The guy skipped town with other people's money and his only goal in life now is not to be found.'

I looked at Saltz and then turned my gaze on the other men in the meeting. They were all white, middle-aged guys with so much money they couldn't keep from throwing it away, which was exactly the state to which I aspired. Along with Saltz were another doctor, an owner of a plumbing supply company, a jewelry seller named Lefkowitz, and two partners in some sort of import/export thing that I never quite could figure out. There were two other plaintiffs who couldn't make the meeting but had given their proxies to Saltz. I was trying to convince them all to accept Prescott's settlement offer. Prescott had told me the check was already cut. If my plaintiffs said yes that afternoon, I could have the forty thou in our account by Tuesday.

'And even if we find Stocker,' I continued, hammering home my point, 'we don't know what he'll say. He could bury us.'

'No way,' said Saltz. 'The guy's crooked as a corkscrew.'

'Can't we just say how dishonest their accountant was?'

134

asked Benny Lefkowitz, the jeweler. 'Isn't that enough to prove they lied on their projections?'

'What he did in other situations doesn't prove he cooked the books here,' I said. 'The judge will never let the jury hear it.'

'Let's cut through the bullshit,' said Leon Costello, one of the import/export guys. He was a fat, well-dressed man with some sort of dragon ring on his left pinky. 'What are you thinking here, Victor? I mean, with your percentage you got the most at stake, right? What do you say we do?'

'My gut says jump at it,' I said. 'If we go to trial now, we'll probably lose. When they were only offering five grand I was ready to roll the dice. But now they've put some real money on the table.'

'If their position is so strong, why offer anything?' asked Lefkowitz.

'It's the way big firms work,' I said. 'They bill the hell out of a case until it gets near to trial and then they settle. That way they suck out all the money they can without ever risking a loss.'

'I don't think we can make this decision until we find Stocker,' said Saltz. 'Or at least give it one more shot. What's to lose? If we don't find him by the trial we'll just take the money.'

'If we don't agree quickly, Lou,' I said, 'they're going to pull the offer.'

'What was that?' said the other doctor, a podiatrist.

'They are offering us this amount so they don't have to spend the money to prepare for trial,' I explained. 'If they have to spend that money, then they might decide to screw the offer and try the thing. And if they do, I believe they're going to beat us.'

'That's not fair,' said the podiatrist, a stricken look on his face. 'They offer us a hundred and twenty thousand, that's what we should get.'

'The only way to make sure we get it is to agree to the settlement now.'

135

'How much time do you think we have?' asked Lefkowitz.

'Not much, a few days, maybe a week. But they could pull the offer at any time.'

'All right,' said Costello. 'I heard enough.'

'Maybe we should talk a bit privately, without you, Victor,' said Saltz. 'Is that all right?'

'Sure,' I said, standing. 'You're the clients.'

I stood in the hallway outside the room and again mentally spent the settlement money. With the fifteen-thousand-dollar retainer for the Chester Concannon case we were almost current with our bills and had paid Ellie what we owed her. We had even gotten Vimhoff off our backs by paying rent. My share of the forty thousand would be enough to start getting my financial life in order, to almost bring me current on my student loans, to even start paying back my father. Down the line there would be more money from CUP for my defense of Concannon, not to mention the fees I would make on the Valley Hunt Estates deal with the Bishop brothers, from whom that very day I had accepted the outside counsel spot, with enough work promised to keep Derringer and Carl going for half a year. Oh man, yes, things were looking up.

I had played the meeting perfectly, I thought. Saltz was my biggest problem, seeking as he was the big hit, but I figured the others would each take the ten thousand and run. As soon as I told them of the offer, I knew it was as if the money was already in their pockets. Then, at the end of the meeting, I raised the possibility of the offer being withdrawn, as if a pickpocket were reaching into their wallets and pulling out ten one-thousand dollar bills. These guys didn't build their fortunes by giving back ten grand here and there. At last I was starting to learn the secrets of the rich: whenever you have a chance for money grab it, quickly, clutch it to your chest as if it were life itself. That's how the rich got rich and that's how I would get rich too. Their signed releases were my first step. I had already instructed Ellie to prepare the documents so as to waste as little time as possible and they were now in the conference room, in a maroon folder, sitting in the middle of the table like a glorious centerpiece.

It was Saltz who came out to get me.

'We've reached a consensus,' said Saltz when I was seated back at the table.

'We're gonna accept the offer,' said Costello.

'Terrific,' I said, reaching for the file with the releases.

'But not just yet,' said Costello.

'We want you to try one more time to find Stocker,' said Saltz.

'There's a private investigator I use,' said Lefkowitz. 'The diamond business is full of swindlers and you get taken now and then no matter how careful you are. This guy always comes through for me.'

'We're going to give this guy three weeks to find that accountant son of a bitch,' said Costello.

'We'll cover his cost,' said Saltz. 'We think the offer will still be good in three weeks.'

'And if it's not, they can go to hell,' said Costello. 'We don't like being pressured.'

'If he comes up empty,' said Saltz, 'we'll take the hundred and twenty grand. But if he finds him, we'll nail those bastards to a cross.'

'Frankly, Victor,' said Costello. 'We're all in agreement. Ten thousand dollars plus or minus is not going to change our lives. But these guys took us for a ride and now if we can make them pay big time, it's worth the risk. This goes way beyond money.'

'It's the principle of the thing,' said Saltz. 'And we know you'll want us to stick to our principles.'

'Do you have a piece of paper for me?' said Lefkowitz. I reached into the file and took out one of the unsigned releases. He turned it over and scribbled on the back. 'This is the name of my guy. I'll call him tonight and set up a meeting for you tomorrow. Tomorrow's Friday, so

137

sometime early is better. About ten? Fine. He'll be here at ten.'

He slid the release back to me. I read the name out loud. 'Morris Kapustin? What kind of private eye has a name like Morris Kapustin?'

'He's tougher than he sounds,' said Lefkowitz. 'Morris is something special.'

'Give him the three weeks,' said Costello. 'If he craps out then take the money, quick. We don't need another meeting.'

'Is that all right?' asked Saltz.

'I don't have much choice, do I?' I said.

'That a boy,' said Saltz.

'I'm an easy guy to get along with,' said Costello. 'But I hate being taken and those bastards took me.'

'You and Morris will get them,' said Lefkowitz.

'That's right,' said Costello. 'Pound a stake through their fucking hearts.'

16

I was walking Saltz through our small reception area, feeling almost desperate about having to wait for my cut of the settlement, when I saw Veronica sitting on the Naugahyde couch by the door. She was wearing her short black dress with dark stockings and black high heels. Her legs were crossed in a way that was hard not to notice. When Saltz saw her he stopped walking and stared.

'Veronica,' I said. 'This is a surprise.'

'Your receptionist told me I could wait here. Is she always so unpleasant?'

'Unpleasantness is Rita's special talent,' I said. 'Give me a minute.'

I dragged Saltz out of the office. He didn't seem to want to talk about the case anymore. 'Is she a friend of yours?'

'A client of sorts. She has a landlord problem.'

'If she needs a doctor,' said Saltz, 'give her my name.'

'She's a little young for a cardiologist,' I said.

'I'm versatile,' said Saltz. He leaned backwards to peer through the windowed door. From where we were standing we could only see her long stockinged legs. 'Besides,' he said, tapping me on the chest, 'that girl's a walking heart attack.'

'So, Veronica,' I said when I came back into the office. 'Another critter turn up dead on your doorstep?'

She was fiddling around in her little black purse. 'I was just in your part of town and I thought we could have a drink together.'

'I have too much work.'

'When can you get free?' she asked.

'December.'

She placed her feet beneath her and stood up gracefully. 'I'm supposed to meet Jimmy for dinner tonight at eight. Let's have a drink beforehand.'

'I can't,' I said. 'I have too much work. There's the trial and . . .'

She placed her hand on my arm. 'I have two hours free. It's so sad when I am forced to drink alone.'

'Then don't drink. Go to a bookstore. Catch a movie.'

'But it's happy hour, Victor.'

'I really can't.'

'Of course you can. Didn't you have fun last night?'

'Yes,' I said, and I did.

Despite the overt threat of that limousine parked on Church Street, I had let Veronica take me to the Society Hill Bar and Grill, where we drank cocktails and listened to the bearded piano player and talked about nothing and laughed and talked some more and were both ever so clever. There was something about Veronica, a certain carelessness maybe, that brought forth a depraved charm I didn't know existed within me, and I liked it. I had always seen myself as a social cluck, dull witted, slow, my conversation frozen with indecision during blind dates or cocktail parties. But sitting at the bar with Veronica, being raked with the gazes of the other men there, all wondering what a jerk like me was doing with someone like her, feeding off her sweet perverseness, my self-confidence blossomed. I was something more than I had ever been. I told stories and she laughed. I kept up my end of a sparkling conversation. I was Henry James, I was James Bond, I was a raconteur.

'Do you have another engagement this evening?' she asked. 'A date?' Her pretty lips twisted into a smirk as she stood before me.

'No,' I said. 'That's not it.'

'Well then,' she said. 'Let's go. Carolina's is just up the street.'

I hesitated for a moment. I was weakening and she could

see it. She moved a step closer and lifted her face up to mine and then the phone rang.

I pulled away, turned my back on her, and answered it. 'Derringer and Carl.'

'What are you doing asking questions about a corpse?' said the familiar, high barking voice on phone. 'You're forgetting your role.'

'Screw you,' I said to Chuckie Lamb, suddenly defensive about my visit to Slocum and examination of the murder evidence, all contrary to my client's firm instructions. 'I'm just doing my job.'

'Your job is not to sneak into the DA's office and plot. Your job is to sit quietly and shut up. That's what they're paying you to do.'

'I know what my job is,' I said. 'What I don't know is why you are so pissed off that I'm doing it. Although I have my suspicions.'

'Oh, you're a brain all right, Vic,' he said. 'You keep looking and you might find something you don't want to find, something that could get you hurt.'

'So that's the way it is,' I said. 'What this call is all about.' I tried to sound hard but I could feel the flutter of fear rise along my spine. I had never been threatened before, not like that, not by someone like Chuckie Lamb, who I had no doubt could turn murderous if he wanted to, who maybe already had.

'I just think you should know exactly what you're getting into, Vic.'

'You're doing me a public service, is that it?'

'Now you got it.'

'Give me one reason I should listen to you and be afraid.'

'I'll give you a quarter of a million reasons, you small-time loser.'

I turned around suddenly. Veronica was standing by the far wall, looking at a print of some flowers, but it wasn't a very interesting print. Vimhoff had bought it for fifteen bucks, framed, and I doubted if it grabbed all of Veronica's attention. Did she know who I was talking to? I didn't want her to know, didn't want her to have anything to do with my role in this case. I lowered my voice. I knew there was a $250,000 discrepancy between the funds claimed to be given to Concannon by Ruffing and the funds apparently received by CUP, though until that moment I hadn't focused on it. But Chuckie had made a slip, had inadvertently let me know that it was important.

'So where are they?' I asked, still looking at the pretty curve of Veronica's back. 'All those reasons.'

'Lay off and you'll live longer,' said Chuckie Lamb.

'So it is a threat, isn't it?' My hand started to shake and I couldn't stop it. I grabbed the receiver with the other hand. That helped, but not much. 'It's been a pleasure, but I can't talk anymore now,' I said. 'There's someone here.'

'Someone I might know?'

'None of your business.'

'Someone involved with the case?'

'Not really.'

'Long legs, thin hips, the face of a spoiled child?'

Just that instant Veronica turned around and looked at me. 'Yes, actually,' I said. 'That's it exactly.'

'Then you are as good as wasted already,' he said.

'Anything interesting?' asked Veronica after Chuckie had hung up and I held the telephone in a still shaking hand.

'No,' I said, putting the phone down slowly. 'It was nothing. Just another debt collector.'

'Oh, the terrible strain,' she said. 'I can see it on you. You simply must come with me for a drink. To calm your nerves.' It was not a question, it was a statement of fact, and before I could convince myself that I really ought to refuse she said, 'Besides, Jimmy wants you to join us for dinner and he insisted I don't accept no for an answer.'

Carolina's is one of those places where suits congregate after office hours to pretend their lives are worthy of a beer commercial. There's a restaurant that serves squab and monk-fish and asparagus bundles tied with a yellow silk ribbon, but the real action is off to the side, where women with flat bellies go to have their drinks bought for them by Italian suits standing three layers deep at the bar. Guthrie and I used to go to Carolina's when we were still partners and still friends and we'd laugh at the scene, even as we scanned for a pair of willing eyes. Guthrie is a handsome dog, broad and swarthy, and he'd usually end up leaning over something comely, laying on his saccharine charm as I clutched my beer, my back against the wall, watching. If there was a friend he'd call me over, but that never worked because after Guthrie had his choice the friend was generally not much worth it or, if she was, she'd have her eye on Guthrie. I always associated Carolina's with failure, so I hated everything about the place, the too expensive drinks, the blank white walls, the forced expressions of self-satisfaction that were worn there like a uniform. But I must admit, it felt different to be there with a beautiful woman who laughed at my jokes and leaned close as she whispered her confidences.

'My jaw is too heavy,' she said, rubbing the back of her fingers along her jawbone. 'It's like the jaw of a wrestler.'

'You're being silly,' I said. 'Do you want another drink?'

'Of course. No, it's not silly. I have a jaw like that giant wrestler, what was his name, Alex or something.'

I waved for the bartender. 'Andre the Giant?'

'Yes. I have a jaw like his.'

'No you don't. Your jaw is beautiful.'

'You're sweet to lie for me. Here, feel it.' She took my hand and placed my palm upon her jawline. Her hand was cool and dry, her cheek smooth. My thumb rested in the hollow beneath her chin. She held my hand there for a moment. 'That's why the modeling didn't work. That and my legs.'

'Now you're being very silly. Another Sea Breeze and

Absolut martini,' I said to the bartender, who nodded at me while he stared at Veronica.

'We have to go soon,' she said. 'After this drink. We're meeting them at a place on Tenth Street. A private room. It's all very serious.'

'What does Jimmy want to see me for?'

'Chet will be there,' she said. 'Chet's always there. And I think your friend Prescott.'

'And Chuckie too, I assume.'

'No, not Chuckie. He's off visiting his mother.'

'His mother, huh? He doesn't seem the type.'

'Oh, he's always off visiting his mother. But I think they want to talk about the trial anyway and, as far as the trial goes, Chuckie's out of the loop.' Now that was interesting. So Chuckie wasn't threatening me on behalf of Chester or the councilman. He wasn't authorized to make the call, he was freelancing, threatening me only on behalf of Chuckie.

'How can you drink that?' she said, pointing to the bright purple Sea Breeze in the highball glass the bartender placed in front of me.

'It tastes like summer. Besides, if I started drinking martinis I'd collapse before I could step out of this place.'

'Cheers,' she said, lifting her clear martini glass and downing a swallow. 'Some nights I need a start on the champagne.'

'Victor Carl, Victor Carl,' said a loud nasal voice that I recognized immediately. 'Looking very sharp indeed.' I felt something in the pit of my stomach the moment I heard that voice. Its owner was a tall, handsome man with short black hair, greased and combed straight back. Athletic shoulders filled his olive-green suit. He had a smartass smile and a bright yellow tie and he slapped me hard on the back as if I were a fraternity buddy.

'Guthrie, you bastard,' I said to my ex-partner as flatly as I could manage.

'Looking good, Vic,' he said. I really didn't like being called Vic and I especially didn't like being called Vic by him. 'First I see you popping up on the nightly news and now in Carolina's with the most beautiful woman in Philadelphia.' He turned his smartass smile on Veronica. 'You're coming up in the world, I must say.'

'I'm associating with a better class of people now,' I said, looking at him very carefully, trying to see the violence Lauren said was in him.

'Since Vic has forgotten his manners,' he said to Veronica, 'let me introduce myself. I'm Guthrie. Samuel Guthrie.'

'And I'm interested,' said Veronica, ignoring his outstretched hand. 'Not interested.'

'Oooh. Very tart.'

'Watch it,' I said.

'No offense meant. How's business, Vic? You busy?'

'Busy as hell,' I said. For some reason lawyers always ask each other if they are busy and the response is always that they are busy as hell, even if they're not. 'Funny, things seemed to pick up just after you left.'

'Well, that's grand,' he said. 'I told you my leaving was the best for all of us. How's Lizzie? That biological clock of hers still ticking?'

'Beth's just fine, she's a champ,' I said, suddenly angry. 'By the way, we ran into your wife the night before last at the Art Museum.'

The smartass smile fled like a roach when the kitchen light is switched on. It cheered me to see it disappear. 'I couldn't make it,' he said. 'I've been mondo busy at Blaine, Cox. And it's not just the quantity of the work that's so amazing, Vic, it's also the quality.'

'She said you were separated,' I went on, not taking the segue he offered me about his new firm, preferring to let him squirm.

'What did she do? Sit you down and tell you all her problems? Be sure to charge her the two hundred bucks. Every shrink in the city already has.'

'She seemed pretty happy to my untrained eye,' I said.

145

'It's a mask. Just the other day she said she pined for me.'

'So you're getting back together then?' I asked.

'When I'm ready. I think I'll let her hang for a bit. I'm enjoying being on my own again.' He gave Veronica a patented Guthrie smile, all confidence and innuendo, but this night it seemed a bit wan. 'Listen, Vic, I've been meaning to talk to you. Can we get together sometime?'

'For you I'm booked until the millennium.'

'I'll have Carolyn get in touch with Ellie and set something up.'

'Oh, the anticipation,' I said slowly.

'It'll be worth your while.' He turned back to Veronica and reached into his inside pocket. 'Let me give you my card. If you need anything, a will, lunch, anything, give me a call. My home number's on the back.'

'I'm sorry, Mr . . .' she glanced at the card. 'Whatever. But I don't need any more insurance.'

'I don't sell insurance.'

'Funny, you strike me as someone who would sell insurance.' She ripped his card in half and let the pieces drop to the floor.

'My man Victor,' he said, shaking his head. 'We really need to talk.'

'A friend of yours?' asked Veronica after he had left.

'He used to be, before he deserted us for a big firm paying him lots of money. Stole our best files, too.'

'You're better off without him. He's a cocky little bastard.'

'I used to think he was charming.'

'He still does,' she said. 'But he's torn up about his wife.'

'It seemed like he was taking it pretty well.'

'It was in his eyes. I read eyes, you know.'

'So you told me.'

'His eyes were very sad, very ugly. He's desperate for her.'

146

'For a desperate guy he was coming on to you all right,' I said.

'Since I was fourteen I never met a man who didn't.'

'Now who's being cocky?'

'It's not arrogance, Victor. Every man in this bar would go out with me if he could. Even the gay ones. If I came in alone I wouldn't have had to buy a drink.'

'You didn't buy a drink. I bought them all.'

'That's true. I never buy drinks.'

'Convenient.'

'For an alcoholic. The only difference between men is that though they all want me, some think they deserve me. Take your friend Prescott. He thinks he deserves me. Every time he has a second alone with me his hands are all over my body.'

'I thought he was happily married.'

'He says he can't help himself.'

'That's bullshit.'

'Or maybe I ask for it.'

She laughed and leaned close and languidly rolled the edge of her finger across my mouth and down my neck and then leaned closer until I could smell her sweet, sharp breath.

'Do you think I ask for it?'

'Stop it.'

She gave me a fake pout. 'Don't you want to kiss me, Victor? Don't you want to bite my lip?'

'You shouldn't be talking like that.'

She took hold of my hand and put it on her thigh and I let her. The cool softness of her palm, the textured silkiness of her stocking. My face got hot and I looked around at the bar crowd, deep into the inanities of its conversations, oblivious to us. She rubbed my hand back and forth on her thigh and placed her mouth next to my ear.

'Don't you want to smell the perfume on my neck,' she whispered, 'and kiss my collarbone and reach into my dress and roll my right nipple between your fingers?'

I took my hand away. 'Cut it out.' The phone call from Chuckie had left me nervous, too nervous to play her games.

'Anything you want, Victor.'

'Just cut out the teasing.'

'I'm not teasing.' She laughed. 'Well, not completely.'

'What about Jimmy? Does he think he deserves you, too?'

'No,' she said, turning back to the bar and drinking the last of her martini. 'Jimmy thinks he earned me and he's right. Finish your drink, we should be going.'

On the way out of the bar, as we squeezed through the crowd of suits, an olive-clad arm reached out to grab my shoulder. 'Don't forget,' said Guthrie. 'We have to meet.'

Veronica draped herself around me until she was facing Guthrie and said 'Bye-bye, Fred.'

Guthrie said, 'My name's not . . .' before he realized she was playing with him.

I gave Veronica a signal to let her know I'd be out in a moment and then I grabbed hold of Guthrie's arm. 'Let me ask you something,' I said. 'Last night Lauren was wearing two gold bracelets with runes and diamonds. I was thinking of getting them for somebody.'

'The babe out there?'

'Sure. Where did she buy them?'

'You don't get stuff like that at Sears, Vic. They're custom jobs, from a jeweler in Switzerland.'

'Is there a catalogue or something?'

'Forget it, they were the only two made. She helped design them, she's into design now, you know. Besides, Vic, they're so out of your league pricewise you might as well be thinking of buying the Eagles.'

Outside the bar Veronica clutched at my arm as we walked down 20th, looking for a cab. She leaned her head on my shoulder and I pulled away as I saw an empty Yellow Cab drive toward us. I stepped out into the street and waved. The cab swerved to a violent, Hollywood stop.

'You go to the airport maybe, mister?' said the puffy-faced East Indian driver.

I opened the door before he could get away.

In the back of the cab she sat close and leaned into me. 'I think I'm a martini short of where I ought to be.'

'I think you've had plenty,' I said, shifting away from her until I was leaning against the door. I took her hand off my knee.

'I wasn't teasing you.'

'Yes you were.'

'But don't you want to kiss me?'

'No.'

'Really. Just a kiss?'

'Stop it.'

She pursed her lips and leaned her face toward me.

'Just one kiss and I'll stop.'

'You'll stop without a kiss.'

'If you were Prescott you'd have me stretched out on the back seat already with my legs around your neck.'

I didn't relish being compared to Prescott like that, as if he were the better man in everything. I was on the way up, in my ascendance, but still I couldn't stop seeing myself as a second-rater compared to the likes of William Prescott III. I felt a swift flash of anger and I cupped her chin to give her a peck on the cheek, like she was a little girl, tossing her chin away from me when it was over.

She laughed. 'See, that wasn't so terrible.'

She leaned forward and kissed me quickly and lightly on the lips. And then again, longer this time, pressing her body into mine as she kissed me. Her lips parted and her tongue licked my lips before slipping itself through and rubbing my teeth and then searching like a serpent for my own. By the time the cab stopped she was almost kneeling on the bench seat, pressing her body onto mine like a wrestler struggling for a pin, and my hands were up the back of her dress and down her panties.

'If maybe you finished here now, mister, we're at the

place,' said the driver. We were in front of a corner restaurant with a brown tiled entrance and a well-lighted sign hanging off the wall that read: DANTE'S & LUIGI'S.

Veronica pulled back from me and, still kneeling on the bench, said through a catlike smile, 'See, just an innocent little kiss.'

Then she reached for her purse and told the driver to ride around the block, once, so she could straighten her face.

17

'How's that veal chop, Victor?' asked Jimmy Moore. 'They make the best veal chop in all of South Philadelphia. The best.'

'It's fine.'

'Their gravy's not as good as Ralph's, but Dante's and Luigi's veal chop is the thickest in the city. And they marinate it before they broil it. That's the secret.'

'It's fine,' I said.

It was just five of us in a bare and spacious private dining room, with whitewashed plaster walls and a high tin ceiling. The table was covered with crisp linen and the waiters, wearing red jackets and linen aprons, had piled it with pasta, veal, broccoli rabe sautéed in garlic, a large bowl of chopped greens swimming in oil and spiced vinegar. Prescott sat rigid in his chair, ignoring his meal so he could stare at me. Concannon worked carefully on his scaloppine, elbows off the table. Veronica sat next to Moore, who kept his arm possessively in her lap.

'We're glad you were able to come this evening, Victor,' said Prescott. 'We wanted to make clear exactly the foundation upon which our defense will rest in the upcoming trial.'

'Politics in America, Victor,' boomed Jimmy Moore. 'That's our defense. You've heard the tapes, we can't deny that we were asking for contributions from that lizard Ruffing, and I wouldn't if I could. But everything we did was required by our fine political system. Required. Do you understand?'

'Not exactly,' I said.

'What is politics in America all about, Victor?' he asked.

I thought for a moment. 'The will of the electorate?'

'Money,' he roared. 'America is not about power being bestowed by the people, it is about power being grabbed. Grabbed. This country was built with a revolution, created again in a civil war, nothing comes easy or cheap here. American politics is the fairest in the world because the only thing that matters is the money. Hire the consultants, buy the television time, put a bumper sticker on every car, pay off the ward leaders, grab the electorate by its throat with all your money and take the oath of office. That's the system and that's damn fine. Any Tom, Dick, or Hanna can hand in a petition, but only the real Joe, can raise the dough. And to stay the real Joe, you better aim every day of your term at getting the contributions for the next election, you better never let down, not for a second. For those who want to support me it is not enough that they clap when I speak, they must give me money when I run. When I was demanding money from Ruffing for my political action committee, for my causes, for my future as a public servant, it was in the great tradition of American politics. All politicians do it, they just cloak it with cocktail parties or fancy dinners. But I cloak nothing. I was demanding money from a supporter because the system I love requires me to do it. And if I was asking a little more forcefully than others, it's because I have a greater passion for what I'm doing than the others. Do you understand what I'm saying, Victor?'

'Our strategy,' said Prescott, with a pursed, mournful face, as if he were a presidential flack on *Nightline*, 'is to turn this trial of these two public servants into a trial of the American political system and then to make sure the system gets acquitted.'

'You should be focusing on that strategy,' said Moore. 'Preparing to build on that foundation. Isn't that right, Chet?'

'That's right,' said my client.

'Now we've hired a polling service,' said Prescott. 'We've

studied focus groups, examined the demographics. With the right jurors this strategy will prevail. We're certain.'

'Can I get a copy of that study,' I asked.

Prescott smiled at me, but not his warm smile. 'Of course. The key is to gear everything, the jury selection, the arguments, the testimony, everything to our strategy.'

'What about the murder?' I asked.

'Don't worry yourself about it,' said Moore, reaching for a basket of toasted garlic bread.

'And the arson?'

'Forget it,' said Moore, his mouth now full.

'It's hard to forget about murder and arson.'

'How's your makeup doing, Ronnie?' asked Moore.

'Fine, I think,' she said.

'Why don't you check it?'

She nodded and rose from the table, leaving the room without glancing at me. I couldn't help but follow her out with my gaze. When I turned back, Moore was staring at me with a frightening ferocity.

'What were you doing at the DA's office this morning?' he demanded.

I pulled back from the table. Did everyone know where I had been that day, what I had done, whom I had seen, how many times I had hit the pot? 'I was looking into the murder,' I said. 'Examining the physical evidence.'

'Why didn't you clear it with Prescott?'

'I didn't know I had to clear all my trial preparations with Prescott.'

'Tell him, Chet.'

'You have to clear everything with Prescott,' said Concannon.

Without taking his eyes off me, the councilman fished a cigarette out of his pocket and lit it. Holding it like a pencil, his lips tight and dangerous, he took a deep drag. 'In war you have to pick your battlefields, son,' said Moore, breathing out smoke with his words. 'That's what Lee learned at Gettysburg.' He jabbed his cigarette at me and the syllables of his words came with the precise staccato of gunshots. 'Our battlefield is not going to be Bissonette's murder.'

'The federal indictment,' explained Prescott, with a surfeit of patience in his voice, 'covers the crimes of racketeering and extortion. If the murder and the arson are not linked to the request for money, and if the request for money is legal, the federal case will fail.'

'But if Eggert ties the murder into the request for money,' I said, 'any claim for legitimacy disappears.'

'He won't,' said Moore. 'Eggert's so far down the wrong road he might as well be in Vancouver.'

'But you've been looking into Bissonette's murder on your own, Victor,' said Prescott, 'conducting an investigation without our knowledge or consent, acting contrary to your client's express orders. Risking everything.' He looked at me hard so that I knew exactly what he meant, and he meant everything. 'So tell us, Victor, what exactly have you uncovered so far?'

'Nothing definite,' I said. 'But I have some ideas about who might have killed Bissonette, some theories.'

Moore leaned back and stared at me. 'So you have some ideas, do you, Victor?' he said slowly. 'Some theories.' There was a silence as he took another drag from the cigarette, all the while staring at me. He spread his arms wide. 'Educate us all with your theories.'

'Yes, Victor,' said Prescott, smiling unpleasantly. 'Please do.'

I was being threatened and tested at the same time, I thought. They wanted to see what I had figured out, to determine whether I was ready for all they had to offer me. Well, I was ready. I had been so ready for so long.

'They are just theories,' I started, leaning forward as I spoke. 'But I wondered why Chuckie Lamb wasn't indicted. Chet said it was because only Bissonette had direct knowledge of his possible involvement. That would have given Chuckie a motive for getting rid of Bissonette.'

I didn't tell them about the phone call that evening, didn't want to run to Prescott and Moore like a little boy when the schoolyard bully threatened, but the call had convinced me that I might be on the right line about Chuckie's motive.

'So Chuckie did it, huh?' said Moore.

'Also, Bissonette was apparently a ladies' man,' I continued. 'Lots of women. Jealousy could have been a motive. I have in mind one man in particular who was being cheated on who is known to be violent.'

'Tell us who?' asked Prescott while Moore continued to stare at me.

'I'd rather not say just yet,' I said, but I, of course, was thinking of my ex-partner, Guthrie. There was no doubt now that it was Lauren Amber Guthrie in the photograph I had picked out at the DA's office, those bracelets, and somehow Guthrie must have found out about her and Bissonette too. She had said he could become violent with jealousy, but I knew it would have been more than jealousy, it would have been desperation. Lauren was as domestic as a bobcat, but a tidy package came with her, money, status, entree into a world that kept guys like Guthrie and me out just for the pleasure of the blackball. It was one thing to never have a shot at it, that just caused a slow tightening of the stomach, tying you gradually into knots until you resented everything, hated everybody, held malice and bitterness toward all. But to have it in your grasp, in your bed, to have it all and then to see it slip away as your wife threw herself at some broken-down ballplayer with pectorals, well, that was enough to drive a man to murder. It would have been enough to drive me to murder and Guthrie was no better.

'Any other theories?' demanded Moore.

'Not yet,' I said. 'But I'd like to keep looking.'

'That's not permissible,' said Prescott firmly, as he examined his water glass. 'Besides, it would be a waste of time. We already know who killed Bissonette.'

'You do?' I said, surprised.

'What, you think we are idiots here?' said Moore angrily. 'You think it just slipped our minds the part about finding out who really beat the hell out of that man?' I shriveled from his blast because that was precisely what I had thought. Suddenly I knew I had made a fool of myself. Whatever test there had been I had failed.

'You were right, Victor,' said Chester with a reassuring smile. 'At least about Bissonette sleeping with the wrong woman. And the woman wasn't discreet about it at all.'

'Mooning over him like a schoolgirl with a crush,' said Moore.

'Linda Fontelli,' said Chester. 'Mrs Councilman Fontelli.'

'Fontelli?' I said. 'Councilman Fontelli killed him?'

Moore snorted. 'Fontelli doesn't have the stones for it. Besides, he's got his own little secrets. He didn't care.'

'No, it wasn't her husband,' said Prescott. 'It was her father.'

'Linda Marie Raffaello Fontelli,' said Chet.

'Raffaello,' I said slowly. 'Jesus Christ.' Enrico Raffaello was the head of the Philadelphia mob, a shadowy, legendary figure said to stand astride the city's underworld like a modern-day Pluto. 'And the limousine at the scene, and the ID by Ruffing?'

'The wino saw a basic black limousine, that's all,' said Prescott. 'There are fleets in the city. And Ruffing is lying. With the lighting in the parking lot it was impossible for him to see what he says he saw. He identified Jimmy and Chester to keep Marshall Eggert happy because Eggert was keeping the IRS off his back.'

'So how do we prove it was Raffaello?' I asked. 'Is she in any of his photographs?'

'Yes,' said Prescott. 'But getting them before the jury will be tricky. I have two lawyers working on it. Gimbel won't let us get it in the front door, that's for sure.'

'So how?'

'A trial like this trial,' said Prescott, leaning back now,

putting on the face of a law school lecturer, 'a trial like this, where the government is trying to cram a huge array of facts into a neat and tidy package, is made up of contingencies more than anything else. Every defense has to have a backup and every backup defense has to be backed up itself. Now our main defense is that we were merely working within the system, doing what the system demands of every politician. If the trial starts centering on Bissonette then we use our backup, we'll bring in what we can about Linda Marie Raffaello Fontelli, and even if the judge upholds an objection the name will be floating out there for the jury to grasp.'

'And if that doesn't work, are there other backups?'

'We're building them day by day,' said Prescott. 'If we need to go that route we'll let you know.'

'Shouldn't I know now?'

'No,' said Moore. 'There are things only Prescott is to know.'

'We're building a very complex piece of machinery to get both our clients off, Victor,' continued the professorial Prescott. 'And it's not enough to end with an acquittal. These men are politicians, they must end the trial smelling like virgins, do you understand? Jimmy Moore has to step out of that courtroom cleansed of any taint, risen in stature, ready for a run at the mayor. Now we can't have you going out half-cocked, stirring up Eggert, getting in the way of the construction of our machine.'

'Eggert didn't know I was there,' I said. 'I went through Slocum.'

'Eggert knows,' said Moore. 'The bastard knows everything. He's got more spies in the DA's office than I do.'

'So now we're all on board,' said Prescott. 'Each ready to do our duty. Any further questions, Victor?'

'Just one,' I said.

Prescott closed his eyes in exasperation and shook his head. Moore glared. Chet Concannon continued to avoid my gaze. What they all wanted just then, I knew, was for me to shut up and take whatever they were giving with gratitude. But something wasn't right here. Chuckie Lamb's slip of the tongue had got me to thinking and what I was thinking about just then, like what I thought about most often in those days, was money.

'Ruffing says he turned over half a million dollars before he backed out,' I said. 'CUP's records showed they only received two hundred and fifty thou. What I was wondering is what happened to the rest.'

'Your job here is not to wonder,' snapped Jimmy Moore. 'Your job is to just follow along. I thought Chet made that clear already.'

'I told him,' said Chester.

'Well, maybe you better tell him again.'

'There's no need,' I said.

'You are to do nothing, absolutely nothing,' said Moore, dumping his ashes on top of the ravioli, his voice rising in anger. 'You're getting paid a lot of money to do absolutely nothing and that's all you better do. I'm not going to have some skinny-assed geek with a hard-on for my girl sending me to jail because he gets in the way of my high-priced attorney. The only reason you're here is because Prescott told me you would stay out of his way.'

'I told Jimmy and Chester,' said Prescott, with the false conciliation of a State Department spokesman, 'that I thought you were bright enough to grasp our defense and a sharp enough trial attorney to realize the importance of letting me try the entire case.'

'Do you got it now, asshole?' said Moore.

'That's enough, Jimmy,' said Chester. 'He understands.'

'Oh my,' said Moore with a laugh. 'He's crying. I see a tear.'

'Enough,' said Chet sharply.

'I'm not crying,' I said as I wiped my eyes with a napkin. 'It's just an allergic reaction to the smoke. And I don't have a hard-on for your girl.'

'You could have fooled me,' said Moore. 'Walking in

here with a billy club inside your pants. You better choose here and now. Up or down, boy? It's your choice. You step out of line and you won't be able to find a client to save your life. You play ball and I can send a lot of business your way. A lot of business. It's already started, hasn't it?'

'Did you call the Bishops?' asked Prescott matter-of-factly.

'Yes,' I said, understanding now exactly what the position of outside counsel for the Valley Hunt Estates deal entailed.

'It's a great opportunity for a young lawyer trying to make a name for himself,' said Prescott.

'Not to mention the money,' said Moore.

'We have to work as a team,' said Prescott.

'If that's what my client wants,' I said.

'That's what he wants,' said Moore. 'Isn't that right, Chet?'

'That's what I want,' said Chet, now looking at me square in the face.

'All right,' I said. 'Whatever my client wants. But the jury's going to be asking the same question I just did.'

'We'll tell them there wasn't any other money,' said Prescott matter-of-factly as he folded a red napkin. 'Ruffing simply exaggerated the amount in his testimony. His accountant advised him that money paid to an extortionist is a deductible expense, so like every other American he lied on his taxes and now he's stuck with it.'

'You can prove that?' I asked.

'Just keep out of my way, Victor,' said Prescott coldly.

'So, everything's settled then, right?' said Moore. 'No more trips to the DA's office, right? No more questions. No more freelancing, right?'

'That's right,' I said.

'That's damn right,' said Jimmy Moore. 'Now, have some wine, Victor.' He poured a blood-red Chianti into my glass. 'There's plenty more where that came from. And finish your veal. I insist.'

I had lost whatever appetite I once held, and the sight of Moore's ashes sinking into the ravioli gravy made me positively nauseous, but still I was hacking into the meat with a steak knife when Veronica returned. She smiled as she walked in, glanced at me with a touch of concern, and sat down.

'I hope I'm not interrupting,' she said.

'Not at all,' said Moore. 'Victor was just telling us how much he was enjoying his chop.'

18

'This isn't the way,' I said from the back seat of the limousine. I was alone in the car except for Henry, Moore's driver. With the partition down I could see the back of his head, nappy hair cut short, thick neck, a set of tiny ears. 'I told you Twenty-second and Spruce.'

'I be knowing where you live at, mon, believe me,' said Henry in his lilting island accent. 'But is some business I need first to do.'

'Can't it wait until you take me home?'

'No, mon. Just you sit back and be resting yourself. We be done here quick.'

I was too tired and nauseous to argue. From the restaurant we had gone to a bar and then to a place on the river and then to a private club above a storefront off South Street, where the booths had curtains and the lights were low. Through the whole of the evening, whenever Jimmy wasn't looking, Veronica rubbed her hand across my crotch. Prescott had left us in the restaurant, and I too had tried to leave, but Moore insisted and Veronica smiled and against all my judgment I tagged along. Because the thing was, I knew, somewhere in my weak-willed heart, I just knew that tagging along with Jimmy Moore was exactly what I wanted to do. Jimmy was probably crooked and Chester was most likely his accomplice and Veronica was definitely dangerous, but sitting in those clubs, drinking champagne, laughing my forced laugh, stealing cigarettes, sitting in those clubs, I again felt the knot in my stomach ease and the ice melt. I couldn't actually say I was enjoying myself after the browbeating I had been given at the restaurant, but for all his faults Jimmy knew something

161

about living I had never learned, something I wanted desperately to learn.

'Have another drink,' Jimmy had said as he filled my glass with champagne. There were others at the table with us now, young girls with bare legs who slurped their champagne loudly, two well-dressed black men, doctors in business with the city, I was told, and, of course, my buddy Chuckie Lamb, who glared at me the whole of our time together.

'I've had enough,' I said even as the foam slipped over the top of my glass. 'Really.'

'Your lawyer's very stuffy,' said Veronica to Chester.

'It's the profession,' said Chet.

'Look over there,' said Moore. A thin-shouldered bald man was leaning over a table, talking earnestly to a young woman with pretty, pouting lips. 'Tom Bismark, managing partner of Blaine, Cox, Amber and Cox. Who's that he's with?'

'I think that's his wife,' said Chester.

'How unusual,' said Veronica.

'His third wife.'

'I thought he moved out with his secretary,' said Moore.

'He did,' barked Chuckie Lamb. 'He's here with his wife, cheating on his mistress.'

'You have to admire a scoundrel who can't even be faithful to his unfaithfulness,' said Moore. 'What about you, Victor?'

'Not married,' I said.

'You can still cheat even if you're single.'

'I'm pretty loyal.'

'You're a boy scout, is that it?'

'I was, as a matter of fact.'

'I was never a boy scout,' said Moore. 'I was too passionate for the boy scouts. There was too much I wanted to hold.' He leaned over to Veronica and with his hand turned her face toward him and kissed her with an open mouth. To see it knotted my stomach again.

162

'How's your wife doing, Councilman?' I said.

Veronica's eyes bugged out at me even as she was kissing Moore, but he just laughed when he was through. 'Very fine, thank you, Victor. So nice of you to be concerned.'

'I find her very sweet and very sad,' I said. 'Lonely, I think.'

'She is all of that and more,' said Jimmy. 'But tell me something, Victor, how much sadness can we endure before we run for the light?' He snapped his fingers and one of the young girls with bare legs quickly threw her arms around my neck and her tongue in my ear.

'Hey, Chuckie,' said the councilman. 'Victor here thinks you killed that lousy ballplayer.'

'Oh, he does, does he?' said Chuckie.

'You mean Zack?' said one of the girls. 'He was so sweet. Why would you do something like that, Chuckie?'

Jimmy started laughing, losing control as he laughed harder, so hard he could barely get out the words, 'Victor thinks you're a murderer, Chuckie.'

'Victor better be careful,' said Chuckie, looking at me with an unkind eye. 'He might just be right.'

I had left finally, feeling the tug of too much work and not enough time, the tug of responsibility, downing the last of my champagne and staggering out of the club into the cold misty night. I was looking for a cab on the deserted street when Henry came from behind me and grabbed my arm and led me to the limousine.

So we were traveling north now, across Arch, under the 5th Street tunnel, into the ragged and unlighted sections of Northern Liberties. It was after midnight and still kids sat out on the stoop and young men leaned against boarded up buildings, looking suspiciously into the darkened limousine windows, and teens loitered in groups in the middle of the street, illuminated by our headlights as if caught in twin beams of unreality, unwillingly moving aside as the limousine slid through.

'Where are we going, Henry?'

'We be there soon, no problem.'

'I'm starting to worry.'

'You with me, mon. You safer than safe.'

Northern Liberties was where my grandfather Abraham and his parents, fresh off the boat from Russia, had settled. It was a poor Jewish section then, crowded and hubbubed, Philadelphia's answer to the Lower East Side. Marshall Street: kosher butchers and discount clothiers and vegetable carts parked wheel to wheel, all catering to the immigrant families crowded four to a row house. My great-grandfather had learned to cobble in a *shtetl* outside Kiev and so in America he repaired shoes in a little store on Marshall Street, just north of Poplar, and my grandfather shortened his name and went into retail, working the store the whole of his life, even as the neighborhood changed and he moved with his family to the new Jewish paradise in Logan. Logan is no longer a paradise and Northern Liberties has fallen into such disrepair that Marshall Street is deserted and great swaths of the neighborhood are rubble. In the eighties there was an attempt at gentrification and some restaurants and stores opened up in the old Jewish center, but that too failed. There was nothing left of what my grandfather had seen as a little boy in his introduction to America.

We passed north out of Northern Liberties and through another neighborhood of boarded-up buildings and narrow, crowded streets and finally reached a corner that looked like a marketplace from hell. There were at least a hundred people hanging around, sitting on steps or patrolling the curb or just lolling on the outskirts of the crowd, heads jacking back and forth. In the streetlight the scene held a demented quality, unformed, chaotic, deeply dangerous. In front of us a flat-green Pontiac stopped and three kids jostled each other for a place at the driver's door. Money passed from the car to one of the kids and the kid ran over to an older man with dreadlocks and gave him the money. I watched the man nod to a different kid, who reached for something under a stoop and ran over to the car. In less than a minute from the time it had arrived, the flat-green Pontiac was on its way. Henry stopped the limo and immediately a kid started tapping at the closed window beside my head. Henry turned around and smiled at me.

'I be back, mon. You be taking things slow as they come.'

He left.

I made sure my door was locked as I watched Henry approach the man in dreadlocks. They spoke for a moment. The man nodded and Henry went toward one of the houses, on the front step of which a group of very young women sat. The women wore blue jeans and leather jackets and gold. One woman had huge gold earrings, impossibly, painfully huge. Another had a gold necklace with chain links the size of manacles. When Henry arrived at the house he leaned over and kissed one of the women on the cheek. He patted another on the head and chatted a moment before squeezing through the group and entering the house. Passing him on the way out was a skinny young man with a high nervous step and sunglasses. I was watching Henry enter the house when the front door of the limousine opened and a young black man with the shoulders of a lion jumped into the driver's seat.

'Where's we off to now, Chauncey?' he said in a thin, slippery voice.

'Get out of here,' I said.

He turned and smiled at me and the next moment I heard the click of the door locks and my door opened. A very thin man in a fine brown pinstriped suit leaned in the open door and said, 'Move over.'

I moved over. He sat down beside me.

His skin was dark brown, his fingers long and thin. There was about him a distinct air of elegance, the way he crossed his legs, the way he clasped his hands close to his chest. But more than anything he was thin, spectrally thin, droopy-eyed and gaunt, so thin it was impossible to tell his age; he could have been twenty-five, he could have been fifty.

'What can I do for you, friend?' asked the man in a deep, soothing voice.

'I'm just waiting for someone,' I said. 'He'll be right back. I don't want anything else.'

'Generally, white boys in limousines down here want something.'

'I just want to get out of here.'

'Don't we all.'

'Where we going?' asked the young man in the front.

'Around,' said the thin man.

'Shit,' I said.

The engine shivered quietly to life and the limousine lurched forward, almost running down a young girl carrying a two-year-old boy in her arms as she wandered toward the marketplace.

'Jesus, take the car, I don't care,' I said with panic in my voice. 'Just let me out first.'

'We only going for a ride,' said the kid up front.

'Drive carefully, Wayman,' said the thin man. 'We don't want to scratch the councilman's car.'

'Then you know whose car this is.'

'Oh yes. Let's introduce ourselves. Call me Mr Rogers.'

'Mr Rogers,' said Wayman with a cackle. 'I like that.'

Mr Rogers reached out a hand. Unsure of what to do, I shook it.

'Victor Carl.'

'Well, Victor Carl, welcome to my neighborhood.'

'Mr Rogers,' cackled Wayman again.

'What do you think?' asked Mr Rogers, gesturing out his window.

I looked around at the bombed-out hulks of narrow row houses, some collapsing in on themselves, others boarded up with plywood, crumbling steps, weeds rising like bushes from the sidewalks, empty bottles scattered. An old man, lips working over his toothless gums, sat on a metal chair and stared at the limousine as we passed.

'It's fine, I guess,' I said.

'Fine for us, right?'

'No. I didn't mean that.'

'Calm down, Victor.' He laughed a deep, surprisingly warm laugh.

'I just want to get out of here.'

'And you will. Calm down, enjoy the ride.'

He pulled down a panel on the door, revealing the limousine's bar. There were decanters of liquor and glasses and bottles. He took one of the glasses and looked at the decanters.

'Now which one's the scotch,' he said to himself. He reached for one, took off the crystal top, and poured. He took a sip and smiled. 'That's what I like about the councilman, always the best liquor. Turn here, Wayman, and remember this car is as long as a school bus.'

We turned down a side alley and then back up 6th Street, making a loop.

'I just wanted to have a little talk,' said Mr Rogers. 'Nothing too serious. You like being a lawyer, Victor?'

'How did you know?'

'I would have been a damn good lawyer,' he continued. 'Would have knocked aside your ass in court, I know that, Victor. See, Wayman, man. It's like I've been telling you. You get back in school, you can be anything you want. Even fools like Victor here can become million-dollar lawyers.'

'Would's I also have to dress like him?' asked Wayman from the front seat, looking back at me in the rearview mirror.

Mr Rogers sized me up and down, my scuffed wing tips, my shiny blue suit, my striped polyester tie. 'Point taken,' said Mr Rogers. 'Where'd you get those shoes?'

'You want them, take them. Anything. Just leave me alone.'

167

'Last thing I want is those shoes. Where did you pick those flippers?'

'Florsheim.'

He snickered. 'Turn up here.'

'I want you to stop the car and let me out, now,' I said loudly. The crack about my shoes had somehow set me off. I sat forward in the seat. 'This is kidnapping. I insist you stop.'

'Victor, trust me,' said Mr Rogers. 'You don't want us to let you off here.'

I looked around. Two kids were shadowboxing in a corner under a dim streetlight on an otherwise deserted street.

'Maybe you're right,' I said, slumping back.

'You know, you are messing in things way above your head, things you can't even begin to understand. No sir. All politicians are liars, don't you think?'

'There are some honest ones, I guess,' I said.

'But not Jimmy Moore. He's a hell of a politician, but he lies and he steals and in the end he takes away everything he promised to give. Now I'm a businessman. I sell a product for a fair price and my customers keep coming back. And I make damn sure I get paid for it. But Victor, I sell more than just a product. I sell my customers a reason to wake up in the morning, a purpose for their lives, something to give meaning to everything they do. In that way, Victor, I'm like a god, and Jimmy resents that. You see, godhood was his career goal, but it wasn't working out for him. I went to him after his sweet daughter died. I brought him proof of where she got the merchandise that killed her. It was a white group from the suburbs, from Bucks County, from Bensalem. And you think this is a hellhole. That's where it came from and I had to hurt some people to get that proof. He said he didn't care, that no matter where it came from I would pay the price. We were two men at war. We bloodied each other. But now the war is over.'

168

'I don't understand.'

'There are things you'll never understand, so I will make this simple.' He wagged a long, bony finger at me and spoke slowly, carefully. 'I've been getting reports about you. You've been asking about missing money. Don't. You've been stepping out of your role. Step back in. Listen to what I say, Victor, your health and career both depend on it, though I don't really have any control over your career.'

He opened his eyes wide and peered at me, to be sure that I understood, and I did.

'Besides, Victor,' he continued, 'anything you would do would hurt more than help. That's simply your destiny. We all have destinies, Victor, and yours is to be a fuckup. Now, in addition to all this, it seems you know a friend of mine.'

'No. I don't,' I said.

'How do you know who my friends are?' he said, a slash of anger in his voice.

'I don't, I mean, I'm sorry.'

'Shut up, Victor.'

From the front seat Wayman laughed like a little maniac, first a hoot and then a series of loud snivels.

'This friend is very special to me, do you understand, and I like to keep track of who she is with.'

'She? A her?'

'You are a bright one, aren't you. This friend of mine,' said Mr Rogers, 'she has this way of . . . let's say attaching herself to people. I don't want her to attach herself to you.'

'Who are we talking about?'

'We aren't talking,' he said sharply. 'I'm talking. Who I'm talking about is Ronnie Ashland. It is all part of the same thing. And what I'm saying is you stay away from her.'

'Veronica?'

'I assume you heard me, then. Any part of what I said you didn't understand?'

'Why? What's she to you?'

'He wants to know why, Wayman.'

'It's not such a swift idea to ask why 'round here,' said Wayman.

'I'll tell you why,' said Mr Rogers in a sweet voice. 'Because if you don't I'm going to hurt you.'

Wayman let out his scary, sniveling laugh again.

'I'm going to hurt you bad.'

'That's why enough for me,' I said quickly, almost gaily.

'Good, Victor. Maybe you're not as stupid as you look. Take us home, Wayman.'

'Yessir, Chauncey.'

Mr Rogers took another sip from his glass of the councilman's scotch. 'You know, Victor, the extra twelve years really do make a difference.'

Wayman pulled the limo into the same spot we had been parked in before and killed the engine. Mr Rogers finished his drink, put the glass back in the bar, and lifted up the panel.

'I never want to see you again, Victor, so be sure to remember all I told you this evening. If I leave one of my calling cards you'll know it and I hope for your sake you'll also know enough to be scared.'

He got out of the car and held the door open for Wayman, who skipped out of the front seat and leaned through the open door and smashed me in the face with the back of his hand.

I grasped my head in my hands and dropped it between my knees. Pain shot from my cheek to my groin and my eyeball stung so much I thought he had popped it and the fluid was running down my cheek. I opened my eyes through the pain and saw a blurry car floor and, with relief that my sight was still there, I heaved loudly and started to vomit.

Wayman remained leaning in the open door as I puked. 'Tell me something, Vi'tor Carl,' he said. 'You gots to pay

170

more for two first names?' Then he laughed his sniveled laugh once more.

I was still bent double, hand covering my eye, gasping for a clear breath, when Henry came back to the car. 'Aw, mon,' he said. 'Him a-chucking in the car.'

'Fuck off,' I said.

'Aw, shit, mon, him a-chucking in the car. Councilman Moore, he won't be liking that at all, mon.'

'Just fuck off.'

As he drove away from the corner the limo's windows and the roof opened electronically, letting in the cool of the night. The fresh air only made it worse.

19

My right eye was swollen thick and pretty by the morning, with a dark swath sitting directly atop my cheekbone, fading into a brownish stain that ran like coffee down my cheek. The night before I had fallen into bed with an ice cube wrapped in a towel and that might have helped for a while, but I still woke in my suit pants and shirtsleeves, the towel empty, my sheets wet, the faint taste of vomit in my teeth. When I saw my eye in the mirror I wanted to heave again.

'What happened to you?' asked Ellie when I came into the office that morning.

'I walked into a door,' I said.

'Looks like the door had a left hook.'

'Just do me a favor, all right, Ellie,' I said. 'Call up Bill Prescott's secretary over at Talbott, Kittredge and ask her to send over a copy of the report by some jury-polling service he commissioned for the Moore and Concannon case.'

'Sure thing,' she said. 'By the way, I have that address you asked for, the address of Winston Osbourne's daughter.'

She handed me a handwritten note with an address in Malvern. Malvern, big lawns and old money in the heart of Chester County. I had never been there, but I knew there were horses in Malvern, horses and gentlemen farmers and old stone houses. It was Radnor Hunt country. Not too many synagogues in Malvern, I would bet.

'Perfect,' I said. 'Send a copy of our judgment to the Chester County Sheriff's Office and tell them we think Osbourne's Duesenberg is parked at that address in

172

Malvern. Get the serial number from the file and tell them we want it seized, immediately. Pay any fees required out of the account.' It was nice to have an account out of which to pay any fees required. Solvency felt better than I ever thought it would.

'What should they do if they find it?' she asked.

'Just have them grab it and hold it for me. I'll decide then.'

I was behind my desk when Beth came in. 'Don't ask,' I said in response to her query.

'Did you fall down the steps?' she asked.

'Something like that.'

'Were you drinking last night?'

'Yes,' I said.

'Are you having a problem?'

'Yes, but not with my drinking.'

'If you're having a problem there are people you can see.'

'Stop it, Beth. With what I drink I'd die from hypoglycemia before I became an alcoholic.'

'That eye looks nasty,' she said. 'Let me get you something.' She left the office for a moment, coming back with a wet paper towel. 'Now close your eyes.'

She patted the wet towel to the puffed flesh just above my cheekbone. I meant to tell her not to, but the cool of the towel was so soothing. With my eyes closed and the dabbing coolness and Beth's perfume, a sweet and floral mixture that reminded me of someone, I couldn't remember who, but someone with whom I had once been in love, the whole mixture of sensations took me right out of that office, right out of my present. I was disappointed when she finally stopped.

'That was great,' I said.

She gave me the towel and I continued to dab, but now I was back in my office, back in my life, and it didn't feel half so good. 'How's your investigation going?' she asked.

'I've been called off.'

'By who?'

'By Moore and Prescott and my client.'

'I bet you were called off by Moore and Prescott and your client sort of went along.'

'Sort of.'

'So what are you going to do?'

'Exactly what I've been told to do,' I said. 'Absolutely nothing other than cashing my checks.'

'Nothing is pretty hard to do sometimes,' she said.

'Not this time.' I didn't want to tell her about Chuckie Lamb's threats or Mr Rogers's warnings. She'd look at the situation perfectly sensibly and have me do something like tell the police or withdraw from the case and I didn't want to do either. What I wanted to do was to stay far away from trouble and I knew how to do it, too. I would ask no more questions about Bissonette's murder or the missing quarter of a million. I would sit quietly at the trial and collect my fees and each night go home, alone, like a good little boy, and wait for my prosperity. I would make no waves. That would satisfy Prescott and Jimmy and Chuckie and the strange Mr Rogers. What I wanted to do was to forget the complications that were rising like flood waters about me. What I wanted to do was float safely through the fall into winter and put all this behind me. What I wanted to do was . . .

My phone rang.

'There's someone here to see you,' said Rita, our receptionist.

'You're supposed to tell me who is here to see me,' I said into the phone. 'That's in the job description.'

'Well, whoever it is, he looks like a short Rasputin if Rasputin had eaten too much chocolate pudding.'

'Find out who it is, Rita.'

Over the phone I could hear her ask, 'Who are you, anyway?' and the mumble of an answer.

'Morris Kapustin,' she said.

'Oh, right, the private eye.'

'Funny. He doesn't look like a private eye,' Rita said over the phone, and, as usual, Rita was right.

Morris Kapustin was a short, very heavy man with a long beard peppered gray and a wide-brimmed black hat. He wore a suit badly and he was sweating badly and he breathed with the slight wheeze common to the badly overweight. From out of his pants, over his belt, flowed four sets of cotton strings. He flapped his arms as he walked into the office and without my asking he let out a high pitched 'Whoooh' and dropped into a chair across from me. He sat down so hard a clock on my desk rattled on its base. His little feet barely touched the floor as he sat. He took off his black hat and wiped his forehead with a crumpled and stained handkerchief. Atop his mass of disheveled hair was a yarmulke.

'This office, it never heard from elevators? I'm *shvitzing* from the stairs. And it's October, yet. If it was July you'd have to wring out the carpet. Morris Kapustin. And you're Carl?'

'I'm Victor Carl,' I said, reaching out to shake his damp, pudgy hand. He lightly squeezed the ends of my fingers.

'Accht, that Benny. I didn't mean to be rude, forgive me, I thought Carl was your first name. All Benny said was that I should meet his lawyer, Carl, at ten on Friday. I thought Carl was the lawyer's first name. That Benny, I love him, but sometimes he's so *farchadat* it is a miracle he doesn't walk into a bus.'

'That's all right. This is my partner, Beth Derringer.' He didn't shake her hand.

'I'm pleased that I should meet you both. Especially the pretty lady, no offense to you, Carl. No; Victor, right? No offense to you, Victor, but in mine business, all day it's grumpy old men shouting about thieves. It's enough to give a headache the size of Pittsburgh. Accht, you don't want to hear mine *tsouris*. Benny Lefkowitz said that you needed help. He didn't tell me the what for. That Benny,

175

he's read too much Philip Marlowe. He's always yelling after me, "Off to catch the crooks, hey, Morris?" I say yes, when really all I'm after is a pastrami on rye. He's lucky to have such a business, Benny, and the money he makes, it hurts just to think it, but he likes to imagine I lead a glamorous life, so I let him.'

He wiped his forehead again with the handkerchief, looking as glamorous as a piece of herring.

'I need a towel is what I need,' he said. 'They should make for me a handkerchief towel. Such an idea, a handkerchief of terry cloth, for *shtik fetah* like me who *shvitz* even in October. I have family in the *shmatte* business, I know from what I'm talking. We'll make a fortune, just the three of us.' He turned to Beth and winked. 'We'll retire to Haifa, sit on our balcony all day, catch a breeze off the Mediterranean, sip slivovitz out of clean little glasses. Don't tell anyone our idea, the *gonifs* will steal it in a second. A second. I know, I have family in the business. Bigger crooks they don't have on post office walls. Now, Victor, Benny said I should be meeting with you. So we're meeting.'

'I think there may have been a mistake.'

'We weren't supposed to meet today? I wrote it down, I thought, but he spoke to me only yesterday.' He reached into his suit jacket with his right hand, pulling out a little black notebook, while at the same time he searched an inside pocket with his left hand, extracting a pair of wire glasses, the ends of which he slipped over his ears. With a lick of his thumb he started through the notebook. It was as disheveled as he, loose papers of every sort poking out from its covers. 'Morris, Morris, you're growing so *famisht*, Morris. I was certain it was today.'

'No, Mr Kapustin, our meeting was for today. You were right about that. But I don't think you're going to be able to help us.'

'Good, I was right about the day. Sometimes there's so much it's hard to keep track, and I get more and more confused. But at least I was right about the day, at least that. It's been a week, you don't want to know about mine week, believe me, so I thought the mistake it was maybe mine, but no. See, right here.' He poked at a loose piece of paper. 'Ten o'clock, Friday. Carl. Now that's cleared up. Good.' He closed the book and took off his glasses and stared at me with a squint. 'So, Carl, tell me exactly why I won't be able to help you.'

'What we needed,' I said, 'was to find a man who doesn't want to be found.'

'Such luck you're in, then, that's what I do. What I do, Victor, what Benny thinks is so glamorous, is that I find people, swindlers, crooks, *gonifs* who have taken off with a diamond or an emerald or the money from a cash register. You wouldn't believe how many times a jeweler unwraps his diamond and finds it's been switched. These are professionals, too. There is something about the way it shines, I don't know, but it attracts thieves, all out to steal from each other. Not Benny of course, he's an *edel mensch*, but the others. Me, I never cared so much for diamonds. Too easy to lose, I know. Mine wife, Rosalie, don't even try to buy her a diamond. She doesn't want to know from diamonds, Rosalie. Zero coupon bonds, yes. Diamonds, no. So Victor, this man you're looking for, he's a swindler?'

'Yes, actually.'

'Well, then, there's no such mistake, no such mistake at all. Tell me who he is, what he did, his friends, everything you know, and I'll find him. I'm no Houdini, but then who did Houdini ever find, huh?'

'But the fellow we're looking for, Mr Kapustin, is not Jewish.'

'Good. It hurts me here,' he pounded his chest, 'whenever it's a Jew I'm looking for, and you wouldn't believe me if I told you how many times I been hurt right here. It's a sin. And you know who I blame? Accht, you don't want to know.'

'Mr Kapustin, with all due respect, I just don't think this job is for you.'

'No?'

'To be honest, I didn't realize when Mr Lefkowitz gave me your name that you were an Orthodox Jew. I guess working in the jewelry business, in which a lot of Orthodox Jews are involved, it makes sense because you can move within that world. But we're not looking for a Hassid here.'

He leaned forward. 'Believe me when I tell you this. It's not only the Jews who steal. When it comes to stealing we're such *pisherkeh*, the things we can still learn. You'll be glad to know, Mr Victor, that Morris Kapustin does not just find Jews. You name it and Morris Kapustin has found it. Just last week, an Armenian boy, cleaning up at Grossman's, grabbed from the register and ran. I found him in Teaneck, Teaneck of all places. Who would think, an Armenian thief in Teaneck.'

'I'm sorry, Mr Kapustin,' I said. 'We'll find a different agency to hire. Thank you for understanding.'

'Wait just a moment, Mr Kapustin,' said Beth.

'A moment I have,' he said.

Beth pulled me outside my office. We left Morris Kapustin sitting in the chair, staring out my narrow window, pulling distractedly at his beard. Beth closed the door behind us and turned loose a fierce expression on me.

'What are you doing?' she whispered angrily.

'I'll get someone else, one of those high-tech private eye firms that advertise in the *Legal*.'

'You're not going to give him the job because he's a Jew?'

'It's not in his field. Our guy is in Buenos Aires somewhere, not Crown Heights.'

'I don't think that's it at all, Victor. He's as qualified as anyone. But you don't like the way he looks, do you?'

'Well, he's no Don Johnson.'

'Or the way he talks.'

'What are you getting at?'

'I think you don't want to hire him because he's too Jewish.'

'Oh, come on.'

'No, really, Victor. And this isn't the first time I noticed it. What is it with you?'

I never knew what it was with me, but I knew even as I denied it that she was absolutely right. I doubted whether this Morris Kapustin could do the job, but in reality I didn't care. I'd just as soon Stocker not be found, so that I could get the settlement and take my cut and be done with the case. But I had to admit feeling a touch of revulsion at the sight of Morris Kapustin, sweating that very moment in my office, with his Orthodox hat and tangled beard and the dirty cotton *tzitzis* that flowed over his belt. The great firms in the city from which I sought acceptance would not hire the likes of Morris Kapustin to investigate their cases.

I had often wondered if my failure to land a job in the firms of my choosing was due to my religion. It was no longer like the old days, of course, when the Drinker of Drinker, Biddle decried the influx of 'Russian Jew boys' into the law, men who had risen 'up from the gutter and were merely following the methods their fathers had been using in selling shoestrings,' when the Bar Association thought up the barrier of its prefectorship to handle what McCracken of Montgomery, McCracken called 'the question of the social origins of men.' Aspiring Jewish lawyers in those years who could actually find a prefector to sponsor them were either tapped for the Jewish firm, Wolf, Block, or forced to chew the legal scraps tossed them by their betters, petty crimes and bankruptcies and slip and falls. Do I sound bitter? Now Jews are hired everywhere, in moderate quantities, as long as they dress appropriately and speak without spitting and don't answer questions with questions or sprinkle Yiddish in their conversations. But though I had mastered those qualifications, I still hadn't been able to crack that crowd. In one great moment of clarity the holders of the keys had judged the Jew before them and in a collective voice had said, 'Sorry, no.'

My father was a lawnmower man, cutting other people's grass for a living, surviving without great modesty in a modest house. It was bad enough that my family lived on the cusp of poverty, it was worse that we were Jews living that way, Jews without money. If my father had made a fortune in shoe-strings or plastic hangers or potato chips or something maybe I wouldn't have fought against my ancestry so, but he hadn't and so I fought. I had wanted to become something new, something glorious, but there was still no estate in Bryn Mawr for me, no BMW, I had not yet been invited to play golf at Merion or tennis on the clean grass courts of the Philadelphia Cricket Club. There was nothing new in what I had become. I was still just a Jew without money. And as I sank into professional failure and a financial despair so deep I had been forced to ask my father, the lawncutter for God's sake, for a loan, I realized with a growing horror that my failures were sending me spinning back into everything I had sought to escape. And I didn't need Morris Kapustin sitting in my office reminding me. And I didn't need Beth staring at me with a pained disappointment in her eyes, the look a mother gives her son when he behaves badly, not my mother, who never cared enough to be disappointed by me, but someone else's mother, a kindly loving mother who only thought the best of her child and died a little when she was shown the worst. Who the hell was Beth, as Protestant as Luther, who the hell was Beth to tell me a thing about the curses I felt so keenly? Who the hell was Morris Kapustin, sitting in my office, begging for a job, making me feel lower than a slug? Who the hell needed any of it?

'Just shut up,' I told Beth, even though she hadn't been saying a thing.

'I was thinking, Victor,' said Morris Kapustin when Beth and I had returned to the office, 'now that I know it's your last name Carl not your first name Carl, that I might know your *mishpocheh*. By any chance was your grandfather Abe Carl?'

'As a matter of fact.'

'The shoe man?'

'He sold shoes.'

'Mine first pair of shoes in this country came right from his store on Marshall Street. What a thing. I was just a *yekl* then, thin as a piece of grass, that thin, Accht, too long ago to even remember. Abe Carl, the shoe man. Later we used to go to *shul* together when he moved out to Logan. In *shul* always he was looking at mine shoes, checking if I needed new ones. "You ready for new shoes, Morris," he would say. "For you I run a special." He had a beautiful voice, Abe did.'

'He used to sing me nursery rhymes,' I said. 'And Irving Berlin songs.'

'*Erev Shabbos*, singing L'*cha Dodi*, his voice was like an angel's, only sweeter. Mine first American shoes were good sturdy shoes. You can tell everything about a country by their shoes. Ever wear German shoes?'

'No.'

'You put on one pair of German shoes and you get a whole new understanding of the last hundred years. Believe me. He sold good shoes, your grandfather. Whenever I was needing new shoes it was off to the shoe man for me. You look like him.'

'They say I look like my mother.'

'I see Abe in you. That's not such a terrible thing. Can you sing?'

'Not a note.'

'Too bad that is. Like an angel's, only sweeter.'

I thought about it for a moment, thought about my grandfather too, his round peasant face and shock of white hair that I used to muss with my fingers and then call him Albert Einstein, about how it was my grandfather, not my father, who would read me stories and take me to the ball

181

games at old Connie Mack Stadium, thought about it all and then reached into my desk drawer. I handed Morris Kapustin a thick file filled with all the information I had about Frederick Stocker, including press clippings about his trust fund swindle and flight from authorities.

'Stocker. Stocker,' said Kapustin, as if he were chewing on a piece of gristle. 'Stocker. I know that name Stocker. How do I know that name? Morris, Morris, think. This Stocker, he stole trust funds?'

'That's right,' I said.

'Accht, of course. Stocker. Herman Hoff, a wholesaler, watches and such, gave this very man Stocker money to invest and then it was gone, poof, just like the wind. I've heard of this Stocker. Herman is not a rich man, nothing like our friend Benny, what this man Stocker took was Herman's retirement in Boca. You been to Boca, Victor?'

'No.'

'That's where they go now, Boca. Who needs to *shvitz* so much, I say, still that's where they go. But not Herman, he still sells his watches. Seventy-three already, still selling. He wanted to go to Boca.'

With his glasses back on, he began looking through the file, asking me questions I couldn't answer.

'All I know is what's in the file,' I said.

'Anything about this man's hobbies, his relatives, his friends, where he grew up. It is these things, I've found, it's good to know about.'

'He lived in Gladwyne,' I said.

'I'll ask around. I have mine contacts there.'

'Really?'

He looked at me strangely from under his brow and for an instant his smile disappeared and there was something fierce about this little man. 'I think you have no faith,' he said to me.

'What do you mean?'

'No faith that Morris Kapustin will find this man. For what he did to Herman Hoff, not to mention Benny, he deserves to be found. He's a crook, a *gonif*, finding him will be a *shtik naches*. You think this is a hobby, this finding people. I didn't start this line with jewelry. But this too needs doing. Talmudic justice. It is mine mission. You study Talmud, Victor?'

'No.'

'So now I know why you have no faith. Somehow, I don't know how, but somehow we will find that too. But first we find this crook Stocker, agreed?' He smiled warmly and was back to being jolly Morris Kapustin. He took out a bundle of pages and looked through them quickly. 'What was this Windward Enterprises thing you have so much papers about?' he asked.

'That was Stocker's own stab at real estate syndication. It didn't take and a lot of people lost money.'

'Windward is a funny name for such a business.'

'I hadn't thought about it,' I said.

'Maybe he was a sailor of some sort,' said Beth.

'This one,' he said wagging a finger at Beth, 'this one has *sechel*. Are you married, by any chance?'

'No, I'm not,' said Beth.

He turned to her and his face brightened with interest. 'Are you perhaps Jewish?'

'No, I'm sorry, Mr Kapustin. But I do eat kasha at the deli.'

'That's something at least. Accht, too bad. Not for you, of course, but . . .' He sighed deeply and wearily. 'You see, I have a son. He's in the business with me.' His shoulders dropped from the burden. 'What could I do, he needed a job.' He waved his hand. 'So what for am I *hocking* your *tchynik*? This sailor thing is a good possibility. He might have run off with a boat. Generally they run off with a woman and not their wives most often you wouldn't believe. But with sailors, they sometimes run off with a boat. Me, I never understood that one inch.'

'There are not many Jewish sailors,' I said.

'You may be right, but the amount of Jews who think

183

they are sailors, don't even try to count that high, you give your brain a hernia. What time do you have on your watch, Victor?'

'Ten forty-seven,' I said,

He put his watch to his ear. 'It's stopping again. I have to leave, quickly, one more appointment for this day.' He pushed himself out of the chair. 'Kramer. A set of earrings is missing, gone. It's only him and his wife, so where are the earrings? You tell me, I don't know myself. But I know Mrs Kramer, she doesn't clean. Even with her first husband, Kimmelman, and he wasn't a jeweler, he had a small grocery with no money anywhere and still she wouldn't clean. So who cleaned the earrings? That I must know.'

'We have a deadline in this case, Mr Kapustin,' I said.

'Always complications. So how much time do you have? Six months?'

'Three weeks.'

'Three weeks, Victor, I can't find the toilet in three weeks.'

'Three weeks, Mr Kapustin.'

'Call me Morris. Okay, three weeks. But don't now be expecting miracles. *Vos vet sein, vet sein.* I'll start first thing Sunday morning doing the search.'

'What about tomorrow?'

'On the Shabbos, Victor? Never a shoe did your grandfather sell, Victor, on the Shabbos, that you know. But I should be working on the Shabbos? You're insulting me now.'

'Okay,' I said. 'First thing Sunday morning.'

'By the way, Victor. I didn't want to mention it but now that we're friends, that eye of yours. What happened, *nu?*'

'A little accident.'

'You know, a slice of gefilte, not too thin, from the refrigerator with the jelly. It works nice.'

'Thank you, I'll try it,' I said, without the slightest intention of putting a slice of gefilte fish on my face.

He pointed a stubby finger at me. 'You won't listen to

me, I know, Victor, I can see it. What does an old fat man know about anything, you think. Put some gefilte in mine eye and I look like a fool, you think. But why you should be caring so much how you look is beyond me, Victor. Be your own man. For sixty-six years such has been my secret. So I'm not wearing the newest fashions. Thin ties, wide ties, Victor, I wear mine ties and that has always been good enough. So the gefilte, you try it, you'll see.'

I looked at Morris as he prepared to leave, gathering the papers into a messy pile and shoving it all into the file, grabbing his coat with both arms. A short sloppy Jew who wasn't embarrassed to be a short sloppy Jew. I would try the slice of gefilte fish on my eye. I'd buy a bottle at the deli. Who knew? And suddenly I didn't like the fact that I was being told what to do by Prescott and Moore and Chuckie and the demonic Mr Rogers, that I was being played like a puppet as I reached for what was being dangled. How was it that someone like Morris Kapustin could be his own man but that it was impossible for me? Fuck them all. Rogers had told me that I was in the middle of something that I couldn't understand and I didn't like that one bit. And Chuckie had told me I was already as good as wasted and I didn't like that one bit either. So maybe I'd check out some of the things I had been told by Prescott and Moore, just to be sure. So maybe I wouldn't float safely through this cold and rainy fall, maybe I'd fight the current and lift up my head to look around and figure out some things.

'Before you go, Mr Kapustin,' I said.

He turned. 'Such respect I can't take, it makes me want to dress better and who needs so many suits. Call me Morris.'

'All right, Morris.' I reached into my top drawer and took out the chip with the wild boar's head on it that I had snatched from Bissonette's love chest. 'Have you ever seen anything like this before?'

Morris dropped his coat on a chair, stepped up to my

desk, and took the chip. He put on his glasses and examined it carefully in his small, fat hands. 'This is a casino chip, like in Atlantic City, but with no name and this picture. This is a very strange thing here. Every other chip like this I've seen, it had the casino name on it. That's so you know where to take back your money, what little money you have left. And still they line up for the buses. Who can explain that to me? And Rosalie now has started. She plays blacktop. I would forbid it, absolutely forbid it, except that she brings home more than she takes.'

'Could you try to find out what it is?'

'I could. Is this something to do with Mr Stocker, the thief?'

'No, it's a different case.'

'A different case?' He lifted his head and gave me a flash of genuine smile. 'So, I think maybe you gained a little faith today, Victor. A little faith in Morris Kapustin. No?'

20

I was sleeping, or trying to in any event, feeling a painful pressure on my eye as I burrowed my head into my pillows, the tangy sweet smell of gefilte fish still clinging to my skin, when the buzzer rang. I groped for the clock radio and read the blue-green fluorescent numbers: 2:38. In a heartbeat I jerked awake, remembering that I had been twice threatened with serious harm only a few nights before. I imagined a horde of drug dealing thugs outside my apartment ready to rip out my spleen and decided not to answer the buzzer, but it rang again and then again and so I dared a look out my window. The street was empty and wet, glazed with a heavy rain. I lived in a brownstone converted long ago to apartments and there was no intercom between the small vestibule, where the mailboxes and buzzers were, and my apartment. The only way to know who was buzzing was to go downstairs and see. I pulled on a pair of jeans that had been lying on my floor and carefully, like a cat burglar, slipped down the steps of my own building to get a look at my late-night visitor through the inside vestibule door.

Veronica Ashland.

She was wearing a tan raincoat and jeans, her brown hair falling flatly in damp strands. The mascara under her eyes was thick from the rain, or was it tears, I couldn't tell just then, but her eyes were red and her lips thick, as if she had been crying. I searched the vestibule behind her. She was alone. Without opening the door I shouted, 'What are you doing here?'

She said something from the other side, I could see her

lips move, but I couldn't hear what she was saying through the glass and wood door.

'Speak louder,' I said.

Her lips moved more emphatically, but still I couldn't hear her. She made a motion for me to open the door. I wondered if she was merely moving her lips, pretending to speak in order to trick me into letting her in.

'What do you want?'

She made the same motion. With another nervous glance over her shoulder into the shadowy emptiness of the vestibule, I opened the door.

'Victor, what's the matter?' she said as she stepped into the lobby. I quickly closed the door. She dripped onto the thin blue rug. 'You looked as if you were going to turn me away like I was a Jehovah's Witness trying to convert you.'

'What do you want?'

'I couldn't sleep.'

'Well, I was sleeping fine.'

'Don't be such a grouch. Let me upstairs so I can take off this raincoat and dry out some.'

'I don't think I should.'

'Oh, Victor, you're such a Puritan. I'm sure I'll be safe.'

She leaned forward to kiss me. I didn't pull back, she was too beautiful to pull back from, but I didn't return her kiss, either, so it was like she was kissing a statue, a statue nearly pissing his pants in fear.

'Who's Mr Rogers?' I asked after she had stopped kissing me and backed away with disappointment creasing her face.

'Mr Rogers?'

'Very thin black man, elegantly dressed, droopy eyes. A drug seller, I think.'

'Oh, you mean Norvel Goodwin. Do you know Norvel too?'

'Is that his real name?' I said. 'Well, your Norvel Goodwin took me for a ride Thursday night in the councilman's limo. He told me to stay away from you. That if I didn't he would hurt me. Then he had his goon give me this black eye.'

'Oh dear.' She touched the swelling lightly with her fingertips.

'Who is he?' I asked.

'Just an old friend. I guess he's jealous.'

'Of me?'

'Why not?'

'There was more than jealousy,' I said. 'There's something going on between him and Jimmy.'

'Norvel and Jimmy hate each other, they have ever since the thing with Jimmy's daughter. Jimmy almost killed him once.'

'He said there were things going on with you and this case that I didn't understand. Do you know anything about that?'

'Norvel's a little crazy with conspiracies. Ask him who killed Malcolm X sometime.'

'Who does he say?'

'Are you going to let me up?' she asked.

'What are you really doing here?'

'The Greek left me another dead animal. A bird this time, a dove, pretty white feathers. Its neck was snapped.'

'Jesus.'

'Please.'

I stared at her lovely face for a moment and decided that she had been crying. 'Follow me,' I said as I turned to go up the stairs.

On the way up I asked, 'Would this Norvel Goodwin hurt me like he said?'

'No, he's not like that.'

And then a few steps later, 'Well, maybe.'

And as soon as I opened the door, 'Yes, he would.'

I took her coat and hung it over a chair. She was wearing tennis shoes, jeans, and a sweatshirt, but even in her athletic wear, and even with the damage done to her makeup by the tears, she was too beautiful. 'Can I use your bathroom?' she asked, and I showed her where it was.

While she was in the bathroom I improvised a quick cleanup, tossing waxed cheese steak wrappers, stained maroon with dried ketchup, into the trash can and grabbing all the loose clothes I could get hold of to dump into the washing machine. My apartment came with a little washer-dryer unit off the kitchen and I generally used the washer as a hamper, running the machine only when it was too full to jam in more clothes, and the dryer as a closet, pulling out what I needed day by day. It was a pretty good system, generally the dryer emptied by the time the washer was full, and it saved all the needless folding and putting away of normal laundry. Of course my T-shirts had a pinkish sheen from being washed with my red shorts and everything was creased, but that was my trademark anyway, creases. There was no hope for the bathroom, the gray grunge in the toilet bowl, the slivers of hair caked on the sink as if with glue, but judging from the condition of her bathroom I didn't think she'd mind. In any event, I figured, who the hell was she to judge my apartment when she barged in unannounced at 2:38 in the morning.

When she came out of the bathroom all the makeup had been wiped off her face and she looked like a girl in an Ivory Soap commercial, gleaming with health.

'Do you have a drink?' she said. 'I could use a drink.'

'I might have a beer.'

'That would be great,' she said. 'I'll get it.'

'Isn't it a little late?' but she was already out of the living room into the kitchen. I could hear her opening my refrigerator, imagine her peering into it as if the mysteries of the universe were growing there, which they might have been for how often I cleaned it.

'How old is this milk?' she asked from the kitchen.

'I don't know, pretty old, I'd guess.'

'Old enough so that the ice from the refrigeration cables has grown around it, locking it in place,' she said. 'What's gefilte fish?'

190

'It's medicinal,' I said.

'Do you want something?'

'No. I'm fine,' I said.

She came back into the living room, twisting off the top of a Rolling Rock. She sat down on the couch beside me with her legs curled beneath her and took a long drink.

'Thank you,' she said. 'I didn't know where to go when I saw that bird just lying there with its head like that.' She shuddered. 'On my doorstep. I had to get away.'

'What are you going to do?'

'Get someone to clean it up.'

'Not me,' I said. 'I'm out of the dead animal disposal business.'

'Maybe I'll call Henry on the car phone tomorrow. He'll do it. He takes care of me when he can.'

'He took care of me, too.'

'I'm so sorry about your eye.'

She sort of shuffled on her knees toward me and touched the eye gently with her fingertips and then harder, hard enough to make me wince and pull away. 'Does it hurt much?' she asked.

'Only when you press it.'

She stroked around my eye lightly with the back of her hand, soothing the nerves, and then pressed it hard again.

'Like that,' I said. 'Stop it.'

'When Henry came back for us with the limousine we knew you had vomited. Henry had tried to clean it up, and all the windows were open, but it still smelled like hell. The councilman was livid for a moment and then he laughed and laughed. He told Chester, "Not only does your lawyer cry, but he drinks like a teenybopper." Jimmy and Chuckie thought that was funny as hell. Chester told them both to shut up.'

'It wasn't the drinking,' I said. 'It was the sock in my eye.'

'Now you're being defensive.'

'I'm a good drinker.'

'Of course you are,' she said sweetly.

'I could drink both those bastards under the table.'

'Of course you could.'

'You don't think so?'

'No,' she said. 'What are we going to do about my landlord?'

'Get your friend Norvel to threaten him.'

'He's not a friend anymore.'

She was leaning over me now, still looking at my eye, searching the black and blue as if she were searching tea leaves for hidden meanings. With her makeup off, in her sweatshirt and jeans, there was something innocently collegiate about her.

'Tell me, Veronica,' I asked. 'What are you doing with these guys, Jimmy Moore and Norvel Goodwin?'

'It's a long story. Very sad.'

'Tell me.'

'It started with a boy, a very sweet boy. He's dead now but that's how it started.' I thought I saw something in her eye, but I must have imagined it because as I kept looking at her it disappeared. 'I'll tell you sometime,' she said. 'Just not now, please. What am I going to do tonight?'

'I'll call you a cab.'

'I can't go home with that dead bird on my doorstep. I just can't.'

With a gallant shrug I stood up. 'All right,' I said. 'I'll take you home and clean up the bird. But this is the last time.'

'Can't I stay here?' she asked.

'No. And tomorrow I'll file for a restraining order. Restraining orders are generally useless, but at least it will be something. I'll let you know when the court sets up the hearing.'

'Can't I stay the night on your sofa?'

'No,' I said. 'Definitely not.'

I walked to the closet and was reaching for my raincoat when she came from behind and placed her arms around me. Her hands lightly rubbed up and down my chest. 'Can't I stay, please? I wouldn't sleep knowing that bird was there, and even if you threw it down the chute I'd still see it lying there, its sad little neck bent like it is, a small dribble of blood out its beak.'

Without turning around, with her hands still floating across my chest, I said, 'I really can't.'

'It's Norvel, isn't it?'

'It's everything.'

'I won't let him hurt you.'

I pulled her arms away and turned around. 'I can't,' I said, but it came out more like 'Ay kaaugh' because she had slipped her tongue into my mouth. I tasted the sexy beeriness of her breath and smelled the wetness of her hair and there was something silky and warm about the way she pressed her body into mine and though I said, 'Ay ayeaally kaaugh,' I knew that I would.

Jeanne, my first lover, a funny word to use for a sixteen-year-old girl with braces, was an athlete, a distance swimmer, all shoulders and thighs, trained for long, exhausting efforts that left her shaking with weariness. I was a notable disappointment to her and we both ended up more bemused than satisfied. My experiences with Michelle were more satisfactory, she had patience and clever hands and a willingness to experiment that was just right for a beginner. Sandra was tall and cold and endured sex but I was fascinated by her blondness, white white hair, pale skin, a profound phlegmaticness. Rebecca was a virgin, but eager, and let me play the role of experienced older man, though she was only a year behind me in college. 'Let's try this,' I would say, nervously, and she'd always reply with a cheerful, 'Sure.' Allyn was in love with me, which brought to the table an intensity I found uncomfortable. Sue was blonde and plump and from Wisconsin but still sweetly kinked, with a thing about her feet. And of course my ex-fiancée Julie, the one true love of my youth, earnest and sad, loosing tears when we orgasmed together with silent sighs under her down comforter. Along the way there were Tina and Bonnie and Lauren, who laughed and grabbed and shouted in French. There was a dancer, a cop, a divorced woman from Toledo with a son older than me. There were many many delightful women, every shape, every size, every political party including the Communists, and I screwed them all. Maybe I was no Wilt Chamberlain, but I was no wilting violet either and I had made love to a peck of women in my life. But I had never made love to a woman like Veronica Ashland.

When we were naked, on my unmade bed, rubbing our hands uncontrollably over each other's bodies, she opened the foil packet she found in my drawer, the packet I had stolen from Bissonette's love chest, and popped the condom in her mouth, placing it upon me with her teeth, leaving just the right amount of slack at the tip. Then, like a crazed leopard, she was on top of me, pressing the palm of her hand into my swollen eye, biting my neck, my breast, licking my chest and my ear, pressing my eye and biting so hard I screamed as she worked. She had a thin supple body that responded to everything like a dream, her breasts were small and sharp and prickly hot, entering her was like entering a jar of electric honey, that sweet, that wild. She bent forward and arched back and bent forward like a willow stick, grabbing my hair painfully hard along the way as she sucked a kiss from my throat. She came quickly and ferociously and best of all she came again, and again. I knew it was her, not me, and I struggled to keep up but she was always one moment ahead of me. I moaned my orgasm and she howled, snatching at the air like a lioness and then the willow bent back toward me and she buried her face in my neck and meowed. She sounded like a satisfied house cat, stretched around a newly emptied bowl of milk.

The sound involuntarily brought up a question. 'There was a litter box in your apartment.'

'Yes,' she said.

'But no cat,' I said. 'That was your cat the Greek killed, wasn't it?'

'Yes, it was.'

'But you acted like you didn't care about the cat, just the mess.'

'It was only a cat,' she said with a dismissive laugh.

'But I know about women and their cats, they are like babies to them, their children. A cat gets a hairball, they grow frantic. But you let me drop the corpse of your cat into a Strawbridge bag and dump it down the chute without a tear.'

'How should I have acted?'

'Mournful, distraught, pathetically tearful. Other women would have.'

'I'm not like other women.'

'No, you're not,' I said. 'You are the coldest bitch I ever met,' and, like an incantation handed down father to son from the deepest mists of prehistory, the words made me hard again immediately. I twisted my hips with a violent rush, sending her sprawling on the bed, and I pressed myself into her and held her arms over her head and bit her throat like she had bitten mine and sucked her nipples when she told me to and bit her even after she told me to stop and I made her cry like no cat had ever made her cry and she came rivers.

It was the best sex I had ever had, better than I had ever hoped to have, and no matter the threat and whatever the price, I wanted more.

PART THREE

Witnesses
for the Prostitution

21

Prescott stood before the potential jurors, clipboard in hand, asking questions in his commanding way. There were forty of them, sitting in the courtroom's benches like churchgoers in their pews. It was from this group, summoned from the jury room by Judge Gimbel's clerk, that the twelve jurors and two alternates for *United States v. Moore and Concannon* would be chosen. Prescott had petitioned the court to be allowed to question the jurors himself and Judge Gimbel had grudgingly granted the petition. If you had asked him, Prescott would have told you he was examining these potential jurors in an effort to pick a fair and unbiased jury. What he was really doing, in addition to sneaking in pretrial arguments, was trying to find jurors who would be the most unfair and most biased in favor of Jimmy Moore and Chester Concannon. That's the way a trial works: the lawyers on the two sides pack the jury with prejudices favorable to their clients with the expectation that these attempts at manipulation will balance themselves out. It is why more than a few juries break down in nervous collapse.

I was at one end of the defense table next to Chester Concannon, who sat with his back straight and hands crossed before him. Jimmy sat at the other end. Immediately behind us were three bright-eyed handsome lawyers all in a row, the Talbott, Kittredge and Chase trial team assisting Prescott. Madeline had been left at the office to do research. The Talbott, Kittredge crowd was furiously scribbling notes and conferring in whispers with a tall, bearded man with a brutal case of dandruff who, I was told, was their jury expert, a man named Bruce Pierpont.

Despite repeated promises from Prescott and numerous requests, I still hadn't seen Pierpont's report. Every now and then one of the Talbott, Kittredge lawyers would lean over and whisper something to Moore and he would nod, a look of supreme probity on his face. I wondered how long Prescott had worked with him to get the expression just right. The Talbott, Kittredge lawyers never leaned over to whisper something to me. Except for our proximity in the courtroom, it was impossible to tell we were on the same side. That had been Prescott's idea. 'It shouldn't seem like we're ganging up on Eggert,' he had said, and so Chester and I kept our distance.

Closer to the jury box was the prosecution table where Eggert and a beefy older man, with heavy hands and a neck like an ox, sat representing the government. The ox wore a blue blazer and his hair was swept rigidly into place, the very image of a man who liked his steak still bleeding. He was the FBI agent on the case, Special Agent Stemkowski. Once, in the middle of the proceedings, he cracked his knuckles and the rat-a-tat sounded like gunshots.

Judge Gimbel sat up high on the bench, bowing his hairless head as he worked on documents obviously unrelated to this trial. He was a busy man, Judge Gimbel, and you couldn't expect him to concentrate on something as routine as Prescott's jury voir dire.

'Now, as you may know,' said Prescott to the entire group of potential jurors, 'one of the defendants in this case is a public official, a city councilman. The other defendant is the councilman's aide. Do any of you believe that public officials, like the city councilman here, are usually corrupt?'

No response.

'Now, ladies and gentlemen, I need you to be honest. Don't any of you look at a public official like my client, a city councilman on the government payroll, and say to yourselves, he is dirty somehow?'

Still no response. He smiled kindly, looked down at his clipboard, ran his finger across a list of names of the jury venire, and looked up again. 'Mrs Emily Simpson.'

An older woman raised her hand, thin frame, pale powdered skin, bouffant hair, glasses that looked like they were squinting.

'Mrs Simpson, do you work?'

'Yes. I work the register at a discount store.'

'And you pay your taxes then, of course.'

'Of course.' Mrs Simpson's hands grasped the pocketbook on her lap.

'Do you think the money you send over in taxes is well spent?'

'On the whole? No,' she said, looking around at the others seated nearby for encouragement.

'Why not?'

'The politicians don't listen to us, they listen to the rich folk, the people who have the money to help them.'

'So what you're saying, Mrs Simpson, is that most politicians can be bought.'

'I guess I am.'

'Anyone else? How many believe that politicians as a whole are generally unscrupulous and easily bought and paid for?'

Mrs Simpson hesitantly raised her hand and looked around for support. The woman seated next to her, with thick features and a dignified cant to her head, smiled at Mrs Simpson and raised her hand, and then a man in the front row, crew cut, thick neck, and then another hand, and soon the great majority of potential jurors had their hands raised.

I glanced at Eggert. He was nodding his head, as if Prescott was proving his case for him.

'And why is that?' Prescott looked back at his clipboard. 'Mrs Lanford?'

The dignified woman next to Mrs Simpson said, 'Yes, that's me.'

'Why do you think politicians are so easily bought?' asked Prescott.

'Because they's greedy.'

'And where do you think the money goes, Mrs Lanford, this money that buys them?'

'In they's pockets,' said Mrs Lanford. 'Right in they's own wallets.'

'Those of you who said that politicians are often bought, is that what all of you think?'

'No,' said a man in the back, his gray hair neat, wearing a polo shirt on his day off from the office.

Prescott scanned the names on his clipboard. 'Mr Roberts, is it? Where do you think it goes?'

'To their campaigns,' he said. 'They're always campaigning. It seems every other year there's a new election.'

'Do you think it's the politicians' fault that they need to ask for money?' asked Prescott.

'I guess not,' said Roberts. 'I mean, we end up voting for the guy with the most television ads, so I guess it's our fault as much as anyone's.'

'Does anyone here believe that politicians should not be allowed to ask for campaign contributions?'

No hands were raised.

'I'm going to hold you all to that now. What you all are telling me is that you each believe it is proper for politicians to ask for campaign contributions, that such requests are precisely what the system demands of politicians like my client.'

Before anyone could reply Eggert stood and in his reedy voice said, 'Objection, Your Honor. Mr Prescott's voir dire has again devolved into a lecture.'

'Civics 101,' said Judge Gimbel. 'We don't need citizenship classes, Mr Prescott. Just get on with it.'

'I'm almost through, Your Honor,' said Prescott.

'We're grateful,' said the judge.

'Now, how many of you have your own businesses?'

A small number of the jurors raised their hands. Prescott referred again to his clipboard. 'Mr Thompkins, what kind of business do you own?'

'A printing shop,' said a thin balding black man with extremely long fingers.

'Who's running it now?'

'My employees. I have an assistant manager.'

'Now, Mr Thompkins, if while you're away your assistant manager should do something wrong, would you be responsible?'

'If he messed up a job, sure I would. I stand by all the work coming out of my shop.'

'Suppose he did something illegal while you were away. Suppose, without your knowing it, he started printing up counterfeit money. Would you still be responsible?'

'No way.'

'Does anyone believe Mr Thompkins should be criminally responsible if his assistant manager started printing up counterfeit money in his print shop?'

Prescott scanned the jurors and nodded approvingly when he saw no hands raised. 'I don't think so either,' said Prescott. 'You're off the hook, Mr Thompkins. Thank you very much for your time, I'm sure you all will be terrific jurors.' Prescott sat down at the defense table and formed a huddle with Moore and his trial team and the bearded, snowy jury expert.

Judge Gimbel put down his pen and looked directly at me. 'Mr Carl,' he said. 'Do you have any voir dire?'

'Can I have a moment, Judge?' I asked.

With the jury venire still sitting in the courtroom I calmly broke into the Talbott, Kittredge huddle. 'Mr Prescott,' I said. 'May I speak to you, please?'

He pressed his lips together and said, 'Let's go outside for a moment, shall we.'

I followed him out of the courtroom, passing the rows of potential jurors, the press, the court buffs, old men who hang around the courthouse whiling away their retirements with free entertainment. Once outside in the long cream hallway, Prescott lifted his chin and peered down at me, looking very straight and very stern.

'That last bit, Mr Prescott, sir,' I said. 'The questions about the counterfeiter? I have to admit they caused me some concern.'

'They did?' he said, his voice rising in confusion.

'Yes, sir. It appeared as if you may have been indicating, maybe, that a subordinate, not a principal, is the responsible party here.'

Prescott looked down at me, his eyes wide with an injured innocence. 'It was just voir dire, Victor.'

'But still, sir, it caused me some concern.'

'Walk with me to the men's room,' he said. 'Let's take advantage of the break.'

The men's room was just down the hall and I found myself in the awkward position of standing next to Prescott at the urinals. He was a stern, formal man, not the type, I would have thought, to chatter while grasping tightly to his prick, but I would have been wrong.

'I've tried more than fifty cases in these courtrooms, Victor,' he said as he peed. 'And in the course of those trials I've learned a little about how to win a case. I have spent hours with our jury expert working on the voir dire, on my arguments, on the presentation of our evidence. Everything I do in this trial has been reviewed beforehand by the best minds at Talbott, Kittredge, every question to the jury was scientifically designed to have the maximum beneficial effect for our clients. Now that question about counterfeiting sets up our entire defense. Unlike the counterfeiter, who is cheating the system, these men were not going outside the system's demands. They were only doing what the system required. The contrast is just what I was trying to put forward.'

Through the whole of his speech I was restraining myself from checking out his equipment. There was something about Prescott that forced me to make comparisons, even though I always seemed to come out the lesser man. 'I guess I see that now, sir,' I said.

He gave himself a shake, pulled up his zipper, and moved to the sinks across the other wall. I did the same. Out of the mirror he stared at me and his eyes turned cold. 'I'm in the middle of a fight with Eggert here, Victor. I can't afford to be explaining myself at every turn to you. When you gain a little more experience maybe you'll understand what I'm doing, but right now what you need is enough faith not to get in my way. You are clear about your instructions, aren't you?'

'Yes, sir,' I said, like a schoolboy being reprimanded.

He turned on the faucet and began to wash. I followed suit. 'Now, I don't want you to ask any questions of these jurors,' he said. 'I have them right where I want them and you can only move them in the wrong direction. And I don't want you to get involved in the selection process, I'll tell you how to use your peremptory challenges and I'll make all the challenges for cause. What I need from you, Victor, what I must have is your absolute confidence in me. Can you give me that, son?'

'Yes, sir.'

'Keep your eyes open, Victor,' he said, grimacing into the mirror. He pressed the sides of his hair back with his palms. 'There is no telling how much you can learn. By the way, the Bishops are delighted with your work so far.'

'I haven't done much yet.'

'Well, they've been raving. And there is more to come, I promise. Let's not keep the judge waiting. The old goose hates to wait.'

Side by side, like comrades at arms, we left the bathroom, marched up the corridor, swung open the courtroom doors, and strode back to the defense table.

'Well, Mr Carl,' said Judge Gimbel. 'Are we ready now?'

Something gave me pause. Maybe it was the look of injured innocence in Prescott's eyes. He was neither an innocent nor so easily injured. But I stared down at the yellow pad in front of me on which I had scrawled a few elementary questions for the jury venire and knew I would follow his directions. Most of my voir dire questions had been asked already by the judge, they were form questions taken right out of a trial manual I had been working with over the weekend. None of them had been scientifically designed for maximum effect on our defense. Besides, Prescott was right, I had my instructions.

I leaned over and spoke with Chet Concannon, just to be sure. When we were done whispering he smiled at me reassuringly. I stood up straight again and said, 'I have nothing, Your Honor.'

22

We were in the process of actually picking the jury, or I should say Prescott and his expert were in the process, when I spotted Morris Kapustin entering the courtroom. He saw me notice him and he waved. I gave him the slightest of nods. Morris was dressed particularly shabbily that day, a suit jacket that didn't match his suit pants, his white shirt undone at the top, letting his faded silk undershirt show through. I hoped that maybe no one had seen the connection between us, but one of the bright young Talbott, Kittredge team, the blond bland-faced man with a name like Bert or Bart and a perfect little nose, had spotted him. I couldn't help notice the smirk as he leaned forward and said something to Prescott, who spun around immediately to get a good look. I turned away in embarrassment. When I could, without being noticed, I motioned for Morris to wait for me. He sat down on the back bench and immediately began talking to one of the court buffs, an ancient man in plaid pants watching the proceedings.

Once the questioning was finished, jury selection was an almost mathematical procedure. All forty names were in order of selection on our jury sheets. The judge gave each of the defendants five peremptory challenges in which we could knock any potential juror off the jury for whatever reason we chose. The prosecution had six peremptory challenges of its own, and after the judge had taken seven jurors out of the group because he thought they were unduly prejudiced for one side or the other, including Mrs Lanford, who had said she believed all politicians took money and put it in their pockets, we began the selection. First Eggert, then Prescott, then I, following

Prescott's recommendations, excused jurors. One by one the excused jurors were crossed off our lists, and then we recalculated who would be in. We ended with a predominantly male jury, as Bruce Pierpont, the jury expert, had suggested, which included Mr Thompkins, the printer, Mr Roberts, the man who had believed the voters forced politicians to ask for money, Mrs Simpson, who believed that buying public officials was a natural part of the political process, and a Mr Rollings, who had been a security guard for ten years at a warehouse in North Philly. When the selection was completed Prescott looked over the jury, conferred with his jury expert, and nodded approvingly.

'Opening statements ten o'clock tomorrow,' said Judge Gimbel. 'And then prosecution's first witness. Court adjourned.'

I waited until Prescott and Eggert left the courtroom with their respective teams before I packed up my trial bag and walked over to Morris, who was still talking to the older man next to whom he had sat.

'I didn't expect to see you here, Mr Kapustin,' I said a little sternly.

'Ah, Victor, I want that I should introduce you to Herm Finklebaum. Herm, this is mine lawyer friend Victor Carl. Herm used to sell toys over on Forty-fourth Street, now he spends his time watching in this very building.'

'Pleased to meet you, buddy boy,' said Herm. His face seemed to collapse upon itself where his front teeth had once been and there was a hole in his head, thinly covered with skin, through which I could see the faint pulsing of his blood. 'You're representing that Concannon fellow, right?'

'That's right.'

'Watch your *baitsim*, fellah. Eggert's a tiger.'

'What did I tell you, Herm, you're not listening, no?' said Morris. 'This Victor is no pantywaist, not like some of those other *shmendricks* staggering around. Your Mr Egbert has his own little tiger on his hands.'

'I never seen Eggert lose,' said Herm. 'I never seen him even sweat.'

'He'll be *shvitzing* like an Hassid in Miami by the time Victor gets through with him. You tell me if it's not so, Herm. I'll bet you a pastrami.'

'At Ben's?' asked Herm.

'Where else? McDonald's?'

'With Russian dressing?'

'No, with mayonnaise on white bread. How do you think I eat pastrami?'

'You're on, Morris.'

'You tell Ben, Herm, you tell Ben the sandwich you are buying is for me and he'll stack it extra thick just as I like it. Now stop all this talk about food, it's driving me *meshuggeh*. Three weeks already since Yom Kippur and still I'm hungry. Come, Victor, we have to talk.'

As I started following Morris out of the courtroom, Herm Finklebaum, the retired toy merchant of 44th Street, grabbed my arm and said, 'I'll keep my eye on you, buddy boy. Yes I will.'

When we were alone in the white linoleum hallway of the courthouse, Morris said, 'The lady at your office, the one at the front desk, told me you'd be here.'

'Rita.'

'Yes. Such a *haimisheh* girl, very helpful.'

'Rita?'

'She gave to me this for you.' He reached into his coat pocket and pulled out a pink message slip folded in half.

I opened it and read it and smiled.

'Something good, I hope,' said Morris.

'For me at least,' I said.

'It's okay, I hope, that I came to the courtroom,' said Morris. 'But I had news for you. Windward Enterprises was exactly right. Exactly. Your lady friend, what was her name?'

'Beth.'

'Beth. Such a smart girl. Beth. She was exactly right.

209

Maybe she should be helping you with this fancy trial in federal court?'

'She is.'

'See, you have *sechel* too. Good. Maybe you might just win this fancy trial after all. Now, let's see.' He put on his glasses, pulled out his grimed notebook, and started flipping through the pages. 'Frederick Stocker had a second home down the shore, Ventnor, on the bayside. Such a home, all done up with columns and glass. His wife sold it when he disappeared. She had nothing, of course, just that shore house, and a mortgage on their place in Gladwyne. She told me she didn't know where he was, and I believe her for a very good reason.'

'You spoke to her?'

'How else do you find someone? Talk to people, Victor, you might learn things. She was a very angry lady, this Mrs Stocker, which you can understand of course, angry, angry. She had a tight little mouth, like a *tochis*, that tight, and her fingers were twisting around each other and after talking with her I suspect I know why this Frederick Stocker he disappeared.'

'That bad?'

'You don't want to know how bad. A real *kvetcherkeh*. This woman could pickle cucumbers without the brine. He had a boat, she said. He called it *The Debit*. Such a clever name for an accountant who is also a thief, don't you think? A thirty-foot sloop. What's a sloop, I couldn't tell you if you *klopt mein kop* with an anchor, but that's what it was, a sloop. He cared more for the boat than he did for her, she said. I hate boats, wouldn't get on another for the life of me, but between you and me, I agree with him. Mine guess is that this thief Stocker he sold his boat and bought another and is sailing somewhere full of joy because he is on his boat and his wife is not.'

'So that's it, then. He's somewhere on the high seas.'

'Yes, that's it, but of course who can sail forever without putting in to land? October, the seas start getting colder,

Stocker the thief will want to find a harbor he can dock in, *kibbitz* a bit, find a *bummerkeh* or two, spend some of the money he stole. My guess, Victor, and it's only a guess, is that he is sucking down *schnopps* on his boat in a marina somewhere it is warm.'

'So there's nothing to be done, right?'

'Quiet, now. You hired Morris Kapustin. Morris Kapustin will decide when there is nothing more to be done. There are ways to keep looking, registries of marinas.'

'There must be thousands. How are you going to check all the marinas in the country?'

'By computer, how else? Acch, you leave it to me, I'll do what I can. I tried this once before looking for a boat.'

'Did it work?'

'So once it didn't work, I shouldn't keep trying? Mine son, the computernik. Such a *chachem*, trying to drag the business into the new world and who am I to stop him. He knows from machines, computers, cars, he was a locksmith in his summers away from school. Me, I know from people. You can learn from people things computers never dreamed about. But, of course, trying to find one boat in all of the Atlantic or Pacific, for that you need a computer. Oh, by and by, Victor, *bubeleh*, this is for you.'

He put his notebook back into his jacket and reached deep into one of his pants pockets. He pulled out the heavy gold and green chip with the boar's head on it and flipped it to me. I dropped my briefcase as I fumbled to catch it. The chip eluded me, spinning on the floor in a wide circle that I followed.

'I can see a basketball player you weren't,' said Morris with a deep laugh as I stepped on the rolling chip and scooped it into my hand.

'I was all right,' I said.

'Now I insulted you, I'm sorry. You were a regular Magic Jordan, I see that now. How I could have missed it I don't know? Seven feet four you were in college, but the years have been hard, you shrunk. I too have shrunk. It happens.'

'What did you find out about the chip?'

'A very special chip, that is. I asked around. Yitzhak Rabbinowitz, the accountant? Pearlman and Rabbinowitz, maybe you heard them? Well, it turns out that Yitzhak, and I knew his grandfather too, though he was no prince like Abe Carl the shoe man, it turns out that Yitzhak does work for certain private organizations. I showed the chip to him and he said immediately what it was. Especially made for a gentlemen's club in South Philadelphia. I wrote out the address for you. They play poker there almost every night with these chips. But it's not a club you can just walk into, Victor. It's a very private club. I think maybe you should forget about that chip.'

'What kind of club?'

'How should I say it? It's a club for *taleners*, *alte kockers*, and not all of them were vegetable sellers in the Italian Market, do you understand? A club for retired mobsters, for old gangsters. It's a dangerous place with dangerous men, not a place for a nice Jewish boy like Abe Carl's grandson.'

Before I paid a visit to South Philadelphia I took I-95 to Chester and then followed the directions I had been given to a cracking industrial road ending at a gray trailer with a hissing neon sign set above it that read: PETE'S YARD – TOWING, STORAGE & REPAIRS. CLASSIC CARS OUR SPECIALTY. Stretching out from the trailer was a chain-link fence, topped with barbed wire, circumscribing an expanse of more than an acre, and what was atop that acre was cars. Lots of cars. Shiny ones and smashed ones and new ones and ones without any wheels, parked in long rows spreading out from that trailer, enough to excite the fancier with the sheer number and variety. But I wasn't excited. I never cared much for cars. I figured when I had the money I would see which BMW everyone else was driving and then drive one level better. Until then I'd drive what I could afford, which was my seven-year-old Mazda compact, registered at my father's suburban address to keep my insurance down.

I parked in front of the trailer. Inside there was a young woman reading a magazine behind a Plexiglas guard. Above her was another sign: TOWING $50. STORAGE $10 PER DAY. NO PERSONAL CHECKS. ALL FINES MUST BE PAID AT TIME OF REDEMPTION. PLEASE HAVE REGISTRATION AND IDENTIFICATION READY.

'I'm here about a car,' I said.

'That's good,' she said, without looking up, 'because we don't take in dry cleaning.'

She was cute, in a trashy little car yard way, and the remark had been clever enough so I couldn't help myself. 'Do I know you?'

'License plate number,' she said flatly. I decided then and there I would have to get a better line.

'I'm here about a car seized for the Sheriff's Office,' I said, and then read directly from the pink slip. 'Number 37984.'

She went into a file and searched for the paperwork. 'Oh, it's you, Mr Carl,' she said, suddenly smiling. 'Pete wanted me to get him personally when you came in. If you'll wait just a minute.'

Pete was a big, sandy-haired man, his stomach bursting from beneath his belt. His tie was loose, it had been tied loose, and his jacket was too tight for him, bunching up around the armpits. Just the sight of it made me flex my shoulders in a claustrophobic reflex. Pete was one of those guys who had never accepted the last fifty pounds. He reached out to shake and pumped my hand like a jack handle. 'Glad you made it, Mr Carl,' he said heartily. 'I wanted to show you personally what we picked up for you.'

He led me out the back of the shack into the yard and I followed. He spoke as we passed the automotive detritus that had been towed from Chester County's streets, rows and rows and rows of it.

'The deputy sheriff, he was there already when we showed up,' said Pete. 'Six in the morning. The morning's the best, before anyone gets a mind to drive off. It was quite a house, like some castle. And a lawn that stretched forever, six football fields or something, all fenced in. There was three cars in the driveway, but not what we was looking for. And nothing in the garage, either. Happy as hell to show us the garage, so I knew before we looked it wasn't going to be there. The deputy wanted to leave but there was all that lawn, right. Fenced in, that was the ticket. "You got horses?" I asked. Sure they did, Mr Carl. A place like that. Then when I convinced the deputy to check out the stable, they went a little batty.'

'Was there an old man there?' I asked. 'Round, sallow face, long hair, slightly wrecked looking?'

'Oh yeah, he was there, mumbling something, shouting. You'd think they'd cut his nails for him, wouldn't you? But I didn't take no mind of him, I'd seen it before. You know this type of work is not the most pleasant. People don't like to see you taking away their cars. Take their washing machines, their VCRs, their wives even, fine. But not their cars. We won't do it without the sheriff there and the sheriff won't do it unless he's armed. But then again we don't get too many houses like that one. So we go to the stable, right. There are horses there, sure, hay and barrels of oats. Smells like leather and horse shit, you know. Little strips of yellow hanging down covered with flies. We walk through it slowly. Nothing, right. I look up in the rafters, you never know, right? Nothing.'

He took me inside a large low building in the center of the yard, with a ceiling of corrugated tin. He led me to something big, something long, covered with tan canvas.

'And then, hiding out there in the last stall, Mr Carl, this is what we found.'

He grabbed hold of the side of the canvas and whisked

it off. Underneath was a majestic looking thing, a long, two-seater convertible, with a golden hood and blue wheel wells front and rear. Four shining exhaust pipes snaked out of either side of the engine. There was a high, majestic grill and a spare tire hooked above the trunk and the delicate front bumper was shaped like a woman's kiss.

'I knew we was getting a Duesenberg, Mr Carl, but frankly I expected a wreck of some sort, not a 1936 SJ Speedster in decent condition. This baby's got a twin over-head cam, eight cylinders, a centrifugal supercharger, tubular steel connecting rods.' He stopped speaking for a moment, staring at it in awe. 'This is more than a classic, Mr Carl. This is a work of art. This is a legend. Designed by Mr Gordon Buehrig himself. When it first came out, Gary Cooper and Clark Gable both ordered a special model. A man who cared would give a lot for this car.'

'About how much, exactly?' I asked.

'In mint condition, at a car show, properly advertised, between two and three hundred thousand. This model hasn't been kept up lately, it's got some rust, the leather seats are cracked, the engine's leaking off a little oil, needs a valve job. But it would be well worth it to spend some time and money and fix up this baby until it shines and then sell it at a show.'

'How much would we get if we auctioned it off right now?'

'These things are tough to say, Mr Carl. It would be a distressed price. It would depend on who shows up. Probably something like forty or fifty. But that would be a shame, Mr Carl.'

I was still getting twenty-five percent of everything I collected from Winston Osbourne. Twenty-five percent of the fifty would be twelve five. It was amazing how once money started flowing it didn't stop. Twelve five.

'Sell it, Pete,' I said, turning around and leaving the building.

He followed after me. 'But Mr Carl, that would be a

shame. I'd be honored to work on it for you. In six months, Mr Carl, it would be mint. I promise it. But to just up and sell it like this would be a damn shame.'

I was sure it would be just that. But you see, I wasn't a car fancier. It was just steel and leather and rubber and glass to me. And all in all, I'd prefer the twelve five sooner than anything else later. 'Sell it,' I said, still walking away. Take that, you little blue-blood snot. 'Sell it as soon as you can.'

23

Ninth Street, north of Washington, is the heart of South Philadelphia's Italian Market. On weekends the street becomes a cacophonous melange of vegetable stands and fishmongers and fine meats laid out in glorious pink rows inside the white refrigerated displays. Cannoli so rich it takes a full half-hour to eat them, hoagies thick with spiced ham and provolone, drenched in fine wine vinegar and covered with hot peppers. Fresh squid soaking in their ink, prosciutto sliced so thin you can read the paper through it, okra and bok choy and radicchio, strawberries ripened to burst like flowers in your mouth. 'Please, lady, please, I pick the best for you, I promise, the best in the world, the sweetest, like sugar for you, just do as I say and don't shake the melons.' It's a sweet old-fashioned street when the market is open, and from all over the city they come to buy the freshest seafood, the finest veal, the ripest produce. Families have owned their stalls on Ninth Street for generations, Giordano's produce, Cappuccio's meats, Anastasi's freshest seafood. The Italian Market is a brilliant Philadelphia tradition, a feast for the senses and the perfect place to shop for that lavish dinner party. Just so long as you don't shake the melons.

This happened to a friend of mine. True story. He was in the market one Saturday morning with his parents. A family outing. They were at LiCalzi's produce store buying tomatoes. My friend's mother is one of those women who shake the melons and press their thumbs deep into the eggplant and take a bite of radish before buying the bunch. If there is a best lemon in the rack, a best ear of corn, a best box of strawberries, she will find it.

'Hey lady,' said the vegetable clerk, a tall fat man cloned from tall fat LiCalzi stock. 'The sign says don't touch the tomatoes. They're all good. You want a good tomato, I'll give you a good tomato. Here, take this one.'

'I'll find my own, thank you,' she said.

'Hey lady, do what I tell you and stop squeezing the fucking tomatoes.'

'Don't talk to my wife like that,' said my friend's father.

'I'll talk to her any way I want,' said the clerk, giving him a shove.

My friend shoved him back.

'What's the problem here?' said another, older LiCalzi.

'The lady is squeezing the tomatoes.'

'Don't squeeze the fucking tomatoes,' said the second clerk.

'Fuck you,' said my friend.

And that was it.

The first clerk dived over the stall, scattering tomatoes like large, squishy marbles across the street, and loosed a right cross that broke my friend's jaw. When my friend's father tried to pull the first clerk off his son, the second clerk grabbed him in a headlock and started pounding his face with uppercuts, one after another, like a wrestler on Saturday morning TV, shattering his nose. In the melee my friend's mother was slugged in the eye with the second clerk's elbow, cracking the socket. By the time the ambulance carrying my friend and his parents had left, the cops had dispersed the crowd, the stall had been righted, the tomatoes replaced, a new bin set up for tomatoes, slightly damaged, at a bargain rate, and the fat tall LiCalzi clerks were calmly weighing celery stalks for the new wave of customers. My friend and his parents now do all their shopping at the Super Fresh.

So that is South Philadelphia, a charming ethnic enclave in the middle of the city, small immaculate row houses, terrific restaurants, churches, softball fields, Pat's Steaks, Geno's Steaks, two bars on every corner, little girls in their

Catholic skirts smoking as they walk home from school, old people in T-shirts and shorts sitting on the sidewalk into the night listening to the Phillies on the radio and drinking cold cans of beer. But if a parking spot is marked off with folding chairs don't take it, and if a drive-by shooting splits open the night walk the other way, and never ever shake the melons in the Italian Market because underneath the sweet ethnicity of South Philadelphia is steel.

I was sitting in my car in the gloomy darkness of 7th Street, just east of the Italian Market, watching the entrance to the Sons of Garibaldi Men's Club. It was an old-style storefront with the windows painted in green and gold stripes except for the last two feet, left clear to let in whatever daylight could slip through. Above the door was a wooden sign with the club's name and a boar's head on it. With the painted windows and the closed wooden door it was impossible to see inside, but light shone out of the clear swath at the top of the windows and I saw a shadow slip across the ceiling. A man, bent with age, shuffled along the street and stopped at the heavy wooden door, giving two hard raps with the gnarled handle of his cane. The door opened from the inside and the old man stepped up and into the storefront. The door closed behind him.

What I was doing sitting in my car outside that club was screwing up my courage to go inside. What I had was a chip and some questions about a dead man and I wondered whether those two things alone were enough to get my jaw broken or my nose smashed or my eye socket cracked. But inside that club was still where I wanted to go. Prescott had told me the mafioso princess had slept with the horny second baseman and that was why the second baseman was dead. Whether Prescott was telling me the truth or lying about Bissonette would tell me whether my trust in him would be misplaced. I wanted to trust Prescott, oh yes I did, I wanted more than anything for everything he ever said or ever promised to be true. But after those damn questions to the jury I needed some assurance and I had

219

the feeling that the assurance I needed was inside that dangerous looking men's club. I had no choice but to go in and get it, despite my instructions to do no more investigating and despite the threats that had come backing those instructions. See, I genuinely liked Chester Concannon, admired his calm, good-natured manner and his outsized loyalty, but it wasn't Chester I was worried about, for if Prescott was setting up Concannon for a fall he was maybe setting me up at the same time. And maybe the deals and contacts and the promised advances to my career were as phony as any connection between Bissonette and Raffaello's daughter. If so I might have to do something about it, don't ask me what, but something. So, with not a little trepidation, and not a lot of confidence, I stepped out of the car, walked up to the ominous wooden door, and knocked twice with my knuckles.

The door opened slowly and what looked like one of the LiCalzi brothers stood in the doorway, staring at me while he chewed on something with his mouth open. He wore pressed jeans and a silk shirt, buttoned low enough so that I could see his pectorals, as flat and solid as flagstone. He just stared and chewed and stared some more and then, through whatever he was chewing, he said, 'Yeah?'

'I was hoping I could come in,' I said.

'This is a private club.'

I reached into my suit jacket and, quick as a cobra, he grabbed me by my collar and lifted me two inches off the ground. Slowly I pulled out the chip. 'I have this.'

He dropped me. I did an awkward three-point landing. 'I don't care what you got,' he said. 'This is a private club. Get lost.'

'I just wanted to ask . . .' But before I could finish the sentence he had me turned around and hoisted by my belt, ready for tossing.

'Who is it, Giovanni?' asked a whispery, accented voice from inside the room. The voice was slow as a snake slithering toward its prey.

Giovanni put me down none too gently, gave me a look that would wither a dogwood, frisked me quickly, and, with a tight grip on my arm, brought me inside.

It was a dusty room, bare and beat, with a linoleum floor and whitewashed walls with travel posters of Sicily curling up at the edges. A fluorescent ring spit a white glow from the ceiling. There was a bar in the corner, wooden and battered, with a few bottles with pouring tops grouped together on top. Beside the bottles were six water glasses upside-down on a tray. An ancient radio with canvas over the single speaker hissed out a thin strain of opera. The room smelled of talcum powder, of liniment, of tobacco burned long ago. Along the sides were metal chairs with red leatherette upholstery that looked to have been swiped from an old barbershop. In the center, under the blinking fluorescent wheel, was a large round table topped with green felt, ringed with wooden chairs. In the far chair, directly facing me, was the old man whom I had just seen come in. He was bent over the table, a deck of cards in his hands. His face, twisted by deep canyons of wrinkles, was as skinny and as sharp as a hatchet. There was no one else in the room.

'It's some guy with a hundred-dollar chip who says he wants in,' said Giovanni.

'Let-a me see,' said the old man.

Giovanni took the chip from my hand and let go of me only long enough to walk it to the old man. The old man examined it carefully.

'Where did you get this?' the old man asked.

'It belonged to Zack Bissonette. I got it from him.'

'Bissonette's dead,' hissed the old man. He put the chip into his pocket. 'Dead-a men don't have chips. It's a club rule. I have to confiscate it. Show him out, Giovanni.'

I pulled my arm out of Giovanni's grasp. 'Wait a minute. That's my chip. You can't just take it and put it in your pocket like that.'

His hands, long and yellow, the knuckles swollen to the

size of jawbreakers, divided the cards swiftly into two piles and gave them a loud, expert shuffle. 'I must enforce the rules. I'm the president of our club. How would it look if I let-a you break the rules?' He separated the cards and gave them another loud shuffle. 'Show him out, Giovanni.'

Giovanni grabbed my arm again and began to drag me, my Florsheims sliding on the worn linoleum as they headed toward the doorstep, when I said loudly, 'The least you can do is let me play you for it.'

'What you got to play with?' asked the old man in his whispery voice, and Giovanni stopped dragging me.

I pulled my arm out of his grasp, shucked my shoulders, and reached up to straighten my tie. 'The chip,' I said.

'It's not-a your chip no more. I had to confiscate it.'

'I brought it, so it's mine. Any fair club would agree to that. What I'll agree to is to play cards with it, give you a chance to win it off me fair and square.'

'And even if that would be acceptable, it wouldn't be enough.' The old man gave a sharp, bitter smile. 'There's a minimum buy-in.'

'How much?'

'How much you got?'

'Another fifty on me.'

'That would only cover your temporary membership dues.'

'Temporary membership dues?'

'To play you have to be a member.'

'How much are the temporary membership dues?'

'Fifty dollar.'

'But if I pay that I won't have enough for the buy-in.'

'No. You would not.' He separated the cards again and gave them another loud shuffle. 'Of course, we could work something out.'

'I have an ATM card.'

'Is that-a so? How much can you withdraw at one time?'

'Four hundred dollars.'

'Well, since you'll be a member, four hundred dollar is how much it will take to buy in.'

'That means three hundred plus the chip, right?'

'Excuse me,' said the old man. 'I must have been confused. You'll be a temporary member only. For temporary members the buy-in is higher.'

'How much higher?'

'Four hundred plus the chip.'

'I see.'

'Plus the fifty you have on you for your temporary membership dues.'

'Five hundred and fifty dollars, total.'

'That's right.'

'That seems pretty steep.'

He shrugged. 'Don't worry, Mr . . .'

'Carl.'

'Mr Carl.' He shuffled his cards again, loudly, perfectly, merging the two piles seamlessly into one. 'It's a friendly game. There's a cash machine at Eighth and Catherine, two blocks away. Giovanni will walk with you. This neighborhood, you know. It's not what it once was.'

'That's good,' I said. 'I wouldn't want to lose five hundred and fifty dollars to a thief.'

'I understand perfectly,' said the old man, now nodding his head sagely. 'While you're gone I'll call the other members, tell them we found ourselves a game.'

24

'Yes,' I said, looking over my cards, subtly trying to dig out the information I needed. 'Zack told me about your games, said he had good times here.'

'Is that-a so?' said the old man whom I had first seen in the club and whose name I now knew was Luigi. 'That's very interesting, Victor. I'll bet twenty. I don't have nothing, of course, but I like to keep things interesting.'

'You're raising just to keep things interesting?' asked Virgil, a huge man with fists like hams and a big-jawed face slackened by age. His voice was thick and slow.

'That's right,' said Luigi.

'It don't have nothing to do with the two ladies up and the third on her belly?' asked Virgil.

'If I had-a three queens I would have bet forty,' said Luigi.

'If you had bet forty I wouldn't be thinking of staying in.'

'Okay,' said Luigi. 'I'm going to raise my bet to forty.'

'What are you, senile?' said Jasper, a tall thin man with deep wrinkles around his eyes and a full head of bristly gray hair. His nasal voice had the tight, tense quality of a postman on the edge. 'You can't just up and change your bet like that. Once it's down it's down.'

'I'm changing it,' said Luigi. 'What's it to you anyway, Jasper, you were out before the first bet.'

'I didn't have no hand.'

'You didn't have no hand since Truman was president,' said Luigi.

'You still can't raise yourself,' said Jasper. 'There are rules.'

'Let him change it,' said Virgil. 'What do I care?'

'Okay,' said Luigi, tossing in another four red chips with the boar's head embossed in gold. 'The bet is forty.'

'Forty dollars,' said Virgil. 'Now I know you don't got nothing. I'll see the forty and raise ten.'

Luigi wheezed out a laugh and said, 'Fifty to you, Victor.'

There were five of us around the table, four men to the far side of retirement and me. We were playing seven-card stud, high only. Giovanni sat by the door, slumped like a sack of cement in one of the red leatherette chairs, thumbing through a well-worn *Playboy* magazine. I couldn't figure out what he was, guard, bartender. He sat around and got drinks for the players when they asked and sat around some more. I had played my share of poker before, but never at stakes this high. My jacket was off, my tie loosened, the top two buttons of my shirt undone, my sleeves rolled up to my forearms. Every now and then I checked my watch, aware that I had to be in court the next morning. But I had been tossing out asides all night, trying to build a conversation about Zack Bissonette, and still hadn't learned what I had come to learn.

I looked at my hand again, lifting the down cards tightly so that no one could see. Down I had the four of hearts and the four of spades. Up I had two more hearts and the four of diamonds. Three fours wasn't bad but except for Jasper, who had folded early, each of the other four had pairs up and were betting strong. We all had two more cards to go. If it was just the fours I might have folded, but there was still the chance to fill the house or maybe pick up the heart flush. I looked at my chips. I had only about a hundred and fifty left of my original five-hundred-dollar stake and it was thinning fast.

'Let's go, Victor,' said Virgil. 'This ain't brain surgery.'

'I'm in,' I said, tossing in two twenty-five-dollar chips.

Dominic, sitting next to me, a short dour man with forearms like bricks and a tight beer gut, tossed in another fifty. Dominic hadn't said two words together all night, just bet money and scooped up pots. There was now over three hundred dollars in the middle of the table.

'So you were buddy-buddy with Zack,' said Jasper. 'Is that what you been trying to tell us all night, Sport?'

'Something like that,' I said.

'Zack was some distant relative of Dominic's, like a second cousin twice removed, or something,' said Jasper. 'I can never figure those things out. So we let him play with us when he wanted. Nice fucking guy.'

'Lousy ballplayer,' said Virgil. 'Lousier poker player.'

'That's why we let him keep playing,' said Luigi, and he let out another wheeze of a laugh that devolved into a spasm of coughs.

'Nice fucking guy, good loser,' said Jasper. 'And the girls he had, I'll tell you, Sport. What do you think? They loved him.'

'He had to beat them off with a baseball bat,' said Virgil.

There was a quiet, awkward pause and then Dominic spoke in a voice hard as slate. 'That's enough,' he said.

'You know what you are, Virgil?' said Jasper. 'You're an idiot.'

'I didn't mean nothing by it.'

'That's your problem, you never mean nothing by it,' said Luigi. 'I'm raising twenty.'

'Three queens,' said Virgil, shaking his head as he tossed in another twenty. 'I knew he had them queens.'

'In,' I said.

Dominic put in his chips and Luigi dealt the next round. No one tripled their pairs but I pulled the seven of hearts, leaving me four to the flush.

Dominic tossed in twenty-five dollars and Luigi saw it.

'What happened to Mr Forty Dollars?' asked Virgil. 'Where's he gone?'

'You in or not?' asked Luigi.

'In,' he said, tossing in his chips.

'I'm in too,' I said. 'What I heard about Zack was

that he was stepping out with the wrong girl at the end.'

'Where'd you pick that up, Sport?' asked Jasper.

'That's just what I heard.'

'Is that what you heard?' said Jasper. 'Well, maybe you heard right.'

Dominic threw in his chips and then, without looking at me, said in his harsh voice, 'Haven't I seen you on TV or something?'

'*Wheel of Fortune*?' I said.

'Maybe that's it,' said Dominic. 'You on *Wheel of Fortune*?'

'No.'

'Funny guy,' said Dominic without a smile. 'Deal them cards.'

Luigi dealt out the last round of cards face down. I slipped mine on top of my other down cards and pulled them to my chest. Slowly, carefully, I looked at my down cards. The four of hearts. The four of spades. I glanced around at the old men looking at me and then I looked at the new card. King of hearts. I had flushed, king high. I was finally going to win a hand. I let out an involuntary sigh.

'What's that?' said Virgil. 'What was that, did you hear that?'

'I didn't hear nothing,' said Luigi.

'You been deaf in your left ear since 'fifty-nine.'

'I heard it too,' said Jasper.

'What was it?' asked Luigi.

'He sighed,' said Virgil. 'Victor sighed, three hearts up and he pulled his flush. That was a flushing sigh if I ever heard it. Something high too, an ace. He's got an ace high flush.'

'Can't be, no way, no how,' said Jasper, searching through and then turning over one of his folded hand. 'I got the ace of hearts right here.'

'You cannot-a do that,' said Luigi. 'You're out, you cannot-a say what you had.'

'Aah, stop that,' said Jasper. 'All of a sudden now it's Hoyle from the guy who raises himself.'

'Believe it or don't believe it, I don't care none,' said Virgil. 'But he's got his flush.'

'I don't-a believe it,' said Luigi. 'Whose bet?'

'Dominic,' said Fred.

Dominic put twenty-five in the pot.

'I see it,' said Luigi.

'Count me out against the flush,' said Virgil.

'I'll see the twenty-five and raise twenty-five,' I said.

'Told you,' said Virgil.

Dominic tossed in another fifty.

'Another raise?' said Luigi.

'You and your queens,' said Virgil. 'You and your queens are worth zippo. You should have folded with Jasper.'

'Jasper bent over the day of his first-a communion,' said Luigi, 'and he's been folding ever since.'

'What? You want I should bet like you, Luigi?' said Jasper. 'You want I should blow my check staying in like a douchebag with three queens against a flush? I don't got no rich son-in-law running a funeral parlor in Scranton. I got to be careful or by the end of the month I'm eating Alpo.'

Luigi looked at Jasper, sneered gently, and said, 'I see Dominic.'

'Is that what got Zack killed, the wrong girl?' I asked nonchalantly as I looked over my cards for the final bet. I only had fifty dollars left.

'Let's just say,' said Jasper, 'between you and me, Sport, his luck wasn't rotten only in baseball and poker.'

Still looking at my cards, I said, 'I heard he was playing around with Raffaello's daughter,' and after I said it a silence crashed into the room.

I looked up. Around the table the four men were staring at me like I had blasphemed the virgin mother. Giovanni sat up in his chair. I started to sweat.

Finally I said, 'I'm in,' and to break the silence that

228

followed that declaration I said, 'and I'll raise my last twenty-five.' But the game didn't continue just then.

'Hey, *stugatz*,' said Luigi. 'Don't be talking about things you should not-a be talking about.'

'It's just what I heard,' I said, trying to shrug it off.

'From who?' asked Jasper. It had turned into an inquisition, four against one. 'What greaseball you hear that from, Sport?'

'I just heard it,' I said. 'It wasn't like a secret.'

'You must not be from around here,' said Jasper, 'because if you was from around here you would know you talk about a man's family like that you might just wake up to find yourself dead.'

'It's been known to happen,' said Dominic in a flat, cold voice.

'Some men don't like nobody talking about their family,' said Virgil.

'You should learn to keep-a your mouth shut,' said Luigi.

There was a long quiet while the men stared at me and I stared at my cards and then Dominic said, 'Let's play.'

Luigi shook his head at me. 'No more talk, hey. Enough with the talk. I'm in,' he said, tossing in his chips.

Dominic put in his twenty-five.

'Now,' said Luigi, turning up his down queen. 'Show me that-a flush.'

'Sure,' I said as I turned over my cards. I reached to rake in the pot but Dominic's hand grabbed my forearm and squeezed.

He squeezed so hard I felt it in the bones.

'Full house,' he said, without turning over his cards.

'Of course he had the boat,' said Virgil. 'Why else would he have stayed in against the flush?'

Dominic pushed my arm away and then slowly began transferring the chips from the middle to his piles. He still hadn't turned over his cards.

'Let's see it,' I said.

Dominic froze at the table, his hands still on the chips,

and I could hear his breathing, slow, steady, dangerous as a leopard's.

'If Dominic says he's got a boat, Sport,' said Jasper, softly, 'he's got the boat.'

'I'm not saying he doesn't,' I said. 'I just want to see it.'

'What you are saying,' said Luigi, the coldness back in his whispery voice, 'is that you don't-a believe him.'

'I'd just like to see it.'

'This is a gentlemen's club,' said Luigi. 'And since you have no more money your temporary membership is revoked.'

Giovanni rose from his red leatherette chair and moved to the table behind Luigi, his arms crossed in front of him.

'You're ripping me off,' I said.

'It's time to go,' said Giovanni.

I looked around at these old men, who had seemed harmless just a few moments ago, and what I saw was not a group of geriatrics needling each other in their weekly poker game but something much more ferocious. Luigi had the sharp hatchet face and Sicilian accent of a Mafia underboss. Virgil was an aging enforcer, collecting for loan sharks, breaking legs when necessary. Jasper was the negotiator, the dealmaker, the man who set up the lucrative arrangements that the others enforced. And Dominic, silent and stolid, was as dangerous as a hit man. I never had a chance in that game, the goal of that night was to fleece me of all my money and I was lucky that was all they were after. But I had learned what I had come to learn, that Bissonette had played around with the wrong girl and had been killed because of it. And though these aged gangsters had refused to talk about it, their silence and threats and the absence of denials loudly confirmed that it was Raffaello's daughter Bissonette had been playing with and that it was Raffaello who'd had him killed. And I wondered, for a moment, if it was one of these old men who had done the deed. Maybe Dominic, Bissonette's second cousin, twice removed, whose grip, I knew, was still strong enough to wield a Mike Schmidt autographed bat.

I stood up and nodded at the men around the table and, without saying a word, self-consciously walked to the door.

'You're forgetting your jacket, Sport,' said Jasper. 'We don't want you should forget your jacket.'

I returned to the table, avoiding the angry gazes of the men as I took hold of my jacket, and walked again to the door, moving as quickly as I could without running.

'Hey, kid,' I heard from behind me.

I stopped and turned around. Dominic was staring at me with a scary squint in his eyes. Slowly he turned over his down cards, one by one, first the ten of spades, then the ten of clubs, then the six of diamonds, which gave him a sixes over tens full house.

'No one calls me a cheater, kid,' he said. 'Leastways no one who wants to keep breathing.'

I looked at him and expected him to smile at his joke, but he didn't, his face was as hard as the squint in his eyes. And then I dropped all pretensions of calm and ran out of the club, ran to my car, and tore the hell out of South Philadelphia.

I was filled with relief when I drove north past South Street, into the safety of Society Hill. It was relief at being out of that grubby little men's club, away from the gangsters there with murder in their eyes. And, just as much, relief at learning that everything Prescott had been telling me might actually be the truth. He was right about who killed Bissonette and he would do his best, which was far better than my best, to make sure the jury knew about it too. I could now, with whatever good conscience I could muster, stay safely silent, following his orders as he tried my case, collecting my fat hourly fee by merely sitting next to my client, keeping my mouth shut and my tie clean as I slipped into my prosperous future.

I had just left the front door of my apartment building

the next morning, heading for the Broad Street subway to take me to the courthouse, my body still suffused with the soft elation of relief, when the rear window of a parked car exploded in front of my face.

25

It was a hatchback, Japanese I think, and I was just in front of it when the rear window shattered into a constellation of diamonds that hung in the air for a brilliant incandescent second before falling. It was such a startlingly pretty sight that I didn't move, just stared at the now jagged opening yawning from the back of the car and the sparkles spinning on the pitted asphalt. Then I saw someone across the street pointing down an alley and a man in front of me dropping to the ground, like a soldier under ambush, and I realized that the window hadn't spontaneously exploded of its own accord but had been shot out in front of me. That's when I dropped to the ground too.

There were no more shots. There were the sounds of footfalls and a car stopping suddenly and more footfalls and people shouting, but no more shots. By the time I had picked myself off the sidewalk a crowd had formed and a policeman was coming over to look at the damage and to ask his questions. There was a group of us now, the man I had seen hit the ground, the man who had seen someone run away and had been pointing across the street, an old woman from my building, out for a morning walk with her purebred dachshund, the dachshund barking rabidly, the woman laughing wildly. I had seen nothing but the explosion of the window and so I wasn't much help, but the officer took down my name and address just the same.

'What do you think it was?' asked the pointer.

'Probably just some random shooting,' said the cop, a peach-fuzzed kid with a holster and an attitude, trying to speak over the dachshund's barks. 'Happens all the time.'

'In Beirut maybe,' said a passerby.

The dachshund growled into my crotch.

'Quiet, Oscar,' said the dog woman, no longer laughing, giving her dog a tug on the leash. The dog sniffed my ankle and growled again.

'Maybe someone was trying to damage the car?' said another man in a tan raincoat.

'That's possible,' said the officer, who for the first time took note of the car's license plate. 'Anyone know who owns this vehicle?'

No one knew, so he called in the license plate on the portable radio attached to his belt.

'All right now,' he said as he was waiting for a response. 'I have your names. Let's get on our way.'

I left, and took some comfort in the officer's nonchalance, but not too much. I stepped quickly to the subway. I took a seat in the corner of the first car and hid myself behind a newspaper. Back on the street I was careful to stay within the bosom of the crowd on my way to the metal detectors in the lobby of the Federal Courthouse. And all the time I couldn't help but carry with me, along with briefcase and raincoat, the suspicion that the shot had not been random or aimed at the car, but fired at me. Oh yes, I was not completely blind. I could feel the danger rising about me, from the threatening Chuckie Lamb, from the paranoid Norvel Goodwin, from my new and fervent relationship with Veronica, from Jimmy if he ever found out about the two of us, from Prescott and the power he could use to break me, from the poker playing gangsters with murder in their eyes and full houses in their hands, from the shadowy Raffaello.

This I knew about myself: I was not the most courageous of men. I was comfortable with that fact. I left the heroics to those who were paid for it, policemen, Brinks guards, inside linebackers, paparazzi. That's one of the reasons I was attracted to the law, I guess. By its very nature the law is a hedge, boom or bust, mergers or bankruptcies, there is always work. And so the shot had only confirmed for me the decision of the night before, confirmed it in a way that was more than intellectual, in a way that was visceral. And whether the bullet was aimed at me or not was no matter; I had learned the lesson of the lead. Whatever was to come, whatever humiliation, whatever ugliness, whatever betrayal, I would do nothing to stop it. My instructions were to follow along, and follow along I would. Whatever you want, Mr Prescott, sir, you can count on me.

Outside the courtroom that morning I was talking to Beth about my opening statement when we were approached by one of the Talbott, Kittredge coterie working with Prescott. It was the blond bland man with the perfect nose who had sneered at Morris the day before. His name was Bert or Bart, something harsh and efficient. I knew nothing about him, really, didn't know whether he had a family, a child, whether he read poetry or Proust, whether he felt deeply for the disadvantaged or whether the pains in the world had turned his viewpoint cynical and his humor wry. But what I did know was that he held a Harvard law degree and I didn't, that he had the job I wanted, that he owned the future of which I had dreamed, and for all of that I hated him.

'Bill asked me to give you this,' he said, reaching into his shiny silver case and pulling out a sheet of paper with a few lines printed out in bold capital letters.

'What is it?' I asked.

'It's your opening,' he said.

'We prepared an opening,' Beth told him, her voice showing incredulity at his nervy assumption that we weren't ready.

After the poker game I had spent most of the night practicing my delivery of a lengthy and blistering attack on the government's case against Concannon. It had been written primarily by Beth, so I knew it was quality. Beth's opening highlighted the gaps in the case against Concannon: There were no tapes capturing Concannon's voice, no pieces of physical evidence directly involving him in any of the transactions, no photographs showing him with Ruffing or Bissonette. The case against Concannon would depend solely on the testimony of Ruffing and certain financial records from CUP, and Beth had laid out a viciously effective argument against Ruffing's credibility. I understood that I would be following Prescott's lead in every sense, but I still expected that I would be saying at least something of my own to the jurors.

'We're sure that it's a fine argument,' said Bert or Bart. 'But what we want you to do is to give the opening we have prepared for you.'

'Who wrote it?' asked Beth, grabbing the paper from my hand.

'I did,' he said, his chest puffing out slightly. 'Bill looked it over, discussed it with the jury expert, made a few changes, and decided you should go with it.'

'Is that what he decided?' I said.

'That's what we decided.'

'I think we'll stay with what we worked up already,' said Beth.

'I was told you were with the program, Vic,' he said to me, ignoring Beth. 'That you wouldn't be any trouble.'

'What's your name?' Beth asked.

'Brett Farber. Brett with two t's.'

'Well, Brett with two t's,' she said. 'The only program we're with is our client's and as best I can tell, from a quick look through this little statement of yours, it's a piece of shit.'

Brett didn't pull back from the attack like I would have. Instead he brought out his sneer and leaned into me until I could smell the coffee in his breath and he said, 'Shit or not, Vic, your client approved it and it is what you are going to give.'

Before Beth could reply he had turned on his heels and was gone.

Fucking Brett with two t's, I thought as I watched his back disappear into the courtroom. Maybe there was a reason other than luck that he was an up-and-comer with Talbott, Kittredge and I was not.

'Such a pleasant young boy,' said Beth. 'His mother must be so proud. So tell me, Victor, how does it feel to have assholes like William Prescott and Brett with two t's as your colleagues?'

'For two-fifty an hour I'd sleep with an orangutan,' I said. 'This is only slightly worse.'

'What are you going to do?'

I took the piece of paper from her and read it quickly, eight sentences typed in bold capital letters so that I wouldn't stumble as I read it to the jury. 'What I'm going to do,' I said, 'is discuss it with my client and then, Beth dear, I'm going to suck it up.'

'You suck it up any more, Victor, you're going to start looking like a chipmunk.'

I hadn't told her about the shattered hatchback window and didn't intend to, nor about Veronica, nor about Chuckie's call, nor about Norvel Goodwin, nor about my disastrous poker game. If there was danger to be ducked, it was mine and I would do the ducking. So all I did, as she looked at me with disappointment flashing in her sharp, pretty eyes, was shrug.

When I sat down at the defense table I showed the paper with the eight sentences to Concannon. 'Is this what you want me to give as an opening?'

'Is that what Prescott showed me last night?'

'Yes.'

He shrugged. 'Is it a problem?'

'It's a big fat zero,' I said. 'It does nothing.'

'The way he explained it to me is that we should make my role in the deal, the arrangements, everything, seem as small as possible.'

'Eggert's not going to let the jury forget you're on trial.'

'If that's what Prescott wants you to give, then give it.'

'You know I checked it out, about Bissonette and Raffa-ello's daughter,' I said. 'It appears to be on the up.'

'Victor, Victor,' he said, his voice slightly scolding. 'You were supposed to stop your interfering.'

'Consider it stopped,' I said just as the door behind the judge's bench opened and the court clerk stood to start the trial. 'From here on in I'm Chuckie Lamb's mannequin.'

'All rise,' said the clerk as the judge climbed the steps to the bench.

We all rose.

26

'Any crime is a betrayal of the trust we have in each other, but when it is a public official who commits the crime, an official who asked for our vote and swore an oath to serve the public, the betrayal is particularly cruel.'

Eggert very slowly walked over to the defense table until he was directly opposite the defendants. He was giving his opening to the rapt jurors, his reedy voice rising in indignation. He pointed at Jimmy, his finger close enough to the councilman's face that Jimmy could have bitten it off if he wanted to, and the moment it flashed there, like a white scimitar, that's exactly what it looked like Jimmy would do. Then he recovered control and the look of deep sobriety returned. Through it all, his eyes never wavered from Eggert's; if there was to be a staredown, it would be Eggert who blinked first. In the front row of the public benches, three different artists were furiously sketching the moment, Eggert's straight back, his accusing finger, the bunched muscles in Jimmy Moore's neck.

'James Douglas Moore is a city councilman, a public official placed into office by the people of this city who looked to him to promote the interests of all of Philadelphia, not just his own. The first requirement of his office was honesty, and that was the first thing he threw out the window. The evidence will show, ladies and gentlemen, that Jimmy Moore used his office to extort money, and when his extortion plan went awry he resorted to threats, which you will hear on tapes legally obtained by the government, he resorted to arson, and he resorted to murder. Murder, ladies and gentlemen, the murder of Zachariah Bissonette, the former ballplayer, who stood up for what was right and refused to be blackmailed. Jimmy Moore took a baseball bat and battered Bissonette so badly he was in a coma for five months, never to open his eyes, to see the beauty of the day, to look into the faces of his loving family, never to recover before he died. That is how Jimmy Moore observed the public trust. And we'll show you where the money went, how it was funneled through his political action committee, how a chunk of it never even got to the committee but was instead skimmed off for his own personal use, how Jimmy Moore used his office to grab enough money so he could ride around the city in a big black limousine and drink champagne and gamble in the casinos along the Boardwalk. That's what the evidence will show.'

Eggert moved on to Concannon and again the finger of the prosecution pointed.

'Chester Concannon is Jimmy Moore's chief aide, a public servant whose duty was to help the councilman achieve his legitimate goals as a public official. But instead of looking out for the interests of the people of Philadelphia, Concannon aided the councilman in each of his extortion schemes. Concannon was the go-between, the bagman, the fellow to see if you wanted the councilman on your side. Chester Concannon took his share of the lucre ripped out of the skin of the people of this city, and Concannon was with Jimmy Moore the night Bissonette was battered with that baseball bat into complete and unwavering unconsciousness.'

When he was finished accusing the defendants he detailed the elements of the crime of racketeering that he would prove, going over what each witness would say and how it would all come together to show so clear a pattern of illegal conduct that the jury would be forced to convict. Then he leaned over the defense table and stared, first at Jimmy Moore, then at Chester Concannon. 'At the end of this trial, I'm going to come back to you and ask for a guilty verdict on all the counts. And instead of the money or the political power or the black limousines and champagne nights and extravagant evenings in Atlantic City, I'm going to ask you to give this corrupt councilman and his corrupt aide all that they truly deserve.' With a final look at the defendants, a look filled with all the weary disgust he could muster, Eggert walked slowly to the prosecution table and sat down.

Prescott didn't jump up to follow Eggert as most lawyers would. He remained seated, his head down dramatically. Judge Gimbel, still at work on whatever opinion he was drafting for some other case, didn't seem to notice the delay and just kept writing. The crowd in the courtroom stirred, one of the jurors coughed, Prescott remained seated.

'It is at a time like this,' said Prescott finally, while still seated at the defense table, 'it is in a trial like this that the genius of the jury system shines through.'

With a great sigh, Prescott stood, his shoulder slightly bent, his head shaking sadly. He looked down solemnly as he spoke and the whole effect was of a profound disappointment.

'My client Jimmy Moore is a politician who is gaining power in this city because he practices the politics of inclusion. His goal is to fight the scourge of drugs, a scourge that has taken the life of his daughter, his only child. The youth home he founded is a national leader in drug treatment for the young. And in pursuit of this noble goal he has brought together all the people of this city, no matter their race, no matter their religion, no matter their economic status, whether they are homeless or HIV infected or children subject to the worst abuses. His political action committee, Citizens for a United Philadelphia, or CUP, has in the last two years spent over half a million dollars informing citizens of their rights and registering the unregistered. His committee has added two hundred thousand voters to the city's polls. And as Jimmy Moore's influence grows, so does the power of his opposition.'

241

Prescott turned to look at the jury and then slowly walked from behind the defense table to a position directly behind Eggert, who was leaning forward in his seat.

'There are powerful men in this city who feel threatened by the inclusive coalition being forged by Jimmy Moore. Fat cats and politicos who want to keep it all for themselves and are not willing to open the system to those they have been able to ignore. Men with enough power that they can use the United States Attorney's Office as a tool for their political designs.

'Now the President of the United States can sweep into town and hold a fund-raiser and leave with a million dollars in his pocket and that is politics as usual. But when Jimmy Moore goes about raising money for his program of healing, it is extortion. Politics has become money, the need to register voters, the need to put up posters, the need to buy buttons and bumper stickers and, most important, the need to produce and put on television commercials. That's why the President takes his cool million when he visits and it is why Jimmy Moore raises money from those like the businessmen who were seeking his help here. Politics is money, and it may not be pretty and it may not be right and it may not be what we would choose if we were starting over, but that's what it is. And Jimmy Moore was doing nothing more here than any politician ever does as he tries to raise the money to run for office.

'So if Jimmy Moore was doing just what every other politician does, why is he on trial? As you listen to the evidence, as you analyze the government's case, that's the question you have to ask yourselves. If Jimmy Moore was a business-as-usual politician, not ruffling the feathers of the powerful men who can control a United States Attorney's Office, would he be on trial? The answer, at the end of this case, will be a resounding no. You examine the evidence, you figure out what was really going on here, you decide who actually committed the crimes alleged by the government. You decide if the government is seeking

242

justice or is seeking to pull out a political thorn in the side of the status quo. You look it all over very carefully, and in the end you'll decide to acquit Jimmy Moore and let him continue in his good work.'

It was my turn now, my chance to speak to the jury on behalf of my client. In front of me was a yellow legal pad with the lengthy and impassioned opening argument Beth had drafted and I had rehearsed the night before. But as I rose, I left it on the table. In my hand was a single white sheet. On it was written the following little speech:

> My name is Victor Carl. I am representing Chester Concannon in this case. Mr Concannon is Jimmy Moore's chief aide. He has been indicted as part of the government's vendetta against Jimmy Moore. You won't hear Chester Concannon on any tapes. There is no correspondence linking him to any of the crimes alleged here. I expect you won't hear much about him at all. Try to remember, whenever you hear his name, how little he is involved, and at the end of the case I am sure you will acquit him of all charges.

I glanced at Prescott, who was jotting down notes upon his legal pad, purposefully avoiding my gaze. I glanced at Concannon, who was staring at his hands clasped together on the table. I twisted to look at the audience. The courtroom was packed. Beth was frowning at me. Chuckie Lamb was pinching his lips together as he shook his head. In the aisle I saw Herm Finklebaum, the toy king of 44th Street, smiling at me with encouragement. I walked to a spot just in front of the jury box, surveyed the jurors one by one, and then read the anemic piece-of-shit opening that had been written for me by Brett with two t's.

When I sat down I was actually embarrassed.

*   *   *

The first witness was Special Agent Stemkowski, the WWF reject sitting with Eggert at the prosecution table. For a bruiser Stemkowski was very well spoken, calm, and deliberate, able to keep a straight face as he used phrases like 'I exited the vehicle' and 'I effected implementation of the interception of Mr Ruffing's phone conversations.' He wore a camel-colored jacket, a white shirt, a calm blue tie. On his thick pinky he wore one of those flashy gold class rings, undoubtedly commemorating his graduation with honors from the FBI Academy. He had played football in high school, tight end, he said, and when Eggert drew out this insignificant piece of testimony, three of the men in the jury box nodded with approval. His demeanor on the stand was evidence that the country was in good hands, the soft competent hands of a receiver with biceps like great ragged chunks of pig iron.

Stemkowski explained how the FBI had been investigating a drug operation being run out of Bissonette's by a bartender, an operation not in any way involving Bissonette or Ruffing, when it had begun wiretapping the club's phones. It was through those wiretaps that the Bureau had discovered the extortion scheme. Special Agent Stemkowski authenticated the cassette tapes, identifying the marked date and time on each cassette as being in his handwriting and accurately based on FBI logs maintained during the surveillance. Eggert then produced thick loose-leaf binders containing all the transcripts, which were first authenticated and then distributed to judge and jury.

An FBI audio man had set up a sophisticated tape playback device with microwave transmission to headphones placed at the counsel tables, on the judge's bench, beside each seat in the jury box. I would have liked to hear Bruce Springsteen pour out of those headphones, the Grateful Dead, the Rolling Stones, I would have liked to hear Jimi Hendrix's version of the national anthem strip away the wax from our ears, but that's not what we heard through those government approved high-fidelity headphones. What we heard, playing clearly, numbingly, for the whole of two full days, were the taped conversations of Michael Ruffing and City Councilman Jimmy Moore.

Moore: Don't do this, Mikey. You back out now, your project's dead. Dead.

Ruffing: My new investor don't think so.

Moore: It's that cookie baker, isn't it?

Ruffing: Shut up. You were taking too much anyway, you know? You were being greedy.

Moore: So that's it, is it, Mikey? I'm sending my man Concannon down.

Ruffing: I don't want Concannon.

Moore: You listen, you shit. You talk to Concannon, right? I ain't no hack from Hackensack, we had a deal. A deal. This isn't just politics. We're on a mission here, Mikey, and I won't let you back down from your responsibilities. You catch what I'm telling you here? You catch it, Mikey?

I had heard the tapes before, knew every line now almost by heart. I knew what had been said, but the jury didn't. When Moore threatened the hell out of Michael Ruffing on the tape the whole of the jury, headphones firmly on, reacted like I had reacted the first time I had heard it: their necks reared, their eyes fixed on both Moore and Concannon, and the squints in their eyes were like squints of a posse intent on a hanging. Not an encouraging sign after just one witness.

27

'Tell me how you got involved with Jimmy Moore,' I ordered Veronica. 'Tell me how.'

She was stretched beneath me, her wrists tied stiffly to the headboard with long silk scarves, her legs pinned down by my bent knees. She snapped at my belly with her teeth, at my chest. I stretched my body over hers, pressing down hard, and we clawed each other with our mouths. It wasn't kissing in any way I had known kissing to be before, there was a violence to it, a rapaciousness. We stirred each other's hunger and satisfied it at the same time. When she bucked her hips and raised her knees, opening herself for me, I sat up again and grabbed her hair and laughed at her.

'Tell me.'

'After,' she breathed.

'Not after. Now.'

'Let me loose and I'll tell you.'

'Tell me and I might let you loose.'

She jerked her hands trying to get free but the scarves, long and soft and creamy maroon, were strong and the knots I had tied with boy scout accuracy and enthusiasm held. In the light of the candles we had set around the loft bed her flat stomach flickered yellow as her hips rose violently. She tried to kick me off but I rode her like a bucking mule and stayed right where I was. I stretched my weight on top of her and we clawed each other with our mouths and again she tried to open herself to me and I wouldn't let her. It was my turn on top and I had control for once and I was going to keep it.

These scarves and pseudo-violent acts, this outbreak of

forced control and mock desperation, this was not my usual thing. I had liked my sex slow and soft, an easy glide, a dance of the lips and the hips, rising and falling in a series of synchronous crescendos, Fred and Ginger swaying together in black and white as he tapped out a subtle mysterious rhythm and the feathers of her boa floated about them in sensual waves. If the sex of my earlier life had been a movie, it would be *Dancing in the Dark*. But it had turned with Veronica. We weren't in the middle of a light romantic comedy. Sex with her was more like *Marathon Man* and she was the dentist. But we had tried it my way and we had tried it her way and believe me when I tell you this – her way was better.

I knew I shouldn't be there in her apartment, but the danger of it all drew me as much as the sheer addictive kineticism of our sex. That I had been warned, that a car window had shattered in front of my face, that if Jimmy found out about us everything might be lost, all that and more drew me there. Even as I banged the steering wheel of my car with my palms at my foolishness, I still drove to that Olde City building, coming at her beckon, where I would rise up in that Plexiglas windowed elevator and knock on her door, knock quietly, head bowed, as reverent as a supplicant before the Pope.

That night she had pulled the scarves out of the drawer beside her bed and floated them across her chest like a harem girl teasing her eunuch. 'I don't think you're ready for these yet,' she had said.

'I don't think so either.'

'There are places you're not ready to go.'

'You're right.'

'But aren't you in the least bit curious?'

'About what?'

'About what it's like to tie me up?'

'I can imagine it.'

'But that's the point, Victor. With me you don't have to

247

imagine. You can do anything you want to me. It's too bad Roberta is out of town.'

'Roberta?'

'She's a friend of mine. A model. You'd like her, Victor. She's very thin, very blonde. All the boys just die for Roberta.'

'You're fine enough for me.'

'I'd be there too. It's about appetites. The more you get, the more you need. It grows like a marvelous cancer. A week in Cancun with me and Roberta and you'll never be satisfied with just one again.'

'Cancun?'

'Roberta likes to travel.'

'How about just you and me?'

'Where?'

'Someplace exotic.'

'I'm not sure I trust your taste for the exotic. You're not a very adventurous boy.'

'Someplace you've never been.'

'Cleveland? You want to take me to Cleveland?'

'Tahiti.'

'I've been to Tahiti. Too long a flight for a beach.'

'Thailand.'

'Too hot.'

'Burma. Have you ever been to Rangoon?'

'No, take me to Rangoon. Yes, Rangoon.'

'But first Cleveland. The best hotel in the city.'

'Motel Six?'

'Sure, and a bottle of Bud from room service.'

'When?'

'After this trial.'

'Could we bring Roberta?'

'I don't need anything more than you.'

'Not for you, for me.'

'I'm not enough?'

'In case you tire.'

That's when I tied the half hitch to the bed post, a solid

sailing knot, and wrapped the scarf tightly around her wrist, so tightly that her wrist purpled when she gave it a solid yank. 'Not so tight,' she said with a laugh and I ignored her, as I was sure she hoped I would. There were enough scarves to bind her ankles too, but I thought it would be more acrobatic if I left her legs free to wriggle about. 'Really, you should loosen them,' she said, 'they're too tight.' But no matter what she said I did what I wanted. 'Stop it, you'll leave a mark.' She was taking me to a strange outer world where no meant yes and stop meant go and all that I had learned about political correctness and sexual courtesy was meant to be breached. There was something clicking in my brain stem, something primordial, something with the glorious confidence of the unselfconscious, something that had existed long before the forebrain swelled and turned sex into an intellectual exercise, something that had been pounded down in my years of politeness in bed, my years of caring if it was good for her, my years of striving for joint satisfaction. 'Stop it. Please. I'm begging you, please. God stop stop no stop it now.' The ultimate, I had always believed, was the simultaneous orgasm, the instantaneous joinder of passions and fulfillments, where two became one. But the part of my brain stem stimulated by Veronica, as if she were an electrode buried deep into a mass of long dormant neurons, cared nothing for simultaneity. It was selfish and violent and brutal. It was Neanderthal, prowling with a club in each hand, one wooden, one swollen flesh, searching for satisfaction, demanding it, objectifying anything that could be grabbed and placed beneath it, anything whose sole purpose was to sharpen desire at the same time it satisfied it in a painful gut-wrenching burst. It wasn't pretty what I felt gurgling inside my brain stem, it wasn't something that was pleasant to admit was within me, but there was nothing pleasant about sex with Veronica. It was closer to hell than to heaven, its power was buried in the genetic memory of the past, but once discovered, it was a place I couldn't leave. And even after I came I stayed impossibly hard inside her, my brain stem allowing for no respite. I sucked a bruise out of the base of her breast and bit her earlobe and with my knees spreading her knees and my hip bone grinding into her hip bone her voice broke into a torrent of ancient cries and while I drove on and on into the mist of my predatory history she came despite my caring not at all and I kept on despite her cries and she came again in a yelp, scraping my neck with her lower teeth, and the back of my neck burst apart in a maddening orgasm and she sucked my Adam's apple and flipped her loose legs high until her feet kicked my head and she screamed murderously.

When I collapsed on top of her, my weight pressing her legs onto the mattress, she jerked her arms as high as the scarves would allow and let out a howl that sounded like the baying of a great wounded cat, golden, striped, saber-toothed.

I rested there, just like that, still inside her, lying atop her like a corpse. I might have dozed off, I couldn't tell, but it seemed like I lay atop her for the longest time. She said nothing, made no movement to shrug me off. There was a silence about us, a haze that only slowly lifted as the sounds of cars slipping along the cobblestones of Church Street edged their way through the quiet. In my chest I could feel a strange asynchronous heartbeat – ba ba boom boom, ba ba boom ba boom, boom ba ba boom boom, ba boom ba boom, ba ba boom boom. I worried for a moment, thinking the intensity of the sex had chased me into arrhythmia, but then I realized my chest was pressing so hard onto hers that I was feeling both our beats. I pushed myself up with weary arms and squatted atop her. She was still tied up and the fact that I remained in control thrilled me. I cupped her left breast with my hand and squeezed her nipple between my fingers. Her eyes stayed closed but her pretty face twisted into something carnal and pained.

Without opening her eyes she said, 'God, I'm sick of old men.'

And that was when I ordered her to tell me about how she ended up with Jimmy Moore. She struggled a bit, and tried again to yank her arms loose. I kissed her gently on her lips, on her cheek, on her eyes, on her lips again, the softness of my kisses calming her. Her eyes were still closed. I rubbed my hands across her sides and said, 'Tell me,' and so she told me.

She was born in Iowa, she said as I rubbed my tongue across the lower edge of her breast, in a small town west of Cedar Rapids called Solon. In Solon the kids used to hang out at Jones's House of Pork and eat fried tenderloin sandwiches as big as a head and play pool, a quarter a game, and grow fat and pimply. It was a small town, not far from a lake where they swam on sweltering summer days, and there was a city park and an American Legion baseball team and once a year the town would gussy itself up for Solon Beef Days and people would come in from all over eastern Iowa and there would be carnival rides and a parade and a steak dinner with corn and salad for $2.79 served under a tent.

Her father taught at the university, about thirty minutes south of Solon, medieval history, and at night he would tell her tales of kings and queens and bloody princes until she knew more about the House of York than the House of Pork. Her dream, always, as long as she could remember, was to marry a prince and live in a castle and hold court. She didn't know if there were any princes left in the world or if they had grown extinct, like dinosaurs, but she knew for sure that there weren't any princes in Iowa.

Her mother she remembered only from photographs, tall, plain, an intense concern grooved into the flesh around her eyes. Maybe she could see into the future, Veronica said, and see her early, painful death from a burst

251

appendix. She was a fine woman, Veronica's father had told her, strong, gentle. Veronica's father was on a trip east, lecturing at Princeton, and her mother hadn't told anyone about the pain, certain it would go away like an upset stomach, unwilling to leave her baby daughter to find a doctor. Her father had flown to Princeton a promising young scholar and had flown back a widower with a baby daughter to raise alone. He was totally gray before he turned forty.

She went to the University of Iowa and pledged a sorority and dated football players and golfers and in the homecoming parade sat decked out like Princess Di on a sorority float made out to be Buckingham Palace. When she had the chance to go to London for her junior year she jumped at it. Her father died while she was away, a sudden heart attack, and she returned just long enough to bury him and sell the house in Solon and cash out his pension before returning to England, an orphan with money to spend. That's where she met a boy named Saffron Hyde.

'He was a poet,' she told me. 'I met him in a pub in Southgate, a rock club. He came up to me and asked me to buy him a pint and I did. He was skinny and nervous and unlike anyone I had ever met before. There were no Saffron Hydes in Iowa. I had an apartment in the North End and he came home with me that night, more like a stray puppy dog than a seducer, but he moved in the next day. We drank a lot, I quit school, he wrote poetry about me, we made sweet love, but he wasn't really interested, which was fine, actually, and every night we went to the art films at the museum.'

'What was his poetry like?' I asked.

'Dark, jittery. Much of it was very funny, but there was always a black loneliness behind the jokes. I thought it breathtaking.'

'Did he publish it?'

'No. He let me see it, some of his friends, but that was

it. He said it was the poetry that mattered, not how many people read it.'

'That sounds like an excuse.'

'Well, he was a great one for excuses.'

'How did he live? How did he support himself?'

'I supported him.'

'And before you?'

She shrugged, an absurd little shrug, calm and matter-of-fact, despite her wrists being bound to the bedposts. 'I didn't ask, he never said.'

'Did you love him?'

'More than anything before or since. He was the love of my life, the prince I had been dreaming of since my girlhood. So when he burst in one afternoon, drunk and full of excitement, and said we just had to go to India, I said "When," he said, "Right this instant," I said, "Fine." '

They took the ferry and backpacked through Europe, Spain, France, Holland, Germany, Italy, Yugoslavia, living like royalty, for backpackers, staying in pensions and rooming houses, eating in restaurants with tablecloths. They took a meandering route, flitting off to wherever seemed the most interesting, but always heading east, taking trains, hitchhiking, boats, Greece, Crete, Turkey, Iran, always on a route toward India. He had to see the Ganges, he said, bathe himself in the holy river, tap into a spiritual source centuries older than his Saxon heritage. He had read Hermann Hesse, it had changed his life, he needed to immerse himself in the sacred waters, he said.

'Remember when Hermann Hesse used to change lives?' I asked.

'You have to read it at a certain age,' she said.

'I read *Siddhartha* when I was fourteen,' I said. 'I think I was too old even then.'

'That's to your pity.'

It was a wonderful trip, she continued, revelatory actually. She was ecstatic and the further away she moved from Iowa the freer she became, swimming naked in the public beaches on the French Riviera, trading her blue jeans for peasant skirts in Corfu, buying drugs in the open-air markets outside Constantinople.

'Drugs?' I asked.

'Yes, that was Saffron at the start, big spliffs of hash in the rock clubs in Amsterdam, then later cocaine in Florence and Greece. I didn't join in at first, but as we continued, the trip seemed more and more dreamlike. Drugs just seemed to fit in.'

'That was pretty stupid for an American.'

'Yes, but after a while we seemed to have stripped away our nationalities, we were just travelers. It was no longer the goal of India propelling us forward, it was just the urge to move, to see more, to go ever further on. Then in Iran, on the way to Pakistan, we had the accident.'

They had tried to catch the bus from Teheran but it was full, and the next day's was full too. They didn't know when there would be an opening, but at the bus station there was a man, black silk shirt, gap-toothed smile. He sidled up and said he was going to the border and would take them for a small fee, less than the bus, only 2,000 toman. The next thing they knew they were in the back seat of a battered blue Mercedes van, sitting on stiff seats with no padding, the van filled with women in black chador holding babies, unshaven men sweating in their grimy shirts, two handsome young men drinking orange Schwepps. With the top of the van piled high with luggage they barreled down the hills outside Teheran, past signs with warnings of falling rocks, into the salt desert on the ancient silk road into Pakistan. They discovered shortly into the trip that the other travelers were being smuggled out of the country, dissidents, young men trying to skip the army service, and the surreptitious nature of the journey thrilled Saffron no end. In a late evening rest stop just outside Isfahan they had drunk some bad water and now Saffron was throwing up, to the amusement of the other passengers, sticking his head out a window, banging his cheek on the frame, heaving loudly, the van shaking like a carnival ride. At a narrow switchback just through one of the tunnels south of Isfahan on the way to Shiraz, the driver barely braked as he swung wildly around, descending into the darkness, the van tilting over the hill as it rushed into the turn. A truck coming up the other way blared its horn and the driver swerved right, the wheels slipped off the road, and, like a gymnast in slow motion, the van tumbled down, down the slope, falling down until it broke apart on a rocky desert ledge.

Veronica had been fine, a bruised shoulder, a sprained wrist, but Saffron, sitting beside the window, had been a mess. In the Shiraz hospital where they had been taken, the doctors set his broken arm and stitched up the gashes in his face, but the real problem was his back, a compression fracture of three vertebrae, which Saffron was adamant about not letting the Iranian doctors set. Instead he gritted his teeth through the pain and, once released, took the next bus out, a modern bus with padded seats and shock absorbers and a bathroom in the back. By the time they reached Pakistan, Saffron was delirious with pain, crying out for drugs, limping alone into the first market he could find and bringing back a reddish gray powder, a local herb, he said, which he snorted first and then mixed with tobacco and smoked and which seemed to give him some measure of blessed relief. She tried it too, mixed with the tobacco of a cigarette.

'It was sweet, numbing, terrific really,' she said. 'Later I found out it was heroin, but I didn't know at first and when I found out it was too late.'

'You really didn't know?'

'I was from Iowa. Within a week he was shooting up three times a day and I was joining him. Everything after that turned into a nightmare, unreal, smoky, disastrous.'

'Jesus.'

'Untie me, Victor.'

I untied her. Without rubbing her wrists she pulled her

arms tight into her torso and turned away from me. I put my hand on her arm to reassure her but she shrugged me off. I didn't want to hear any more, I wished I had never asked the question about her and Jimmy, wondered how the councilman entered into her story anyway.

'Through Pakistan and India he grew thinner and thinner, he was skinny to begin with, but he turned into a ghost. All night he shook, he sweated, his teeth started falling out. He was feverish. I begged him to come with me to America to get treatment. I told him they would fix his back, get him off the drug, we could live in Iowa, I told him, or New York, but he insisted on reaching the Ganges. His arm got infected, it swelled, it began to stink, he started limping from an abscess in his foot. His fever made him delusional in the nights. He was too weak to carry anything, so I emptied out half my stuff and put his clothes in my pack. He stopped eating anything but fruit, drank only water. He could barely talk when we arrived in Varanasi. We went right to the river and he wrapped himself in a white sheet and stepped down the ghat, slowly, mournfully. He turned and waved at me and then stepped down into the water of the Ganges until he was submerged.

'It was filthy, they were washing clothes, dumping sewage, it smelled like a latrine, shit and foam floated by, just upstream they were dumping ashes from the corpses ceremonially burned on the great pyres by the river. He was submerged for a long time, too long a time, and then I knew he would die in the river, his final wave was a wave good bye, and I started running down after him. But he emerged, filthy, the white sheet covered with mud, his face serene, his eyes calm. His fever had broken. When he climbed out of the river he said, "Okay, Ronnie. Take me to America."

'I put him in one of the whitewashed boarding houses they have just off the river and ran to a travel agent. There was just enough left in my account to buy two tickets to Cedar Rapids, Iowa, by way of New York. We would leave

256

the next day. Thrilled, I rushed back to the room and discovered him dead. I found out later that the boarding house was primarily for old men who were coming to Varanasi to die and have their ashes scattered in the river. Before I left I arranged for him to be burned like the others, in his muddy sheet, and to have his ashes shoveled like manure into that fucking Ganges.'

'My God, Veronica.'

'I didn't wait for the funeral.'

'That is awful.'

She stayed on her side, facing away from me, silent, and I knew enough not to say anything. She lay there for five minutes, for ten. I lay on my back, my head atop my hands, thinking about the skinny dark poet with a name like Saffron entering the river bit by bit until he wasn't there anymore. Suddenly she flipped over until she was facing me and ran a finger lightly down my side.

'So I cashed in his ticket,' she said. 'It was money, you know. I had to change planes in New York and realized the last place I wanted to go was Cedar Rapids, so I stayed. I got a job as a paralegal, hated it, I waited tables, hated it, I worked in a gallery, hated it, I tried modeling, they hated me, so I decided to go back to school. I got into Penn, which is how I ended up in Philadelphia, and how I met Norvel.'

'How did a Penn student meet a drug dealing scum like Norvel Goodwin?'

'I looked for him.'

'I don't understand.'

'I was still hooked, Victor. Just because Saffron died didn't mean I was cured. I had a source in New York, but when I ended up at Penn, in West Philadelphia, I just walked into the neighborhood and started asking. He wasn't hard to find. He liked me right off, this pretty white girl stepping into his place and asking for a fix. We became a thing.'

'What about Jimmy in all this?'

'Well, Norvel had a place in West Philly, about six blocks from campus. It was on Fifty-first Street, a shooting gallery of sorts, but not as bad as some of the places up north. Jimmy had lost his daughter only a few years before and was in full battle cry. A neighborhood group came to him about the house. He raised a mob of concerned citizens and raided the place with clubs and shovels and axes and baseball bats. I was there the night Jimmy smashed his way through the door. You should have seen him, his eyes fired, bashing anything in his way, knocking out windows, busting doors, slamming a television screen with a hatchet. He almost killed Norvel, dragged him out of a closet where Norvel had been hiding and started beating the hell out of him with his fists and then with a chair. Norvel's a big man, stronger than he looks, but Jimmy beat the hell out of him. And then he torched the place. He later said the drug dealers had set it on fire, but his people had quietly cleared the surrounding houses before they burst in. Two boys died in the fire, lost in a stupor in a hidden attic. They found them later, after the ashes had cooled.'

'What about you?'

'He found me in a daze in a small room on the third floor and gave me to Chester to take to his car. Chester left me with the driver, who watched over me, made sure I didn't leave until it was over.'

'Who was that, Henry?'

'No, Henry was inside. He was Norvel's partner at the time.'

'No.'

'Sure. And after that, after Henry cleaned himself up, Jimmy gave him a job, turned him into one of his models. Everyone Jimmy hires had a problem. That's so when he gives his speeches he can point with pride to his workers and lecture about how possible it is to change your life.'

'But what about you?'

'After the fire, after the police came and went, after Jimmy had given his speeches for the news reporters in

258

time for the eleven o'clock news, after everything was over, Jimmy came back to his car and took me to a private drug treatment center. He knew by then that I had been Norvel's girl. At the center they told him they didn't have any openings but then he started yelling about city council funding and I was admitted that night. I told him I didn't want it but I really did. I was ready. When I saw that house burn down I knew I was ready. I thought that would be it with Jimmy, but he kept on visiting me, my only visitor, hectoring me to kick my illness, taking me out for ice cream. It may sound strange, since it was more than a year later, but that raid and the fire, that whole night was part of that accident south of Isfahan. It was Jimmy who pulled me from the twisted wreckage of that van. With his help I got clean – he saved my life. By that time, though, school was finished for me, I had incompleted everything. Jimmy got me the apartment in Olde City, he got me a job.'

'And he got in your pants.'

'That was my choice.'

'And if you said no?'

'Believe it or not, if I wanted nothing to do with him I bet he would have done everything the same. When he pulled me out of that house he didn't know me from Eve, all he knew was that I was in trouble and needed help.'

'And pretty as hell.'

'Well, maybe yes, but I had been pretty for a long time and in trouble for a long time and only Jimmy stepped up to take care of me.'

'And for that you owe him the occasional roll in the hay.'

'No, Victor. For that I owe him everything.'

28

'I had known the councilman as a friend and customer for many years,' said Michael Ruffing from the witness stand. 'About twice a month him and his party would come into my club and order drinks and food. He was a very good customer.'

'Did he spend a lot of money?' asked Eggert. He stood behind the podium, his body still, his voice calm, his questions short and non-leading. Eggert was a good enough lawyer not to steal the spotlight from his star witness.

'He was a very good customer, like I said. He never bought the cheaper wines. He always ordered the Dom, every time he came in. No matter how many were with him, that's what he would order. Bottle after bottle.'

'What is "Dom"?'

'Dom Perignon, one of the finest champagnes made. It's like drinking love, or at least that's what I would tell the customers.'

'Is it expensive?'

'The price depends on the year. The 'seventy-eight you can't even get, the 'eighty-five is about one-fifty a bottle, sure, but worth it.'

'And that's what the councilman would order?'

'Nothing but the best, he told me. "Mikey," he used to say, "you're either class or you're shit." That's what he used to say, and then to prove he was class he'd order another four bottles of the Dom.' Ruffing looked at the jury and gave a little wise smile and whatever that smile was saying it looked like the jury agreed with him. The jurors had already heard the tapes, they had already heard a series of witnesses testifying about the waterfront deal

260

and the City Council's involvement, and now they were hearing the story of a shabby shakedown straight from the victim, a law abiding Center City businessman.

Michael Ruffing was a short, energetic man with thick hands and curly gray hair. He was one of the guys who grew up in the neighborhood and kept his neighborhood ways, his Philly accent, his rough talk, his way of shooting his cuffs and fixing his tie between questions. He had grown rich in real estate and lost everything in the bust and grown rich again with a series of nightclubs, the last and largest of which was Bissonette's, which made him a name in the city. He was one of those developers who believed he could build anything he could envision, and he had envisioned a hotel and shopping complex on the waterfront that would draw tourists from five states and would be riverboat-ready when the governor, the only remaining obstacle to legalized gambling on the river, left office. But more than one visionary developer had run aground on the shoals of the Philadelphia waterfront, a cement-encased stretch between the Delaware River and I-95 that had defied commercial development on a grand scale. Ruffing was now testifying as to how his vision died and the part Jimmy Moore and Chet Concannon had played in its death.

'Now on these expensive outings of his at your club,' continued Eggert, 'how did the councilman pay?'

'Cash. Sometimes he would put it on a tab when he was short, which was okay by us because he was in about twice a month like I said, and if he was short one visit he would make up for it the next. Actually it wasn't the councilman that paid, it was Chet.'

'You mean Mr Concannon.'

'That's right. It was Chet who carried the money. Or if not Chet then it was the councilman's media guy, Chuckie Lamb.'

'And he tipped well?'

'The councilman, sure. Chet too. But Chuckie wasn't a

great tipper. Whenever the councilman would catch him shorting one of the servers he'd give Chuckie hell, call him the cheapest bastard this side of Trenton.'

Everyone laughed at that and I did too. I turned around. Chuckie was sitting in the back of the courtroom. Well, almost everyone was laughing.

'Now, Mr Ruffing, did there come a time when you entered into business discussions with Councilman Moore?'

'Yes.'

'And how did that come about?'

'One night, when Jimmy was in with his girlfriend and Chet . . .'

'Objection,' shouted Prescott from his seat.

I turned around again, quickly. In the row behind Jimmy sat his wife, Leslie. Her eyes were closed, her face tense, she was breathing deeply. Then she opened her eyes again and looked forward calmly. Chuckie had been right, Leslie Moore had known about Veronica all along.

'I ask that the answer be stricken,' said Prescott.

'I'll so order,' said the judge. 'Now, Mr Ruffing, try only to answer my question. How did you enter into business discussions with Councilman Moore?'

'He was at the club one night and he called me over and made room for me to sit down next to him. I was actually busy and I tried to beg off but he insisted, so I sat.'

'And what did he say, Mr Ruffing?' asked Eggert.

'He was angry. He told me he had heard I was setting up plans for the waterfront development and was seeking help in the council but that I didn't talk to him first. He told me he had been a good customer for a long time and that I had insulted him by not going through him to get approval for my plan. I told him I didn't mean to insult him and that, sure, I'd love his help. So he said if we worked together he could be the best friend I ever had and that I should call him and I did. That's when he told me he thought my plan would take off like a rocket ship and

I thought that was great, that got me all excited. It was a good plan, it would have been good for the city, and I thought that Councilman Moore saw that too. So he told me to set up a meeting with Chet Concannon and I did.'

'When was that meeting?'

'A few days later. Chet sat down with me on a bench at Penn's Landing and told how the legislative process worked with the council and how the councilman would propose the enabling legislation I needed for the development and shepherd it through a political obstacle course to get the legislation approved.'

'What did you say?'

'I told him I was excited about his help and was very optimistic. Then Chet started talking about CUP, that's the councilman's political action committee, and about all the good work it was doing, sponsoring drug treatment facilities, registering voters, organizing neighborhoods, general political stuff, you know. Now I'm no young kid from the suburbs, I knew what he wanted. So I told him, I said sure, how much do you want? That's when he flabbergasted me.'

'What did he say?'

'He said one percent of the cost for the entire project. The thing was budgeted at one hundred and forty mil, if we got both the hotels we wanted and the shopping strip. So what he was demanding was a million four.'

'Did you agree?'

'Not at first. I couldn't. How was I going to come up with a million four right off the books? I wasn't making enough on the club to cover it all and the financing was too tight to work with, really. The banks had it down to the penny. But Chet told me that I had to think of the future, how much could be realized if the waterfront plan went through. How much money I would make. And he said the councilman didn't expect it all at once, he'd take it over time, which would make it easier. I still didn't figure

I could make it. But then he told me that the councilman had a lot of power on the zoning committee and would be looking very carefully at the plans and he told me that unless the councilman was certain of my commitment to help all the neighborhoods of the city he would kill the plan and any bills introduced to get it done.'

'How did you take that?'

'As a threat, sure. He was telling me I pay a million four or the plan was dead. I had been in real estate a long time, I knew the shakedown when I saw it, but I had already invested over a million in the design and initial purchasing of lots and I had mortgage commitments with penalties that I had signed personally, options that were costing me a fortune to keep up. I couldn't afford to let it die.'

'So what did you do?'

'What could I do? I paid.'

'How much?'

'Chet said he would take a hundred grand to start, and then the same amount each month or so. And then he said the councilman would like a large part of it in cash so he could pay it out to the neighborhood organizers that were instrumental in running the programs.'

'How did you pay?'

'About once a month the councilman would call and give me an update on the project, how the bills were progressing through City Council. And then he would set up a meeting for me with Concannon. I would meet Concannon at various places around the city. We'd talk about the deal, sometimes we'd have lunch. Everything was very friendly, you know. And then I'd pay him.'

'What would you give him?'

'A check made out to CUP for fifty thousand and the rest of that payment in cash in a manila envelope. What I did was set up a credit account at a couple of the casinos in Atlantic City and take out enough chips in bits and pieces over an evening to make up the fifty thousand. Then I'd cash out, asking for hundreds. Concannon told us the councilman liked the cash to be in hundreds and cleaned through the casinos.'

'To pay the neighborhood activists?' asked Eggert with a wry smile.

'That's what Chet said.'

'And what happened in Council?'

'Oh, the councilman was true to his word. The project was moving through the system. It got stalled here and there, which you got to expect, it's the city after all. And I was already running short of cash because of the delays, but the councilman was doing his part. But then, along with my money problems, Zack found out about the payments.'

'You mean Mr Bissonette?' asked Eggert.

'Yeah, right. I had given him a small piece of the club in exchange for his name and every now and then he'd take a look at the books. When he saw these payments to the casinos and CUP he went crazy. He was a good guy, Zack, and I couldn't really blame him. Said he wouldn't be involved in anything that wasn't completely legal, said he wouldn't let profits from his club be used to bribe a councilman.'

'Objection,' said Prescott. 'We don't need to hear Mr Bissonette's interpretation of the legality of Mr Ruffing's campaign contributions to CUP. In any event, it's hearsay.'

'Sustained,' said the judge.

'Fine,' said Eggert. 'Did Mr Bissonette get involved in the waterfront deal?'

'Yes,' said Ruffing. 'When I told him I needed to keep paying Concannon because I couldn't afford any more delays he said he could raise all the bucks I needed as long as I stopped giving any payments to the councilman. I was running out of cash for development. It didn't help that I was dishing out about a hundred grand a month to Moore and Concannon. I needed a partner, so I said sure.'

'And he came up with the money.'

'Surprised the hell out of me, don't know how he did

it, but yes, he did. Enough to keep the options alive and the mortgage commitments going, which was what I needed. So I agreed to stop paying the money demanded by Moore and Concannon.'

'By that time, how much had you paid?'

'I had given CUP half a million dollars, exactly.'

'How did you stop making the payments?'

'I called up Moore and told him it was over.'

'What was his reaction?'

'He was apoplectic, what do you think? He told me he would send Chet over to talk with me.'

'Did you talk to Chet?'

'Sure, I told him I had no choice. I explained the thing with Bissonette. Chet told me if I stopped paying the deal was dead and that was just the start of it. He told me to think of the poor and the underprivileged, the drug addicted youth who had begun to rely on my payments. And then he told me if I stopped paying it wasn't only the deal that would be dead. He told me the club could have licensing problems and other problems. He told me the councilman could no longer guarantee my safety. When he left, I was shaking I was so scared.'

'What did you do?'

'I didn't have no choice. I had sunk everything I had into the development project and the only way it could go forward was with the money Bissonette brought in and Bissonette said no more payments to Moore. So I stopped paying. I thought maybe they was bluffing. Boy, was I ever wrong about that.'

'Objection,' said Prescott.

'Sustained,' said the judge. 'Just tell us what happened after you stopped the payments, Mr Ruffing.'

'One night, about two weeks after I stopped paying, in the club, we were closed then, it was after two and we were closed, I saw the councilman's limo pull up and it looked like Moore and Concannon getting out. Bissonette was still there. I told Bissonette that I was getting out of there, but he said he'd stay and talk to them. As they approached the back door I got out the front. My car was in the back but I didn't dare go back there. I took a cab home. Later that night I was called by the police and told that Bissonette had been beaten to near death and was in a coma. Just a few days ago he died, poor guy.'

'Anything else?'

'Yeah. A month later my club burned down. Arson.'

'And what happened to the waterfront development deal, Mr Ruffing?'

'It's gone, like the club. With Bissonette in the hospital and the plan delayed in Council I ran out of money. It would have been beautiful, but it all turned to crap. So I ended up with nothing, which is what I got right now, a lot of nothing. You know, when the councilman called me over, told me to sit with him, and said he could be the best friend I ever had, I was on top of the world. I had a hot club, I had a partner I admired and trusted in Zack Bissonette, you know how hard it is to find a partner you can trust? I had a waterfront deal in the works that was going to make me a name as big as Rouse, as big as Levitt. I had everything going for me. Nine months after getting the councilman on my side I'm broke, the club is gone, the development deal has disappeared, and Bissonette is dead. With friends like that, Jesus.'

29

The night before Ruffing's cross-examination I was in the offices of Talbott, Kittredge and Chase, sitting at the long marble conference table, drinking one of those free Cokes, enjoying the luxury of it all. But I wasn't there to work on the Concannon case. The Bishop brothers had insisted we spend that very evening going over the paperwork for their Valley Hunt Estates deal, so I was once again reviewing the documents that we would be putting into the prospectus, spreadsheets, pro forma projections, performance data on prior Bishop Brothers deals, a list of limited partners who had already committed to purchasing shares. I was sitting there alone at that conference table, drinking my Cokes, when a secretary opened the door and ushered Beth into the room.

She looked around. 'Fancy,' she said. 'Like a mausoleum.'

'Never been here before?' I asked when the secretary had left. 'Look at all this stuff. Pens with Talbott, Kittredge and Chase embossed in gold, all the yellow pads you could ever want. Why don't you take some back to the office in your briefcase? You want a soda?'

'No, thank you,' she said.

'It's free. Come on, have one. Diet Coke?'

'Doesn't this place give you the creeps, Victor?' she asked. 'How many trees had to die to panel these walls? How many deserving plaintiffs were screwed to pay for all this? I don't like it here.' She shivered. 'I feel like I'm in a wax museum after hours.'

'We should get ourselves a marble conference table,' I said. I pointed to the antique prints of Philadelphia landmarks, City Hall when it was still young and clean, Independence Hall, the Second Bank of the United States. 'And some artwork just like this. What do you say?'

She sighed. 'I have enough faith in you, Victor, that if you ever got any of this you'd hate it all too much to keep it. Rita told me you were here. I came over because I thought I could help you prepare for Ruffing tomorrow.'

'That's not what I'm working on. It's this Valley Hunt Estates prospectus.'

'What about Ruffing?' she asked.

'I have my instructions, and my instructions are to do nothing. How can I justify billing for preparing to do nothing?'

She sat down across from me and sighed again. I was beginning to fear her sighs. She looked around. 'Is this place bugged?'

I shrugged. 'Probably.'

'Well, screw it,' she said. 'Victor, if Prescott is going to point the finger of blame on Chester he's going to do it tomorrow.'

'He won't,' I said. 'He told me he was going to get Chet off.'

'Like his old boss Nixon said he wasn't a crook. You should be preparing just in case. Prescott's whole defense is based on the legality of asking for political money, right? If he tries to distinguish Concannon's meetings with Ruffing from the phone conversations between Ruffing and Moore, Chester could be in serious trouble. Prescott could claim that what Moore was doing was perfectly legal but that Concannon extended it to the illegal.'

'Concannon was Moore's top aide. No one would believe that.'

'Remember about the missing money? A quarter of a million that never ended up at CUP? Money like that can erode anyone's loyalty and don't think the jury won't believe it. If Prescott can pin the missing money on Concannon, then Chester is going to take the fall for his boss.'

I took a sip from my Coke. It was in a tall glass, filled with ice cubes I had lifted with pewter tongs from the ice bucket sitting on the marble credenza. 'There is no missing money,' I said. 'Ruffing's lying about the numbers to get a bigger tax deduction.'

'Who told you that?' asked Beth.

'Prescott.'

'So it must be true.'

'You know what I think,' I said, suddenly angry. 'I think you're jealous. I think you're worried that I might just make the big time here and leave you behind, that I might pull a Guthrie. And frankly, it pisses me off that you would think that of me.'

She stared at me for a long moment. I thought I might have seen something terribly sad in her face but then was sure I hadn't because she was too tough to let me see anything she didn't want me to see. 'What I think of you, Victor, is that you're drunk on this marble conference table and these fine prints of Old Philadelphia and these free Cokes. And that when you sober up, you're going to be very sorry for all that you did while under the influence.'

She stood and stared down at me. 'Morris wants you to call him,' she said coldly before she left, stranding me with the embossed pens and piles of yellow pads and antique prints. I took another sip of soda.

I turned back to the Valley Hunt Estates papers and read again the list of limited partners who had already agreed to buy into the deal. There was an entry that puzzled me, a partnership purchased by one set of initials for the benefit of another. I was still looking it over, trying to figure it all out, when Jack and Simon Bishop came into the room.

'How's it all looking, Victor?' asked Simon.

'Great,' I said. 'There's only one thing that troubles me.'

'I don't fancy the numbers in the five-year pro forma, either,' said Jack, holding in his hand the financial projection prepared for the prospectus. 'The numbers are too high.'

'It's not that,' I said. 'The numbers look fine.'

'They look smashing to me,' said Simon. 'We'll sell out within a week.'

'And be sued within a year if things don't work out,' said Jack.

'They'll work out, Jack,' said Simon. 'They always do. But let's deal with it later. Right now we're off to dinner. You coming, Victor?'

I looked at them, their round faces as open to me as an invitation, and whatever concerns I might have had disappeared in the warmth of their generosity. 'Sure,' I said. 'Dinner sounds great.' I followed them into the elevator for the ride to the parking garage and their Rolls-Royce Silver Shadow.

They took me to a fine French restaurant, a small place in a fancy suburb. It was a long drive but Simon told me it would be worth it and it was. The place was full, a mob of swells waiting at the bar, but the man at the door knew the Bishops and led us right to an empty table by a window. They were actually a jolly pair, these Bishops. I had first thought them to be very stiff and very formal, but that was just their surface manner. Underneath they were great fun, full of rollicking appetites and a taste for fine wines. Halfway into our second bottle I excused myself to make a call.

'Victor, is that you, Victor?'

'Yes, Morris. It's me.'

'You have a cold or something, Victor? You don't sound yourself.'

'I'm just a little tired, but I wanted to return your call.'

'You must take care of yourself, Victor. That's number one. What I do when I'm *oysgamitched* from all the work, I pick up a bottle of Manischewitz that's good and thick like a medicine, I lie in bed, turn on the news, drink the wine, fall asleep to Peter Jennings, and when I wake up I'm the old Morris. You should try it.'

'What about chicken soup?'

'Forget what they tell you. Chicken soup in bed it creates such a mess, all that splashing. News I have for you, Victor. Mine son, the computer genius, he has a phone right in his computer and he pulls out a register of marinas and starts looking for our man.'

'Any luck?'

'Calm your *shpilkehs* and let me tell you. So first he looks under the thief's name. Stocker. Plugs it in, the search takes an hour, more, the cost of the call is so high I don't want to say it over the phone.'

'We'll cover it.'

'Of course. I'm in this business to lose money to AT&T? So word finally comes back, no Stocker. So I think that our friend the accountant might not have sold his boat so fast so we looked up *The Debit*, and sure enough we get the listings of five boats called *The Debit*. Five accountants with the same idea, a conspiracy of accountants. So we check them all and, what do you know, there is only one thirty-foot sloop. I still couldn't tell you what a sloop is, but mine son, he says he knows, and *The Debit* anchored in a marina just south of St Augustine, Florida, is a thirty-foot sloop. Owned by a man named Cane. So I happen to know that cane in German is *stock*.'

'You happen to know?'

'I just happen to know, so I think maybe it's the same man. So I call the marina and they get hold of our Mr Cane.'

'And it's him?'

'Accht, let me finish.'

'Morris, you're a genius.'

'Victor, so you've finally caught on. Yes, with all modesty, I confess that I am. But no, Mr Cane was not Mr Stocker. He's Mr Cane, Nathan Cane, his father was a Cantowitz. He sells real estate and he sold a big house or something so he says he splurges and buys this boat, *The Debit*.'

'From who?'

'Funny, that's exactly what I asked. He says he bought it from a Mr Radbourn, a little *pisher*, he tells me. All the papers were in order. So I ask him who Radbourn got it from and he looks on the bill of sale and it turns out Mr Stocker sold it to Mr Radbourn, and if you ask me, from the description, Mr Stocker and Mr Radbourn are one in the same. He transferred it to himself to make it harder to find him.'

'So what we have now, Morris, is the boat but no Stocker.'

'Exactly right. You're very quick there, Victor.'

'So what do we do?'

'Well, of course, I figure our friend the thief he likes boats too much not to have one, and he has the money, so I figure he bought himself something else, and this time something bigger. *A chazer bliebt a chazer*, right? So we check the marina records again for a Mr Radbourn. *Gornisht*. We check the records for the sale of a boat larger than thirty feet at around the same place and time and you know what we found?'

'What?'

'Hundreds. Too many to check. To check them all would take us six months.'

'So we're done.'

'Not yet, Victor. We talk again to our friend Mr Cane, a nice man, really. He promised to set me up with a condo deal if I decide to move south for mine retirement. When it gets colder like it is now I start thinking that maybe *shvitzing* is not the worst thing in the world. So he seems to remember Mr Radbourn mentioning something about going across the state and buying something on the west coast of Florida, where he heard prices they might be cheaper.'

'So what does that tell us, Morris?'

'It narrows it down. Our friend Mr Stocker, I tell you with much confidence, our friend Mr Stocker is right now, right this instant, in a boat larger than a thirty-foot sloop,

273

living under some other name, docked in a marina some-where on the Gulf of Mexico.'

When I returned to the table, the Bishops were laughing loudly at something. The laughter died slowly when they saw me. 'Who died, Victor?' asked Simon. 'You look like the plague.'

'It's nothing,' I said. 'Everything's fine.'

My veal was on the table now, three delicate medallions in a light lemon sauce. I finished the wine in my glass and Jack quickly filled it again. For a moment I felt a slight sense of disappointment. I had almost believed that the strange and mystical Morris Kapustin could do anything he put his mind to, and his finding Stocker would have opened a different door for me, more difficult yes, confron-tational yes, but also less reliant on the *them* that had always disappointed me before. It had been a nice belief, Morris as savior, warming in its way, like a Jimmy Stewart movie, but Stocker was lost somewhere on the Gulf of Mexico and that door was closed and I was here at this prime table in this exclusive restaurant with two of the richest men in the city buying me dinner. The future was shaping up with great clarity. I would settle out *Saltz* and follow along sheepishly in *United States v. Moore and Con-cannon*. I would avoid all bullets aimed at rear windows of imported cars. I would placate the paranoid Norvel Good-win and the suspicious Chuckie Lamb with my inactivity. I would keep screwing Veronica in secret and write my opinion letters for Valley Hunt Estates and collect my fat fees and step into my future and all would be right with the world.

But still.

'What say we do the town tonight?' said Simon.

'Find us a high-class knocking shop,' said Jack.

'Just a pleasant night out with the boys,' said Simon.

'I noticed something curious in the partnership list,' I said. That got their attention fast. 'That's what was troub-ling me before. There were two partnership shares held in trust by W.P. on behalf of W.O. Any idea what that is all about?'

'An old friend of Prescott's,' said Simon. 'A prep school mate, being hounded by some cackhanded fool for a million dollars or so. Something to do with his divorce, I think. Seemed to be a sad story, actually, when Bill told it to me. It's always sad to see a sot being chased for his money. Prescott owed him something so he bought two shares to be held in trust, until the legal problems settle.'

So that's the way it was, I thought. William Prescott and Winston Osbourne, friends from the start, prep school mates, one helping the other hide his money from me. Well, now I knew where to find a little bit more for my twenty-five percent share. But all of a sudden I wasn't hungry for the last of Winston Osbourne's dollars. I was tied up with William Prescott in a very real way, which meant I was tied up with Winston Osbourne too. And I guess that was the price for joining the club, that we all help each other out, even the destitute. I could be munificent, sure, if that was what was required of me, I could be munificent as hell. Simon was right, it was so sad to see a sot being chased for his money. I had taken enough from him, I figured. Whatever he offered in final settlement after the car would be enough. Good. My first case as a lawyer would finally be over. It was time to move on.

'Well, what do you say, Victor?' asked Jack. 'Boys' night out? A few cigars, a few cheap thrills?'

'Or maybe not so cheap thrills,' said Simon.

'Sure,' I said with a shrug, shucking off all concern that Beth had raised about the Ruffing cross-examination, ignoring the worries about the connection between W.P. and W.O. that should have been hammering at my consciousness but were instead only tap, tap, tapping there, tapping so lightly they couldn't break through the spell of the alcohol and fine food and rich company. 'Why not,' I said. 'I've got nothing better to do.'

'More wine, Victor?'

'Yes, please.'

I drank the wine, a crisp Chablis, and ate the veal and laughed along with Simon's jokes. The waiter brought another bottle and my glass was filled again, the two Bishops so attentive to my goblet they might almost have been trying to get me drunk, and as the wine danced on the back of my tongue my spirits rose. This wasn't so bad, this veal, this wine, this ambience of money. I could get used to this.

30

Prescott was impressive on cross-examination. Even without saying a word he could be unnerving. He leaned slightly forward, his hands gripping tightly to the sides of the wooden podium, his eyes fixed like laser sights on the witness. As he stood there, tall, in a solid navy blue, pitched forward, his posture angry, the polite smile on his stern face tight and angry, as he stood before the court a tension grew and then out of that tension came questions, soft at first, full of incredulity or certainty, rising and falling in pitch and volume, questions that compelled answers.

'Now, Mr Bissonette was a ladies' man, wasn't he, Mr Ruffing?'

'Yes, that's right.'

'He went out with lots of different ladies, isn't that right?'

'That's right.'

'Older ladies and younger ladies and single ladies and married ladies.'

'He did all right, he was a ballplayer, after all.'

'And the married ladies had husbands?'

'By definition, right?'

'And the single ladies had fathers?'

'I would guess so.'

'And Mr Bissonette with all his lady friends was sure to have made some enemies, isn't that right?'

'I don't know about that.'

'Are you married, Mr Ruffing?'

'Yes.'

'Do you have daughters?'

'Two.'

'Would you have let your two precious daughters go out with Mr Bissonette?'

'Not on your life,' said Ruffing with a broad smile at the jury.

'No, I'm sure you wouldn't, Mr Ruffing. But plenty of men, without giving permission, had their precious daughters go out with Mr Bissonette, right?'

'Yeah, sure.'

'And Mr Bissonette used to talk about these girls, didn't he?'

'Occasionally.'

'He'd tell stories.'

'Sometimes.'

'He'd entertain his friends at the bar with his stories of all these ladies.'

'Now and then.'

'Stories about these ladies he took to bed, these wives and daughters he took to bed and fucked.'

The jury leaned back as if they had been slapped. The word was all the more shocking coming from the upright and austere personage that was William Prescott III.

Eggert said, 'Objection to the language and the relevance.'

The judge turned to Ruffing and said simply, 'Is that what Mr Bissonette would talk about?'

'Sometimes,' said Ruffing. 'Yes, sir.'

'Watch your language, Mr Prescott,' he said. 'You can continue.'

'Now, Mr Ruffing, did Mr Bissonette ever tell you the names of these women?'

'Sometimes.'

'And was one of them the daughter of Enrico Raffaello?'

'Objection,' shouted Eggert, jumping to his feet before Ruffing could answer, and the judge picked his head out of his papers and stared long and hard at Prescott and then said, 'The jury is excused for fifteen minutes, the bailiff will lead you out,' and everyone stayed still as the jury rose and filed out, Prescott gripping the podium, Eggert standing, his arm raised in protest, the judge staring at Prescott.

When the jury had left the courtroom the judge said in four sharp and precise syllables, 'In my chambers.'

I rose as steadily as I could and followed the other lawyers into the judge's book-lined office. I had drunk far too much wine the night before with the Bishops, graduating later in the evening to Sea Breezes. We had never gotten back to the marble-tabled conference room. Instead, Simon knew of this place on Admiral Wilson Boulevard in Jersey where the women dance on your table and sit on your lap, so long as you buy them twenty-four-dollar glasses of fake champagne cocktail, which we did. One of the women in this place had the longest legs I had ever seen, bacon and eggs Jack called them, legs she could wrap twice around the pole that bisected the stage, and the Bishops bought her three champagne cocktails just to keep her on my lap. Her name was Destiny, she wore golden spikes, her breasts were like porcelain, that white, that smooth, that immobile as she danced. I liked her smile. Destiny. With real red hair and golden spikes. It was a good thing that my orders were to let Prescott do the whole of the examination because that morning my brain was so fogged and my tongue so thick I doubted a single word would have been understood by the jury.

'Mr Prescott,' said the judge, with more than the usual tinge of anger in his voice. He was sitting behind his desk in his chambers while the rest of us stood around him in a semi-circle. The court reporter had brought his machine from the courtroom and was sitting serenely next to the desk. 'What kind of question was that?'

'A probative one, Your Honor,' said Prescott.

'I won't let you bring up all the names of the women Bissonette might have been with. I gave you more than enough latitude with your questions about his stories as it was.'

'Your Honor, we believe Mr Bissonette was murdered by Mr Raffaello because he was having sex with his daughter.'

'That's ridiculous,' said Eggert. 'I demand an offer of proof.'

'I don't think,' said the judge sourly in his brutish rasp of a voice, 'that you should ever demand anything in my chambers, Mr Eggert. However, I appreciate your concern. Do you have any proof, Mr Prescott, to back up this charge?'

'I can prove Bissonette was sleeping with Raffaello's daughter, and we all know that he's a killer.'

'Is that so?' asked the judge. 'Are you going to prove that Mr Raffaello is a killer in this trial?'

'Every one of those jury members knows who he is. Just let me ask the question, Judge.'

'Not if you can't prove he's a killer. Now, Mr Eggert, is this Mr Raffaello under investigation by your office?'

'Under federal law, Your Honor, I can't confirm or deny that.'

'I hereby make a formal request for all the evidence you have against Enrico Raffaello,' said Prescott.

'On what grounds?' asked a surprised Eggert.

'Based on what we know, anything you may have is *Brady*,' said Prescott.

'We don't have anything exculpatory and you know it. We've found absolutely nothing linking Raffaello to Bissonette's murder, nothing at all.'

'Mr Eggert,' said the judge. 'Do you have enough evidence to indict Mr Raffaello?'

'No, sir. If we did, we would have already.'

'I'm going to formally deny your *Brady* request, Mr Prescott, and I am going to forbid you, under threat of contempt, to ask any more questions about Mr Raffaello's daughter or anyone else whom Mr Bissonette might have slept with. Do you understand, sir?'

'Yes, Your Honor,' said Prescott.

'I'm not going to allow gossip and inadmissible innuendo

to act as a defense in any trial in my court, this is the federal courthouse, not the offices of the *National Enquirer*, do you understand, Mr Prescott?'

'Yes, Your Honor.'

'Do you understand, Mr Carl?'

'Yes, sir,' I mumbled.

'All right, then let's go out there and try this case as if the rules of evidence were still in existence.'

'What do we do now?' I asked Prescott in the courtroom as we waited for the jury to return.

'We scramble,' he said.

And scramble he did. He asked Ruffing about the waterfront deal and why exactly it had collapsed. He asked about the phone conversations with Moore and the meetings with Concannon, the exact locations, the exact words spoken. He asked about the discrepancy between the amount Ruffing claimed to have given to Concannon and the amount actually received by CUP and whether Bissonette had deducted the full amount claimed on his tax returns, and Ruffing said he had. It took Prescott almost all of that day to ask his questions. He asked about the lighting in the back parking lot the night of Bissonette's beating and how far away the limousine had been when he saw the men stepping out of the car and he got Ruffing to say he wasn't totally sure who the men were but that it looked like the councilman and someone else, a black man, and to say that though he recognized the limousine as the councilman's he couldn't exactly say how that limousine was different from any other long black limousine with a boomerang on the back. And he asked about the back taxes that Ruffing had owed and the deal Ruffing struck with the IRS and how part of the insurance money on the burned down club went to the IRS to keep up Ruffing's part of the deal. In all it was a solid cross-examination by Prescott, indeed he had asked almost all of the questions I would have asked had I spent the night preparing instead of drinking. But in the end, with all his bluster, all his questions, all his intimidation and insinuation, he did nothing to make Ruffing seem like a liar in front of the jury.

The swelling in my head had subsided and what was left was a deep exhaustion as Prescott asked questions about areas traversed twice or thrice already and Ruffing answered them with the very same answers he had produced before. The rhythm was repetitive, drowsing, hypnotic. I could barely keep my eyes open as Prescott asked his last series of questions.

'All of your conversations with Councilman Moore were on the tapes, isn't that right, Mr Ruffing?'

'Most of them. Some were made on untapped phones.'

'Were the unrecorded conversations any different than the taped ones?'

'No, substantially the same.'

'Now I noticed something peculiar on the tapes of your conversations with Mr Moore. What I noticed, Mr Ruffing, is that nowhere in those conversations did Councilman Moore mention a specific amount of money.'

'I thought he had.'

'There was no mention of it in the tapes.'

'He mentioned contributions.'

'But never amounts and never how it was to be paid.'

'He might have mentioned it in the unrecorded conversations.'

'But you said those were substantially the same just a second ago, isn't that right?'

'Yes, I did.'

'So we can assume if he didn't mention specific amounts in the taped conversations, he never mentioned them at all.'

'I guess so.'

'In fact, it was only Chester Concannon who gave the specifics about money.'

'That might be right.'

'And those conversations weren't taped.'

282

'No.'

'Now those checks you gave Concannon, did they come back from the bank?'

'Sure, cashed out by CUP.'

'But you didn't get anything back from CUP for the cash? No receipts?'

'No, nothing.'

'So CUP only acknowledged payments of the two hundred and fifty thousand dollars that was duly reported on its books.'

'I don't know about their books.'

'And the councilman never mentioned that he got the cash?'

'No. He didn't want to talk specifics about that.'

'It was Chester Concannon who talked the specifics.'

'That's right.'

'It was Chester Concannon who told you how much to pay, how to pay it, that some should be paid in cash.'

'That's what I said.'

'And it was Chester Concannon who threatened you after you stopped paying.'

'Yes, that's what happened.'

'And as far as you know, that cash might never have reached CUP.'

'As far as I know.'

'And it might never have reached Councilman Moore.'

'As far as I know.'

'It might have gone no further than Chester Concannon.'

'That's possible.'

'I have no further questions,' said Prescott.

Judge Gimbel lifted up his heavy prune face and, peering hard at me over his half reading glasses, said, 'Do you have any questions for this witness, Mr Carl?'

Still sitting, I looked around the courtroom. Prescott was back at the table, conferring quietly with the councilman, ignoring me. Eggert was looking at a yellow pad, taking notes. Concannon's eyes were closed, like he had been put to sleep by the questioning himself. I shook my head to wake myself and stood up slowly. I found it difficult to phrase the words, my mouth dry, my tongue thicker than before, my stomach turning over. Finally, after trying to squeeze them through my lips, the words fell out in a tumble. 'I'd like a few moments with my client.'

Judge Gimbel smiled condescendingly at me. 'Good idea, Mr Carl. Court is recessed for twenty minutes.'

31

What had stunned me by the last series of Prescott's questions to Ruffing was not just that he had turned on Concannon, shifting blame to him, but that he had done it so blatantly. I would have expected him to do his damage subtly, a question here, a remark there, I would have expected Prescott to slip the knife into Concannon surreptitiously, silently, the razor-thin blade sliding through the vertebrae so cleanly that Concannon himself wouldn't have known he was dead until his knees collapsed beneath him, and even then not be sure. But Prescott had discarded all subtlety. He had looked at the jury, smiled, and said it wasn't my guy, it was his guy, and all of a sudden the strategy imposed upon me of trying to make my client seem not a part of the proceedings was revealed to be a sick joke.

My first reaction was to sit down at that counsel table and put my head in my hands and try to keep from crying. It is undignified for a lawyer to cry at a trial, unless it is in front of a jury and then only for effect. But the jury was out of the room, the spectators were milling, my client had left for the men's room, in that situation crying was not a trenchant strategy. Even so, I couldn't stop my eyes from watering. I heard Prescott laugh to my left, not a loud laugh, but loud enough.

I felt a hand on my arm and I turned around as quickly as my hangover would allow.

It was Herm Finklebaum. He was back on his heels, smiling thinly at me. 'You feeling all right, buddy boy?' he asked.

'Not so good just now,' I said.

'I been watching you, like I said I would, but I ain't seen much.'

'By design,' I said.

'By whose design? Eggert's?'

'It's a very complex strategy, Herm. You wouldn't understand.'

'A toy company came out once with a doll that pooped in its diapers,' said Herm Finklebaum, the toy king of 44th Street. 'I asked the sales rep, "What's the fun in that? I've changed diapers. Changing diapers is not fun." The rep told me I didn't understand but that the doll was hot hot hot, that it was going to sell like flapjacks. I bought fifty for the Christmas season, sold three. He was right, I didn't understand, didn't understand that I was being a *schmuck* for buying fifty.'

'What's your point, Herm?'

'Point? There's no point,' he said, turning away from me and starting to walk away in his jaunty, splayfooted walk. 'It's just a story I like to tell on myself.'

As I watched Herm walk to the rear of the courtroom I saw Beth sitting in the back row, staring at me, not triumphantly or angrily, just staring. She stood and gestured me to meet her in the hallway. I nodded and turned around again.

I didn't have much time to figure out what I was going to do. Judge Gimbel would be asking me if I had any questions for Ruffing at the end of the twenty-minute break and then and there I would have to know for sure. But I really needed to figure it out for myself before then, before I faced my client, before I faced Beth.

After the shock of Prescott's questions had worn off, I realized I shouldn't have been surprised at all. Of course Jimmy would betray Chester, he was a politician, after all, and the only difference between a politician and a viper is that a viper's fangs retract. And how could I ever have assumed that Prescott's offer of opportunity meant anything other than opportunity at a price? But the price was so damned high. To shuck all the principles of my profession with the ease of shucking an ear of corn and let my client suffer an unrebutted attack that would leave him imprisoned for the rest of his life was almost unthinkable. But then again there was money to be made, bonds to be forged, opportunity to be seized. Valley Hunt Estates was just the first of a myriad of projects that would be offered me as I rose to the upper echelons of my profession. Prescott would make it all happen for me, he had as much as promised it. They say behind every great fortune is a great crime and I had always been waiting to find mine to commit. Now here it was, and all I would have to commit was nothing. And even if I tried to do something, what could I do, stand on the table and holler that the mobster Raffaello had killed Bissonette? That would get me nothing more than a contempt citation. And what about the threats from Norvel Goodwin and Chuckie Lamb? And what about the exploding hatchback window and the message of the lead? And what about . . .

But even as I debated it all in my mind, I knew what the answer would be, never truly doubted it for a minute. And right in the middle of deliberations I shut off my thoughts like I shut off a faucet, stood, and left the courtroom.

Chuckie Lamb was waiting for me in the hallway. He grabbed my arm and pulled me aside and his fish-lipped grin was unpleasantly dark. 'You going to ask Ruffing any questions, Vic?' asked Chuckie.

'I don't have time for this,' I said. 'I need to talk to my client.'

'You going to ask any questions, Vic, or are you going to be their good little boy?'

I leaned into him and stuck a finger in his chest, like my Uncle Sammy would have. 'Look, Chuckie. As far as I'm concerned you don't exist, your threats, your opinion of me, it's like you're on Mars. I'm going to do what I have to do.'

I turned around and walked away from him, on my way to meet Chester and Beth, but his voice chased me down the hallway. 'We all do what we have to do, Vic.'

The room we found had pale green walls and a formica table with steel legs. Metal chairs were jumbled there and here. Beth gestured toward a chair and Concannon sat. She stood over him. I sat at the table across from him. Even though there were only the three of us, with a trail of ashes fallen out of the tinfoil ashtray and sprinkled over the table, with the too many chairs, with the stale air in the room, it felt crowded.

'There's nothing to worry about,' Chet said. I looked at him carefully, wondering whether he truly didn't know there was a six-inch blade buried knuckle-guard-deep in his back.

'Are you really this stupid, Chester?' said Beth. 'Or is this all an act?'

Chet didn't get angry or start to shout. He clasped his hands together on the table and stared at them for a moment. 'The councilman told me about this line of questioning last night,' he said finally. 'If Prescott couldn't get into evidence that Raffaello's daughter was sleeping with Bissonette, then the councilman told me Prescott was going to do whatever he could to make it seem like the whole thing might not have happened the way Ruffing said it happened.'

'Well, did your friend Jimmy also tell you,' said Beth, 'that if Prescott convinces the jury that you were taking money on the side and were the one making the threats, he could walk out of here smelling like a violet while you got the jail time?'

'He told me he was taking care of me,' said Chet.

'Sure he is, Chester,' she said. 'He's going to take care of you all the way to a twenty-year racketeering sentence.'

Chet stared at her without saying anything. I turned

around to look out a window, but there were none in the room. For a moment I felt I was in a coffin.

Beth said, 'With your prior convictions, Chester, Victor and I had no intention of putting you on the stand, so we didn't want you to tell us what happened. But now we need you to. How much would Ruffing give you in that envelope?'

He shrugged, but he answered her. 'A hundred thousand each time, like he said, a check for fifty and fifty in cash.'

I turned away from the wall and stared at him. 'And you let Prescott lie to me about the money?' I asked.

'You said you were asking the same question the jury would ask,' said Chet. 'Prescott told you exactly what we were going to argue to the jury, that's all.'

'Why not the truth?' I asked.

'Because the truth looks bad,' said Chet. He shrugged, like a boy caught at a prank, and I turned away from him again.

'Who told you to get it in cash?' asked Beth, continuing her interrogation.

'Jimmy.'

'And what did you do with it once you got it?' she asked.

'I gave it to him.'

'All of it?'

'Yes, all of it. He sometimes gave some back to me. He liked me to have cash for his expenses. And sometimes he gave me cash for Ronnie.'

'You never took any out for yourself?'

'Never.'

'Come on, Chester,' she said. 'Never even a little?'

'I didn't keep my job for five years by stealing from the councilman.'

'Were you there the night of the murder?'

'No.'

'Who did it?' she asked.

'Raffaello.'

'Who told you it was Raffaello?'

'The councilman.'

'And you believe him?'

'Absolutely.'

'Chester, listen to me,' she said slowly. 'Jimmy Moore is selling you out.'

There was a pause then. Chet sat straight-backed in his chair, his hands clasped before him, clasped tightly, his fingers twisting around each other like knotted ropes, and Chet was staring at those clasped hands, saying nothing. I tapped my fingers on the formica tabletop, fatatatap, fatatatap, fatatatap.

'Chester,' she said finally. 'We have to fight back. If we act now we can still mount a defense. We have to point the finger at Jimmy and let the jury choose between you and him. My guess, everything being even, they'll go after him.'

There was another pause, and then Chet looked my way. 'What do you think, Victor?' he asked. 'What do you think I should do?'

Here it was. Beth was staring at me, a sad uncertainty in her gaze. Chester was looking at me and I could see that boy again, the lonely one inside of him that all his careful manners had been hiding for so long, and the little boy was scared. I had to be careful here, I knew. I had to phrase it just right.

'It appears, on the surface,' I said, looking only at Concannon as I spoke, 'that the councilman's lawyer may be planning to make you a scapegoat. But it's also possible that Prescott is simply trying to cast any doubt he can on Ruffing's story to show the weakness of the prosecutor's case. If so, he would argue in front of the jury that Eggert hadn't proven whether Jimmy was at fault or you were at fault and therefore reasonable doubt existed. That's exactly what defense attorneys are supposed to do, raise reasonable doubt. And, frankly, it might not be a terrible strategy. So what we should do, Chet, really depends on whether or not you trust the councilman.'

I kept looking at Concannon, only at Concannon, even after I finished speaking. I was almost disappointed to see the relief spread across his features.

'That makes it easy, then,' said Chet. 'I'm going to trust Jimmy. He's the closest thing I've ever known to a savior. If he says he's going to get us both off, I'm going to trust him to do it.'

Beth banged the table with her hand. 'You're his sacrificial lamb, Chester,' she said. 'He's feeding you to the government to save himself. And it doesn't stop here. After this trial there's the trial in state court. You remember that, don't you? The murder trial where ADA Slocum is going to ask for the death penalty?'

'I didn't kill that man,' said Chet. 'And Jimmy didn't either.'

'It doesn't matter who did what,' she said. 'If you go down here, you're going to go down there too, do you understand? Don't throw your life away.'

When his answer came it was slow, precise, but the anger in it was clear and hard. 'I was wasting away to nothing when the councilman took me from the street and gave me something to be. You don't know what it's like, feeling the frustration of wanting something so bad and knowing there is no way in hell you're going to get it. And then along comes Jimmy Moore like an angel of God and he gives it all to me. We get one shot, that's the rule for us, one shot if we're lucky, and the councilman's my shot. Victor says it's all about whether or not I trust him, well, I do. More than anything else in this world. And I will continue to trust him until you can prove to me, I mean prove it in black and white so there is no doubt, until you can prove to me that his strategy is to dump me to save himself.'

'We can't get proof like that,' said Beth.

'Then I want Victor to keep following Prescott's orders. Prescott doesn't want Victor to ask any questions of Michael Ruffing.'

291

'Is that right?' I asked.

'That's what he wants. The councilman's a loyal man, all he demands is loyalty in return. I've seen it over and over, people doubting him and him coming through for them. Get me the proof or do what Prescott tells you.'

I slapped the table lightly. 'Well, I guess that's that,' I said. 'The decision's made.'

'Why don't you give us a minute alone, Chester,' said Beth.

After he left we stayed there in silence for a while, Beth and I. I couldn't bring myself to look at her, afraid of what I would see in her eyes. I thought she'd start out by screaming at me, but she didn't. Her voice when it came was soft and even, but I could still feel the emotion in it.

'You should get the hell out of this case,' she said. 'Cause a mistrial, leave Prescott holding a leaking paper bag with his spoiled strategy inside.'

'The judge won't let me go,' I said.

'Then you should get Chester back in here and convince him that he's getting screwed.'

'He's the client,' I said. 'He made his decision.'

'You could convince him,' she said. 'What you told him was absolute bullshit and you know it. He listens to you, God knows why, but he does. You could change his mind, give him a fighting chance.'

'And then do what? What evidence do I have? What can I ask Ruffing that will change anything? It would be different if I had something concrete to use.'

'Would it?'

I didn't say anything.

'So what are you going to do now, Victor?'

'Just what my client wants me to do,' I said. 'Nothing.'

'I can't accept that,' she said.

'It's not your case.'

'It's my name on the letterhead.'

'Yes, but it was the retainer I got in this case that finally paid the stationery bill. The decision has been made,' I

292

said. 'Whatever happens, it's my responsibility.'

She gave me that damn sigh again and I shuddered as if I had been hit about my shoulders with a stick. 'They've been trying for years to get me to work down at Community Legal Services,' she said. 'Perillo called me again about CLS just last week. He has an opening for me. The pay's steady, and there's plenty of work.'

'Beth,' I said, but that's all I could say, because when I finally looked up at her she was facing away from me and in the hunch of her shoulders was a sadness I had never seen in her before, a sadness that shocked me into silence.

'I think I'm going to accept his offer,' she said, and I knew then why she was turned away from me; Beth would sooner have me see her naked than have me see her cry. 'Don't you know, Victor, haven't you learned yet that the one thing we're never allowed to do in this life is nothing?'

'Beth,' I said again, and again that was all I could say, because before I could say anything else she was out the door.

This is what I realized just then. I realized that the difference between those who got what they wanted and those who didn't was not merely talent or brains or grace under pressure, the difference was that those who got what they wanted simply wanted it more than those who didn't. Well, dammit, I knew what I wanted and I knew just how bad I wanted it, too. I was sick of our outdated law books, of our scruffy copier, of the dunning letters and collection calls and my same three suits and my frayed collars and the worry over small change that had kept me tossing on the sofa as the late show droned. I was sick of our second-class practice, sick of my second-class life. I wanted my share of the wealth and glory in this world, I wanted money, and if my wants were shallow then sue me, dammit, for I was third generation now, American to the core, and what I wanted was only what this country had taught me to want. And it taught me how to get it, too. As Beth walked out of that room I learned that she simply didn't want it all as much as I did. Too bad for her. Maybe she belonged at Community Legal Services, working in a cubicle, handling landlord-tenant disputes for families on welfare, but not me, no sir.

When Judge Gimbel came back on the bench and brought the jury into the courtroom and asked me, 'Now, Mr Carl, do you have any questions for this witness?' he might just as well have been asking whether I had any doubts about how badly I wanted the success that Prescott was promising, because the answer would have been exactly the same.

'No, Your Honor,' I said without hesitation. 'None at all.'

When I sat down again Prescott was smiling at me. It was a warm smile, and what I interpreted that smile to mean was, 'Welcome to the club.' I smiled too.

Now, when I think back on that smile of mine, full as it was with hope and anticipation and deference to my patron, I think of the chuckle it must have given to that bastard and I can't help but wince.

32

I was in my office alone, late, checking through my mail and making calls, when Morris phoned with the bad news. I had spent another awful day in court, the only kind I seemed to allow myself, another day where I sat silently beside my client and let the evidence spill over him like ocean waves unchecked by any reef. And afterwards I had come back to the office to find it deserted again. I had not seen Beth since the afternoon of Ruffing's cross-examination. She was conveniently absent when I was around but I noticed that the personal effects in her office, the photograph of her father, the photograph of her sisters, the little outhouse whose doors opened up with the touch of a button that she got such a kick out of, one by one the personal effects were disappearing. She was leaving, no doubt, she had meant what she had said, Beth always meant what she said. And so we would no longer be Guthrie, Derringer and Carl or Derringer and Carl but just plain and Carl, and each night thereafter would be like that night, where I was left alone with nothing but the emptiness of the office and a pathetic stack of mail. On the high road to success.

My mail that day was much like my mail every day, letters confirming conversations on the telephone that in no way matched the descriptions in the letters, advertisements for legal journals and continuing legal education courses, an accounting firm's brochure listing all the exciting ways it could make my practice more successful, when in fact the success it was seeking was its own. And then, in an ominous manila envelope, on crisp paper backed with a blue piece of cardboard, I found an answer. No, it wasn't an answer to life's more perplexing questions, like why we exist or how to drink beer and laugh at the same time without getting suds up your nose. What it was, actually, was an answer to the motion for a protective order I had filed on Veronica's behalf against one Spiros Giamoticos, Veronica's landlord, who had been leaving dead animals in front of her doorway in an effort to chase her out of her bargain lease.

Giamoticos was being represented by Tony Baloney, which was a surprise since Anthony Bolognese, Esq., dubbed Tony Baloney by the admiring press, was one of the more successful and expensive drug lawyers in the city, an interesting choice of counsel for a deranged landlord. You wouldn't see Tony at the Philadelphia Bar Association dances or lunching at the Union League, even though he outearned most of the big-time corporate types. There is a certain pungency to drug lawyers, to mob lawyers, to those attorneys who represent society's outlaws, a smell that makes such lawyers unwelcome in the more hallowed hallways of the bar. Where you saw Tony Baloney was on the evening news, his cheeks jiggling beneath his wide walrus mustache as he explained in overwrought language the details of still another acquittal for one of his clients.

The answer Tony had filed stated very simply that Spiros Giamoticos had not done any of the things Veronica had claimed he had done, which was not a surprise because Tony's clients always pleaded not guilty, even when the cocaine was found inside their intestinal tracts, wrapped in greased prophylactics swallowed before boarding the plane from Bogotá.

'Yes, Victor,' said Tony Baloney into the phone, after I had waited on hold for a solid five minutes. 'Not surprised you are calling. This nasty Giamoticos matter, I assume.' His voice was high, exuberant, punctuated by the deep breaths of the asthmatic. 'My daughter resides in that very building. Giamoticos brings your motion to her. Like a devoted father I agree to take the case. I expect you'll do your best to make me regret it.'

'Is he going to stop the animal killing crap?'

'It's not him, Victor. He says he didn't do it.'

'You sound like you've said that before.'

He laughed. 'Yes, well,' he said. 'Maybe I have. That's the speech for the lummoxes in the DA's office all right. But sometimes it happens to be true.'

'He killed her cat,' I said. 'I know. I was forced to clean it up. The tenant I represent has a bargain-basement lease and he wants her out so he killed her cat.'

'"Courage, man. What though care killed a cat, thou hast mettle enough in thee to kill care."'

'You speaking Spanish?'

'Not a devotee of the Bard, hey, Victor? Too bad. There's more to learn of law from Shakespeare than from all the digests put together. So tell me what it is your client wants.'

'What she wants, Tony, is to be left alone.'

'Well then, darling, how about a deal?' he asked. 'You withdraw this scabrous motion. My guy will swear to be a perfect gentleman. Follow the letter of the law. Stay forty paces from your client.'

'Like he's on probation?'

'Just like.'

'No skulking around hallways, no more dead birds from him?'

'I'll vouch for him. He didn't do it. He wants no trouble. The whole legal thing scares the *ouzo* out of him. It seems the law is different in Greece. I keep telling him there are no firing squads in America.' I could hear him pound his desk as he shouted, 'There are no firing squads in America!'

'Deal,' I said.

'Good, Victor. Good. Now this Veronica Ashland. She's Jimmy Moore's friend, isn't she?'

'I have nothing else to say.'

'Discretion is good, Victor. I like that. I need to be discreet too. But even so, Jimmy and I used to be buddies. A drink or two together now and then. But after what happened to Nadine he wrote me off. The wrong side, or some nonsense like that. She was a good kid too, Nadine. Her biggest problem was her father. Jimmy thinks he's a new man, that what's past is prologue. "But love is blind, and lovers cannot see." *Merchant of Venice*, Victor.'

'I don't understand,' I said, and I didn't. All I could catch was that he was trying to threaten Jimmy through me and I didn't like it. I had received enough threats in this case to last me a lifetime.

'I can't say anything more at the moment. Discretion, right? Just tell him what I said. And if he wants to call me, he can.'

'Sure,' I said, but I didn't feel very messenger-boyish just then, especially not for fat Tony Baloney. I figured I would let him threaten the councilman on his own.

So it was back to the mail, reviewing letters, dictating missives of my own into the little tape machine for Ellie to butcher on the typewriter the next day, marking it all down on my time sheets in six-minute increments to be billed. That's what I was doing when Morris called.

'*Vey is mir*, Victor. It pains me to have to call you this evening, I hope you appreciate that. During the short time we have worked together, Victor, and I mean this with all sincerity, you have become like *mishpocheh* to me. I wouldn't say like a son because, frankly, we haven't become that close, but a nephew, maybe, a distant nephew, a nephew from a foreign country, a Czechoslovakian nephew, yes? And so, being that you have become as dear to me as a Czechoslovakian nephew, it pains me to tell you what I have to tell you.'

'What is it you have to tell me, Morris?'

'First I want you to know that we left, mine son and I, not a single stone but that we turned it and not a single path but that we followed it to nowhere.'

'Just tell me, Morris.'

'Your Mr Stocker, your thief, I know he is somewhere

298

on the Gulf of Mexico, I know it, I can taste it, he is so *trayf* you wouldn't believe, but still I can taste him on his boat, floating happily, bobbing up and down, as happy as a Cossack on a sea of vodka, that happy, Victor. He is there, I know it, but where I can't tell you. If I could tell you where he was then I'd be a happy man, but such is life that we are not to know such happiness until we find *ha'olum haba'ah*. Do you know what such is that, Victor? *Ha'olum haba'ah*?'

'No.'

'How will you get there if you don't know what it is?'

'What is it?'

'The world to come.'

'Heaven?'

'Of a sort, but better. No angels with wings, no annoying harp music, and the food, Victor, all the food is kosher.'

'I assume they have pastrami there.'

'What, you think you go all that way for egg salad?'

'So what you are telling me, Morris, is that you can't find Stocker.'

'I'm calling tonight because you gave me three weeks and tomorrow is exactly three weeks to a day from when you hired me and so mine time is up. I would spend the extra day and call you tomorrow but it's Friday and preparing for the Shabbos I wanted not to forget.'

'Don't worry about it, Morris, you got farther than I ever expected, you even got farther than the FBI in finding the guy.'

'So that's such a challenge? Being as mine investigation has come to a close, I will be sending along a *tzatel* with my charges, sending it tomorrow, in fact. Now, just as a point of curiosity, to who should I send mine *tzatel*, to you or to mine friend Benny Lefkowitz who told me to see you?'

'You should send it to Mr Lefkowitz, Morris. He'll ship it over to me, but he and the other clients are paying it.'

'Perfect, I just thought I should know. So, Victor, that

is that. Do you have anything else you need investigating? Anything you want Morris Kapustin to look into?'

'Nothing right now, Morris.'

'You keep me in mind, Victor, and I would be very appreciative. I feel very bad about this, Victor. Anything you need, any help at all, you give Morris a call.'

'Sure.'

'*A gezunt ahf dein kopf, mein freint.* And don't be a *shmendrick*, call me sometime. We'll do lunch.'

'We'll do lunch?'

'A guy like me, I could have been in Hollywood, why not? John Garfield, Jewish. Goldwyn and Mayer and Fox, all Jewish. So why not Morris Kapustin?'

'No reason, Morris. No reason at all.'

I wasn't feeling the same pain as Morris over his news. What it meant was that the deadline for finding Stocker had passed without a positive result and I could now settle the *Saltz* case for the $120,000 offered by Prescott, from which I would immediately deduct my one-third share, forty thousand dollars, forty thousand sweet smelling, crisply crinkling, beautifully off-green, satisfyingly stiff new dollar bills. I could feel the rough texture between my fingers already. In anticipation of Morris's failure I had sent out release forms to the clients with self-addressed, stamped return envelopes. One by one the envelopes had come back and I opened them gleefully, like a child receiving birthday cards. Eight releases, each of them duly executed and ready for turning over to Prescott in exchange for a sweet little check made out for one hundred and twenty thou. With Morris throwing in the *tallis*, I was ready to settle.

And the man with whom I had to settle was ready for me.

'Good morning, Victor,' said Prescott as he strolled into court the morning after Morris's final call. As always, he was followed by his legion of natty and intense Talbott,

300

Kittredge lawyers. 'This morning I'll carry the cross-examination of the crime scene search officer. I've gone over the reports with my own experts and I think I'm best qualified to minimize his effectiveness.'

'That's fine, sir,' I said.

'Splendid,' he said as he looked through a sheaf of documents handed him by Brett with two t's.

'By the way, sir,' I said. 'I have those releases for the *Saltz* settlement. I'm sorry it was so late but I had a hard time getting them back from all my clients, vacations and such.'

'The *Saltz* settlement?'

'Madeline sent us over the final settlement agreement and we've signed that too.'

'Did my clients sign?' he said, still looking through his documents.

'Not yet.'

'Hmmm. Well, Victor, I'm sorry, but I don't believe that deal is still operative.'

A sickening fear rose from my groin and grabbed my throat. 'What are you talking about?' I said. 'We had a deal.'

'We reached an agreement, yes, but that was with the expectation of an immediate settlement. When you hadn't gotten back to us we thought the deal was off and proceeded accordingly.'

'Accordingly?'

He lifted his head out of his papers and stared straight at me. 'We've been preparing for trial, Victor. Haven't you?'

'I'll enforce the settlement,' I said. 'Judge Tifaro likes his calendar clean, he won't let you yank the offer back.'

'Oh, he'll holler and shake,' he said, his gaze again upon his papers, as if I were no more consequential than a buzzing fly. 'But it's been over three weeks, Victor. You can't expect my clients to wait forever. That offer has expired, it is gone, disappeared. It is as dead as Bissonette.' Then he looked at me again and one of his sly, diplomatic smiles

301

spread onto his face. 'However, Victor, I'm sure my clients would be willing to rethink the settlement and to pay what had been previously agreed under certain conditions.'

Here it was, I thought. Whatever the conditions, Prescott had been waiting to lower them upon me for a while, waiting as patiently as a spider having already woven his web.

'It seems,' said Prescott, putting his arm around my shoulder and leaning in close so that he could speak in his lowest voice above a whisper, 'that my clients happen to be very interested in this case. They have made certain deals with Councilman Moore concerning certain of their real estate ventures and it would be very inconvenient for them if Councilman Moore was convicted here and stripped of his council post.'

'I'm not quite sure I understand.'

'Don't be a cowboy, Victor. What they want is for you to keep staying out of my way. You do and, win or lose, you'll get your settlement.'

'But I've been cooperative,' I stammered.

'Yes, you have, Victor. We've all been extremely pleased with you. And if you remain cooperative we won't have any problems, will we?'

'This sounds something like blackmail,' I said.

'Don't,' said Prescott quickly, his voice dipping to a ferocious whisper, his hand now squeezing my shoulder harder, so hard it hurt. 'Don't even think of using such language with me. For the rest of this trial you're just going to sit back and let me do whatever I have to do. I want you out of it. The *Saltz* offer was generous beyond belief, we both know it, you sit back and it is yours. But you act up in any way and it is dead and you'll get your balls handed to you at the trial. I want you silent and docile for the rest of this trial, that's what we're paying you for. You step out of line and I'll absolutely destroy you.'

With his grip still tight around my shoulder he pushed me down and I fell hard into my seat. I looked at the empty

302

jury box, the dark maroon chairs swimming in the tears that had sprung to my eyes. In a pleasant voice Prescott said, 'I think we understand each other now, Victor.'

I didn't answer, but I didn't have to. We understood each other perfectly. Prescott believed he could read me like a comic book. He believed he could buy me for a mere forty thousand dollars, our cut of the *Saltz* settlement. He believed that for a minor monetary gain, and the hope of future deals, I would sit back and take a dive in the biggest trial of my life. He believed he understood all that burned inside me, all the hidden dreams and pent desires, and from that knowledge he thought he knew my price.

And so what if he might have been right, dammit, I didn't have to like it. I thought I was becoming a member of the caste by going along, but Prescott had just dressed me down like I was a cabana boy. I had a half a mind to spit it all back in his face, but only half a mind. After all, what could I do, realistically? Disregard my client's orders, defy the judge, try to slip in more references to Enrico Raffaello and his daughter's sad and deadly affair with Bissonette? That would leave me with nothing but a citation for contempt.

No, William Prescott III had turned me into his cabana boy and I was helpless to fight it. What else could I do but sit back and take the money?

33

I was lying on the couch in my apartment with the lights off, drinking a beer and occasionally banging the wall with my fist, when she called for me. I was banging in frustration at allowing myself to be bought, banging at whatever it was inside of me that kept me from fighting it. And I was banging at the way Prescott was playing me. It rankled. *'Oh, cabana boy, bring me a drink. Oh, cabana boy, sit down and shut up and let me have my way with you. Oh, cabana boy . . .'* I drank my beer and stared at the shadows of light that swept through my window from the street and bang, banged, waiting for the phone to ring. From the first trill I knew who it was.

'I'll be right over,' I said into the handset and within thirty seconds I was out the door.

Even before my fall into outright whoredom I had been running to Veronica whenever she called. She was like a drug to me, an addiction, and even when I wasn't with her, when I was sitting in the courtroom supposedly concentrating on the testimony I was not permitted to challenge or rebut, I couldn't keep my mind from drifting back to the salty smell and soft soft skin and the electric tongue. Jimmy, preoccupied with the trial, still slipped out now and then for a quiet rendezvous with his mistress, though his nights of carousing through the city with his entourage were on hold pending the verdict. Whenever he was with Veronica I worked late on Valley Hunt Estates or whatever else I could find to suck up my time and on those nights, whenever the Bishops weren't taking me out for dinner and filling me with wine, I would stop at the corner grill for my evening cheese steak and fall asleep to the brilliance of late-night television. But on the nights Veronica called I would hang up the phone and rush out the door and drive enthusiastically to Olde City.

For a while we had been meeting at bars for a drink or two before retiring to her apartment. There was something reassuring about that, a restaurant for a late dinner, a bar for a nightcap. On those evenings out we could pretend that we were dating, as if we were a normal couple in a normal relationship satisfying our normal desires. But after the rear window of that hatchback exploded in front of my face I grew cautious of public places. And then there was that night in Carolina's.

'Oh, Jesus,' she said, turning her head quickly away from me. 'Jesus, Jesus, Jesus.'

We were at the far end of the bar, drinking our martinis and Sea Breezes, sharing cigarettes. She had begun smoking on our nights out, Camel Lights, and a cigarette was between her fingers now when her eyes widened with a shot of terror and she said, 'Oh, Jesus,' and she turned away from me.

I thought for an instant she was gasping at my face, which was a gasper, really, but that wasn't it. Behind me was the entrance and when I swiveled to grab a look, whom I saw walking in that entrance was Chester Concannon. I spun around again before he could see me.

'Oh, Jesus,' she said. 'We have to get out of here.'

'Would he tell Jimmy?' I asked to the back of her head.

'Of course he would,' she said. 'And that's not all he'd do. Jesus. He has a wild crush on me, didn't you know?'

'No,' I said.

'He told me on one of our nights out when he was bearding me. We got drunk together and he made a pass and told me. Jimmy and me is one thing,' she said, sliding off her stool. 'But if Chester knew about you he'd go nuts. Come on, follow me.'

Without turning toward the entrance she headed for the rear of the room and I followed, hunching down so I might

305

not be recognized from the back. We entered a short hall-way with two lavatories and, at the end, an unmarked door. Veronica went to that door and opened it. Inside were shelves filled with supplies, toilet paper, and towels. There was just enough room for two to stand inside the closet.

'Did you know this was there?' I asked.

'No,' she said, with a laugh. 'But good thing it is.'

'And you want us to hide from Chet in there?'

'I'm not the type to stay in closets,' she said. 'I want you to hide from Chester in there. Thirty minutes.'

She left me in that closet, telling me that she would get Chet out of there before he saw me with her. I stood tall in the darkness, surrounded by the sweet menthol smell of urinal cakes, wondering at how far I had fallen that I had to hide from my clients in closets. This Veronica thing was impossible, I had told myself before and repeated it to myself inside that dark mentholated cave, but even as I swore to end it I knew I wouldn't. It was something obses-sional and foolish and perverse, but it had evolved into something else too, it had evolved into something close to love. Twisted, yes, forged from depravity and desire, yes, but there it was, like a nugget in my chest. And no matter how impossible it might have been, no matter how doomed, I would stay in that closet to keep it alive as long as I had to. When by the green glowing hands of my watch I could tell a half-hour had passed, I straightened my jacket and opened the door.

A woman standing in the hallway waiting for the ladies room saw me emerge from the closet and screamed.

'Funny,' I said with a shrug. 'I thought it was the men's room.' And then, with all the dignity I could muster, I walked past her back into the bar.

So, for safety's sake, we didn't meet in bars or restaurants anymore. When she called for me I came running to her apartment, straight as if on a string, and the night I was bang banging on my walls in frustration was no different from any other night. She called, I ran, and we rolled around her bed like cats, sometimes playful, sometimes lupine, always carnal, and it was worth everything.

And when it was over it was always the same.

'You have to go,' she said.

'Why?' It came out in a half-moan, dragged from the recesses of my sleep, a sleep that was eluding me in my own apartment but that attacked me as I lay in the warm muskiness of her bed.

'Because you do,' she said.

'Let me stay. Let me sleep just a little bit more.'

She pushed me hard, rolling me over toward the end of the bed, and I jerked awake in a panic of falling. 'What?'

'You have to go,' she said,

'Just one night,' I begged. 'Let me spend just one night over.'

'Absolutely not.' She rose from the bed and put on a heavy terry cloth robe. She took a cigarette from the pack on her bedside table and lit it, inhaling deeply, and then leaned against a wall with her arms crossed. Smoke leaked out of her mouth, covering her face like a veil. 'Your clothes are scattered here or there. Pick them up on your way out.'

Generally, I had always believed there was no greater luxury after sex than to be alone. It is something about men, about the way our bodies work, about the physiological effects of orgasms in our brains. The neurotransmitters that are released by sex trigger those neurons that say turn over, pretend to sleep, maybe she'll just go away. Give us a beer afterwards and a remote control and an empty bedroom and we're halfway to heaven. Which is why men have invented the great after-sex lies: 'I have to be at work early,' or, 'I'm allergic to your cat,' or 'I have to pick up my laundry before the dry cleaner closes.' The problem had always been getting away. Now I was desperately disappointed that she wouldn't let me stay.

The reason for the desperation was clear to me that

night, and it was more than just that nugget of love in my chest. Nothing existed in my life that I could yet be proud of and nothing ever had. Who I was just then, Prescott's cabana boy, was no one I ever thought I'd ever want to be. But in her touch, her warmth, in her wet embrace, with Veronica I could lose myself. Her apartment had become a magic wonderland of sensuality and vice, a place separate from the rest of the world, which had suddenly turned even uglier for me. With her I was not Victor Carl, the shady lawyer who had been passed over by the profession, first duped and then bought by those he would have had as peers, instead I was part of something wild and lost and satisfyingly perverse. With her I metamorphosed into a piece of a puzzle that promised so much and that only the two of us could possibly solve. With her I . . . let's just say with her I was someone else and someone else was very much what I wanted then to be. To force me to leave was to force me to become myself again. She didn't know how cruel she was being.

'Don't do this to me,' I pleaded.

'I'm doing.'

'You can't just use me and then toss me out. I'm not a tampon.'

'No, you're not as useful.'

'Why do you make me leave each night?'

She sucked smoke. 'I like to wake up alone.'

'Well, tonight I'm staying.' I lay back in the bed, my arms crossed beneath my head.

'Then tonight's your last night.'

I sat up. 'You're not serious.'

'I'm as serious as celibacy.'

'I bet Jimmy stays over.'

'Never,' she said.

'Really? What's he like in bed?'

'The thing about men,' she said, holding the cigarette in her lips while she stooped to pick up my T-shirt and then tossed it into my face, 'is that they see sex as a competitive sport. They want scores from the judges, a set for technical merit and a set for artistic impression.'

'I'm just curious,' I said, starting to dress.

'Well, how do you think he is?'

'Passionate. He's a very passionate man.'

'He is.'

'Yes?'

'So are you, Victor.' With one of her bare feet she nudged a sneaker toward me. 'Now put on your shoes and go.'

'When will I see you again?'

'When I call,' she said.

'I'll be waiting.'

'Surprise me sometime, Victor,' she said dryly, holding the cigarette in front of her face. 'Let the phone ring more than once before you answer it.'

Ever since the incident with the hatchback I had developed a small ritual upon leaving Veronica's apartment. There were no windows in the hallway, but the elevator had a scuffed Plexiglas side from which the residents could see out as they descended to the cobblestone plaza. When the elevator opened for me I slipped in and searched through the Plexiglas to see if anyone was waiting for me outside. My plan, if I saw anything suspicious, was to get off at a lower floor and cower, but that night, as best as I could see in the uneven light, the plaza was deserted. When the elevator reached the ground floor I looked carefully out the front glass door before I opened it. Again there was nothing.

Slowly I slid out the door and walked along the shadowy edge of the plaza to Church Street, the little cobblestoned street on which Veronica's building sat. Like a little boy I looked both ways. Nothing, no car idling malevolently, no shadowy pedestrians lurking, no stray raccoons. Relieved, I walked down Church Street to 3rd, where my car was parked. I was leaning over, my key in the driver's door, when I felt the hand clamp onto my shoulder.

I jumped, or I tried to jump, but the hand kept me pressed down on the ground like the gravity of some giant planet. I turned to see who was there. It was a tall bruiser, an older man with sallow yellow skin, a tan fedora, a loud plaid jacket, yellow pants, white shoes, a nose that had been run over by a forklift. He looked like an aging heavyweight retired to Miami Beach.

'You're Victor Carl,' the man said in a ragged, nasal voice carved by one too many shots to the schnozzola.

'No,' I said. 'You got the wrong fellow.'

Without taking his hand off my shoulder, the man reached into his plaid jacket and pulled out a piece of newspaper that he showed to me. It was a picture of Jimmy Moore and William Prescott talking to the press outside the courthouse, and there, behind Moore's shoulder, inside an ominous circle drawn with black, was me. Not a bad likeness, I thought as I stared at it. The paper made me look heavier and more handsome.

'No, that's some other guy.'

'It sort of looks like youse.'

'I got that kind of face,' I said, and it would have been a pretty brave line if my voice hadn't cracked in the middle of it.

'Maybe it's not youse after all,' said the bruiser. 'Maybe not, you know, because the guy here in the picture, this guy looks like a handsome guy and you, you look like a punk. But there's a man wants to see youse. If it turns out youse ain't you then I'm sure he won't want to see youse no more.'

'Huh?'

'Whatever. He's waiting up the block, here.'

He squeezed the hand on my shoulder, yanking me away from my car and toward Arch Street.

'What about my keys? I left them in the car door.'

'From what I hear,' said the bruiser without slowing down, 'this here's become a very safe neighborhood.'

That was the sum of our conversation as he led me to

Arch Street. The front, squared-off nose of some big white American car parked on Arch jutted out from behind a brick wall. I didn't know whose car it was, I couldn't tell if it was a limousine from what I could see. I expected it was Norvel Goodwin inside, or maybe Jimmy, but no matter who it was there waiting for me I knew it wasn't a good thing to be snagged by a bruiser outside Veronica's apartment after sticking my thing in her thang. I thought about running, but the hand was tight on my collarbone, squeezing so hard my shoulder rose as we walked. When we were closer to the car more of it came into view. It wasn't a limousine, it was a Cadillac, long, shiny, dangerous with chrome. Its windows were up and tinted black so that it was impossible to see inside.

The bruiser stopped me just in front of the rear door. He knocked on the window and slowly the door opened. For a moment I saw nothing but the blackness inside. And then a man stepped out and smiled at me.

'How's it going there, Sport?'

It was Jasper, the gregarious poker player at the Sons of Garibaldi Men's Club, and he was smiling at me in a way I didn't like.

'We want you should come for a ride with us,' he said.

'Thanks, but I'd just as soon go home alone.'

'C'mon, Sport, a short ride. I got someone here you need to meet.'

As he was speaking the darkened window on the front passenger side opened slowly, electrically, and appearing like a ghost at some boardwalk house of horror was Dominic, Bissonette's second cousin twice removed, the hit man whom I had falsely accused of cheating. 'Get in, kid,' he said softly and, with a push from the bruiser, I was in the car.

There was an old man on my left and Jasper got in so that he was on my right. It was a big car, with a wide bench seat in the back, and there would have been plenty of room if Jasper hadn't jammed himself next to me. The bruiser closed the door and immediately went around the car to the driver's seat. The bench seat was black leather; the car smelled of Brylcreem. The old man on my left was looking out the window, out into the night. He wore a cream-colored suit, his thick hands were carefully laid one on the other in his lap. There was a diamond in his lapel. Slowly, easily, we pulled out on Arch Street and the bruiser turned up 2nd Street and we drove on for a while, south, toward Society Hill Towers, without anybody saying anything. And then the old man spoke.

'I wanted to meet you, Victor.' His voice was soft and lightly sprinkled with an old world accent. When he turned I saw his face, pitted ugly, his hair gray but pulled back elegantly and heavily greased. 'I thought it was time we should talk. Do you know who I am?'

'Yes,' I said. The word came out in a gush of breath that I had been holding once I recognized the man. I had seen his face in newspaper photographs, on mug shots flashed on TV, in gory hard-boiled articles in *Philadelphia* magazine. The man sitting next to me, his swollen hands calmly resting on his lap but close enough to my throat so that he could have reached up and strangled me before I let out a yelp, that man was the boss of bosses, Enrico Raffaello.

34

Philadelphia has five major spectator sports: football, baseball, basketball, hockey, and the Mafia wars. Whenever one of the subtle mob hits occurs somewhere in South Philadelphia or in the new ganglands of New Jersey, the papers and the television stations go crazy with coverage. There are photographs of the victim, sprawled in an alley or in his car, puddles of blood leaking from his newly created orifices. There are statements from the victim's neighbors saying what a stand-up fellow he had been and that no, they hadn't known, had no idea he was associated with the mob. The necrologies are printed in the papers like an honor roll. Speculation as to who ordered the hit and who performed it is rampant. And the charts come out; the deceased's name is crossed off the list and everyone below rises a notch. The mobsters have nicknames, just like ballplayers: Chicken Man, Shorty, Weasel, Tippy, Chickie, Toto, Pat the Cat. We root for our favorite as he rises and drink a beer to him when he winds up on the front page of the *Daily News*, slumped over the wheel of his Cadillac, his once handsome and arrogant face disfigured from the force of the bullet that came in the back of the neck at close range and exploded out the front of his face, taking the jaw along for the ride.

For a long time there was peace in the city's mob and folks followed the Phillies and the Eagles. But one night Angelo Bruno, the boss of Philly bosses, the man who kept the peace, was sitting in his car when his driver, a Sicilian named Stanfa, powered down Bruno's window, through which a wiseguy with a shotgun blew apart Bruno's skull. After the Bruno hit the necrology began to grow. 'Johnny

Keys' Simone, Bruno's cousin, shot dead somewhere and dumped in Staten Island; Frank Sindone, Bruno's loan-sharking capo, found stuffed into two plastic bags in South Philadelphia; Philip 'Chicken Man' Testa, blown apart on his porch with such savagery that Bruce Springsteen wrote a song about it. And after that, about once every quarter, as regular as 10Qs from a Fortune 500 company, another one fell. Chickie Narducci, gunned down outside his South Philly home; Vincent 'Tippy' Panetta, sixty, strangled along with his teenage girlfriend; Rocco Marinucci, found a year to the day from the Chicken Man's incineration with fire-crackers stuffed in his mouth; Frank John Monte, shot to death next to his white Cadillac; 'Pat the Cat' Spirito; Sammy Tamburrino; Robert Riccobene; Salvatore Testa, the Chicken Man's son; 'Frankie Flowers' D'Alfonso. And after each of these unfortunate accidents the charts came out, names were crossed off, one by one the bigger players fell off the list and the smaller players rose. Nicky Scarfo was on top for a while, but the killing continued and soon Scarfo was indicted in federal court for racketeering and in state courts running from Delaware to New Jersey to Pennsylvania on numerous charges of murder. There was quiet during this period of uncertainty, but after Scarfo was shipped to the federal penitentiary in Marion, Illinois, the high-security jail that replaced Alcatraz, and left there to rot, the battle for power began again.

Enrico Raffaello wasn't even on the charts at the start of this second war. He had been peripherally involved with the mob, a friend of friends who were cousins to some of the boys, like almost everyone in South Philly. Enrico was a merchant. He sold pastries in the Italian Market, content, it seemed, to bake cannoli shells and mix the ricotta custard and sprinkle the filled shells with freshly ground cinnamon until he died. It was his son, 'Sweet Tooth' Tony they called him, who was the comer. He was one of the guys you saw in the pictures of Scarfo as the boss walked triumphantly into court to pick up another twenty years here or forty years there or a Lucky Strike bonus of life without parole. Sweet Tooth was in the back, carrying the boss's bag, smiling like a sweet fat kid from the neighborhood who was thrilled to be hanging around the downtown boys. But when it was decided finally that Scarfo was through, decided not by the feds or the DA but by the guys underneath who were sick of waiting, and a new war of succession broke out, bit by bit Sweet Tooth Tony's name started rising up the charts. First he was just on the list of mob associates, then he was in the group of enforcers, then he was one of the lieutenants, and then he was listed as a possible successor, number four on the charts, but rising fast, number four with a bullet.

That bullet finally came in just below Sweet Tooth's ear while he was waiting for his driver outside his father's pastry shop on 9th Street. He had a pig's ear in his mouth and was reading the sports section of the *Daily News* when a woman with a baby carriage passed behind him and stuck a silenced .45 into his neck just below the ear and pretty much blew Tony Raffaello's head right off his body. Enrico rushed out of the store and found his son on the ground, his head twisted grotesquely, the blood filling cracks in the sidewalk and falling in a viscous stream into the gutter. The picture of Enrico on his knees, covered in his son's blood, staring up at the sky and bellowing in agony as Sweet Tooth's head lay cradled in his apron, made the front page of the *New York Times* and was nominated for a Pulitzer.

About ten days later there began a brutal flurry of killings. Mob leaders and lieutenants up and down the charts were wiped out in a veritable plague of violence until the charts themselves became obsolete. Businesses closed, people stayed home, every night another picture of a sprawled and bloody corpse made the papers as the city sickened from the spreading pool of blood. And then after a month of horror, after a month in which more mobsters died than in any previous year, after a month that forced the police commissioner to resign and the Pennsylvania Crime Commission to throw up its hands and the United States Attorney General to set up a special task force to investigate, after a month in which even those fans who bet in pools on the next mobster to fall turned away in disgust, after a month that put Philadelphia on the cover of *Time* and *Newsweek* and *National Detective*, after a month that has gone down in history as the 'Thirty-Day Massacre,' after a month there was quiet.

It took the attorney general's special task force and the newspapers a full year to reconfigure the charts, and it was a year of peace. No more bodies were discovered floating face down in the Delaware, no more bodies found in the trunks of abandoned cars under the bridge in Roosevelt Park, no more corpses sprawled on the cover of the *Daily News*. The government sent out its informants like an infantry of spies and they came back with word that there was a new boss with support from New York and a series of interlocking agreements among the city's mobsters that kept everything peaceful and profitable. He was a strong man, a respected man, he was called the 'Big Cannoli' by the cognoscenti, he was not a man to be trifled with, but he was an honorable man who through his strength would keep the peace. In one short year he had become a legend and his power flowed from Philadelphia through Atlantic City into New York and Pittsburgh and as far away as Las Vegas. He was the most powerful man in the city, in the state, he was the Big Cannoli, and on the first Monday of every month he visited the grave of Sweet Tooth Tony and left a pig's ear on the mound of earth rising above the specially ordered oversized coffin.

'I want you to know, Victor,' said the Big Cannoli, sitting next to me in the back seat of that Cadillac, 'I want you to know that I am not a violent man by nature.' His voice was soft, genteel even with the accent, a grandfather's voice, a voice without obvious menace. It was the voice of Geppetto. I would have thought him a harmless old man, ugly but harmless, if I hadn't known who he was. 'I think I would have been happy as an artist, painting flowers on canvases. But such was not my fortune. I tell you this so you should not be frightened of me. The newspapers, they exaggerate so. Now my friend Dominic . . . You know Dominic, I believe, Victor.'

'Yes.'

'Dominic is a violent man. It's in his nature, it's in his blood. Even though he's retired now, it still takes everything in my power to keep him under control. And Jasper, too. Such a nice man, Jasper, but there is a streak in him that is very hard to restrain. Lenny, my driver, was a boxer for years. You'd think a boxer would be violent, but not Lenny. He's a sweetheart. Isn't that right, Lenny?'

'That's what my grandchildren say, Mr Raffaello, so long as I treat 'em to taffy.'

'What Lenny did as a profession Dominic and Jasper do for pleasure. Such is the way of mankind. But that's not my way, Victor. I am more like Lenny.' Suddenly his voice hardened. 'It's a good thing that I have people like Dominic and Jasper because without them, Victor, without them, I tell you, I don't think I would get any respect in a world such as this.' He was almost shouting now. 'Without them, Victor, I'd just as well be baking cookies.'

'You listen to Mr Raffaello, Sport,' said Jasper.

Raffaello threw up his hands in a kindly shrug and when he spoke, his voice was soft and grandfatherly again. 'I had two children, Victor. We wanted more, of course, but two was all we had. A boy and a girl. A millionaire's family. Anthony and Linda Marie. You might have heard about Anthony,' he said, looking at his nails. 'It was in all the papers.'

'I'm sorry about your son, Mr Raffaello,' I said in a voice as soft as a whisper.

'Yes, well, these things happen. That leaves me with

317

Linda Marie. Linda Marie is a sweet girl, a wonderful girl. I love her totally, believe me. Do you have a daughter, Victor?'

'No, sir.'

'Well, have a daughter and hold her in your arms and then you'll know how much I love my Linda Marie. So it is with this much love that I say in all honesty my daughter is troubled. She is married to a man who doesn't love her, a man who'd sooner keep the company of other men than sleep with his wife. Do you know her husband, the councilman?'

'I know of him.'

'Well, he is one of her troubles. And sadly, I am another. She has difficulty accepting my current position. I pay for a psychiatrist for her, an hour a day, five days a week, but it doesn't seem to help. You see, along with her husband and father she has another problem, the fact that she's a slut.'

Dominic quickly said, 'Enrico, no, don't say such a thing,' and Jasper started demurring to his boss, but the Big Cannoli lifted up his hand to stop them and they quieted immediately.

'I say this with a heavy heart. It hurts me to call my daughter such a thing. But it is the truth, a truth I can live with. Now, Victor, I can call my daughter a slut.' His voice suddenly deepened. 'But don't you ever.'

'You listening, Sport?'

'You see,' said Raffaello, his voice slowly falling back into calm, 'I'm very touchy about my family. What do you think of my daughter, Lenny?'

'A very fine girl, a sensitive, pretty girl,' said Lenny without turning from the road, tilting his head up as if he were talking into a microphone in the ceiling of the car. 'A princess, a queen.'

'It is well known among my associates,' said Raffaello, 'to only speak well of my family. There were once men who treated my family with disrespect, Victor, and they're not around anymore. Now there was a poker game not too long ago in which you were involved, along with Dominic and Jasper and certain other friends of mine, and in that game you treated my family with disrespect.'

'I didn't mean to . . .'

Raffaello held up his hand and I shut up quick.

'You sound scared, Victor, and that is not what I want. I am not a violent man. I'm more of an artist, like I said. I should have been a poet. Do you read much poetry, Victor?'

'No.'

'Neither do I. I'll be frank with you, I don't understand it. Sea-gulls and clouds. But even so I feel, in my heart, that I have the soul of a poet. I should have had an education. There is so much I wanted to do. Now in this poker game you implied that Dominic's cousin Zachariah . . .'

'Second cousin twice removed,' said Jasper.

'Yes. You implied that Zachariah was having an affair with my daughter and because of that I killed him. Such a rude comment is unforgivable, really.'

'I'm sorry, sir,' I stammered, but before I could go on he quieted me with a soft gesture from his right hand.

'Now one reason for our visit,' said Raffaello, 'is for me to tell you that this is not true. There was an affair, yes, and it pains me to say it. Zachariah was like a dog without any control, but I didn't have him killed. If I killed all the men Linda Marie slept with over the years the Schuylkill would run red.'

'I understand,' I said into a pause.

'Besides, if I was going to kill Zachariah it would have been for the way he butchered second base.'

Jasper laughed, like a horse with a wheeze.

'You see,' Raffaello continued, 'when I was told of the conversation at the poker game I realized you might have mistaken the silence and lack of denial by my associates as agreement that I had ordered the killing. That would have been a mistake. The silence was just that, silence. My

319

associates know not to speak about my family. They have learned that over the years.'

'I believe you, Mr Raffaello,' I said quickly. 'I do.'

'That's good, Victor. Now you may be wondering who did kill Zachariah. Well, the answer is that we don't know. The federal prosecutor, as usual, has it wrong. It was not part of Jimmy Moore's extortion of Ruffing, I am certain.'

'How are you so certain?' I asked.

'Victor, Victor,' said Raffaello, shaking his head. 'You have to trust me, Victor. Jimmy is not a stupid man. A passionate man, yes, which he never fails to tell me when we break bread together, but not stupid.'

'If not Jimmy, then who?'

'Dominic, tell Victor what you told me,' said Raffaello.

Dominic twisted around in the front seat so he was facing me. 'Zack told me, before he died, that he was in love in a way he had never been in love before. He told me it was dangerous and he had to be careful but that he was going to stop whoring around because this girl was so special.'

'Who is this girl?'

Dominic shrugged. 'We don't know, but when he told me this I could see that he was scared.'

'Victor, what we are telling you is the truth. Use this information however you want. But what I don't want to hear anymore, Victor, is anything about my family in this trial. Do you understand?'

'I didn't bring it up.'

'No, Jimmy's lawyer did. But I have had representatives speak to Jimmy already and he has given his assurances. What I want from you is your promise that you won't bring my daughter into it either. Can you promise me, Victor?'

Jasper leaned over and whispered in my ear, 'You should promise the man, Sport.'

'I promise,' I said.

'That's good, because I know you to be a man of your

320

word. I know that, Victor. And the reason I know that is because Dominic and Jasper also heard that promise and these are men who believe nothing is more important than keeping one's word.'

'Nothing,' said Dominic.

'I understand completely,' I said.

'Yes, I think you do,' he said calmly. 'I am not a violent man, you must believe that. I should have been a sculptor or a farmer, anything but what I have become. I don't really have the temperament for it. But sometimes, when it comes to my family . . .' He shrugged. 'When that happens, I become like an animal. Listen when I tell you this, Victor. It's been known to happen. Now there is something else. You know that while we do much for the community . . .'

'We protect and serve,' said Jasper. 'No different than the cops.'

'Though we do much good,' continued Raffaello, 'we are not a charity. Like all businesses, we are forced to take our share of the economic benefits our protection allows.'

'A modest sum,' said Jasper.

'And we require that those involved in activities that aren't government sponsored and thus not subject to normal taxation pay an even larger share.'

'Think of it like a baseball game,' said Jasper. 'And we're home plate. No matter how big a hit, you need to touch base with us before you score.'

'Do you understand the concept?' asked Raffaello.

'Yes, sir,' I said quickly.

'Now, our information tells us there is a quarter of a million dollars unaccounted for, money that was given by Mr Ruffing but never received by Jimmy Moore's organization. A quarter of a million dollars. Whoever ended up with that money never touched home plate. Inadvertently, I assume.'

'Mr Raffaello is a very forgiving man,' said Jasper, shifting closer to me and leaning so close to my face that I could smell garlic and a touch of rosemary on his breath.

'But still,' said the boss of bosses. 'We expect our share. Now one third of a quarter of a million dollars is . . .'

'Eighty-three thousand,' said Dominic. 'Three hundred and thirty-three.'

'Let's call it an even hundred thousand,' said Raffaello. 'I always liked clean numbers. So, Victor, we're missing one hundred thousand dollars. It is as if someone walked into my house, opened a drawer, and took one hundred thousand dollars from me. I'm a forgiving man, Victor,' but now his voice rose until he was screaming once again, 'but to just march into my home and open a drawer and take from me, that I cannot forgive.'

'What happened to the money, Sport?' asked Jasper, still leaning close to me.

'I don't know,' I said.

'Find it for us, Victor,' said Raffaello, 'and I'll forget all about your disrespect for my daughter. You see, I can be forgiving.'

'You should thank the man,' said Jasper into my ear.

'But I don't know where . . .'

'Find it, Victor,' said Raffaello, interrupting my pathetic whine. 'And we'll forget about the unpleasantness at the poker game. Otherwise . . .' He shrugged.

'Thank the man, Sport.'

'Thank you,' I said obediently.

'All right, we've taken care of our business,' said Raffaello. 'Lenny, do you have something for our friend Victor?'

'Sure thing, Mr Raffaello.'

Lenny pulled the car over and reached down for something and then turned around quickly. I ducked, expecting another shot to my eye. I was getting sick of these rides around town. But Lenny didn't turn around to sock me with the back of his hand. When I recovered and opened my eyes he was holding a small white paper sack with slight grease markings on the bottom.

'This is for you, Victor,' said Enrico Raffaello. 'It's a

cannoli, from my own special recipe. I hope you like vanilla custard. Now take my advice, Victor. A cannoli this rich you must not eat too fast. I never created the great art I dreamed of, but my cannoli come close. Eating one is like having sex. If it's too fast, you just end up nauseous. But eat it slowly, carefully, let the custard melt in your mouth. You eat it right and the joy you experience will fill you with an unaccountable joy. You like sex?'

'Yes, sir.'

'Well, trust me, Victor, you eat it right, you'll like my cannoli better. We'll be hearing from you, I assume.'

With that the door opened and Jasper jumped to the street and jerked me out with him. 'See you later, Sport.'

I leaned back into the car. 'Thank you for the cannoli, Mr Raffaello. By the way, sir, you didn't, by any chance, just sort of happen to take a shot at me a few days back, did you?'

Raffaello leaned forward in his seat and smiled as sweetly as he could with a face such as his. 'Victor. If we had taken a shot at you, you wouldn't be around to ask such a question.'

35

Enrico Raffaello was almost right about his cannoli, it was heavy and crisp and I ate it slowly, letting the white custard slide down my throat like sweet, perfumed oysters. It wasn't quite as good as sex, but after an evening with Veronica it was all I could have asked for. I sat in my car and ate the cannoli and let the cinnamon tickle my nose and bite after bite my spirits fell because, along with giving me that superb cannoli, Mr Raffaello had opened a door I'd rather have remained shut. On the other side were danger and loss, but there it was, open wide and waiting for me. I didn't have much choice. I ducked my head and stepped through and found myself the very next morning at the Sporting Club.

The Sporting Club was swank, which wasn't exactly what I wanted in a gym. Gyms should be sweaty, smelly places, where muscle-bound lugs grunt as they move around great discs of metal and the rubbery thwack thwack thwack of a basketball echoes from the court. That wasn't the Sporting Club. The Sporting Club was swank.

'I'm interested in joining,' I said. 'And I wondered if I could look around for a bit.'

'Of course,' said the woman in the membership office. She wore white, her top stretched by a very fit pair of breasts, worked out, I was sure, on a Nautilus breast machine until they were every bit as taut as her thighs. 'Why don't you fill out this form first.'

They wanted to know my name, my address, my credit card, they wanted to know what I did for a living, who I worked for, my estimated yearly income. It was almost like the way potential dating partners sniff each other out at a party or a bar. Out of pride, I lied to make myself sound like a better candidate for their club, even though I had no intention of joining.

'Well, Mr Carl,' she said, 'let me give you a little tour.'

'How about if I look around myself, get a feel for the place, would that be all right?' ·

'Of course,' she said. 'Take this pass and go right through there. The men's locker room is on the left and there are signs to the various rooms.' Her gaze drifted down to where my chest would have been had I had one. 'Be sure to check out our free weight room.'

I smiled back anyway and left the office, waving the pass casually at the beefy man in white guarding the entrance.

It wasn't very crowded at seven in the morning, a few haggard souls trying to sneak their workout in before they were awake enough to realize how crazy it was to take an elevator seven floors just to bound up an endless flight of mechanical stairs. In the men's locker room I grabbed a couple of towels and found a locker and stripped. I couldn't help but look at myself in the mirrors that surrounded the room. What I saw was pathetic. I would need to join a gym someday, but not this one, not one so swank.

With a towel around my waist, I followed signs to the men's sauna and steam rooms. The sauna was empty but in the steam room, lying on one of the tiled tiers, was a hard mound of flesh with a towel around its waist and over its face. I sat on a lower tier where it was still possible to breathe and waited for a moment as the steam floated about me and the sweat started sucking from my body.

When sweat dripped from my nose to my knees I said finally, 'Enrico Raffaello didn't kill Bissonette.'

'Good morning, Victor,' said Jimmy Moore, without lifting the towel off his face.

Concannon had told me that Moore worked out at the Sporting Club every morning, primarily by sweating out the alcohol from the night before in the sauna or steam room, depending on his mood. It was directly to the

325

councilman that the door Raffaello opened had led, it was Moore whose answers to the big questions I needed to hear.

'Where did you gather your startling bit of information?' he asked.

'From Raffaello himself.'

'So you had an audience with the pope and the pope told you he's innocent.'

'And I believe him,' I said. 'No reason for him to lie, his hands are already crimson. Which raises the question I have raised before and to which I still don't have an answer. Who killed Bissonette? Did you?'

He grabbed the towel off his face, sat up, and let out a long grunt that was like the baying of a great wounded mammal.

'If you want, councilman,' I said, 'you can have your attorney present when we have this conversation.'

He pushed himself off his tier and stepped down, loosening the towel from his waist and letting it drop into the puddled steam slipping across the tiled floor to the drain. Beside the door was a cold-water shower and he turned it on. His muscles were turning slack and what was once a formidable chest was dropping, but what I noticed most clearly was the size of his prick, which was big, huge, like a bull elephant's, it flopped down and hung there and the size of it was sickening. I wrapped the towel more tightly around my waist.

'I think I can handle this without Prescott's help,' he said from inside the shower, water streaming down his face and body. 'So you want to know if I killed the ballplayer. If I am a murderer. Because the way you figure it, it was me who beat him to death with a baseball bat.'

'You've lied to Chester and me about who did it and you're setting up Chester for a fall. It doesn't make sense unless you killed him.'

'Get dressed,' he said, wiping his face with a towel and opening the steam room door. A blast of frigid air swirled in. 'We have time for a morning drive before court.'

'Do you know how I was first elected to City Council, Victor?' asked Jimmy Moore. We were inside the limousine now, driving north on Broad Street. Henry and the car had been waiting in the alley next to the old Bellevue Stratford, where the Sporting Club was situated. Inside the limousine was a tray of danish and a steel thermos, out of which Jimmy poured us each a cup of coffee. 'Cream?' he asked.

'No, thank you,' I said.

'I ran on an anti-busing platform,' he said. 'I opposed integration. I promised to keep our neighborhoods crime-free, which is political shorthand for white. You don't have to use Klan language to grab the racist vote. Talk about maintaining the integrity of the neighborhoods, talk about the scourge of crime, talk about protecting the American dream of home ownership and maintaining real estate values, talk about busing and the electorate understands. I even got into a fist-fight in the Council chamber over a Gay Pride Day. I was opposed to it, of course. In my district the politics of hate were good politics and all I wanted was my city post, my city car, the power to make deals, so they were my politics too. The papers hated me, I was a joke, except that I carried my district with seventy-three percent of the vote.'

'Where are we going?' I asked.

'Drugs were the other people's problem,' he said, ignoring my question. 'You know much about the gospels? No, of course not. Saul, an agent of the Jews and the scourge of Christianity, on his way to Damascus has a vision, hears a voice. "Saul, Saul, why persecuteth thou me?" It is the voice of Jesus. At that moment he becomes a new man, he changes his name to Paul, he becomes Jesus's messenger on earth. Well, I didn't hear any voice. What I heard was a silence. My own daughter's silence. But it spoke to me just as clearly. "Daddy. Daddy. Why forsaketh thou me?" And I didn't have an answer for her. Not a one.'

He took a sip from his coffee and another, looking out the side window into the desolation of North Philadelphia.

'Now I do,' he said.

'One of our most important programs here at the Nadine Moore Youth House,' said Mrs Diaz as she led Jimmy Moore and me through a tour of the facility, 'is our community outreach program. Actually, it was at the councilman's insistence that we began the program and it has become the cornerstone of our effort. So often the only place children in trouble can receive help is through the criminal justice system and by then it is often too late. Through our education and outreach programs we can get hold of these children and deal with their problems before they enter the criminal system. That makes all the difference, we've found.'

Mrs Diaz was a handsome woman with broad cheekbones and strong hands. We were walking down a hallway running around the perimeter of the building. All the classrooms had windows facing the hallways, which gave the construction a large and airy feel, more like a fine office building than a prison school. We stopped in front of a classroom where a group of twenty teenagers, dressed alike in white shirts and navy pants, were sitting in a semicircle around a teacher in goggles performing a chemistry experiment.

'The day for our children starts early in the morning,' said Mrs Diaz. 'We have a regular school curriculum, supplemented in the afternoons with classes designed to meet the specific needs of the individual child. The afternoon classes include group therapy. What we have found is that these children go back to school with their scholastic skills improved to such a point that they excel, which is primarily why our graduates generally do so well on the outside. Through our monitoring and counseling program, which continues long after the children leave here, we have found that almost ninety percent have stayed off of drugs and out of trouble.'

'Explain to Mr Carl where our funding comes from, Loretta,' said the councilman as we continued our walk down the hall.

'We get some support from the city,' she said. 'Councilman Moore has been able to secure for us some federal funds. And of course there are private donations. Whatever you'd like to give, Mr Carl,' she said with a warm smile, 'would be greatly appreciated. And then CUP, Citizens for a United Philadelphia, has been extremely generous. In the past, whenever we have anticipated a shortfall, CUP has balanced our budget.'

We followed Loretta Diaz up a flight of stairs into a gym where a large class of young men and women in their blue pants and white shirts were marching, in short-order drill, like soldiers on the parade ground. A teacher was barking out commands, 'Left face. Right face. Quarter-turn. About face,' and the marchers were chanting together, to the beat of their footsteps, *We got to go home on our left, our right, we got to go home on our left, our right.*'

'There's a consensus growing around the country,' said Mrs Diaz, 'that army-type discipline helps build self-esteem. So-called boot camps. I'm not so certain about whether it works or not, but the President is enamored with the idea and so it helps with the grant monies. As our plans for the future are ambitious, everything we can do to increase our funding we do. Besides, the children seem to actually like it.'

'What exactly are your ambitions?' I asked as the footsteps of the marchers and the chanting rose around us. *Left. Left. Your left, your right. Left.*

'Oh, I'm sorry. I thought the councilman explained all that to you. The Nadine Moore Youth Home is a pilot program. We only have room in this facility for one student out of every thirty who are referred to us. Our goal is to build fifteen more here in Philadelphia and then expand into other cities. This home acts not only as a center for these children but also as a laboratory, and we expect our success here will serve as the model for a great bloom of healing. Our great hope,' she said, as the councilman surveyed the troops marching to and fro on the basketball court, something wet and glistening in his eyes as they chanted, *Sound off, one two, little louder, three four, kick it around, one two three four one two — threefour,* 'our great dream,' she said, 'is that for every child in this country struggling with drugs there be a Nadine Moore Youth Home to help her through her time of deepest need.'

'This is our next one,' he said. Henry had driven us to a vacant lot on Lehigh Avenue, across from a stream of crumbling row houses and boarded-up stores. A school was up the avenue just a bit. 'The Art Museum fund-raiser gave us just enough to complete the effort. We start construction in two months. This will be twice the size of the facility you saw.'

'It certainly is a grand ambition,' I said.

'It will be her immortality,' said Jimmy Moore. 'After she died I realized that what had killed my daughter was not someone else's problem. It was everywhere. And I was in a position to do something about it. Something. For the first time I saw what politics could be about and it was not about hating or getting. That was when my passion reared and my mission began. First fight the dealers, then heal the children. We are making progress on both fronts and when I become mayor we'll win it all. We'll put the lords of death out of business and build those youth homes throughout the city. And not just homes, youth centers, boys' clubs and girls' clubs. I can do it. I will do it. It was as good as done before they set me up.'

'Who set you up?'

'I don't know exactly. Maybe the mayor, maybe the dealers. I was in danger before the indictment. Why do

330

you think I ride around in that limousine? My City Council car was shot up more than once by my enemies. But my black beauty is bulletproof now and I continue on. Then the feds, after consulting with the mayor, determined my fund-raising extortionate. And even if it is, so what? The money is going to the right place. But then came the murder and the arson and they decided to pin that on me too.'

'So you didn't kill Bissonette?'

He turned to me and looked me square in the eye. 'No,' he said without a flicker of his eye, without a hesitation in his voice. 'Absolutely not. Why would I kill that boy? For money? That's the problem with prosecutors, they're so willing to sell out for a small piece of change they think everyone else is too. I'm on the track to something big, huge, and you've just seen the tip of it. Besides, did you know that the money Bissonette was able to mysteriously raise for Ruffing came from Raffaello?'

So that was what Raffaello had meant when he said Jimmy was too smart to kill as part of the extortion plot. What he meant was that Jimmy was too smart to fight him. 'If you didn't kill him, why are you setting up Chester to take the fall?' I asked.

'Because I don't have a choice,' he said quickly.

'Bullshit.'

He let out a sigh, took out a cigarette, tapped it on its box, and lit it. 'Maybe it is bullshit. Maybe I'm just a coward, I don't know. I hire a lawyer, the best in the city, and I tell him to do anything he has to do to get me off and save my dream. He's a hard bastard, clever, and what he tells me is that if he can't prove who actually did the killing, the only way to get me off is to go after Chet. He told me we needed an attorney to represent Chet who wouldn't get in the way. Someone he could control. First it was McCrae. But then he took his ill-advised trip to Chinatown and so we needed someone else.'

'And that was me,' I said bitterly. The cabana boy.

'He told me it was my only choice. That if it works right

331

it will make the government's case look so weak we might both get off.' Jimmy took a deep drag from the cigarette and let it out slowly. 'So I told him to go ahead.'

'Even if Chester ended up behind bars for good.'

'What do you think, I like this? I don't have a choice. No choice at all. We're in a war here, fighting to build something grand and noble, but as in any war there will be casualties. Concannon might be one. I'll take care of Chet, and he knows it. But my enemies are coming after me. I won't let them win. If they do, it is the children who will pay the price. We need you to stick with us, to follow Prescott's direction and foil the government's plot against me. I brought you here so you would be aware of all you are endangering if you oppose us. Together we can make a difference.' He flicked his cigarette onto a tuft of weeds sprouting through cracked brick and it smoldered there. 'If you want, I'll put you on the board of CUP. A terrific position for a young lawyer. Together we can change the world for the better.'

That would be a terrific position for me, I knew. It was on charitable boards and political committees that lawyers found clients. Serve on enough boards, get enough clients, and you become a rainmaker, with the power to go to any firm in the city and name a price. I didn't jump right away onto my hind legs and say, 'Okay,' but I was thinking.

'So who killed him?' I asked.

'I don't know,' he spit out. 'God, I wish I did. You're the man with the theories, you find out. See if you can do any better than we did.'

I looked out over the vacant lot and then the neighborhood. There was something eerily familiar about it. 'What number is this?' I asked.

'Nineteenth Street.'

Now I knew where I was. The old baseball stadium had been a block away. Connie Mack Stadium. Where the park had been was now a big modern brick church, like a giant McDonald's, but when it had still been a ballyard my grandfather had brought me there to watch the Phillies play. He called it Shibe Park, its old name. We'd sit in the bleachers and chant, 'Go Phillies Go,' and watch Willie Mays beat the hell out of the home team. Richie Allen and Clay Dalrymple, Jim Bunning and Johnny Callison. And Gene Mauch sitting in the dugout, his dark face in the pained squint that became permanent after the team collapsed in '64. But what I remembered right then was not just the baseball but the young boy holding his grandfather's hand, walking past the parked cars on 20th Street to get into the park. How had he become me?

'Where's the rest of the money?' I asked, suddenly tired of the dog-and-pony show, tired of Jimmy Moore's self-righteousness. 'The missing quarter-million.'

'I don't know,' he said, his arm spreading over his vacant lot. 'But it's going to end up here, I'll make damn sure of it, and in the others we will build. I'm working on it as we speak.'

'Mr Raffaello wants his share.'

'Not a penny,' he shouted. 'They sell their poison right under his nose and it's fine so long as he gets his cut. He's a disgrace. I'd sooner die.'

'I'm sure he could arrange it.'

'Let him try. If he wants a war that's what he'll get.' He pointed a thick finger at me. 'I'm ready to take him on and take on anyone else who gets in my way. We're going to fill this vacant lot and fourteen like it with facilities that will heal a generation. It is my mission, and I will do anything to protect it. Anything. My mission is all I have left to care about now.'

I guess it all was getting to me, the false nobility, the lies, the inevitable bribes, a deal here, a settlement there, a position on an influential board. Was it so clear that I could be bought, was a 'for sale' sign printed on my face, unmistakable above my watery eyes. I hated it, especially here, where I felt haunted by the little shoe merchant and the young boy holding his hand. I couldn't help my anger from bubbling out. Even so, I might have kept quiet if his prick hadn't been so damned thick. But when he got all self-righteous on me I thought of the sight of him in that cold shower and I got even angrier and I said, 'But that's not the only thing to still care about, is it, councilman?'

'What else could there be?' he asked, his voice as plaintive as if there could be nothing.

'Fucking Veronica,' I said.

I regretted it immediately, regretted it all the more when he turned his startled face to me. It was twisted strangely into a mask that proclaimed both helplessness and need and, for the first time since I met him, Jimmy Moore was speechless.

But from what Veronica had told me and from the mask on Jimmy Moore's face I could piece it all together. Still in a rage from his daughter's death, he bursts into a crack house and sees her on the floor, helpless and high, about the same age as his daughter would have been, this pretty young girl on drugs, as pretty as his daughter. She might even have looked like her. And he shelters her in his car and takes her to a treatment center and saves her life, like he had been unable to save his daughter's life. And he visits her, his surrogate, and he makes sure she is cured, and bit by bit some deep desire starts rising from the forbidden, locked portions of his soul and he finds that he can't help himself, the unthinkable has become real, the impossible had become inevitable, and it is finer than any imagining.

36

You can learn everything about a man by learning what he truly wants. I had seen the bricks and glass of Jimmy Moore's greatest ambitions; they dwarfed my own in grandeur and worth. I felt a strange, sad sympathy for Moore, with his grand dreams of healing and his own hopeless love for Veronica Ashland, both built on a foundation of tragedy, and truly I hoped his grand dreams could all come true. But not over the rotting carcass of my client.

'We need to talk,' I said into the pay phone, taking no chances on a tap.

'My office, at five,' said Slocum.

'Forget it,' I said. 'Last time I went there it made the front page of the *Daily News*.'

'You got some heat, huh?'

'Like Las Vegas in August.'

'Never been.'

'Hot,' I said. 'Let's find a bar.'

'Dublin Inn?'

'Too many ADAs. How about Chaucer's?'

'Fine,' he said. 'Make it later then. Eight o'clock. Something interesting?'

'You'll think so,' I said, and I knew he would.

See, Prescott made a mistake, really. Had he treated me with the respect I craved, had he taken me to lunch as his guest at the Union League, at the Philadelphia Club, had he welcomed me with open arms into the fraternity of success, I might have sat quietly, willingly, and let Concannon eat whatever shit Prescott served him. But the bastard had threatened me, given me orders, turned me into his cabana boy, and that was his mistake. In the rush of my late-night prowlings with Jimmy Moore and his entourage, of my society functions, of my mentorship with Prescott, of my sexual obsession with Veronica, of my work and play with the Bishop brothers, of this new life that had seemingly been granted me, in the midst of it all I had lost my resentment for a while. But it was back, with a vengeance. It slipped over my shoulders like a favorite old sweater and it felt damn good. Even if the orders from my client prohibited me from actively engaging in the trial, even if my cut of the *Saltz* settlement and my deals with the Bishops and my directorship of CUP required my formal obeisance in court to Prescott, even if all that, my resentment still demanded I do something, anything, something, no matter the consequence. Concerning the mystery of who killed Bissonette, Jimmy Moore had said, 'You're the man with the theories, you find out.' So maybe I would.

What I had discovered from Raffaello was that Bissonette might have been killed because he was playing around with the wrong woman, so now all I had to do was find Bissonette's final fatal love. Lauren Amber Guthrie and her jangling gold bracelets? Maybe. Some other woman with a husband bent for revenge? Possibly. Or was it Chuckie Lamb after all, silencing the one witness who could connect him to everything? And what about the missing quarter of a million dollars, two-fifths of which was owed to Enrico Raffaello and the rest of the downtown boys? I wanted answers and quickly, before Eggert started nailing the shingles on the roof of the jail Prescott was building around Chester Concannon and before Raffaello started pressing me for information. Which is why I had called the man with the grand jury subpoenas, my old friend K. Lawrence Slocum, ADA.

Chaucer's was a friendly sort of neighborhood saloon with a famous shuffle bowling game, cheap paneling, stained-glass windows in the doors, and deep booths where groups of kids right out of college could sit and drink pitchers and gossip about other kids right out of college. When I first started going there it was filled with older, blue-collar types, with truck drivers, with lesbians who dressed like truck drivers, with college dropouts who ruefully discussed their dubious futures. But it no longer had that type of charm. Now the boys wore their baseball caps backwards, ponytails spilling out beneath the brims, the girls sheathed their long legs in black leotards, and they were all college graduates, discussing their dubious futures with pride. I still drank there, but now I felt too old to be a part and that was scary and sad both. I still remembered when it was a thrill just to be inside a bar, when the soft lighting and cigarette smoke and strangers on the stools whispered something so seductive I couldn't believe I could just walk in, sit down, and order a beer. But now I was one of the older and the sadder and the people slipping in were younger, gayer, more vibrant than I. Now I knew what the older people in the bars used to think of me because I knew what I thought of this new generation. I wished they all would just go home to their mamas.

Slocum and I were sitting in one of those deep booths toward the rear of the bar. The waitress had given us each a bottle of Rolling Rock and a glass and each of us had ignored the glass. I almost liked Slocum. He took it all very seriously, as one would want a public prosecutor to take it all very seriously, but he had a sense of humor, too. It was a weary sense of humor, that was the only type a prosecutor would ever allow himself, but even a weary sense of humor put him leagues ahead of the rest. I told him the whole story of my meeting with Raffaello, although I left out the part where he called his daughter a slut. I still remembered that Jasper and Dominic believed nothing was as important as keeping one's word, and though I almost liked Slocum, I wasn't willing to bet my life on whether or not he had a connection to Raffaello. Everyone else seemed to in this burg.

'He said it was a jealous husband?' asked Slocum.

'He didn't give me specifics.'

'So right now it's just a mystery girl.'

'Right,' I said.

'And you want me to check it out?'

'Yes.'

'To send out my detectives to find that girl?'

'That would be terrific.'

'You want me to send out my detectives to find this mystery girl, the existence of whom was disclosed by the biggest criminal in the city, all in an effort to destroy my murder case against your client.'

'Exactly.'

'I don't think so.'

'Larry, an innocent man is getting railroaded here.'

'Or maybe Raffaello's lying. You ever consider that gangsters sometimes lie? Nothing happens in this town without him getting a cut. Maybe he was part of the whole thing and now he's throwing out false leads to take the heat off his *compares*.'

'I don't believe that,' I said. 'Not for a minute. What I believe is that you've got the wrong guys facing death row and you don't want to admit it.'

He shrugged, like he wasn't certain that I was wrong. 'Maybe, Carl. It happens. But you're going to have to do your own investigating. How much you getting an hour for this case? No, don't tell me, it'll just make me ill. Earn your money, find the girl yourself.' He rubbed his hand over his mouth and looked at me for a moment. 'But maybe I can help.'

I just stared at him and waited.

He leaned forward and lowered his voice. 'All right, I'm going to tell you something. I'm telling you this because I think there's a chance, small, but a chance you may be right. But if it comes back in my face in some motion or in a newspaper article I'm going to be very disappointed, do you understand? And you don't want to disappoint me.'

He paused and took a drink from his beer.

'When we showed you the physical evidence,' he continued, 'we didn't show you everything. There was a book.'

'Shakespeare?' I asked.

'More like Ma Bell.'

'A phone book?'

'A personal phone book.'

'You withheld Bissonette's little black book?'

'Now don't get like that,' he said, raising a hand in protest. 'The office made a determination that it wasn't appropriate to release Bissonette's personal phone book, as it might tend to embarrass certain, how should I phrase this, certain well-known and highly placed women in the city. These women and their families have privacy rights. This wasn't like a hooker's book with the names of her johns. There were no crimes committed here.'

'So there's this book.' I pressed on.

'You want another beer?'

'Tell me about the book.'

'I'd like another beer.'

I raised my hand for the waitress like I was in grade school and ordered two more Rocks when she came. 'All right,' I said. 'Tell me about the book.'

'Well, this book has the names of the usual suspects, a lot of women with reputations.'

'Let me see the book.'

'Are you listening to me, Carl? I said we're not disclosing the book. There are names in there that if you saw them your jaw would drop to your knees, world-famous singers, athletes, wives of heavy politicians.'

'Like Councilman Fontelli's.'

'This was his book. But there aren't just phone numbers there. He rated them, gave them stars, one to five, like a damn critic.'

'Just like a baseball player to be obsessed with statistics.

But that's good, then,' I said. 'We can use that book to find the girl he fell in love with. She was a five-star for sure.'

'There's more than one five-star name.'

'Just give me the five stars to check on, then.'

'Some are just initials, some without numbers.'

'Well, whoever this mystery woman is, it's someone in the book,' I said. 'A man falls in love, he puts the number in his book.'

'You sound like you have a book of your own, Carl.'

'More like a few paper slips with hand-scrawled numbers.'

'You ever find a number you don't know whose it is?' asked Slocum, taking a long gulp from his beer, his eyes, behind his thick glasses, showing amusement.

'All the time.'

'What do you do then?'

'I call it. "Hello, anyone there single and under fifty-five?"'

'Oh man,' he said. 'I can't tell you how glad I am to be married.'

The waitress came with two more Rolling Rocks, the green long-necked bottles fogged with cold. 'Two more,' I said.

'So this is what I'm offering here,' said Slocum after the waitress left. 'You give me the name of any woman whose possible involvement you're investigating and I'll tell you if she's in the book and her rating. You can take it from there.'

'Linda Marie Raffaello Fontelli.'

'Three stars,' he said. 'I would have figured more with all that practice . . .'

'How about Lauren Amber Guthrie?' I said quickly.

'Where did that name come from?'

'I recognized her photograph in the love box.'

'And you withheld relevant information about a homicide from me?' He shook his head at me sadly. 'I'll let you know if she's in there tomorrow. Any others, you just give me a call.'

'Tell me something else,' I said. 'Tell me what you know about a drug dealer named Norvel Goodwin.'

He stared at me for a long moment, took a drink from his beer, and then stared at me some more. 'What the hell are you into?' he asked finally.

I shrugged.

'Norvel Goodwin,' he said, shaking his head. 'One of the worst. We're onto him, but he's tough as hell and he's got a good lawyer. Bolognese.'

'Tony Baloney,' I said. 'I have a case with him.'

'Well, no matter how good a lawyer Tony is, it's only a matter of time. You don't step up like he is stepping up without paying for it. He was big in West Philly for a while and then dropped out of sight.'

'When Jimmy Moore burned him out?' I asked.

He gave me another long look. 'That's right. Now he's back. There's been a lot of violence in the East Kensington Badlands as he pushes his way into other people's territories. Fights over street corners. The five-year-old who got a bullet in her head last week, cover of all the papers?'

'That was terrible.'

'That was Goodwin. A stray bullet from just another fight over another corner. But all of a sudden Goodwin has a lot of muscle and he's taking over a lot of territory. He's a stone-cold killer.' He shook his head. 'What the hell are you into now, Victor?'

I wouldn't have told him even if I knew.

37

Josiah Blaine was a shriveled old scoundrel who huddled before his rolltop desk late into the night in his second-floor law office two blocks away from the courts in City Hall. I'm speaking now of a different time, when the law was a less pervasive thing and a ten-thousand-dollar case was as big as they came. Josiah Blaine practiced law at the turn of the century, representing envelope makers and hat blockers, collections mostly, first the dunning letters and then the confessions of judgment, attachments of the bank accounts, foreclosures, all for fifty or a hundred dollars, plus interest, plus costs. He owned a building at 6th and Green in the old Jewish section and once a month, on the first of the month exactly, except on Saturdays when it was impossible to get the Jews to pay him because they couldn't touch money on Shabbos, an excuse to get away with an extra day he would have told you if you asked him or even if you hadn't, he would roam the hallways, bent at the waist, banging on the doors and shouting at Mr Pearlstein and Mrs Himmelfarb and Mr Carlkovsky, my great-grandfather Carlkovsky, to come up with the rent or face eviction the very next day. His wanderings through the hall were in the early mornings, too early for his tenants to escape his dreaded monthly knock on the door. And true to his word, those who were late would find the men in their apartments hauling out the mattresses, rolling up the rugs, tossing pots out the window to the street, where they clanged to great effect, clearing the place for a new extended family that had come up with the deposit and first month's rent.

When Josiah Blaine grew too arthritic to march through

the hallways of his slum on Green Street, he sponsored Everett Cox to the bar so he would have someone to collect his rents on the first of the month and to file his confessions of judgment with the court. When Everett Cox, incapacitated by great quantities of alcohol, found himself unable to rise early enough to effectively collect the rents, he hired Samuel Amber as a clerk to do it for him, promising to study him in the law, a promise he was unable to fulfill because of the great quantities of alcohol. But Amber studied on his own and it was finally Josiah Blaine, now over eighty and rapidly losing his mind, who sponsored him before the bar. It was this Amber, of the Bryn Mawr Ambers, though in those early days they were not then of elegant Bryn Mawr but of Fishtown, it was Amber, Lauren Amber Guthrie's great-grandfather Amber, who began to add some semblance of modernity to the office's practice of law. He hired clerks to do the menial labor, he bought drinks for fellow lawyers in the bars surrounding City Hall, he obtained a position with the city from which he was able, for a small percentage to the city solicitor, to shuttle a nice piece of the city's legal work to the firm. Everett Cox insisted that the firm hire his son, Everett Jr, who embezzled city funds, a crime that it cost a considerable amount for Amber to buy his firm out of, but there was now enough work for more clerks and more lawyers and eventually more partners. By the time Josiah Blaine died, mad as a hatter, threatening his nurses with eviction, the offices had moved to the Fidelity Building, a corner suite, and there were eight names on the door.

In the firm's offices now there was a painting, on the frame of which a brass nameplate read JOSIAH BLAINE, FOUNDER. The face in the painting was noble, blue eyed, a ferocious moustache like the elder Holmes, a fine head of hair. It was a face of solidity, of propriety, a founder's face, but it was not the face of Josiah Blaine. Lauren Amber had told me the truth one late night as we lay together in my bed. Her great-grandfather had found the painting among the bric-a-brac of an estate he was administering and thought it projected the proper image.

On an afternoon when our trial was recessed due to a pressing engagement Judge Gimbel had with his dentist, I was sitting in a tapestried wing chair directly under that very painting of Josiah Blaine. The offices of Blaine, Cox, Amber and Cox were not in One Liberty Place but in one of the older, less obtrusive buildings in the city. Blaine, Cox was one of Philadelphia's older, less obtrusive law firms, with well-monied clients and estate lawyers managing the wealth of the city's grandest grandes dames. The firm's two hundred lawyers practiced respectfully, discreet litigation, sensible corporate work. The bankruptcy department was exiled to a lower floor so as not to make the corporate types nervous. There was something so solid in the dark wood paneling, something so white-shoed and blue-blooded, something so foreign to me that I felt as if the fake Josiah Blaine in the painting above my head was staring down at me with those cold blue eyes, demanding my monthly rent, threatening me with eviction if I didn't come through.

'Mr Guthrie will see you now, Mr Carl,' said the receptionist. 'He's sending his secretary up to get you.'

That was the way they did it in the big firms, they sent emissaries for the visitors to summon them into the meetings. I didn't like being summoned, but Guthrie had said he wanted to meet and I had some questions to ask my dear former partner, a cuckold prone to violent rages, questions about his wife, from whom he had separated, and about a man with whom she was cheating while they were still together, a man who now was dead. I was out to find a murderer, so with the afternoon free I had told Ellie to set up the meeting and she had.

When the emissary from on high came I recognized her.

'Hello, Carolyn,' I said. She was a tall African-American, pretty, competent, and an awesome typist. I knew about the typing because she had been our secretary before

Guthrie brought her to Blaine, Cox, along with the files he stole.

'It's good to see you, Mr Carl,' she said as she began to lead me through the wide hallways of her new firm.

'How are they treating you here?'

'They pay us for overtime.'

'Terrific.'

'And we work plenty of overtime.'

I followed Carolyn through winding hallways of wood and secretaries, remarkably busy for seven in the evening. When Carolyn worked for us she was always out the door at 4:58 on the nose. 'I have to catch the train,' she'd say, 'or there's nothing else to get me home at a reasonable hour.' Now, getting paid for overtime, she seemed to have no trouble catching the later West Trenton Local. It's funny what a little thing like time-and-a-half will do to a train schedule.

'Guthrie, you bastard,' I said after Carolyn had led me into his office.

'You look like crap,' he said.

'Thank you.'

'Hey, what are friends for? Sit down, Vic. So this is your first time in my new digs, right? What do you think?'

What I thought was that this was everything I had ever wanted and I resented the hell out of him for it. The big office, the leather couch, the burnished desk, the window overlooking City Hall, the freshly painted walls and fancy phone and computer on his desk for his e-mail. I recognized the painting behind his chair. I pointed at it and said, 'Wasn't that in our offices?'

'As a matter of fact, yes.'

'Excuse me a moment while I call the police. You must have stolen it along with the files.'

He winked. 'I'll messenger it over tomorrow if you want.'

'I want. Along with the files.'

'If only I could, Vic. Truthfully, they've been more

headache than anything else. I'd love to dump them. But the clients all wanted to stick with me. Hell, there's more than enough work here to keep me busy.'

'What about the *Saltz* case?'

'I asked Lou what he wanted to do and he said he thought I was a prick for leaving and to let you have it.'

'He said that?'

'What did I care, it was a dog. But I heard you got a settlement anyway. You guys ever find that accountant?'

'No.'

'And a settlement even so. I should get a part of it, don't you think? After all, I brought it in. A referral fee?'

'Sue me.'

'I don't sue friends, Vic.'

'No, you just screw them in the ass.'

'Still sore, huh?'

'What gives you that idea?' I asked while looking out the window.

'Maybe I can make it up to you?'

'I never figured you for a suicide, Guthrie.'

'So hostile, Vic? Have you considered therapy?'

'I'd rather buy a gun.'

'It was only business. I understand Lizzie is finally hooking up with Community Legal Services.'

Word traveled fast, especially when the word was bad and it was about me. I didn't want to go into the whole sorry mess, especially not with Guthrie. 'It's a consentual thing,' I explained. 'I've been doing more criminal and investment work than she felt comfortable with. When she found they had an opening she decided she would take it.'

'That's terrific for her,' said Guthrie. 'It's where Lizzie belonged all along. And it makes what I wanted to meet with you about easier for everyone. The reason I wanted to get together is that Tom Bismark was asking about you. You know Tom? The managing partner here?'

'I don't think so,' I said, though I did. Not personally, the Tom Bismarks of the city didn't waste their time with second-raters like me, but I had seen him in one of the bars with Jimmy. He had been out with his wife, cheating on his mistress, or so Jimmy had said.

'Tom caught you on the news with this trial of yours, the Jimmy Moore case. How did you get that, anyway?'

'They scoured the city for the most desperate shyster they could find and my name naturally came up.'

'No, really.'

I shrugged. I didn't want him to know that what I had said was the absolute truth.

'Well, he saw you on the news and asked me about you. It seems they're trying to build up their white-collar crime department here and are looking for some laterals with trial experience. I told Tom you'd be terrific.'

'You said that? Why?'

''Cause you're a friend, a buddy.'

'Skip it.'

'It's the truth, Vic, nothing but. I gave him a glowing report and he wants to talk to you about joining the firm.'

'This firm?'

'Of course. After the trial.'

'Why would this firm be interested in me?'

'Frankly, I don't know, Vic. I thought they'd have more sense. But you're in a high-profile case, I lied about your ability, things are just breaking right. Don't let this opportunity slip through your fingers.'

'I'm doing pretty well by myself right now,' I said. 'It wouldn't be so easy to just up and join here. Leases and stuff.'

'Hey, Vic. No pressure. Forget it if you want.' He leaned back at his desk and smiled at me. 'But I know you. You're just like me. This is something you've always wanted, and when it's offered to you you're going to jump for it. Like a show dog. Look at this office, look at the paneling on the lobby walls, paneling an inch thick. Look at what you

347

can be a part of. You're just like me, Vic. You want it. Set up a meeting with Tom after the trial.'

God, how I had hated Guthrie. I had hated his clothes and his shoes and his handsome twisted face and his supercilious manner and his slicked hair and his ability to absorb insults as if they were compliments. The idea of ever again becoming his partner was unthinkable, but now here I was about to be offered a job at his new firm, the job of my dreams. When he said it was something I had always wanted he was right. When he said I would jump at it he was right again. And when he said I was just like him I hated the very idea of it, but I guess, dammit, he was right about that too. Beth could have convinced me otherwise, maybe, but she had gone off to serve the poor and so I was left with becoming Guthrie. God help me.

Although he didn't know it, by reminding me how very alike we were Guthrie was confirming all the more my suspicions about him and Bissonette. I knew how angry I would have become if everything I had gained in a marriage to an Amber was falling from me in an affair between my wife and some broken-down ballplayer, I knew how desperate, how irrationally ruthless, how murderous. And I knew something else, something I had learned with great gusto from my own carnal knowledge of his wife before she was his wife and which was confirmed by Slocum after consulting with Bissonette's little black book. Lauren Amber Guthrie was a five-star in bed, someone almost worth dying for.

'What's really going on between you and Lauren?' I said, steering the subject to where I wanted it. 'I was really saddened to hear about the problems.' I lied, yes, but with sincerity.

'They're only temporary, trust me,' he said, but the way his face fell into a strange, sad cast I knew he was lying too.

'Were you playing around on her, Sam?'

'Jesus, no,' he said quickly. 'It wasn't like that at all.'

'Then what?'

He swiveled in his chair to look out the window. 'It just happened. Come on, Vic, you of all people know what she's like.'

'Which is what?'

He took in a breath of frustration. 'Flighty. Maddeningly independent. With the attention span of a mosquito.'

'So she was cheating on you, was that it?'

'I don't think I want to talk about it, Vic.'

'You don't think your problems with her will affect you here at your firm, do you?'

He didn't answer right off, but I had suspected the answer. Married to an Amber, the partnership decision on him, two or three years hence, was assured. If he was just a Guthrie, with no name, no contacts, nothing but ability, he would be out on his butt within six months. 'We'll work it out,' he said. 'I know we will.'

'Well, at least Bissonette's out of the way, right?'

It was the way he turned and looked at me that said everything I wanted to know. His head swiveled and his eyes were so full of pain and fear. His jaw quivered, his face paled, the sweat on his forehead glistened with an oily sheen. It was on his face as clear as an affidavit. His wife had been screwing Zack Bissonette and he knew it, he knew it, he knew all about it, and the knowledge was killing him. I was ready to bet then and there that it had killed Bissonette, too.

I walked into the courtroom the next morning deeply distracted. It wasn't just that I suspected my former partner of being a murderer. That was almost a pleasant thought. I had no idea of how to prove it, of course, except by talking it over with Lauren, with whom I had already set up a dinner at a far too expensive restaurant, but I figured that when I found out enough I'd simply put Lauren on the stand, have her identify the picture, have her tell about her husband's violent rages, and then stand back and let the jury draw its own conclusions. Afterwards, I'd turn whatever I had over to Slocum and let him do the legwork to clear up the murder charges. But that wasn't all that was on my mind. My distracted air that day arose from the offer that had been magically bestowed upon me.

The night before I had lain in my bed thinking of being at Blaine, Cox. Veronica hadn't called and I hadn't been able to sleep, but I didn't miss her or my sleep that night. I stayed warm into the early hours thinking about my own burnished desk and leather couch, thinking about my visitors waiting for me under the fake portrait of Josiah Blaine, thinking of my name on that letterhead. It was coming, it was coming, late maybe, but coming all the same. I would call Bismark, Tom, now that we would be working side by side, I would call Tom when I had a chance and set up an interview.

'Good morning, Victor,' said Prescott as I set my bag on the table. 'Eggert's putting on an accountant who did work for Citizens for a United Philadelphia today. In a few days it will be the executive director of the committee. We have to be very careful in questioning these witnesses, since CUP is in a very sensitive position. It's almost here as a defendant. I'll handle both examinations.'

'Of course, sir.'

'Fine. And I don't expect you'll be speaking to my client outside my presence again, do you understand?'

'I asked the councilman if he wanted his attorney there and he said no.'

'Do it again and I'll pull your ticket,' he said rather sweetly. 'And don't doubt that I can.'

I set out my notebooks and papers and pads and placed my briefcase underneath the table. When I was set I turned around to scan the audience. Chester was standing in the corner of the courtroom talking with the councilman and Chuckie Lamb. I noticed Leslie Moore and her sister, Renee, seated side by side behind the defense table. There was Herm Finklebaum, the toy king of 44th Street, in the back. And then I saw someone I didn't expect to see at all.

On the aisle, alone, sitting erect, a tall bald man, wearing a very fine suit. I recognized him right off. He was Tom Bismark, managing partner of Blaine, Cox, my new boss to be, here, I assumed, to see me at work. He would be disappointed to find I was asking no questions today, or any day really. I smiled and he smiled back, so I went over to formalize our introduction.

'Mr Bismark, hello. I'm Victor Carl.'

He stood and shook my hand. 'Yes, I know, Victor.' He spoke quite crisply. 'Or is it Vic?'

'Whatever.'

'Sam Guthrie has spoken very highly of you, Vic.'

'Good old Guthrie,' I said. 'If you're here just for the show, I won't be doing much today. We've agreed that Mr Prescott will be handling today's examinations.'

'That's fine,' said Tom Bismark. 'Just fine. That's exactly as Bill and I discussed it.'

'Bill and you? I don't understand.'

'Oh, I'm not here for the show, Vic,' he said. 'I'm working. Blaine, Cox is corporate counsel to CUP. I'm here to make sure the reputation of our client is not besmirched in this trial.'

'I see.'

'I'm certain, Vic, that you'll cooperate in every way possible.'

'Sure, Tom,' I said, and I actually winked. 'Anything I can do, you let me know.'

I sat down at the defense table and started doodling on my yellow pad. So it wasn't just the *Saltz* money, or my fees, or my deal with the Bishop brothers that were at risk. And it wasn't just my prospective directorship on CUP or the councilman's grand dreams of good works, either. A job had been added to the mix, not a job at Talbott, Kittredge, no, that would have been a bit too obvious, but at Blaine, Cox, yes. Stay quiet, smile, stop asking those foolish questions, stop barging in on the councilman's morning *shvitz*, just sit back and let Chet take the rap and the future was mine. I could do that, yes I could. I could play ball, yes I could. Yes I could. May be.

There was something so wrong here, and not just the idea that I was for sale. I knew what I was, knew it in my pained heart: I was small-time. There are those in the world destined to be names, those who might fight their way to near namehood, and those, like myself, who would give it all up for a handful of change. And that's what troubled me here. I wasn't being offered a handful of change, I was being offered everything. The price was far too high. Play ball and your dreams will all come true could only mean that playing ball involved something bigger and dirtier than I could now imagine. Dreams don't come true on the cheap. And it could also only mean that there was an opportunity for me not to play ball. I didn't see it yet, couldn't see any other option but to follow along in court like a lap dog, but it was there, it had to be, or so much pressure would not have been brought to bear. As I drew ferociously on that pad, circles and diamonds and six-cornered stars, I decided then and there to keep looking for answers. See, I could play ball, I could sit back and keep my mouth shut and be the best little cabana boy these pricks had ever seen, but only when I knew all that I would have to kick under the carpet for my lucre. If I had any nobility at all it was this: I would not sell myself short.

38

That very evening I drove through the wilds of Northeast Philadelphia, huge shopping plazas and multiplexes and rows of stores selling pizza and pharmaceuticals and Buster Brown shoes. As I searched for one specific address on Cottman Avenue I passed the Toys 'Я' Us, passed the Herman's World of Sporting Goods, passed the Clover discount store, passed the John Wanamaker's department store. This was the part of the city that looked like every other place in America, strip malls and chain stores, glowing plastic signs held high over the landscape by great metal stanchions. I passed the Northeast High School grounds and then spied the numbers I was looking for and turned left into the lot. It was a low brick building, L-shaped with only one entrance, right in the crook of the L. I drove around the lot a bit, just to get my bearings, and then parked near the entrance. The metal letters bolted into the brick above the door read: ST VINCENT'S HOME FOR THE AGED.

There was a lobby with hospital lobby furnishings, plush orange chairs, bare coffee tables, nondescript prints of flowers on the green walls. Out of that lobby was one door that led inside to the home and in front of that door, behind a counter, was a guard. He wore blue with a cop hat and as I got closer I could see the gun. A large register squatted atop the counter.

'I'm here to visit one of the patients,' I said. 'A Mrs Connie Lamb.'

'Are you family?' asked the guard. His nametag said James P. Strickling. He was an older man, with deep lines of dissatisfaction fanning out from either side of his pinched mouth.

'A friend of the family,' I said.

'After eight I can't let you in unless you're family,' he said.

'I'm sort of a cousin,' I said.

'Well, then, I sort of can't let you in,' he said.

I knew what that meant. I could read it in that dissatisfied face as clear as a tabloid headline. I slipped my wallet from my back pocket and pulled out a twenty. 'I just want to say hello.'

He looked at me.

I pulled out another twenty. 'Just to cheer up the old lady.'

He looked at me.

I opened my wallet wide and stared inside. I pulled out a five and two ones. 'That's all I have.'

'That's not enough,' he said. And then he laughed, a big hearty laugh that shocked me, coming as it was from this dour-faced man behind the counter. 'Take your money back, son. If I could be bought I wouldn't be worthy of this uniform, now would I?'

I took a closer look. It was a private security agency uniform, some sleazy outfit that hired retired guys off the street, gave them a gun, and stuck them behind a booth as fodder should anything go wrong. What I figured, as I embarrassedly picked up my money, was that the uniform wasn't worthy of this Mr Strickling.

He picked up his phone. 'I'll get an attendant, we'll see if a visit's all right.'

While a heavy woman in a nurse's outfit waited for me on the other side of the door, I was required to record my entrance in the register. Strickling checked my driver's license and then pointed out where I should sign. I signed and he filled in the date and time.

'You'll have to sign out, too,' he said. Then he winked. 'Enjoy your visit, Mr Carl.'

I followed the heavy woman down the hallway, past a meeting area with a television on, past a recreation area

354

with men and women sitting in their chairs and playing chess or crocheting or just plain shaking. And there were the rooms, of course, many with their doors open, the residents lying in bed, waiting.

'I'm sure Mrs Lamb will appreciate your visit,' said the woman attendant. 'All she ever sees is her son.'

'He here today?' I asked.

'Not today,' she said.

'Are visitors allowed to stay overnight?' I asked.

'Of course not,' she said, looking at me sideways.

'I didn't think so.'

This is what I had been told by Veronica and Chester both. I had been told that Chuckie Lamb was visiting his mother the night that Bissonette had been beaten to comatosity, that he had stayed overnight because she was especially ill that day, that he had been in the nursing home the whole of the time of the beating. I didn't buy it. Chuckie didn't seem the type to care that much. And did I mention the smell? It was a medley of favorites: cat piss and overcooked string beans and the sharp scent of the alcohol swab they give you before they prick you at the doctor's. I couldn't see Chuckie spending more than five minutes at a time in that smell.

'Mrs Lamb,' said the attendant in a loud voice, leaning over the bed once we were inside her private room. Chuckie Lamb, the dutiful son, had sprung for the best. There were flowers in a vase and nice curtains and on a table was a boom box and a stack of cassettes, opera. 'Mrs Lamb. You have a visitor.' She straightened up, smiled at me, and stood by the door while I approached the bed.

Mrs Lamb stared past me, up at the ceiling, her gums working one against the other, her eyes darting back and forth, back and forth, not seeing me in their journeys back and forth. She was a small, toad-faced woman, shriveled, her skin, even with its deep cracks, tight against her face.

'Hello, Aunt Connie,' I said.

Just the gums worked in response to my greeting.

'She likes it if you hold her hand,' said the attendant.

It sat atop her sheet like a withered claw. I leaned over and touched it, barely able to hide my revulsion. 'You look good, Aunt Connie.'

Just the gums working. She seemed as delighted to have her hand held by me as I was to hold it. I had wanted to ask her some questions, see if I could get anything definitive from her about her son's alibi, but I wouldn't get it out of that face, those lips, those god-awful gums.

'Doesn't say much, does she?' I said when we were out of there.

'Not anymore,' said the attendant. 'Your aunt's been very sick. There were times we didn't think she'd make it, but she's stronger than she looks.'

'When she gets seriously ill, is it possible then for a visitor to stay over?' I asked.

She didn't stop walking me back to the lobby as she spoke. 'If we believe the end might be imminent, and there is a private room, then sometimes we let immediate family stay. But no nephews, Mr Carl, just spouses, siblings, or children.'

'Does cousin Chuckie come often?' I asked.

'All the time,' she said with a smile. 'He's a very devoted son. I'll be sure to let him know you were here.'

'That's not necessary,' I said. 'We're not so close anymore.'

'I can't do that, Mr Carl,' said Strickling when I had been deposited back outside into that lobby. 'Those books are private records.'

'But it's very important,' I said, reaching again for my wallet and then stopping when he shook his head. 'Listen, Mr Strickling. I'll level with you. I'm a lawyer.'

'Well in that case . . .' said Strickling, laughing at me.

Being a lawyer might have meant something at some time, but not anymore. I knew I was in trouble when I was forced to resort to the truth. 'I'm representing a man accused of a murder, Mr Strickling, a murder I think Mr

Lamb might be involved in. He says he was here overnight the night of the murder. I just want to check it out.'

'Oh, right. I seen you on TV,' said Strickling. 'You're representing Councilman Moore.'

'His aide, actually. I just want to know if Chuckie was here the night Zack Bissonette was beaten into a coma.'

'I saw Bissonette play down at the Vet,' said Strickling. 'What a bum. I remember once, ninth inning of a tie ball game, slow bounder to second, the guy kicks it. He kicks it. Like he thought he was playing soccer. Two runs scored.' He took a deep breath. 'Well, seeing as you were on TV and all, what's that date again?'

That was it, I guess. Lawyers were as nothing in the new scheme of things, as were scholars and doctors and businessmen. But have your face flashed for a few seconds on TV and all of a sudden you were somebody to be trusted, to be revered, someone to do favors for. I gave him the date and he searched below the counter for the applicable register. With a heave he lifted it up and turned it around to let me look. There it was, Chuckie's signature going in at 9:37 p.m. the night of the murder and not leaving until 6:45 the next morning.

'Could this have been faked?' I asked.

'No, sir,' said Strickling. 'In fact, I signed him out. That's my writing there. I was on the late shift. So I can tell you for a fact he didn't leave between midnight and six-forty-five.'

'Any other exits?' I asked.

'Just emergency exits, and alarms go off if they're used. We've had some thefts and we have lots of drugs here, so we're pretty careful.'

'And that's his signature?'

He turned the book around and looked. Then he opened the most recent register to a few days back. There was Chuckie's signature signing in and out. It was the same.

So that was it. I shrugged at Strickling and he smiled at me and wished me a good night. I left the lobby and stood outside at the entrance and thought a bit. I believed the registers because I believed Strickling. He had two jobs at that place, to carry a gun and to keep the registers, and Strickling would do both jobs with an integrity I could only admire, not match. So Chuckie Lamb hadn't been threatening me because he had killed Zack Bissonette. Maybe he had ended up with part of the quarter of a million and was trying to protect his stake, as likely a possibility as any, Chuckie the thief. But he wasn't Chuckie the killer. Too bad, too, because I would have liked nothing better than to nail Chuckie Lamb for murder. Well, maybe one thing would be better: nailing that bastard Guthrie.

39

I was in my office, working late revising my opinion letters to be appended to the Bishop brothers' prospectus for Valley Hunt Estates, when the phone rang. I didn't have time to answer, I was already late for my dinner date with Lauren Amber Guthrie, but thinking it might be Veronica wanting to change our plans for later in the evening, I picked up the receiver and said, 'Victor Carl.'

It wasn't Veronica.

'Victor. I need to talk with you. It is extremely urgent.'

From the soft, rounded tones, from the precise pronunciation, from the lockjawed superiority of the voice, I knew who it was.

'I don't have time to speak to you now, Mr Osbourne.'

'You took my car, Victor. My father's Duesenberg. I must have it back.'

'It was lawfully seized by the sheriff, Mr Osbourne. There are papers you can file if you believe the judgment we have against you is improper. Otherwise it is going to be sold.'

'My car, Victor. It is a classic, the only memento I have left of a more glorious time.'

'If you want, Mr Osbourne, you can have your daughter bid for it at the auction.'

'After having the police stomp through her property she has refused to help me any further. I have offered you all the money I have. Victor, you must stop this harassment. You simply must. You don't know what you are doing to me. I have prospects, grand prospects, but you are ruining them. You are making me feel like a hunted animal. I am not an animal, Victor.'

'We need to sell the car, Mr Osbourne.'

'Have you no compassion? I'm a man, Victor. If you prick me, do I not bleed?'

'I believe that is my line,' I said flatly.

'If you poison me, do I not die?'

'I'm not trying to hurt you, Mr Osbourne. Make me a final settlement offer in writing and mail it to me and whatever it is, no matter how low, I will urge Mr Sussman to accept it. I promise.'

'If you wrong me, shall I not revenge?'

'Good-bye, Mr Osbourne. I have to go,' I said, and then I hung up the phone.

It rang immediately afterwards, but I didn't pick it up again. Since learning from the Bishops that Winston Osbourne was an old school chum of William Prescott's, I hadn't enjoyed my moments with him as I had in the past. I think it was the grayness of it all that did it. The dun-colored skies of that bleak autumn, the haziness of my own prickly moral dilemmas, of my own twisted arrangements with Prescott, it had all turned the crisp blacks and whites of the world into a muddle. Things just weren't as simple as I had pretended them to be when I sat down with Winston Osbourne's wife and destroyed his life. Though at that moment, with the phone tolling on my desk, I didn't want to judge myself for what I had done in the now-distant past, I couldn't help but know I had done something deep within the gray. And I couldn't help but sympathize with Osbourne's plight and his attempts to maintain his position in the club that I was still desperate to join. Whatever it was that was working its way through my spine and into the recesses of my intellect, I found I could no longer gleefully despise him. I would indeed call my uncle Sammy. I would tell him the whole situation. I would advise him to leave it at the car, to cash in the Duesenberg, and then mark the note as satisfied. My uncle Sammy, surprisingly, was what Morris would have called a *mensch*. He would do it if I asked him, and I

360

would ask him. I would let Winston Osbourne off the hook.

Lauren was waiting for me at Restaurant Tacquet, a small bistro nestled in a Victorian hotel smack in the middle of the Main Line. It was suburban chic, large bay windows, almond and blue walls with a stenciled border, pale green ceilings. Charmingly informal and gallingly expensive, it was a very in place for the horsey set, just down the road from the Devon Horse Show grounds. Lauren sat at a trapezoid table by one of the windows. Beside her on the table were long fuchsia flowers in a narrow black vase. She had ordered a red wine and was deep into the bottle already by the time I showed up.

'I was afraid you were going to stand me up, Victor,' she said in her soft, breathless voice, reaching out her braceleted arm, fingers pointing down for me to take hold of. 'I was feeling like one of those sad blue-haired ladies who dine alone each night, as if I had jumped into my future. It was too horrible to bear, so I ordered some wine.'

'Chateau Lafite Rothschild, 1984,' I read from the label.

'Appropriate, no? Pour yourself a glass and we'll toast.'

I did as I was told.

'To the renewal of our . . . Well, to the renewal of our whatever,' she said with a gay laugh.

We clinked glasses and I took a sip. True to its name, it was rich and powerful and slightly exotic. I let it linger on the back of my tongue for a moment before I swallowed and took another mouthful right away. Even with my Rolling Rock palate I could tell it was magnificent.

'So how is your friend Beth doing these days?' she asked.

'Fine,' I said, content to leave it at that, and as far as I knew she was. It was I who was missing her terribly. We still hadn't talked since she walked out on me from that witness room. But her office now was sadly empty of all her personal effects. Just a file cabinet and a desk and a wastepaper basket.

'It's too bad about Alberto.' The 'r' rolled lightly off her tongue.

'What happened?' I asked.

'She dropped him. It looked like things were going so well and she just up and ended it. And no one knows why. Poor Alberto was devastated. It appears he was in love. He's a very serious young man but apparently your Beth made him laugh.'

'She has that talent.'

'A simple thing like that and Alberto was lost. If I had known that was all it took, I would have learned to tell a joke.'

'You do all right.'

'But not with the serious ones. I could never have gotten Alberto to laugh.' Lauren stared at me and twisted her head slightly, giving me the impression her eyes were boring into mine. 'I could never get you to laugh much either. But I'm still willing to try.'

I broke the moment by dropping my gaze and taking a sip of wine and then another. 'Actually, Lauren, I'm here on business.'

'Please, no. Victor. Don't tell me you are only wooing me as a client. Do you do divorce work now? All right, darling, you can represent me, but only if you promise to forget all about that silly old precept against sleeping with your clients.'

'That would be against the code of ethics.'

'Which would make it all the more fun, no? The best sex is always surreptitious. If nothing else, marriage has taught me that.'

'I don't do divorce work.'

'Good. I've already hired Cassandra. She's a tiger, I hear.'

'Guthrie deserves something for his years with you, don't you think?'

'I let him sleep in my bed for a good part of the time, Victor. What more could he want?'

'Money.'

'Don't be vulgar. Besides, Cassandra says we have a case.'

'Was he cheating on you?'

'Men don't cheat on me, dear.'

'So it was the violence.'

'Something like that.'

'How violent is he? I was just wondering, you know. What exactly do you think Guthrie is capable of?'

'That's the second time you asked about Sam's violent tendencies.' She looked at me with a touch of appraising coldness in her blue eyes. 'I'm beginning to see a pattern.'

Lauren was a lot of things, dissolute, depraved, dissipated, but she was far from stupid. If not born with the twin handicaps of being very rich and very pretty there is no telling what she could have accomplished.

The waiter came over to our table before Lauren could say what was on her mind. His accent was French but I suspected it was fake. Lauren ordered the mixed greens and a fish. I ordered lobster ravioli in a vodka cream sauce and a *steak au poivre*. She ordered more wine. When the waiter left, Lauren sat back in her chair, crossed her arms, and frowned at me.

'Frankly, I'm insulted, Victor. Pumping me for information like I was a common street tart.'

'I could never accuse you of being common.'

'Sweet boy. How did you find out about Zack?'

'He took a picture,' I said. 'From a remote-controlled camera, I think. The police have it, along with scores of others.'

'It's a good likeness of me, I hope.'

'Actually, no. The camera was up high. The picture is only of your back.'

'But you recognized me anyway. How encouraging.'

'It was the bracelets,' I said, indicating the diamond studded, rune engraved gold bracelets that lay spectacularly on her delicate forearm. 'And a certain way you grabbed at his balls.'

'Darling of you to remember, Victor. You told the police, of course, who the unidentified figure was.'

'No, I didn't,' I lied.

'My Galahad.'

'I just want to know what happened,' I said.

'You just want to know if my taste for beefcake had something to do with the beefcake's murder, is that it? You want to know if my husband killed him, is that it? Because if it is my husband, then your grubby little politico client might just get off, is that it?'

'That's it,' I said.

'Once again, Victor, the girl from Bryn Mawr is going to disappoint you. Pour me some wine, please.'

I poured her the wine from a new bottle the waiter had brought. She drank it quickly, too quickly for its price. She was still drinking it when the salad and ravioli arrived. My ravioli were light and radiant. I sopped up the dregs of the cream sauce with thickly buttered bread. I could feel my arteries clench. Lauren merely picked at her greens between deep drafts from her wineglass.

'How much do you want to know?'

'As much as you want to tell me.'

'Wonderful. We won't discuss it at all.'

I shook my head and she reached out a hand and cupped my chin.

'All right then, I'll tell you everything. It was at that vile little club he put his name on. We went there now and then. Guthrie had run off to the bathroom. He was always running off to the bathroom. They don't make men with bladders anymore, Victor. It's true. All the good bladders are gone. While he was away Zack came over and asked if everything was satisfactory. He asked it with a smile that I recognized from my own mirror. So I told him no. Which was the truth, Victor. I had married Sam with the best intentions. My little piece of rebellion. I mean, he wasn't a Biddle or a Pepper, but then he wasn't anything scandalous either.'

'Like a Jew,' I said.

'Maybe you should go to the men's room and straighten yourself, Victor. Your chip is showing.' She smiled at me, a broad, cold smile. 'My intentions with Sam were always honorable, but things simply weren't working out. I had thought him insouciant at first. But that was an act. Underneath he is very earnest. I don't like earnest, do you?'

'That's not how I think of Guthrie.'

'Marry him and find out. A very perspirable, very earnest young man. We should have lived together first. I would never have made such a mistake. But Mother wouldn't have it. So instead I married him and found myself sadly disappointed. I began to dally. Discreetly, while he was at the office. Just minor bits of fun here and there. Decidedly dry, decidedly unearnest fun. So when this very handsome, very well-built man asked me if I was satisfied, I said no. He had the most marvelous apartment, a real bachelor pad. All kinds of wonderful toys.'

'I saw them.'

'Yes, I suppose you did. We had a wonderful few afternoons together.' She laughed in spite of herself.

'How did Sam find out?'

'Oh, so you know that too. A detective, hired by my earnest husband to discover if I was cheating on him.'

'And when he found out he went apeshit,' I said.

'What a pleasant term. Yes, he went apeshit. He hit me in the face with the back of his hand, knocked me clear over the bed. I had a perfectly beautiful bruise. I must tell you, Victor, it was the most passionate I had ever seen him. What a night we had.'

'And then he went off to find Bissonette.'

'No, Victor, I'm sorry.'

'Yes, he did. You're protecting him now.'

'No.'

'How can you be sure?'

'By the time Sam got the report I was already through with Zack. He had broken it off, actually. Some foolishness

365

about being in love. No, after Zack there was my personal trainer and then a heating contractor, working on our pipes, and then a florist, a sweet Englishwoman named Fiona, and they were all listed in the report too. And they're still very much alive. By the time Zack was beaten we were in the middle of an earnest but ultimately futile reconciliation. So you see, Victor, it wasn't Sam after all.'

I didn't respond. Instead I sort of grunted with disappointment. The waiters whisked away our appetizer plates and brought our main courses. My steak, thick filets in a deep brown pepper sauce, seemed too much to eat just then.

'Suddenly,' I said, 'I'm not hungry.'

'Doggie bags are such bad form, Victor. Eat. You look a little peaked. But I must say it is charming that you think me worth a homicide.'

She smiled at me, her impossibly wide, sexy smile, but then it withered into something arctic.

'But it wasn't me you thought he would kill for, was it, Victor? It was the name, it was the money, it was the slot at the family firm. You're a monster, do you know that? Both of you bastards. You belong together. At least poor dead Zack was honest. All he wanted from me was my body.'

I dropped my gaze down and saw my steak sitting there, charred and thick in its sauce, malignant with peppercorns. I cut into the meat. It was blood-red inside and I realized I was more than not hungry. I was nauseous, lost. I was adrift without a clue.

Someone was lying about killing Bissonette: Enrico Raffaello lying to throw us off the scent, or Jimmy Moore lying to save his political career, or Lauren lying in one last gallant gesture to her soon-to-be-former husband. Or maybe no one was lying. Maybe the murderer was someone else, a jealous husband I hadn't yet stumbled upon. Or Norvel Goodwin, threatening me off the case to try to keep his drug-related murder of Zack Bissonette a secret.

It could be anyone or no one, as far as I was concerned, because all my hunches had been all wrong and I had no more hunches to follow. Prescott would have his way with his cabana boy after all and there was nothing I could do about it.

'Excuse me,' I said to Lauren as she sadly separated the flakes of her trout with her fork and I rose to go to the men's room. But once I reached the glass-enclosed bar, instead of turning right and heading into the hotel lobby, where the lounges were, I turned left, out the door, down the ramp, out and across the side street to the parking lot and into my car. I could see Lauren's back through that bay window. So what if I stuck her with the check, she could afford it. I had someplace I had to be. Lancaster Avenue to City Line Avenue to the Schuylkill Expressway to 1–676 to Race Street into Olde City and the converted sugar refinery and the loft bed where something golden awaited me and where, like a convict leaping the fence, I could escape from my life.

40

Veronica is waiting for me, naked, languid in her bed, legs slung carelessly about a twisted sheet, arms resting on a pillow above her head, breasts leaning on either side of her narrow chest. Her hair is wild, tangled, the room smells of her, it smells of deer in suburban forests, of raccoons. She doesn't turn her head to look at me as I stand over her bed, staring at her, overcome.

'You took so long to get here,' she says.

'You shouldn't leave your door unlocked.'

'How did you get in the building?'

'An old lady with grocery bags.'

'You took so long to get here I started without you.'

'It looks like you finished, too.'

'It is never finished.'

I undress hurriedly, like a schoolboy at the pool while others are already splashing. I yank off my shoes without untying them, my pants end in a pile. A sock lies limply against the leg of her bed. A button pops as I fumble with my shirt. With her I feel young and clumsy, competent only as long as she tells me what to do. I want her to watch me undress, but her head is turned away, she is lost somewhere. Wherever she is is where I want to be.

'Mr Lee, what is your position?' asked Eggert from behind the courtroom podium.

'Executive Director of Citizens for a United Philadelphia.'

'And what exactly is Citizens for a United Philadelphia?'

'We are a political action committee. We collect funds and then support political candidates we feel have the best chance of ensuring that Philadelphia prospers and that this prosperity is shared by all members of the Philadelphia community, not just the privileged few. We also spend money organizing community groups and on voter registration drives, not to mention our prime charitable project, the Nadine Moore Youth Centers, providing full-time drug rehabilitation for troubled teens.'

'Is your organization connected with Councilman Moore?'

'The councilman is chairman of our board of directors.'

'And Mr Concannon?'

'Mr Concannon is also on our board.'

'And have you supported Councilman Moore in his previous elections?'

'The councilman is exactly the type of public servant we are looking for, a forward thinker who is determined not to let anyone get left behind.'

'Yes, I see,' said Eggert. 'Are you aware of any plans of the councilman's to run for mayor?'

'We have asked him to run.'

'We?'

'The board of the committee.'

'On which the councilman sits?'

'Yes, but he abstained from the formal vote. There is a lot to be done in this city and we believe he is the one to do it. The youth centers are just the start of his plans.'

'Has the committee been raising money for the councilman's mayoral campaign?'

'Yes, and we have been surprisingly successful. The support out there is way beyond what we had expected. There is a great excitement citywide for the councilman.'

'How much have you raised so far?'

'Over two million dollars.'

'Was Mr Ruffing a contributor?'

'Oh yes, a very generous contributor.'

'How much did he contribute?'

'That is confidential, sir.'

'I ask the court,' said Eggert, 'to instruct the witness to answer the question.'

'Answer the question,' growled Judge Gimbel.

'But, sir, that is precisely the type of question I can't answer and be faithful to my duty to our contributors.'

'Answer the question, Mr Lee,' said the judge, 'or you will go to jail.'

'Two hundred and fifty thousand dollars.'

'Not five hundred thousand dollars?' asked Eggert.

'No, sir, two hundred and fifty thousand dollars.'

'Did you ever receive any cash contributions?'

'Never. We made it a policy never to accept cash. In fact, the councilman insisted on that. Everything had to be by check, everything had to be on the straight and narrow.'

'How did you get Mr Ruffing's check each month?'

'Mr Concannon brought it over.'

'You mean the defendant Concannon.'

'Yes, the man sitting right over there.'

'Did he ever bring you cash from Mr Ruffing, too?'

'Never.'

When I slip beside her she turns from me, showing me her back, long and slender, the vertebrae marching with precision down the shallow valley. I reach over and take hold of her breast and bite the lobe of her ear. She stretches like a house cat and snuggles back until her buttocks are spooned against my groin. She twists to make herself comfortable and lets out a soft purr. Her arms are still above her head. I brush her hair away from her neck, it smells wild, abandoned. It is a mustang's mane. I kiss her there, on the wild-smelling neck, soft oyster kisses, wetting the down on the nape. It quivers beneath my tongue, turns febrile. I rub her nipple between my fingers, it swells slowly, like a bruise, as I rub. I squeeze harder. She shifts her position once again. Her nipple grows hard as a tack, my fingers hurt, I squeeze harder. Her neck rears and I begin to suck at its side. She reaches

*down between her legs and takes hold of me and squeezes. She
is wearing a ring, the metal bites into my flesh. I suck harder
at her neck, I play with her skin between my teeth. She yanks
her neck away.*

'You'll leave a mark,' she says.

'Let go of me.'

'No.'

*I grab her hair and again pull it away from her neck and
bite at her back. She locks her legs behind mine and squeezes
harder. I take hold of her ankle. We are shackled together, like
prisoners, chained together like lifers at a slag heap. I pull her
leg back, she breathes in sharply and then squeezes hard. I can
feel myself deflate.*

*'You let go and I'll let go,' I mumble through teeth still in
her neck.*

'I don't want you to let go,' she says.

*So I immediately open my teeth, let go of her ankle, release
her nipple from between my fingers.*

*'No,' she says with a disappointed shrug, even as she pulls
her knee up to her chest, turns toward me, curls into a
ball, and, without ever letting go, places me, bruised, deflated,
lolling, places me into her mouth. As before a judge, I
rise.*

'Now, Mr Petrocelli, what were you doing on Delaware
Avenue the night of the fire at Bissonette's?' asked Eggert.

'Sleeping in my cab.'

'Why were you sleeping in your cab on Delaware
Avenue?'

'I was tired. It's a long shift.'

'And when did you wake up?'

'About five in the morning, when I heard the sirens.'

'What were the sirens from, do you know?'

'The fire trucks.'

'Where were the fire trucks going?'

'To the fire.'

'Where was the fire, Mr Petrocelli?'

'At that club.'

'Bissonette's?'

'That's it, yeah.'

'Now, when did you fall asleep, Mr Petrocelli?'

'About an hour earlier.'

'That would be four in the morning?'

'Something like that, yeah.'

'It's not unusual for you to catch a nap on Delaware Avenue at four in the morning, is it, Mr Petrocelli?'

'It's a long shift.'

'Just before you went to sleep at four o'clock in the morning, tell the jurors what you saw that night, Mr Petrocelli.'

'I saw the car.'

'Where did you see the car?'

'It was leaving from behind the club.'

'Bissonette's?'

'Like I said, yeah. It flashed its brights at me as it came out.'

'What kind of car was it, Mr Petrocelli?'

'I got a good look at it under the streetlights there.'

'What kind of car was it, Mr Petrocelli?'

'I couldn't help but notice it.'

'What kind of car was it, Mr Petrocelli?'

'It was a black limousine.'

Her mouth is silk, her tongue, her soft lips thick with passion. I run my hands through the tangles in her hair, the strands are thick, greasy. I am on my back, she is on her knees, crouching over me, her hair spilling down, obscuring her face. She is working, like a squirrel over a nut she is working. Her legs, smooth as felt, rub against my legs. Her head bobs in her work. My hands in her hair, over her ears, I pull her off and up so that she is stretched over me. The smell of game is in the air, quail. As I kiss her I taste my own saltiness. We lay like that, her stretched out on top of me, kissing gently, sweetly, passing the saltiness back and forth, suspended as in a hanging prism, but

*even as our mouths lay upon each other just as gently, even as
our tongues dance about each other just as sweetly, like waltzers
floating arm in arm across a wooden floor, even as we try to hold
on to the moment our bodies are picking up the tempo, her hands
pressing into my side, my grip on the thick muscles of her thigh,
her foot, toes splayed, pressing down on my own, my knee, her
knee, my teeth, her hip. I grab her tight and spin around and
she is beneath me now, reaching for me. I pull my hips away,
away from her gropes, and drag my tongue down from her neck,
between her breasts, down.*

'And what did your investigation of the fire find, Inspector
Flanagan?' asked Eggert.

'A hot spot in the basement, just underneath the bar
area.'

'What exactly is a hot spot?'

'It's a place where there is damage beyond that which
we would expect to see from a normally spreading fire.
The hot spot is where the fire started.'

'What kind of damage did you find to indicate this was
a hot spot?'

'Well, in this basement, for example, there were pots
and pans being stored, metal racks, cans of food, that
sort of thing. A normal fire, there maybe would have
been some damage, but since a normal fire rises, not
as much as we found. There was an area down in the
basement where certain metal objects had just melted, not
charred at all, just melted, as if they were made of clay
and someone had stepped on them. You wouldn't see that
as part of a normal fire. And the lower walls of the basement were singed. A regular fire goes up, a fire set with
chemicals spreads out and down, which is what this looked
like.'

'Did you perform a chemical analysis in the basement?'

'Yes, sir.'

'And what did you find?'

'There were trace elements consistent with a great deal of kerosene being burned in the basement. We checked with Mr Ruffing and he stated that there was a small amount of kerosene kept in the basement, but not a sufficient amount to have left the quantity of trace elements we found.'

'Why would a fire in the basement burn the whole building, isn't the basement floor cement?'

'Actually, yes, it was, but the walls were wooden and, more importantly, the joists in the basement were all wood. Once the joists catch the entire foundation is weakened and most likely the building will collapse.'

'Is that in fact what happened to Bissonette's?'

'Yes.'

'Did you, in the course of your investigation, come to a conclusion as to when the fire started?'

'Based on the evidence, as we could best put it together, it started sometime between three and four-thirty in the morning. It wasn't called in until ten to five.'

'Did you come to a conclusion as to how this fire was started, Inspector?'

'Yes, we did.'

'And what was that conclusion, sir?'

'Arson.'

She tastes of prairie dogs and coyotes, angry, taut and electric, oily, ancient, of something untamed and dangerous. Salt pork. Beneath me she quivers, she howls, soft, ominous, inhuman. I am biting into the flesh of a live snake. She digs her thumbs into my biceps, her heels kick at the small of my back. I fight to maintain control, first with my tongue, spelling out mysterious words in dead languages, then my arms, straining as they grab at her clavicles, her neck. My head leaps forward and like a wrestler I am on her, pinning her arms, my face pressing into hers. We breathe together in the struggle, hot wetness passing from her lungs to mine and back again. I slip an arm around her body and flip her over. Her legs

*tangle about themselves as she spins. With my arm I sweep
her knees to her chest and then I am atop her, one arm across
her breasts, the other hand grabbing tight at her elbow. I
spin around her from one side to the other. I am in a classic
riding position. Two points for the takedown. She tries to lift
up with her arms and I break her down. She growls when
I enter her. Our rhythms are in opposition. There is thickness
there, resistance, despite my ferocity I drop into her slowly
and a force in opposition rises as I pull back. She straightens
her legs and suddenly I fly into the air, lost for an instant,
then we are back to the slow insistent pounding. I fall on top
of her and bite her shoulder. She takes my hand and starts
to suck at my fingers. It accelerates, the pounding, the breaths.
I am igniting atop her. She straightens her legs and I fly once
more through the air, ungrounded, untethered, suspended, lost
somewhere above the unceasing Colorado.*

'And what did Chester Concannon say then, Mr Grouse?'
asked Eggert.

'He said some of the city's finest citizens had already
contributed to the committee, this CUP. I asked him
who.'

'Did he give you names?'

'Yes, sir. He rattled off a whole list of prominent
businesspersons. It was a very impressive list.'

'Did you agree then to make the contribution?'

'Well, no, not really. I'm a Republican, you see.'

'What did the defendant Mr Concannon say then?'

'He mentioned a few other contributors, including Mr
Ruffing.'

'Did you know Mr Ruffing?'

'Oh, yes. We worked on a development deal in Hatboro-
Horsham once. His place had just burned down and I told
him that it was a terrible shame what happened.'

'What did Mr Concannon say then?'

'He told me that, yes, it was a great shame. And then
he said, and I remember because it gave me chills, he said

it was a great shame but that Mr Ruffing had fallen behind in his contributions to the committee.'

'What did you do then, Mr Grouse?'

'Then and there, Mr Eggert, then and there I wrote out a five-thousand-dollar check to CUP.'

I lay beside her now, my legs stretched, my arms resting on a pillow above my head. The sweet cloak of sleep slips across my brain and my head turns to the side. There is a sharpness to the room, it is hot, moist, it smells like the Carnivora house at the zoo. I want to sleep, I don't have much time, I know, before I will be evicted, but with her leg tossed carelessly over mine, I want to sleep.

'Let's try something,' she says.

'Too tired,' I mumble. 'I'm exhausted.'

'But that's the point. To get so exhausted that everything else disappears, until it all fades silently away and nothing matters but the fading away.'

'I'm there.'

'I'm not.'

'Let me sleep.'

'I can still hear the traffic, I still know my name.'

'Veronica.'

'Yes, that's it.'

'Let me sleep, please. Just a minute.'

'Yes, sweetheart.'

'I love you,' I say as I slip away into a shifting dreamy thickness. She curls her head on my chest and brings up a knee to rest on my hip and I smell the wilderness in her hair. The slight weight of her body presses me down and I slip beneath her unbridled scent and drift and I know with a searing certainty that the nugget is real and I do love her and I want her with a gnawing pain and she will never be there for me and I love her and there is nothing I can do about it because I am asleep and dreaming.

*   *   *

'Your Honor,' said Eggert, standing erect, his voice infused with satisfaction. 'Ladies and gentlemen of the jury. The prosecution rests.'

41

THE LAW OFFICES OF ANTHONY BOLOGNESE, P.C. was printed in gold letters above a rendering of the scales of justice on the plate glass window of the storefront at 15th and Pine. The lights were off in the front waiting area, but I could see a glimmer of light traveling from the back part of the office, through a hallway, spreading like an invitation into the waiting room. I switched the heavy plastic bag from my right hand to my left and buzzed the buzzer. When nothing happened I buzzed it again and again. I kept buzzing it until the light widened in the waiting area and Tony Baloney, stuffing his shirt into his pants with one hand and leaning on a cane with the other, came limping along the very same path that the light had traveled. At the window he peered out at me.

'We're closed,' he shouted. 'What do you want?'

'We have to talk,' I shouted back.

He looked at his watch. 'It's after eleven. We're closed. Who are you, anyway?'

'Victor Carl.'

He cocked his head to give me what looked like an evil eye and then twisted open the lock on the door.

Tony Baloney was a tall man with the face of a walrus, the belly of a bear, and the tiny feet of a ferret. His outsized suit pants were cinched to his stomach by a thin belt, his pink shirt open at the collar without a tie.

'That's right,' he said. 'I recognize you now from the evening news.' He glanced at his office and stroked his thick mustache. 'My apologies, but we're closed. Whatever it is, we can discuss it at length in the morning.'

'We'll talk about it now,' I said as I marched past him and started down the hallway to his office.

'Wait, Victor. Stop,' he said as he rumbled after me as quickly as his leg would allow. He grabbed an arm and said, 'What the hell are you doing?' but I shrugged it off and kept going.

The hallway was lined with legal books, *Pennsylvania Digests*, *Federal Reporters*, fully updated, I was sure, with pocket parts right in place because Tony, I was sure, took in enough cash up front to keep his books current. Past the hallway was a partly open door, through which the light had been streaming. I pushed it open and found myself in Tony Baloney's office.

It was big and rather simple, with a white couch and a huge desk. Bookshelves climbed halfway up the wall, filled with even more legal tomes, digests, hornbooks, compilations of decisions by ancient British courts. Between the books on one wall was a television set. The rest of the walls were painted blue and covered with artwork, good stuff, too, by the looks of it, colorful abstracts and bright impressionistic oils. No doggies playing poker on Tony Baloney's walls. And then, so motionless I almost missed her, sitting on the couch was a startlingly beautiful woman, dark and small, in a tight white dress, her legs crossed and the veins in her dangling foot pulsing out of a white high heel.

Tony finally made his way back into his office. 'What in fucking hell is going on, Carl?' he said between gasps.

'I thought your client was going to be a good boy.'

'Who? The landlord? Giamoticos?'

'That's right,' I said. 'Well, Spiros flunked his probation.'

'What are we talking about?'

I took the plastic bag over to the desk, littered with stacks of papers and files, and dumped its contents onto the desktop.

'God, man,' shouted Tony. 'Jesus Christ. Now what did you have to go and do that for?'

What lay now on Tony Baloney's desk was a dachshund, Oscar I think its name was, owned by a woman in my building, the dog chocolate brown and very dead, its neck snapped, its belly slit open, its intestines oozing out like thick glossy eels. I had found him on my doorstep that night when I had straggled home after an evening with the Bishops and knew immediately from where he had come. Veronica's landlord, Spiros Giamoticos. He must have picked my name off the motion I filed and was trying to scare me off from helping Veronica. I thought old Tony should see firsthand the crap his client was pulling. From out of the dog's entrails a dark viscous liquid was puddling over Tony's papers.

I looked over at the woman on the couch, wondering if I had gone too far, but she wasn't screaming, she wasn't even flinching. A smile appeared on her dark pretty face and between her painted lips I could just glimpse an array of twisted brown teeth. Her smile was scarier than the dead dog. I turned away from her as soon as I saw it.

'Giamoticos left this for me on my doorstep,' I said.

'On *your* step?' asked Tony.

'That's right,' I said. 'You were going to keep him under control, remember? You vouched for him, remember?'

He looked at me closely, like he was looking for something, then he loosed a sharp, quick stream of Spanish and the woman on the couch stood up and walked out the door. On her way out she grabbed hold of the bottom of her dress and yanked it down.

'A client,' said Tony Baloney with a shrug. ' "So lust, though to a radiant angel linked, will sate itself in a celestial bed, and prey on garbage." Hamlet's ghost.'

'Cut with the quotes,' I said.

'Look, take a seat.' He gestured to the couch.

'I'll stand,' I said.

'Well, I'll sit, if that's all right,' he said, dropping onto the couch. He carefully leaned his cane beside him. 'These late-night conferences consume much of a man. Now, how shall we clean up that mess?' He casually gestured at his desk, as if a carcass lying on its top was not an unusual sight.

I held out the plastic bag still in my hand and dropped it onto the floor. 'Use this if you like.'

'No, you'll clean my desk, Victor,' he said.

'Not in this life,' I said. 'Do something about Giamoticos and make sure it sticks.'

'You know, this whole sorry chain of events, Victor, is putting me in a difficult position. There are attorney-client considerations that are putting me in a very difficult position. Not to mention my obligations to the bar. Come on. Sit down.'

I remained standing. 'What are you going to do to stop Giamoticos?'

'I shouldn't have taken the case,' he said as if to no one in particular. 'My daughter calls me and right off I know what the story is. And it's just getting more complicated.' He raised his head to me. 'You're an esteemed member of the bar, Victor. Let's do a hypothetical.'

'I'm not here to play law student.'

'Humor me,' he said. 'A simple hypothetical, like in the ethics exam we all cheated on. Let's say, hypothetically speaking, we are representing a client accused of doing something deeply nefarious.'

'Like a Greek accused of killing cats.'

He pointed at me like I had guessed a word in charades. 'Exactly so. Hypothetically, of course. And we also have another client who has nothing to do with the first. And this other client tells us, with the full protection of the attorney-client privilege, that he does as a practice what the first client is wrongly accused of doing. See where I'm going here?'

'Not exactly,' I said.

'Been feeling a bit sluggish lately, darling? Any troubles concentrating? No sinus clogs?' He sniffed loudly twice. 'No sniffles?'

'What are you talking about?'

'Let's expand our hypothetical a bit. Struggle to keep up, if you can. Now let us say a lawyer shows up accusing the first client of doing something to him, something which we figure was not done by the first client but by the second client. Right-o? And now we have a problem. Because if it was done by the second client then in all likelihood the lawyer is involved in activities that he shouldn't be involved in. Activities that can impinge upon his fitness to stand before the bar. Now tell me, Victor. Do we have a duty to inform the bar association about this lawyer?'

'What kinds of activities?' I said, starting to get the horrifying idea behind Tony Baloney's hypothetical.

'You don't see me chairing any bar association committees, do you, Victor?' he said in a calm, quiet voice. 'They don't take my photograph two-stepping at the Andrew Hamilton Ball with the other high-flying members of our bar. I'm an outcast. And you know why, Victor, don't you? It's my clientele. Can you guess now what type of activities this hypothetical second client is involved in? I'll make it very simple for you.'

He leaned forward, smiled at me, and shouted, 'DRUGS!'

I jumped back at the shout.

'You see,' he continued, 'we, hypothetically, have one client who has a wide distribution network. When he distributes on credit, and bills aren't paid, he leaves what he calls his calling card. And that calling card happens to be dead animals. Furry little things generally, with their necks snapped and their bellies slit. And then, funny thing, he generally gets paid what he's owed. It's so much more effective than a dunning letter, wouldn't you say? So in all likelihood, it is not a hypothetical Greek landlord leaving these little calling cards. It is a hypothetical drug dealer and he's leaving these calling cards for his hypothetical drug addict clients.'

I pulled a chair around and sat down because I had to. 'Norvel Goodwin,' I said quietly.

'Hypothetically, of course. I gave you a message for Jimmy and I expected you would pick up on it.'

'I thought it was a threat,' I said.

'Yes, judgment is the first thing to go. I've been there before you. "How use doth breed a habit in a man." '

'It's not what you think,' I said.

'It never is. Clean my desk, Victor. There are supplies in the back closet.'

I didn't move, didn't respond. I just sat there staring at him.

'What kind of asshole would come into my office,' he said, 'and dump a gutted dog on my desk to advertise that he is a drug addict? What kind of asshole would do that unless he is crying out for help and wants me to report him? And I will tell you, Vic, right now you look like you could use some help, you know. I mean, right now, Vic sweetheart, you look like hell.'

I was sure I did just then. I was blanching. What Tony Baloney had just explained hit me like a short quick blow to the stomach, one of those shots you subconsciously know is coming but takes your breath away just the same.

'So clean up my desk, darling,' he said. 'Clean it now.'

I tried to stand, but I couldn't. I was helpless, in shock, because what I realized just then was that Norvel Goodwin had risen like a specter to once again threaten my life. And what I realized just then was that Veronica, with whom I had fallen in love, was once again hopelessly addicted to drugs. And what I realized just then was that in all our wild and brutal sex this drug addict whom I loved might have given me the plague. And what I realized just then was that it was over with me and her and I didn't I didn't I didn't want it to be over at all. I couldn't stand just then because I realized all of that, but it wasn't only all of that. I couldn't stand just then because at the same time I was realizing all of that I also realized exactly who had murdered Zack Bissonette and all that I would have to give up to prove it.

PART FOUR

The Defenestration

42

I grew up with my father in a Spanish-style bungalow in a suburban enclave of Spanish-style bungalows the developer had enthusiastically titled Hollywood. There was the Hollywood Tavern, where the working men of Hollywood escaped to a cool, red-tinged darkness and twenty-five-cent beers, the Hollywood Drugstore, dusty plate windows with small, hand-lettered signs, and an all-night donut shop that broke the tradition and was not called Hollywood Donuts but instead Donut Towne, the final 'e' the only bit of class remaining in the neighborhood. It wasn't a terrible place to live, this Hollywood, and after the war when it had just been built it had been quite a thing, but it wasn't much compared to the sprawling five-bedroomed manses with rolling lawns that surrounded it.

There was something about my neighborhood that I had always thought pathetic. Maybe it was the way the houses seemed to have been built rundown, maybe it was the way a scrappy flora had risen through the sidewalk cracks, turning the concrete slabs into rubble, and nobody did a thing about it. Maybe it was the whole idea of there being a Hollywood in the middle of this suburb outside of Philadelphia, as if in that little six-block area of cracked and decaying bungalows there lived John Wayne and Jimmy Stewart and Vera Miles and Yvette Mimieux, making movies and throwing barbecues in their seedy little back yards. I guess if the whole of the school district had been made of places like Hollywood I wouldn't have minded it so much, but it was a rich school district and my classmates were rich and I wasn't. Though we had a television and heat and always enough food, I could never shake the feeling that I grew up in a slum.

The Sunday after my meeting with Tony Baloney I drove past Donut Towne and the Hollywood Tavern and into the maw of my childhood. The trees that had been big and sturdy in my youth were now ancient and twisted. Many had fallen, taking the sidewalk with them, and this, along with the surviving trees having just shed their autumn leaves, had the effect of letting fall a cold, hard light so that the neighborhood seemed brighter than I ever remembered it to be. Every time I came back home the neighborhood seemed brighter than I ever remembered it to be. Nome, Alaska, during the six-month darkness of winter would be brighter than I ever remembered my old neighborhood to be. There, in front of that ranch house, there was where Tommy DiNardo used to beat me up after elementary school. Oh and there, over there, was where Debbie Paulsen jumped on top of me and, holding me down, kissed me and licked me and felt up my chest. Was I the only boy in my neighborhood to be raped by Debbie Paulsen, five feet and 180 pounds of frustrated Catholic flesh? And yes, there, right there, in a gap under that porch, fixed now so that you'd never know, but there was where I hid the day my mother left, shouting curses at my father as he snarled silently back at her from our front stoop. Ah, childhood in Hollywood, did ever shit smell sweeter?

I guess I was coming home for perspective. I had a decision to make and I figured here was where I would make it. I had to decide what I wanted, what my obligations were, how to attack my future. I had to decide what I should be when I grew up, and so home I came, to my father. I hadn't called but I knew he'd be there. The Eagles were on television, which gave him a fine excuse to do that which he did every night after work and all day Saturdays and Sundays: sit in front of the tube, drink beer, cough. I dropped the knocker twice onto the door. There was a button there to press, but it hadn't worked since I was nine.

'What do you want?' my father said when he opened the door and saw his son standing behind the screen with a sickly smile on his face.

I lifted the six-pack of Rolling Rock beer I had brought. 'You watching the game?'

He turned from me without opening the screen door and shambled back to his seat. 'No. There's golf on Channel Six.'

In case you missed it, that was my father's idea of a joke.

I think to understand my father you had to have understood my mother, all that she wanted, all that she felt she missed out on in her life because of marrying my father, the reasons that she left us for a trailer in Arizona. Unfortunately I had never understood anything about my mother beyond the fact that she was committably crazy and so my father remained something of a mystery too. He was a big man, bristly white hair, thick fingers, a quiet, hardworking, unambitious man with a bitterness cultivated by his ten years with my mother, a bitterness that had now bloomed into an ugly overripe flower he wore pinned to his breast like some beastly corsage. It was this same bitterness, I believed, that had manifested itself as the spots on his lungs that the X-rays were not erasing, just holding in check. The doctors all said he should be dead by now, he told me over and over, and I could never tell if he said it out of pride or disappointment.

I sat down on the sofa and twisted off the top of a Rock. He was in the easy chair, a can of Iron City in his hand. You could buy Iron City in the deli for $1.72 a six-pack. My father always had a taste for the finer things.

'How are they doing?' I asked.

'They're bums.'

'The Eagles or the Jets?'

'They're all bums.' He coughed, a loud hacking cough that brought up something. He spit into a paper towel on the table beside the chair and didn't look at it. 'And the money they make. These bums couldn't hold the jock-straps of players like Bednarik and Gifford.'

'Then why do you watch every week?'

'To have my judgment confirmed.'

'I haven't seen you in a while. You look pretty good.'

He coughed again. 'The doctors all tell me I should be dead by now.'

'Yeah, but what do they know, right?'

'That's what I always say.'

'Is that so?'

'Now you're being a smartass.'

'One of my inherited traits.'

'From your mother.'

'No. From you.'

His face grayed and he hacked out something else for the paper towel. 'Ah, what do you know?'

'What's the score?' I asked.

'Fourteen-seven, Eagles.'

'They're not playing like bums today.'

'This is the Jets. Let's see them play the Cowboys. In their hearts they's bums.'

We watched the game in near silence, throwing out charming bons mots as the play progressed, things like 'He's got hands like feet,' when a receiver dropped a ball, and 'He couldn't tackle his sister,' when a running back spun off a safety's hit, but basically keeping our thoughts to ourselves, the television commentary interrupted only by my father's coughs. We even sat in front of the halftime show, snippets from the band, hyperactivity from the commentators in the booth, a string of commercials about cars and beer. Sometime during the third quarter I realized that my beer was warming, so I took the now half-empty six into the kitchen. What I saw in the refrigerator was depressing. There was beer, there was an old milk carton, there were things I couldn't identify in the back. Ice was growing from the refrigerant cables. What was so depress-

ing was that the inside of my father's refrigerator looked
very much like the inside of my own.

'You should clean out your fridge sometime,' I said when
I sat back down.

'Why?'

Why indeed? Stumped again, I thought. Stumped again
by my father.

'What about that five thousand you owe me?' he asked
after the game, when the only thing on was the golf tournament on Channel 6, which my father had decided to
watch rather than do the unthinkable and turn off the set.

'That was what I came about,' I said. 'Or something like
it.'

'Well, do you got it or not?'

'Do you need it?'

'I could use it, sure,' he said.

'I could get it if you need it.'

'I didn't say I needed it.'

'You said you could use it.'

'It's not the same thing. Everyone could use it. Donald
Trump could use it, but he don't need it.'

'Bad example,' I said.

'Yeah, well, maybe.'

'Do you need it?'

'No.'

'Good,' I said. 'Because I don't have it.'

The tournament leader pulled a five-footer past the hole.

'That's not to mean I couldn't use it,' he said.

'I'll get it for you, then.'

'Look at that putt he missed,' my father said, waving
disgustedly at the screen. 'Bums. For fifth place they get
fifty thou. Who the hell cares about winning anymore?'

So we watched golf for a bit, seduced into somnolence
by the rhythm of the game, the setup, the waggle, the
step back, the waggle, the swing, ball disappearing into the
screen only to reappear as a tiny speck spinning forward
on the fairway. The shadows in the house were getting

longer now, the room was darkening. I glanced over during one of the crucial putts and my father was asleep in the chair, head back, mouth open, breathing noisily through his diseased and rotting lungs. He woke up with a start when Greg Norman made a long twisting putt and the crowd applauded wildly.

'Who? What?' he stammered.

'Norman just made a putt.'

'There's a bum. You want to know how to become a great golfer? Play Norman in a playoff.'

'The trick is getting to the playoff in the first place.'

'There's always a trick,' he said. 'I'm just telling you how is all.'

'Tell me about Grandpop,' I said and that quieted him for a moment.

'What about him?'

'I met someone who knew him from the *shul* in Logan. Someone who used to buy shoes from him.'

'Yeah, well, he went to *shul* and sold shoes,' said my father. 'What else is there?'

'And sing, right?'

'Sure, he used to sing all the time. He had a voice, but it still drove me crazy.'

'How come you stopped going to *shul*?' I asked.

'Old men singing sad songs in a dead language. Prayers in Aramaic. You know what is Aramaic?'

'No.'

'Nothing in the world is deader than Aramaic,' he said.

'What happened when you stopped? Didn't Grandpop try to make you go?'

'What was he going to do? I outweighed him when I was twelve. He didn't have much control over me. I was a bad kid.'

'Did you love him?' I asked.

'What kind of question is that?'

'I'm just asking.'

'He was my father. What do you think?'

A few holes went by on the television, a few drives, a six iron to the green, a sand shot, a putt from three feet that missed, a twenty-footer that found the cup.

'When did we stop going to synagogue?' I asked.

'All of a sudden you care?'

'I'm just asking.'

'It was your mother who kept that stuff going. She wanted to belong to the fancy place with all the rich dressers. She thought belonging there would give her class. She could have married the Queen of England she still wouldn't have had no class, and believe me, I ain't the Queen of England. The dues were killing us but that's what she wanted so that's what we did. When she left I didn't see any point.'

'I should have been *bar mitzvahed*,' I said, and I don't know why I said it because I had never thought it before in my entire life.

'And I should have been rich. So what's life but regrets.'

'If Grandpop had still been alive, he would have made sure I got *bar mitzvahed*,' I said. My voice seemed to fill with a great bitterness whenever I came home and it did again just then.

'You always were a whiner, you know that,' said my father. 'It was always "I hate this" and "I hate that," I just wanted to smack you all the time. Two people in the world knew how to get at me and they got to be my wife and kid. Well, quit being such a little whining snotnose already and grow up. Everything doesn't got to be done for you, you can do it yourself if you want. There ain't no age limit. Do it, I don't care, just quit whining about it. Look, I did it and believe me, you didn't miss nothing.'

'I didn't know you were *bar mitzvahed*.'

'Yeah, well, there's a hell of a lot you don't know,' he said.

'Did you have a big party?'

'It wasn't like that then. My mother made a brisket and we had a cousin or two over, that's all. Nowadays, shit,

they set up tents and serve lobster Newburg. Lobster Newburg, clams casino, a band with a colored singer. How do
you figure that?'

'I would have liked a party.'

'You didn't have no friends. Who would we have
invited, the President?'

After golf there was *60 Minutes*, the little ticking clock,
the talking head, the reporter with his incredulous tone as
though the scam he discovered was anything but expected.
I am shocked, shocked, he seemed to say, that there are
companies out there defrauding the government. It was
dark now, the shadows had spread to cover everything.
My father's face, slack in its thralldom of the television,
was illuminated in a shifting light.

'I have a problem I need to talk to you about,' I said.

'How much do you need now?'

'It's not like that.'

'This time, maybe,' he said.

'I have to make a decision about something. I have this
case, the one I've been on television with.'

'You been on television?'

'Don't act like that, you've seen me. I know you have.'

'I thought it was you but I wasn't sure. You look better
on TV.'

'So I should have been a television star, then?'

'You'd be better than that Bryant Gumbel, I'll tell you
that,' he said. 'There's a bum if ever I saw one.'

'In this case I have a client who's in serious trouble. It's
a criminal case and it looks like he is going to lose, but he
doesn't want me to do anything about it. Now I think I
know who did what he is supposed to have done, and I
think I know how to prove it, but it would cost me.'

'Cost you? How much?'

'I've been offered a job, a really good job, a job like I've
always wanted, but the job will come through only if I
don't rock the boat. And I've been offered a lot of money
for another case, enough money that I could pay you back

with interest, but again only if I let my client go down. There are deals that I'm on that I won't be on if I do it. And the group who is paying me to represent this guy probably won't pay me if I cause trouble, or that's just the way it seems. So the whole thing could mean a lot to me, the money and the job. But on the other side of the ledger, I'm like a lawyer and my client is going down and I feel that I have to do something about it, anything, even if it costs me. So I'm not sure what to do.'

There was a long silence between us, ably filled by the television set, an interview with an old entertainer, Morley Safer shaking his head over and over in amazement. Then, without turning from the television, my father spoke.

'Take the money,' he said.

He coughed loudly, hacking something big and weighty into the paper towel.

'Take the money,' he said. 'It don't come around that often.'

There was another long pause as a string of commercials played out and then the annoying skirl of Andy Rooney. My father switched the channel, surfing to find something, ending back in failure with Andy Rooney. Rooney had a pile of products before him and he was reading the labels.

'That's what you could do on television,' he said. 'You could whine as good as him.'

'You ever have a chance for real money?' I asked.

There was a long pause before he said, 'Marty Sokowsky.'

'I don't know him.'

'Sokowsky Chevrolet and Subaru out on 611. I grew up with Sokowsky in Logan. Right out of high school he had a proposition for me. Meat. He was going into the meat business, you know, not growing meat or chopping meat but selling meat. He wanted to be a salesman.'

'What kind of meat?'

'Pigs, cows, chicken, meat. The whole thing was a little shady, you know, selling second quality as first, bait and switch, it wasn't nothing about meat, really, it was about sucking out the money. I wasn't sure about it and the idea of telling your grandfather that I was selling pork was too much. I had decided on the army anyway, so I said no. Well, Sokowsky just misses getting indicted but he makes a ton, goes on to buy a car dealership where he is minting money, just minting money, and I come back from the army and start cutting lawns for that *schmuck* Aaronson. I missed out. It could have been Sokowsky-Carl Chevrolet and Subaru, that could have been me. Everything would have been different had I had a car dealership. I been waiting here for another chance ever since, but nothing never came. So what I learned is that with screwups like us it only comes around once and when it comes take it. No matter who you have to fuck.'

When the slangy little music for *Murder She Wrote* came on I told my father I had to leave. He followed me to the door.

'Take the money,' he said.

'Yes, I heard you.'

'You ever hear from her?' he asked quietly.

'Now and then. She's taken up golf.'

'I'm not surprised,' he said bitterly. 'I think her whole life she aspired to golf. She wanted me to join Philmont Country Club, the ritzy Jewish place down Huntingdon Pike. You know what that fucking place costs? Sokowsky belongs there.'

'She tells me to say hello.'

'I don't want to hear it.'

'I know.'

'The bums are in Dallas next week. They're going to get killed in Dallas.'

'Are you inviting me?'

'No, I was just saying.'

'"Cause if you're inviting me.'

'I'm not inviting you. Shut up. I'll be busy anyway.'

'Really?'

'Yeah. I got a tee-off time at Merion. Tell the bitch I'm taking it up too.'

It was a sad drive out of Hollywood and the suburbs and back into the city. My father was dying but that wasn't what was sad. I drove right up Broad Street, through the worst parts of North Philadelphia, bombed-out moviehouses, boarded-up stores, congregants of the homeless under elevated train bridges. I drove through Temple University and past the *Philadelphia Inquirer* building and then right around City Hall, past that building that had been decimated by fire but was still standing, a high-rise shell with plywood for windows, and I felt sad the whole way. It wasn't my father's certain future that was upsetting me so, it was the uncertainty of his past. But it had been a good visit; it had clarified things. My father had always been a barometer for me, the rebellions of my youth only mattered in relation to him. He was quiet, so I talked too damn much. He was uncomplaining, so I complained. He wore his hair in a crew cut, mine flowed past my shoulders all through high school. He was a laborer, I became a lawyer. He was poor, I would be rich. But I wouldn't be rich his way. 'Take the money,' he had said, and in those three swift words he had pointed out my direction as clear as a road sign. 'Take the money,' he had said, and I would, but not his way. I wanted nothing of my life to be his way.

Jimmy Moore had killed Zack Bissonette. I knew that with as much certainty as my father knew the Eagles were bums. Jimmy had gone to that club looking for Zack Bissonette and when he found him he grabbed a baseball bat from a display on the wall and with it he beat Bissonette senseless, faceless, comatose, beat him to death. Even as I cleaned up the dachshund mess, scrubbed the bloodstains from Tony Baloney's wooden desktop and leather blotter with Murphy's Oil, even then I could see it all, the flashing bat, the fury in Jimmy Moore's face, the blood bubbling as Bissonette breathed through it. And with a little luck I could prove it all happened just like that, too. I knew what it would cost me. Blaine, Cox, Amber and Cox would not be calling. The Bishop brothers would not be calling. My sweet forty-thousand-dollar cut of the *Saltz* settlement would not be resting gently in my bank account. From affluence to poverty in the blink of an eye.

But all my life I had resented the fact that what I had wished for had not been bestowed upon me. My father had not been rich, the law firms had not been hiring, that slam-bam-in-your-face case had never come walking in my door. I had been waiting too long for someone to give me my share. Enough already of waiting. Jimmy Moore had said America was not about what was bestowed but about what was grabbed, and now I was grabbing. Make no mistake, I still wanted it all, the money, the prestige, the best tables, the best cars, the youngest and prettiest women. But I wouldn't end up like my father, embittered because the myth of opportunity had not come knocking on my door. By going up against Jimmy Moore I would surely be losing that which was being bestowed upon me by William Prescott, but I didn't want to be given anything by anybody anymore. What would Clarence Darrow, the greatest trial lawyer of all time, what would Darrow have done in my situation? What would Lincoln have done, or Daniel Webster, or Andrew Hamilton, the first of the great Philadelphia lawyers? They each would have spit in Prescott's eye and then gone out and taken what was rightfully theirs. They didn't rely on gifts bestowed, and no longer would I.

So this is what I would do. I would shit on Blaine, Cox, Amber and Cox. I would shit on the Bishop brothers, on CUP, on the goddamn defendants in *Saltz v. Metropolitan Investors*, on Norvel Goodwin and his bloody calling cards. I would convince Chester Concannon to let me fight for his freedom and then I would take down Jimmy Moore. And in taking down Jimmy Moore I would make a name for myself. I would win the case for Chester Concannon, I'd save his life, I would, and when I did I'd shout it to the press and watch the clients come roaring in. I would seize opportunity by the neck and wring it, oh yes. I would make a name for myself and from my name, and no one else's, would flow my power and my wealth and all my worldly success. I would make a name for myself, dammit, and in so doing I alone would make my dreams come true.

43

'How's your pastrami, Morris?' I asked.

'*Goot*,' he mumbled through a mouth full of meat.

'Not too lean, I hope.'

'No, *goot*,' he said, fighting to swallow so he could snatch another bite.

'You want more coleslaw, maybe?'

With his mouth again full he nodded his head and lifted the top piece of rye bread off his sandwich. I placed a layer of coleslaw over the thickly sliced spiced meat.

'And more Russian dressing?'

He shrugged, but with the top of his sandwich still off I took a knife and slathered the coleslaw with Russian dressing from the little bowl in front of us.

'I hope it's not too lean,' I said as Morris was in the middle of taking a bite. 'I told the lady not too lean.'

Morris nodded at me, his eyes wide in satisfaction, the sandwich still at his mouth.

'Oh, look,' I said. 'This is great. Here come our French fries.'

We were in Ben's Deli, Ben's Kosher Deli, a block away from Jewelers' Row in Philadelphia. Ben's was a long, low restaurant with one aisle down the middle flanked by booths. The walls were painted white and the floor was white linoleum and the leatherette on the booths was dark green and in the back of the store, on two large planks of plywood, like the tablets from Mt Sinai, was the menu, writ in dark blue on white. Hot pastrami was a specialty, thick slices of meat with dark peppered crusts and veins of fat that melted on the tongue as you chewed. There was also corned beef, roast beef, tuna fish, chicken salad, egg salad, though no cheese or yogurt or ice cream. Ben's was a *flayshig* place, which meant that the cholesterol that oozed out on their platters and into your heart came directly from the very muscles of the twice blessed then slaughtered animals as opposed to indirectly, from their milk. Old Hassids sat at the booths yelling at each other in Yiddish, slick young diamond sellers talked out the sides of their mouths as they snapped the complimentary pickles in their teeth, young boys in yarmulkes sat morosely over their egg salad sandwiches and Cokes. Two nuns squinted at the menu on the wall, searching for the toasted cheese sandwiches they had mistakenly stopped in for.

We were in Ben's because I had a favor to ask Morris and I astutely figured the best time to ask Morris for a favor was when his mouth was full. 'Ketchup?' I asked as the waitress spun the plate of thick-cut fries in front of him.

He shook his head no.

'Beer, how about a beer? A beer would go great with this, wouldn't it?'

Morris, his mouth once again joyously filled with pastrami and coleslaw and rye bread, shook his head vigorously but then stopped all that shaking and shrugged.

'Miss, could we have two beers? Is Heineken all right, Morris?'

He nodded.

'Two Heinekens.'

When the beers came I poured Morris's into the little water glass she brought with the bottles, making sure the head was a perfect inch thick.

'How's your lunch, Morris?'

His glass to his lips, he nodded again.

'Take another bite.'

He took another bite.

'I've got a favor to ask.'

He fought to finish swallowing what was in his mouth,

took a long drink from his beer, and said, 'Tell me, Victor, why am I not surprised by this?'

'Because you're a wise man, Morris.'

'Wise to you, mine *freint*, and your obvious attempt at bribery. But Morris Kapustin is a righteous man, he cannot be bought by a simple pastrami sandwich on rye. I am not so easily taken as you think, Victor. Please pass the coleslaw. Sometimes when I take a bite it slips right out of the sandwich and pffft, onto mine lap. These paper napkins they give you now, such *schlock*. They do nothing to protect you from coleslaw. So tell me what you want from Morris.'

'I need to break into an office.'

He stared at me and shook his head. 'I am an investigator, not a thief. You want to find a thief, that's very simple. Go to a prison, any prison, and you will find many thieves. And the funny thing, even in those prisons there are some thieves who are lawyers, do you understand what I am saying, mine *freint*? But not here will you find a thief, not at this table at Ben's. Now you're insulting me now. All of a sudden I don't want no more your sandwich. Take it away. Take it. It's like *trayf* to me now.'

He pushed his plate away from him. There was still almost a quarter of a sandwich left. He looked at me. I looked at him. He looked at the plate and then pulled it back.

'Give me the coleslaw, please,' he said. 'Just a *pitsel* more is all it is needing.'

I refilled his beer glass.

'Thank you,' he said. 'Careful there is not too much head. Who wants to be drinking all that *shum*? It gives gas.'

'I need to break into an office.'

'Again with the office?'

'I have no choice,' I said.

'Okay, Victor. Tell me now what is so important that you have to become a thief and break into some poor *shnook's* office. Wait, don't yet tell me.'

He quickly finished his sandwich and downed the entire glass of beer. He snatched a French fry and ate it in two quick bites. Wiping his mouth with a napkin, he said, 'Okay, now. I was hurrying up to finish mine eating so that I wouldn't lose appetite from what you are going to tell me.'

'I need to break into an office.'

'So I have heard three times already. Whose office, if I may ask?'

'William Prescott's.'

'The other lawyer on that trial you are losing. Oh, don't protest like that, I know everything. Mine new friend Herm Finklebaum, he has been watching the trial for me, keeping me up to date on exactly how lousy you are doing.'

'I'm in a difficult position,' I said.

'Herm says you are dropping faster than his mother's *kreplach*. I don't know his mother, never met the poor woman, but I can imagine.'

'I'm in a very difficult position.'

'And breaking into this fellow's office, it will help? This I want to hear. This will be better than cable.'

'You get cable, Morris?'

'What, I alone in this country, I don't deserve to watch our favorite movies on TNT? What crime have I committed, Victor, what? Tell me.'

'I just never thought of you sitting back with a beer watching Sports Center.'

'That Berman fellow, he cracks me up. Jewish actually, you know that? I can tell. Such a *punim*. So tell me why I must to help you commit a felony.'

And so I told him about Concannon and how he wouldn't let me defend him like he needed to be defended without proof that Jimmy Moore was dumping on him and how I thought that proof was in William Prescott's office.

'You need proof in black and white to convince this client of yours?' asked Morris incredulously.

'That's right.'

'And you think that proof is in this office you want to break into?'

'That's right.'

'Are you sure you won't find nothing there but *bubkes*?'

'I think it's there. Prescott is a very scientific trial lawyer. He checks every argument with focus groups before popping it on a jury. He had a jury survey conducted before the trial and I asked him for it five or six times. Each time he said he would send it right over, but I never got it.'

'And you are sure that is your proof?'

'That's all I can think of.'

'And let me ask you this, mister felony, mister three to five years if you are caught. Even if you find this sheet and use it to convince this client to fight back at this fellow Moore, what then? Is there something you can do to save him?'

'I think there is,' I said, 'but I can't do it without his consent and I can't get his consent without some proof.'

'It seems to me, Victor, and this is just mine professional opinion so you don't have to follow it because what do I know, but it seems to me that you are taking a very big risk to help this client.'

'You don't know the half of it.'

'I know more than I want to know already by a half, believe me. Is this client of yours, is he worth it?'

'Actually, yes,' I said. 'He's a good man who is being taken advantage of and deserves someone to stand up for him.'

'And that needs to be you?'

'If not me,' I said, 'who?'

He paused and ate a French fry and stared at me for a moment. 'You've been studying Rabbi Hillel maybe?'

I shrugged and nodded with a shy smile, all the while wondering who the heck was Hillel.

'Maybe you have gained a dollop of faith on us after all,

404

44

I had been instructed to be at the bar of the Doubletree Hotel at 10:30 p.m. and to wait there for little Sheldon. The Doubletree was a modern cement and glass structure just south of City Hall. The bar there was open and airy, with rows of tiny tables, a ring of circular booths on a riser around the edge, and glass doors looking out at the hookers on Broad Street. A two-man band played on the tiny stage, a short guy in a tux on guitar and a tall good-looking woman singing and playing synthesizer, standards like 'I Will Survive' and 'Cherish,' the Madonna version, but no one was dancing. As I sat at the bar, waiting for little Sheldon Kapustin to come and get me, I wondered what he would look like. Small, round, a young Morris but maybe skinnier, hopefully skinnier. He would have to be skinnier, having made it through two years in the Israeli army, but it wouldn't take too many pastrami sandwiches to beef him up again. My image of Sheldon was not exactly comforting, young, small, fat, a computer nerd. 'Give him a chance,' Morris had asked and give him a chance I would because I didn't have much choice, but I hoped giving little Sheldon his chance wouldn't land me in jail.

Morris had told me to draw up a rough plan of Prescott's floor and I had, very rough. It was folded in my jacket pocket. Prescott's office was on the fifty-fifth floor. I wasn't quite sure how to get up there. I hoped Morris had worked out a plan. I also didn't know how to get in the office door if it was locked, but Sheldon was a locksmith, so he would have to take care of it, as well as the desk and file cabinets, which might also be locked. And if I couldn't find the actual document, it would probably be somewhere on the computer, which Sheldon would have to hack his way onto. Already, I realized, I was too dependent on little Sheldon, and if little Sheldon was even only twice what I expected him to be, I would be lost. I ordered a beer while I was waiting and, on a spur, also a gin and tonic. This was not a night to get drunk, but it was a night for calm, natural or chemically induced, so I drank the G&T quickly and then the beer and ordered another of each.

'Mr Carl?'

I turned around and immediately flinched. Behind me was an enforcer type, big, solid-necked, arms like legs, a real bruiser with curly black hair and a weightlifter's pinched nose. He wore a hat, a gangster's fedora raffishly cocked forward. He held a little leather briefcase in his right hand. It was another Raffaello summons and that briefcase, I thought, was a nice touch in the hotel. 'What now?' I asked.

'Is there a problem?'

'I'm sick of it, is all. I'm sick of being dragged into cars for little chats with big-time mobsters. I'm sick of being whipsawed in your boss's little fights with Moore and the feds.' Maybe I had drunk too much, or maybe my renewed resentment was getting the best of me, but it felt fine sounding off against this lug. 'Tell your boss I'm busy, that tonight's not a good night, that if he wants to talk to me he can just call me on the phone like everyone else. Tell him that.'

'I don't understand, Mr Carl.'

'Just tell him what I told you to tell him. You don't need to understand. That's not what you're made for, understanding, is it? Brawny boys like you are made for something else. Just tell him.'

'Maybe some other night would be better.'

'Yeah, sure. Tell him to have his girl get in touch with my girl and we'll set something up. We'll do lunch. I know an Indian place.'

'I'll tell him, Mr Carl, but my father won't be too happy about it.'

'Your father, huh? Funny,' I said. 'I thought you were dead.'

'Not yet. I'll give Morris the message.'

'So you're little Sheldon,' I said. I looked him up and down. 'Tell me, Sheldon.' It was the first thing that popped into my mind. 'Your mother, Rosalie. I don't mean to be rude, but your mother is she by any chance a big woman?'

'She can be imposing.'

'I bet. I'm sorry, I thought you were someone else. Sit down. Can I get you a drink?'

'A ginger ale.'

I waved down the bartender. 'A ginger ale and another beer.'

'Make that two ginger ales,' said not-so-little Sheldon Kapustin. When the sodas came he took his and led me to a booth in the rear, where we sat across from each other.

'Are you drunk, Mr Carl? I'll be frank, I'm not going up with you if you're drunk.'

'I'm not drunk at all,' I said.

'You sounded drunk back there at the bar.'

'Fortified is what I am.'

'Let me see your floor plan.'

I pulled out the sheet of paper on which I had sketched the hallways and offices, as best I could remember, of the fifty-fifth floor of One Liberty Place. In the corner, as big as I remembered it, was Prescott's office. I had drawn in the couch, the desk, the oblong table. He looked at it for a while.

'Which way is north?' he asked.

'I don't know.'

'Do you remember the view out the window?'

I closed my eyes and saw the rivers of row-housed streets leading to Veterans Stadium, and catercorner to it the Schuylkill and Franklin Field. 'I think this was south and this was west.'

Sheldon nodded and stared for a long time at my little map. The band was playing the theme from *Beverly Hills Cop*. A waitress came to give us a wooden bowl of tiny pretzel fishes and asked if we were all right and Sheldon said we were. When she left he reached into his briefcase and pulled out what looked to be a road map, but when he unfolded it, one sheaf at a time, it turned out to be a detailed schematic of the fifty-fifth floor.

'How did you get that?'

'My father has friends everywhere. You'd be surprised.'

'I don't think I'd be surprised by anything about Morris anymore.'

He spun the schematic around. 'All right, based on what you are telling me, this is Prescott's office.'

'That looks right.'

'And this then would be the closest freight elevator.'

'If you say so. I can't tell.'

'And this here is probably the custodian's closet. See how it abuts the HVAC system, so they can change filters and do any needed repairs.'

'Okay,' I said, willing to go along.

'And fortunately,' said Sheldon, 'the custodian's closet isn't but ten yards from the entrance to Prescott's office.'

The custodian's closet was small and dank, with the hum from the floor's HVAC unit pushing vast quantities of air in and out like a giant lung. There wasn't really enough room for the two of us, but as long as we staggered our breathing we were all right. We were both in overalls, with caps that read 'Robinson Cleaners,' all supplied by Sheldon.

It was Sheldon who had picked the lock to the freight elevator and gotten us onto the fifty-fifth floor. I had thought the offices would be quiet, as dead as my office after five o'clock, but it wasn't dead at all. There were associates still working, secretaries still typing, copy machines still whirring in the distance. This Talbott,

Kittredge and Chase was a billable-hour machine and I guess, like the best-oiled machines in the world, there was no reason to shut it down for a silly thing like nightfall. For a moment I wondered if Prescott was still there, hard at work, but Sheldon had called him before we left the Doubletree Hotel bar and he was gone for the day, not at meetings or out to dinner, but gone. Just to be sure the coast was clear, we followed the hallway past Prescott's closed door and into the custodian's closet. On the way I had seen light coming from associates' offices and I feared that maybe one of those hard successes would recognize me. The first office I passed I instinctively glanced into, spying at a desk a woman whom I had fortunately never seen before. 'Don't look,' whispered Sheldon, and thereafter, for the rest of the walk to the closet, though my hackles were raised, I successfully fought not to glance into those productive little offices. When we reached the custodian's closet beside the heating, ventilation, and air conditioning system on the fifty-fifth floor, Sheldon opened the door and entered and then yanked me inside.

'His door was closed,' I said.

'That's good. Hopefully it's locked.'

'Hopefully?'

'So long as it's locked we know he's not expecting anyone to use it. If he leaves it unlocked, one of his people might be planning to step in and pick something up.'

He reached into his briefcase, took out a stethoscope, and proceeded to listen through the door.

'Giving it a checkup?' I asked.

He put his finger to his lips and I shut up.

After a long moment he said, 'All right, Mr Carl, you ready?'

'Sure.'

'You just follow me and keep quiet if anyone sees us.'

'Sure.'

'Don't go wandering around without me.'

'Don't worry.'

'And take that with you,' he said, pointing to a bucket with a dirty rag laying over the edge.

After a final moment of listening through the stethoscope, he stuffed it in his briefcase and pulled out a clipboard. One deep breath and he was out the door. Bucket and rag in hand, I followed.

Slowly, calmly, we walked down the hall to the office and made our way around the desk used by Prescott's secretary, Janice. Sheldon tried the knob and it turned. He opened the door. I looked around quickly, saw no one, and scooted inside. Sheldon closed the door behind me and immediately turned on the light. It was as I remembered, the wall of photographs, the gilded desk with piles of papers, the conference table in the middle covered with files, the wraparound couch and grotesque boxing painting and coffee table with papers atop in a neat pile. Behind the desk was the low and long wooden credenza.

'Go to it,' he said.

'Where do I begin?'

'This is your gig, Mr Carl. Just be quick about it. I don't like that the door was unlocked.'

The first place I hit was the long conference table in the middle of the room, covered with thick maroon folders packed with documents. There were titles on the folder dividers that let me know these were indeed Moore and Concannon files, but the system was based on numbers with which I wasn't familiar, so I was forced to search through them one by one. There were transcripts, there was correspondence, which I went through carefully, there were documents from the councilman's files. Much of this stuff I had seen, on many of the letters I had been copied, but there was also much I had never seen before. I especially concentrated on correspondence between Prescott and Bruce Pierpont, the jury expert. I had hoped a copy of Pierpont's report would be in the correspondence file, attached to the cover letter, but though the cover letter was there, the report was not. As I searched, Sheldon glanced around Prescott's desk.

'Anything?' he asked in a worried whispered voice.

'Not yet. Why don't you check the desk?'

'It's locked,' he said.

'Well, open it.'

'If someone comes in and I'm fiddling around inside his locked desk, that's trouble.'

'If someone comes in we're in trouble anyway.'

He looked doubtful and then pulled his picks out of his pocket and went to work on the desk's lock. It yielded to him in less than a minute.

Though I wasn't finding the jury report I had come for, I was learning much I hadn't known. There was a bill from Bissonette to Moore for money owed for club expenditures. There was also a stack of bank receipts showing a series of cash deposits to Veronica's checking account, all in the high four figures but none for more than ten thousand dollars. And then I found a file, number 716, which stopped me cold.

Inside was a copy of the *Martindale-Hubbell* report on Guthrie, Derringer and Carl. Inside was a copy of my law school transcript and the pathetic letter I had sent off seven years before seeking a job at Talbott, Kittredge and Chase. Inside was a copy of my apartment lease, a copy of my car insurance application, listing my father's address as my own to get the reduced suburban rate, a list of all transactions for the last two years on my credit card, copies of my bank statements, copies of my delinquent payment statements from the Student Loan Marketing Association, a copy of my deficient credit report. And then, sitting there like a ghost from my past, a transcript of my deposition of Mrs Osbourne. I paged through it quickly. One section was highlighted in orange.

Q: Perhaps you know the person living in your husband's apartment, a Miss LeGrand?

A: No.

Q: Let me show you a picture. I'll mark this P. 13.

A: What is this? This is a brochure of some sort.

Q: Yes, for a gentlemen's club called the Pussy Willow. Why don't you look through it. I'm referring to the section about the exotic dancers. Let me show you. The woman right there.

A: Tiffany LeGrand?

Q: Oh, so you do know her.

A: (no response)

So my ability to be bought wasn't writ large on my face after all. It was documented in my paper trail, in all of my records, in each step I had taken in the shallow depths of my past. The sum total of my years, the ledgers of my true worth were in that file, all I had wanted, how low I would stoop to get it, how little I had achieved no matter how low I stooped. My chest ached at the very thought of it. I put it down carefully, as if it were a fragile flask filled with the vilest of liquids.

I turned away from the table in disgust. 'Anything in the desk?' I asked Sheldon.

'Not yet, just firm memos, phone bills.'

'We're looking for a jury report, or anything marked Attorney Work Product over the top. I'm going to check the credenza.'

The credenza behind the desk was wooden, a piece of fine furniture really, low like a table. One wooden door, the length of the piece, swung up, revealing files arranged horizontally. Kneeling down, I started going through the files one by one. I hurriedly determined the subject matter of each, checking file tabs, looking inside to make sure the papers corresponded to the tabs, and then moving on. I was finding nothing, and growing frustrated, when the office door opened and I heard a gasp from the woman who entered.

'What?' she shouted. 'What are you doing here?' and

from the tenor of the voice and its unrestrained hostility I recognized its bearer right off. It was Madeline Burroughs, Prescott's drone, who held in her well-hidden breast a deep hatred of me. I kept my head down and froze, not turning around as she spoke.

'Cleaning crew, ma'am,' said Sheldon.

'Cleaning crew left three hours ago.'

'I'm a supervisor. We've been getting complaints about the work, so we're checking up on the crew.'

'What are you doing at the desk?'

'Checking for vermin,' said Sheldon. 'They got them like crazy on fifty-three.'

'I've never seen any insects up here,' said Madeline. 'I don't believe you. Stay right there, I'm calling Security.'

'That's all right with us,' said Sheldon calmly. 'But they're all throughout this desk. That's why the guy left us the desk keys, to check.'

'Mr Prescott left you his keys?'

'I don't know who he is.' There was a rustle of papers from inside a desk drawer and then I heard Sheldon say, 'Here's one.'

'Oh, God,' said Madeline.

'Oops, sorry,' said Sheldon. 'They're slippery little things.'

I turned around slowly, my head down so that, from beneath my visor, I could see only the carpet. A huge roach was rushing right toward a sturdy pair of blue pumps.

'Let me get that,' said Sheldon.

The pumps took a step back and then, as the cockroach approached, the right pump lifted and squashed it. The bug's shell crunched like a potato chip and the innards squished out.

'We're going to have to come back and spray,' said Sheldon.

'I think so,' said Madeline.

'Anything you wanted to get?'

'It'll wait,' she said as the pumps spun around and

stepped out of the office, the door closing behind them.

Sheldon stepped over to pick up the summarily executed roach.

'Jesus,' I said. 'Where did that come from?'

'My pocket,' said Sheldon. 'Now hurry up and let's get out of here before she figures out what I might have done and decides to call Security after all.'

I turned back to the credenza and rushed through the remaining files. Nothing. I went to the desk and rifled the papers in piles on top. Nothing. I went through the drawers, quickly, looking for anything. Nothing. I went back to the table and searched again through the stretched maroon files. I was going through them haphazardly now, desperate from nearly getting caught by Madeline Burroughs, desperate to get out of there, but even more desperate to find my proof for Concannon.

'We have to go,' said Sheldon.

'Look through the desk once more,' I said. 'We're looking for anything by Bruce Pierpont.'

Sheldon once again went through the desk. I kept reviewing the files on the table. I pulled the sheaves of papers bound in those files to check them. There were transcripts from the trial, from the grand jury, accountants' reports on CUP finances, but nothing by Pierpont.

'Well, here's something interesting,' said Sheldon.

'The report?'

'No.'

'Forget it, then. Try the computer.'

'Not enough time,' said Sheldon. 'We have to go.'

'One last look,' I said.

'No.'

He closed the desk drawers and fiddled with the locks. Then he stepped over to pull me away.

'Okay, all right. Just let me straighten up.' I rearranged the files on the table to approximate the way they were when we got there. As I followed him to the door I spied the small pile of papers on the coffee table by the couch.

An old Edgar Allan Poe story somersaulted into my mind.

'Wait one second.'

'We can't,' said Sheldon, but we did, as I leafed quickly through the pile. It was a mishmash of things, letters from other cases, advertisements for continuing legal education courses. And then near the bottom, covered with clear plastic, bound with a thin black fastener, about a quarter of an inch thick, was a report by Bruce J. Pierpont, PhD, entitled: *A Statistical Analysis by Demographic Sector of Community Views on Certain Specific Arguments to Be Presented in the Case of the United States v. Moore and Concannon.* Got you, you bastard.

I rolled up the report tightly and stuck it into the back pocket of my overalls. 'Let's get out of here,' I said unnecessarily, as Sheldon was already out the door.

As we walked quickly for the exit and the elevator we heard the sound of a group coming toward us. Sheldon grabbed my shoulder and we turned and ran, ducking into the custodian's closet before anyone could see us. Sheldon locked the door. We waited there for almost an hour, terrified, waiting as Security came and went and Madeline told her story to an associate here and a secretary there and then, on a secretary's phone, to Prescott. When Sheldon's stethoscope told us the field was clear, we ducked out silently but with pace.

On the way down in the freight elevator I asked Sheldon what he had found in the desk that had interested him so.

'Just a phone bill.'

'So?'

'Well, there had been a series of collect calls from a number in area code 512.'

'Area code 512?'

'Right, which includes Corpus Christi, Texas.'

'Okay, calls from Corpus Christi.'

'Well, Morris told me that this Prescott was involved in your case with Stocker. We had tracked Stocker to somewhere on the Gulf of Mexico. Last time I checked the map,

Corpus Christi was right there on the Gulf of Mexico.'

'You think he's there?'

Sheldon shrugged. 'Who knows? It doesn't matter, though, since Morris told me the time limit had passed for the case.'

'Did you take the bill?'

'No, you told me to forget it.'

'Jesus, Sheldon. I wish you had taken the damn bill. If we could link Prescott to Stocker it could be worth millions.'

'So if I had taken the bill, you would have hired us again to check out if Stocker was the fellow Prescott was talking to in Corpus Christi.'

'In a heartbeat, yeah.'

'At special rates, of course, being that Corpus Christi is halfway across the country.'

'Sure, you could have charged your special rates.'

'That's interesting,' he said, staring up at the descending numbers lighting atop the elevator doors. 'Because although I didn't take the bill, I just happen to have memorized the number.'

'Little Sheldon,' I said, shaking my head. 'When I first met you I couldn't imagine anyone looking more different than your father. But all of a sudden I see the resemblance.'

45

'Good morning, Victor,' said Prescott to me the next day as I set my briefcase on the defense table.

'Good morning, Mr Prescott,' I said.

Prescott had been presenting his case for a number of days now, witnesses testifying about the absolute need for money to run and win political campaigns, witnesses testifying as to the good works CUP was performing in the community, Mrs Diaz testifying as to the crucial ministrations being given at the Nadine Moore Youth Center and the councilman's ambition for a great bloom of healing. Today, I assumed, would be more of the same and I assumed right.

'Most of this session will be spent on character witnesses for the councilman,' said Prescott. 'Political allies, community members whom he has helped. That sort of thing. Eggert was willing to stipulate to much of the testimony, but I thought the jury should be able to hear the full quantity of community support for Jimmy Moore.'

'That sounds fine,' I said. 'I might have a few questions for some of the witnesses myself.'

'Oh, I don't think so, Victor,' said Prescott. 'I think you won't have any questions for these witnesses. And when the councilman testifies tomorrow you won't have any questions either. Talk it over with your client.'

'You know I will, sir.'

'Splendid,' he said.

Prescott's first witness of the morning was the Reverend James T. McHenry, pastor at the 57th Street Baptist Church of Divine Revelation. The reverend was a tall African-

American with a narrow face accented by sharp cheekbones. He wore a flowered tie knotted thick as an ascot and he spoke in beautiful rhythms, as if he were up high on an altar, standing before a gospel choir, preaching. He had known Jimmy Moore for twenty years, he announced from the witness stand, and for much of that time they had been political opponents. But in the last five years, since the death of the councilman's daughter, they had been marching together, ever forward in the struggle for dignity and human rights in this great city. Jimmy Moore had helped him get the funds to finish renovation of the church. Jimmy Moore had been a crusader in saving the children in his community, had been the scourge of drug dealers and healer of the drug dependent. He knew Jimmy Moore to be a fine man, a caring man, a family man who looked out for his God, his community, and his family before looking out for himself. Jimmy Moore, in the crucible of his personal tragedy, had become a great man, a fighter for righteousness who would never do anything to hurt his city or its people.

'What is your opinion, Reverend McHenry,' asked Prescott, in the archaic way required by the Federal Rules to elicit character testimony, 'of Jimmy Moore's reputation as a truthful and honest citizen?'

'The Jimmy Moore I have worked with so closely lo these many years is as honest as Moses, as truthful as a saint, a God-fearing man who follows all the Lord's commandments, including the prohibition against bearing false witness.'

'Objection,' said Eggert. 'The reference to God is inappropriate.'

'God has no place in a court of law?' asked Prescott with false incredulity. 'Isn't that a Bible we swear on before we testify?'

'Sustained,' said the judge. 'Reverend, please just answer the questions.'

'Reverend McHenry,' continued Prescott, 'what is your

opinion of Jimmy Moore's reputation as a peaceful citizen?'

'I have worked side by side with Jimmy Moore to rid the streets of the scourge of drugs, I know all the good he is capable of, and I know in my heart that he is a peaceful man with the gentleness of an angel.'

'And what is your opinion, Reverend McHenry, of Jimmy Moore's reputation as a law-abiding citizen?'

'I'll repeat it, sir. Jimmy Moore is a man, sir, a man above reproach. A man who can look his family, his community, and his God, sir, his God straight in the eye so that all will know he is a righteous, law-abiding man.'

Eggert threw up his hands at the last response but stayed quiet.

'No further questions,' said Prescott.

'Mr Carl,' said Judge Gimbel without looking up from his daily paperwork, 'I assume you have no questions for the Reverend.'

I stood up. 'Just a few, Your Honor.' The judge raised his head and looked at me gravely and then nodded. I could feel Prescott's eyes staring me down from the other side of the table. I buttoned my jacket and strolled to the podium, but before I could speak Prescott was objecting.

'Can we come to sidebar, Your Honor?' he asked.

'If you must,' said Judge Gimbel, and all the lawyers huddled with the judge out of earshot of the jury and the witness.

'Your Honor,' said Prescott. 'I don't believe Mr Carl's intended cross is in conformity with his client's wishes. I believe it is Mr Concannon's desire that he not cross-examine this witness and it is improper for Mr Carl, therefore, to conduct this examination.'

'Mr Carl?' asked the judge.

'Mr Prescott represents Councilman Moore,' I said. 'I don't understand how he can presume to speak for my client.'

'Generally, Mr Prescott,' said the judge, 'I assume a

lawyer's strategy is in conformity with his client's wishes. Is there any reason why I shouldn't assume that here?'

'Yes, sir. I can guarantee that this is not the case here. Absolutely, and Mr Carl's disregard of his client's wishes is going to be prejudicial to my client as well as to his own. I believe you should bring up Mr Concannon and ask him.'

'That's improper,' I said with as much indignation as I could raise.

'How good is your authority as to Mr Concannon's wishes, counselor?'

'Ironclad, Judge,' said Prescott. 'He confirmed his desires to Councilman Moore just last night.'

'Last night?' asked the judge.

'Yes, sir, which means Mr Carl is acting without authority.'

'That's a pretty grave accusation, Mr Prescott,' said the judge.

'Yes, sir.'

'If you're right, I'll have to notify the bar association as to Mr Carl's conduct. If you're wrong, that makes this objection an improper tactic and I'll have to notify the bar association as to your conduct. Now do you want to pursue this further?'

'Yes, sir,' said Prescott, and he slipped a little smile at me.

'Mr Concannon,' said the judge to the defense table. 'Will you step up here, please?'

Concannon stood up from the defense table and walked toward us. At the same time, Prescott motioned for Jimmy Moore to come up too, so the two men walked side by side to our little klatch. Chester was walking with his head high, his shoulders straight, seeming not to notice the way Jimmy was staring at him.

'Mr Concannon,' said the judge when the two men had arrived. 'The question has been raised as to whether or not you have agreed to your lawyer's questioning of this witness and generally participating in this trial on a more than pro forma basis. Without getting into any conversation between your lawyer and yourself, I am going to ask you a question and I would like only a yes or no answer. Now, Mr Concannon, yes or no, do you consent to your lawyer's questioning of this witness?'

All eyes were on Chester, Jimmy especially was staring hard, leaning forward, his jaw thrust out, his head shaking back and forth just slightly, but enough to let Chester know exactly what he wanted to hear.

'Victor has my complete confidence,' said Chester in a clear voice. 'He has my consent to ask any question he seeks fit to ask.'

Prescott twitched when Concannon gave his answer. It was only a slight twitch, a sudden contraction of the corner of his mouth, nothing more than that, but there it was. It brought a joy to my heart that is indescribable. A *mechaieh*, Morris would have called it.

'Fine,' said the judge. 'Mr Prescott, I will be sending a report to the bar association immediately after today's session. Mr Carl, you may continue.'

'You're betraying me,' Jimmy growled at Chester.

'Quiet,' said the judge.

'After all I've done for you,' shouted Jimmy for all to hear, including the jury. 'You were in the gutter when I found you.'

'Mr Prescott,' said the judge. 'Restrain your client or I'll hold him in contempt.'

Prescott grabbed hold of Jimmy's arm, but Jimmy was already in Chester's face, their noses not five inches apart. 'You're stabbing me in the back, you ungrateful bastard,' said Jimmy Moore.

'Go to hell, Councilman,' said Chester. 'And maybe we'll room together there.'

I understood exactly where Concannon's anger was coming from. Before dawn I had been at his apartment, delivering for his perusal *A Statistical Analysis by Demographic Sector of Community Views on Certain Specific Arguments to Be Presented in the Case of the United States v. Moore and Concannon.* The report was written in an obscure technojargon that could only have been invented by a group of PhDs trying to give their bullshit profession the appearance of validity, but even all that jargon couldn't obscure that Pierpont's report was a blueprint for screwing Chester Concannon to the wall.

'It's all there, Chet,' I had said, pacing back and forth as I spoke. 'What jurors to pick, what voir dire to ask, how to present evidence, how to argue, it's all there. The report gives a scientifically designed method for convincing the jury that Jimmy Moore was betrayed by a greedy subordinate who was interested only in taking as much as he could grab hold of, the politics be damned. He's going to climb out of this mess on your back, Chet, leaving you struggling for breath in the deep shit. He is letting you take his fall.'

'He's not going to do that to me,' he said wearily.

'Yes, he is. He's been doing it all along. He told me so himself. And Chester?'

He looked up at me.

'You know it. You've known it from the first.'

Chester didn't give me an answer right then. He needed to think about it, he said. He was in a silk robe. From the bedroom a sweet, drowsy voice had asked, 'Is everything all right, baby?' But everything wasn't all right. I hadn't even asked him his decision before I stood to examine the preacher, but I didn't doubt what he would do. Chet's greatest trait was his loyalty, and the one thing loyalty can never abide is betrayal.

'That's enough from both of you,' said the judge, with steel in his grating voice. 'Another word and you'll both be in contempt. You may continue, Mr Carl. And Mr Carl.'

'Yes, Your Honor.'

'It's good to see you back from the dead.'

'Thank you, sir,' I said.

When the warring parties had been seated and I was

back at the podium, I stood very straight and stared directly into the witness's eyes until he squirmed just a bit. Then I started.

'Now, Reverend, you testified that you believe Councilman Moore to be a righteous man, an adherent to the laws of God and man both.'

'That's right, sir,' he answered.

'Now tell me, Reverend, you've met the councilman's wife.'

'Yes, sir. Leslie Moore is a lovely woman.'

'What about his mistress, Reverend, have you met his mistress?'

Prescott leaped to his feet and bellowed his objection.

Judge Gimbel waved us to the bench, leaned forward, and said in a low rasping voice, 'Explain yourself, Mr Carl.'

'Last I heard, Your Honor,' I said calmly, 'adultery was a violation of both God's law and the penal code. Now the reverend has testified as to his opinion of the councilman's law-abiding character as well as his adherence to God's law. I am now entitled to ask questions about that opinion, as well as to inquire on specific instances of the councilman's conduct. Rule 405(a) of the Federal Rules of Evidence allows this precise question.'

'Rule 405(a)?' asked Judge Gimbel. He snapped at his clerk and a leatherbound volume was immediately brought to him. He licked his thumb and paged through the book. 'Rule 405(a), Rule 405(a). Here it is, Rule 405(a). Hmmmmm.' He slammed the book shut. 'Yes, all right, I'll allow it. Objection overruled.'

'But Your Honor,' protested Prescott. 'This is far beyond anything relevant to the crime charged.'

'That's enough, Mr Prescott. You opened the door, so now don't be surprised when Mr Carl marches through it. Read your rules before you call your next witness.'

'But Judge . . .'

'It's Rule . . . What rule is it, Mr Carl?'

'Rule 405(a), Your Honor.'

'Precisely. Now go back to your seat and sit down, Mr Prescott. You can ask your question, Mr Carl.'

'Thank you, sir.'

I stepped back to the podium and stared sweetly at the jurors as I said, 'Now, Reverend, I'll repeat the question. Have you ever met Councilman Moore's mistress?'

The reverend hesitated just enough so that the whole courtroom knew he was lying and then said, 'No.'

I turned my attention to him sharply. 'You're under oath now, sir,' I said. 'You have sworn on the Bible to speak only the truth. Are you telling me you have never met Veronica Ashland?'

The reverend looked nervously at Jimmy, at the judge, and then said, 'I have been introduced to Miss Ashland.'

'Pretty woman, isn't she?'

'My my, yes.' He paused for a second and involuntarily licked his lips. 'As are all God's creatures,' he added.

'And you knew that Miss Ashland was Jimmy Moore's mistress.'

'I had been told that, yes,' said the reverend.

'Objection, hearsay,' shouted Prescott.

'Sustained, answer is stricken.'

'How did Councilman Moore introduce her to you, Reverend?' I asked.

'As a dear friend.'

'But you knew that to mean mistress?'

'Well, sir, the councilman is a very passionate man.'

'That means you knew her to be his mistress.'

The reverend looked at Jimmy with pleading eyes and then said, 'That's what I assumed.'

'Now you've been with the councilman on one or two of his evenings out with his limousine and Miss Ashland, haven't you?' I glanced over at Chet and the reverend followed my gaze and knew immediately all that I knew.

Staring at Chester, he said, 'Yes, that's right.'

'You drank champagne with the councilman and Miss Ashland.'

'That's right.'

'Good champagne, right? The best.'

'I don't remember the quality of the champagne.'

'And the councilman paid for everything, isn't that right?'

'I don't know.'

'Well, you didn't pay, did you, Reverend?'

'No, sir. The pulpit is not a place for prosperity.'

'Are you aware, Reverend, that the councilman met Miss Ashland, his mistress, at a crack house?'

Prescott leaped again to his feet as the murmuring rose. 'I object, Your Honor. This is pure slander.'

'Mr Carl,' said the judge, 'is there a good faith basis for that question?'

'Yes, sir.'

'Proceed.'

'Answer the question, Reverend. Were you aware of that?'

'No, I wasn't.'

'Are you aware that the councilman has put Miss Ashland up in a luxury apartment in Olde City with a sweetheart lease at far below market value?'

'No, sir.'

'Are you aware that during this trial he has slipped up to that apartment numerous times to visit late into the night with his mistress, Veronica Ashland?'

'No, sir, I was not.'

'Now, sir, adultery is against God's law, is it not?'

'Yes. That is one of the Ten Commandments handed down to Moses on Mt Sinai.'

'One of the big ten of God's laws, isn't that right?'

'You could say that it is one of the big ten, yes.'

'Like the prohibition against bearing false witness.'

'Yes.'

'And the Sixth Commandment is also one of the big ten, isn't that right?'

'Yes, sir, it is right there in Exodus, chapter 20, verse 13. "Thou shalt not murder." '

'And someone who has so easily violated one of the Ten Commandments might just as easily violate another.'

'I can't say that for certain.'

'But all of God's laws are equally vital. I mean, you don't preach it's okay to violate some of the Ten Commandments and not others. You don't preach, go ahead and steal, just don't take the Lord's name in vain, now do you?'

'No, sir, it is all God's law.'

'And both adultery and murder, along with being against God's law, are also against the secular law, isn't that so?'

'I am not a lawyer, sir.'

'Good for you, Reverend, that puts you one up on the rest of us here. I have no further questions.'

As I walked back to my seat I had a panoramic view of the defense table. Chester was sitting calmly, his hands clasped before him on the table, looking straight so as to avoid Jimmy's stare. Jimmy's face was dark with anger, his facial muscles moving like stung slugs beneath his skin. Prescott was in a desperate conference with two of his associates.

The battle had been joined.

Just before I sat down I noticed someone leaving the courtroom. It was Moore's wife, Leslie, head high, posture erect, rushing out of there as fast as she could go.

46

The fistfight started in the men's room before spilling into the hallway. US marshals, stiff and heavy, ears plugged, blazers flapping, lumbered over to break it up, but the ferocity of the combatants kept them at bay. Jimmy Moore had hold of Chet Concannon's neck. Chester held tight to Jimmy Moore's crotch. Their shoes slipped on the smooth tile floor as they struggled in silence. With their free arms they were flailing, one at the other, like hockey players. Chester landed a few mighty hooks into Jimmy's stomach and then Jimmy butted him, a brutal contraction of the arm that left Jimmy dazedly swirling away and Chet bleeding in sheets down his forehead even as he maintained his death grip on Jimmy's crotch. A photographer's flash popped like a firecracker. The picture landed on the front page of the *Daily News* under the headline COURT HALL BRAWL.

After the judge had dismissed the jury early for the day, once again admonishing them not to read the newspapers, and after he issued contempt citations, fining Chester and Jimmy each five hundred dollars and threatening both with jail if anything like that happened again for the rest of the trial, and after the bloodied Chester Concannon headed home in a taxi and the bowed Jimmy Moore stepped out of the courthouse bent over double, as if he had eaten a bad piece of pork, Prescott slipped beside me on the courthouse steps.

'Your client has been fired from the councilman's staff,' said Prescott.

'Evidently,' I said. 'But it was only a matter of time.'

'That's right,' said Prescott. 'Only for as long as the

loyalty shown by my client to a subordinate would continue to impress the jury and keep Concannon in line at the same time. There's no need for it now. It is my understanding that Concannon somehow obtained a copy of our expert's jury survey.'

'You mean the one you had promised repeatedly to send me but never did?'

'Precisely. It is what Chester told Jimmy before their little burlesque broke out. How did he get a copy of it, hmmm? Do you know?'

'I gave it to him.'

'How did you get it, Victor?'

I shrugged. 'I have my sources, Billy.'

He put his arm around my shoulders and squeezed hard enough for me to hear a crack. Looking the other way he said, 'Don't call me Billy again or I'll snap you in two. There was a break-in at my office last night. Nothing was missing except that report. I requested the entire office be dusted for fingerprints. You wouldn't mind giving us a sample of yours, would you?'

'I would, actually,' I said. 'On principle, you understand.'

He let go of me. Like an injured ballplayer, I restrained from rubbing my shoulder.

Prescott said, 'You really stepped in it today, Victor.'

'The day I stepped in it was that first afternoon when I walked into your office.'

'I would have thought you'd be grateful,' he said. 'You were a nothing and I gave you the opportunity to be a something.'

'The opportunity to play your dupe.'

'Really now, Victor. What other role could you play? I'm very disappointed in you.'

'I am crushed,' I said.

'Yes, that's right. I am going to crush you. You know of course that CUP is very dissatisfied with your personal attack on their chairman.'

'I assumed they would be.'

430

'They've forbidden Blaine, Cox to even think of hiring you.'

'I don't need their stinking job,' I said with my best bandito accent, but it came out wrong, like a whine.

'And of course they'll dispute your fees now.'

'I'll get paid. I'm a lawyer. I'll sue them if I don't get paid. That's what lawyers do.'

'Any judge will see the conflict of interest. How could you have expected CUP to pay for Concannon's defense when his strategy at the trial is to betray CUP's chairman? In fact, they have told me they are going to sue you for the retainer.'

'Good luck to them finding it. I've got nothing but debts.'

'Yes, we know. But still, judgments can be inconvenient things.'

I thought of Winston Osbourne and his sad overgrown fingernails. My eyes were involuntarily watering now. It was one thing to anticipate the firestorm, it was another to be in the middle of it. I turned away from him so he wouldn't see tears. Across the steps I saw Chuckie Lamb staring at us, something strange and open in his face. He saw me looking at him and he smiled as Prescott dressed me down, but it must have been an off day for Chuckie because the normal quantum of malice in his smile was missing.

'The Bishop brothers have already begun to look for other counsel on the Valley Hunt Estates deal,' continued Prescott. 'And my clients in the *Saltz* case have withdrawn their offer. Permanently. Trial is scheduled in two weeks.'

'We'll be ready.'

'Ready to lose. You have stepped in it today, my friend, yes you have. Eye deep.'

He started walking down the steps, away from me, and then he stopped and turned. 'After today, Victor, your career is dead. Gone. It has sunk from the weight of your foolishness. After today you might just as well go back to living in that crumbling house with that bitter old man, spending your days cutting lawns.'

Prescott's lawn-cutting remark sent me to the bar. I found a place just a few blocks from the courthouse, a bar called Sneakers, and I figured it was a sports bar, but whatever it was I didn't care. It was empty when I went in, dark, the mashy sour smell of beer, like a frat house the morning after. There was music playing, some throaty folksinger turned up too loud. The bartender was a pretty woman with a pug nose and freckles and a boyish haircut. I asked for a Sea Breeze. She looked at me funny and I shrugged and told her to send over a vodka martini while she was at it. When the drinks came I downed the martini with a quick snap and chased it with the Sea Breeze, and although the combination didn't quite send me off to a tropical paradise as I had hoped it was fine enough for me to order another round.

So Prescott had learned even more than what was in the sad sheaf of papers in file 716. He had researched my lowly family history, my father's lofty profession, he had spoken to my acquaintances, my friends, to Guthrie, that bastard. And of course there would have been the chats over lunch with his prep school mate Winston Osbourne, Prescott getting the lowdown on the greedy second-rater who had hounded poor Winston into desperation. How pathetic that even in his decrepitude, with his fingernails long and his hair stringy, Winston Osbourne was still more welcome at the club than I. But of course he was of noble blood, scion of the Bryn Mawr Osbournes, and so it was squarely within the finest and oldest traditions of his people for Osbourne to lunch at the club with Prescott and plot against the Jew. And then Prescott, after researching the whole of my life, after drawing a detailed psychological portrait, after reviewing his information with the best minds of Talbott, Kittredge and Chase, after all that Prescott had decided to hire me, knowing, *knowing* that I would sell out. Was my weakness that palpable? Well, at least the bastard had me wrong, but at that moment, sipping the Sea Breeze, watching the pretty bartender make up my next round, at that moment I wished he had been right.

It was the flip side of the lawn-cutting remark that was killing me. Prescott was right. My career, in all probability, was dead. Beth had jumped a sinking ship and none too soon. Well, good for her. I mean, who was I to think that I could pull off something as audacious as this? I didn't have the power or the skill or the balls for it. I had chosen to take the opposite tack of my father and, with the inevitability of farce, that choice would lead me right back to the dark crumbling bungalow in Hollywood, Pennsylvania, or someplace very much like it, where I would spend my life sitting alone in a big faded chair, watching TV, hacking my lungs out into a paper towel, cursing myself for what might have been. I was not made for noble sacrifice or for the hard work of self-making. Let the Philip Marlowes of the world sit in sad satisfaction of their nobility. I didn't want to be noble anymore, I wanted to be somebody, and for guys like me it was one or the other.

The bartender placed the drinks in front of me and I smiled at her. I took a sip of the martini, letting out a sigh when I was finished.

'Woman trouble,' she said to me with a knowing smile.

'How could you tell?'

'We get that a lot around here.'

'I bet you do,' I said.

Veronica and her whippet body and her thrilling insatiability. I took a gulp of the Sea Breeze. I had never before met anyone like Veronica, she had taken me someplace I didn't know I could ever find. What had I meant when I said I loved her? What was the nugget that still lay in my chest? I had never felt about anyone else what I felt about her, but was that love? It was more like a thirst, a deep desperate thirst. I took another gulp and felt it even more strongly. I wondered whether Tony Baloney might have been wrong about everything, whether I might have jumped to the wrong conclusions, but even as I let my mind play with the thought I knew better. The cash withdrawals, the way she grew more harried as the evening aged, her kicking me out of bed every night so she could take care of her other needs in private. The wild greasy smell of her hair as she let herself go. She had told me half her story and I could figure out the rest. She had been hooked in Pakistan, cleaned up in Philadelphia by Jimmy, hooked again somewhere, and I was pretty certain where. There was a weakness to Veronica, a softness where she needed to be steel. You could see it in the way she drank, in the way she screwed. There was a need for indulgence that could never be satisfied, no matter how hard she tried. I figured she was up there now, in her apartment, desperately trying to figure out what to do. Jimmy, I'm sure, had called, warned her about what was happening. She was fluttering around her apartment now like a trapped bird. But I had something for her, something that would settle her down. I just needed a few more drinks to get up the courage to slip it to her.

Two women came in, nice looking, sharp-eyed women, women with faces that said they cared about politics and literature and saw the latest movies. That's what I needed, someone to bring me back into the world, someone like Beth. We could go to plays, the ball game, discuss the President and the budget and the Middle East. We could curse out Newt Gingrich together. Life would be just so grand. Veronica was not of this world, she was of her own. There was something sad and lost about her, something unconcerned. Maybe it was the accident outside Isfahan she had told me about, the van twisting down the slope, the fragility of life pressing itself over her face like a damp, smelly pillow. It was enough to drive anyone out of the present and that was precisely what it had done to her. But I wasn't going to follow anymore.

434

I waved at the bartender and she placed two more drinks before me. I was getting drunk and it felt good. Another woman walked in and eyed the place. She was heavy, dressed in jeans and flannel shirt, but with a nice ponytail. I always thought ponytails were sexy. Like back in high school, well, not my high school, Archie's high school. Ponytailed and overweight, what more could I want? She would keep me rooted, I thought. A ton of fun, yes. Someone like her. Jesus, I was drinking too much, but it felt so good. What the hell? It was a Tuesday, no court for another thirteen hours, plenty of time to prepare my cross-examination of Jimmy Moore. He was to be called tomorrow to testify in his own defense and he would bury Concannon. And what could I do about it? *Gornisht.* That was what was so sad about the whole thing. Even as I gave up everything I ever wanted, it wasn't going to do Chester a bit of good, it wasn't going to make the kind of name I needed to make for myself. Clients don't come roaring in to losers. Maybe I could call Prescott, tell him I was sorry, that I would go along, but to give that prick a victory, shit, I'd shoot him first.

Two women came into the bar with matching black leather jackets. Epaulets, belts hanging, zippers on the sleeves. Yes, tie me up with those jackets, wind the sleeves around my chest. One was pretty, one was not, I didn't care anymore. Tie me up with your leather, sweetheart, bind my arms and legs, flagellate, flagellate, dance to the music, tie me up and I'm yours. I downed the martini in front of me. What was that, my third, fourth? And then the Sea Breezes on top of them. Maybe Veronica was waiting for me, maybe she had been calling. I could use it tonight, yes. A few kisses, a few tweaks of those gorgeous nipples, and then slip it to her, that would be something.

One of the black leather jackets sat down at the bar beside me. My poor luck was holding, it wasn't the pretty one. She was thin, angular, her chin sharp, her hair like a sloppy Dorothy Hamill. And what was that on her cheek, that thin white line? It was a scar. Oh, God, now that was sexy. Maybe my luck was changing, a leatherclad vixen with a scar on her cheek.

She leaned on the bar and faced me. 'Enjoying the view?'

A line, I thought. What I needed to do was to give her a line. My thinking had grown thick, but I could come up with a line, at least. 'It's fine,' I said. 'It just got better.'

'Well, that's good,' she said bitterly. 'We just love to provide an evening's entertainment.'

What had I done now, I wondered. I didn't understand what she was saying. Maybe she was for sale, but if so she was a strange looking hooker.

The bartender came over. 'Back off, Sharon, we've talked about this before.'

'I'm just sick of the gawkers,' said Sharon.

'That's not why he's here.'

'Then tell me, J.J., what is he doing here?'

'He came in for a drink. I can tell the ones who are here to look.'

It dawned on me then. It came close to clarity, a thought just hovering out of reach, and then slammed into me.

'I'm sorry,' I said. 'I thought it was a sports bar.'

'You got to change that name,' said Sharon as she slid away from me.

'I was wondering where the televisions were,' I said.

'Let me get you another round on the house,' said J.J.

'Maybe I should get going.'

'There's no rush. Sharon's just a bitch sometimes but basically she's all right.'

So I had another round and by the end of it the place was spinning and I couldn't focus on anyone enough to gawk and so Sharon was finally safe from my gaze. The place filled up quickly, it was Tuesday night after all, and I watched them all as they came in. There were younger women and older women and pretty pretty women and ugly women and fat and fatter and skinny women. There were all kinds of women and for some reason, the drinks probably or the secret knowledge I had or some typical male perversion forcing its way to the surface, but for some reason I found them amazingly sexy. I wanted to date them all, to make love to them all, to each of them become a friend and confidant. I was in love with the whole damn room, J.J. especially, with her cute pug nose and freckles. Even Sharon with that scar, yes, I wanted her too. Every damn dyke there I wanted so much it hurt. Hell is being surrounded by all that you want without any possibility of getting it: hell is pure wanting without satisfaction. Hell was being in that bar, in love with the unobtainable. Hell was my life.

Enough with the self-pity already; I had things that needed doing. I slipped off my stool and crawled to the back of the bar, where there was one bathroom and a phone. I peed a river and afterwards fished in my pocket for a quarter and placed a call. Then I left a sweet tip for J.J. and staggered out of that palace of denial and into the soggy, moonless night.

47

I waited purposely in the shadows of Veronica's building for another old lady with shopping bags to come along, but it was too late for that. The little courtyard was strangely silent, the plastic-encased elevator was still. The drinks started turning in my stomach and a flowering nausea rose in my throat. While I stood there, concentrating on that blossoming bud, it started raining. I panicked for a moment, not knowing what to do, and then sick and wet I rushed into the vestibule and rang doorbells up and down the metal grid, rang all but hers. One by one they shouted at me through the intercom. 'Pizza,' I shouted back in a series of badly accented responses and finally someone, hungry and with pepperoni on the mind, let me in. I walked up the stairs to her floor and then carefully down the thin carpet of her hallway. Her door was locked this time. I rapped it hard with my knuckles. There was no answer but I could see a light through her peephole. I knew she was there, so I rapped on, rapping hard enough and long enough to make my knuckles bleed. Through the alcohol I didn't feel pain so much as a numbed sensation that I knew would evolve into pain. I kept rapping until she shouted at me, 'Go away.'

'Oh, let me in, Veronica.'

'I can't.'

'Jimmy told you not to let me in, right?'

'He's furious.'

'I have to see you. Let me in or I'll throw up right here in the hallway.'

'Do it and go.'

'Let me in,' I said. 'Let me explain, at least.'

'Go away.'

I leaned my head against the cool of her door and shouted, 'Just tell me one thing, one little thing. Tell me one thing and I'll leave.'

She didn't answer, but she didn't tell me to go away again either.

'Just tell me if Bissonette was better in the sack than me.'

There was nothing for a long moment. Then the metallic click of her unlocking the door. By the time I pushed it open she was already walking away from me. She was dressed seriously, in jeans and a white shirt, heavy shoes. It was a different look for her, a good look, I thought as I lurched into the apartment, ever entranced by her shifting appearances. She sat on the couch, demurely, legs drawn beneath her, head turned to look out the back window onto the rear parking lot. The cast to her face was tense, locked. I got a hard-on looking at her.

On my way toward her I tripped over a suitcase standing upright not far from the door. With the little dignity I could muster I pulled myself up from the floor. She was making it a point not to look at me. I grabbed the handle of the offending suitcase and lifted. It was packed, but packed light, a bag packed for a weekend at the shore.

'Where the hell are you going?' I asked.

'Any suggestions?' she said.

'I hear Cleveland is beautiful this time of year.'

She wanted to smile but held back. I walked over to the couch and stood beside her, swaying a bit, my raincoat shedding tears, and then I dropped down hard onto my haunches and leaned back, trying to look natural sprawled on her floor. The room was spinning on me, but she wasn't, she was tightly in focus and breathtaking.

'So what about Bissonette?' I said.

'How do you know about Zack?' she asked calmly.

'The police found his little black book,' I said. She was in there, under the name Ronnie, nothing else, no last name, no address, no phone number, just Ronnie. And five stars.

'He was so proud of that book, like a little boy showing off his baseball cards.'

'Tell me about him.'

'Was he better than you? Be a little different, Victor. That's your problem. You're so ordinary. You want the same things as every other guy and you have the same little worries. Am I big enough, is my girl pretty enough, do I make enough money. There's not one unique twitch in your entire body.'

'They feel unique enough to me,' I said. I would have been angry as hell at her except that nausea tends to drive out all conflicting states and so instead of spitting back something devastating and witty I closed my eyes and lay down on her floor. This was a bad drunk. I was going to be sick. I wanted to get this over with before I got sick. I didn't want to get sick in front of her, I didn't want to be that vulnerable in front of her, kneeling over the toilet, retching uncontrollably while she leaned on the doorjamb, amused.

'So you met Bissonette at the club,' I said, my eyes still closed. 'He was attractive enough and you thought you'd give him a ride.'

'I was bored,' she said. 'Zack looked different, that pony-tail, the sharp clothes. And he had been a major leaguer. I thought there might be something there but he had turned boring too, like the rest. It happens to anyone who spends too much time in Philadelphia.'

I opened one eye and it was like I was on a Tilt-A-Whirl, so I closed it again. 'You dropped him?'

'We played around for a little, then I told him it was over. He didn't like that.'

'I know how he felt. A man in love.'

'Yeah, he fell, but not until I told him to pound dirt. Before then he thought he was doing me a favor. That's how to stir passion in a man, I've learned. Walk out on him. But he wouldn't accept it. He acted like it was all a matter of his will and if he wanted me bad enough I could be had.'

'And I guess he wanted you bad enough.'

'He called incessantly. He sent me letters, flowers, Hallmark cards, like that would do it. A bottle of champagne brought by a bozo in a gorilla suit. He was a real charmer, all right. But one night, Jimmy was out of town with his wife. In a fit of absolute boredom, I called him.'

'One last dance.'

'Well, it was easy, you know. Just lift up the phone, like ordering Chinese food. You're sweating, Victor.'

'It's hot in here.'

'No, it isn't. You look like a sweating ghost. Were you drinking those sweet drinks of yours?'

'And those vodka things of yours.'

'Together? Oh, you're going to be sick all right.'

'Not yet,' I said, though I knew it wouldn't be long. 'And that last night together was when he pulled out the cocaine?'

'Victor, you little detective.'

'Am I right?'

'Yes, Victor, you are right. You have that link ordinary men have with other ordinary men. You can see through their tactics. That's when he brought me my little gift.'

'And he tricked you into getting high.'

'God, no. He held it out and I nearly raped him to get my hands on it. A sweet vial with one perfect chunk.'

'What about your twelve-step program?'

'Twelve steps to mediocrity. It was too boring without it, too sad. I didn't realize what was missing until he held out that vial at arm's length. Then I remembered.'

'But it worked for Bissonette. You stayed with him.'

'You don't understand. Neither did he. I wasn't with him anymore, I was with the drug. He was just the prick who brought it.'

'How did Jimmy find out?'

'It wasn't long before what Zack was bringing over wasn't enough. So I started back to buying from Norvel.'

'And Jimmy found out.'

'Yes. Henry is still somehow connected with Norvel, I don't understand in what way, but that's how Henry found out and he told Jimmy.'

'And Jimmy went crazy.'

'He has a thing about drugs,' she said calmly. But it was more than just drugs, I knew. It was history repeating itself. If it was happening to anyone else Jimmy Moore might have handled it, but not to his surrogate daughter Veronica. He had saved her life, had cleaned her up, and now to see it happen all over again, like it had happened to Nadine, to be threatened with once again losing his daughter was too much to bear, even if it wasn't his daughter, even if it was only the piece of trim who had taken the place of his daughter. What anger he felt was coming from a deep, primal place within him and there was no soothing it with words, no arresting it with reason, no assuaging it with anything other than blood.

'And then he killed Bissonette,' I said.

'I didn't know what he was going to do. He came over in a rage and I told him.'

'Who drove him here?'

'I don't know. He came in alone and I told him. But I didn't know what he was going to do.'

'You knew.'

'I knew he was going to do something.'

'You knew. Shit.' I struggled to rise to a sitting position and felt my stomach fall like it was falling down a shaft. 'What about the series of cash deposits made into your account?' I asked, trying to fight the nausea.

'Jimmy told me what to do. I only did what Jimmy told me.'

'Where did the money end up?'

'I don't know.'

'You're lying.'

442

'I don't know.'

My falling stomach hit bottom with a spasm. 'Oh my God,' I gasped. 'I have to go.' I stumbled to my feet and reached out to steady myself and missed the couch armrest and slammed my head into the side table and fell to my knees. It was already up, in my mouth, held there by clenched teeth and my right hand when I struggled again to my feet and ran, bent over, like a hunchback, to the stairs and up two half-flights to her bathroom.

It came out in a noisy, involuntary series of retches that left my sides cramping and my throat burning and saliva hanging from my mouth in long strands. With each retch it felt like it was coming from deeper inside me, until it hurt as much as if pieces of my lungs and guts were coming up along with the alcohol. The toilet was violet from the drinks, violent in color and smell, and my head hung just above the putridity as I waited for the next round. I was still wearing my raincoat, my suit was damp with a feverish sweat. In a brief moment of peace I turned my head and saw her there, leaning against the doorjamb just as I had imagined, except for her face, which was not smug but sad and concerned. I involuntarily lunged back for the bowl as the retches began again. The next time I turned around she was gone.

When it was finished I stood up and felt instantly relieved, light, spry. I was no longer sweating, the room was no longer spinning, but there was enough alcohol in me to still feel the recklessness of a mild buzz. I cleaned my face with cold water and soap and then opened her medicine cabinet. It was full of cosmetics arranged haphazardly, little red plastic medicine containers, Band-Aids, too many Band-Aids. I pulled out a thick plastic comb and ran it through my hair, I used her toothbrush to scrub my teeth, I rinsed my mouth with her Scope. When I came downstairs she was putting on an overcoat.

'Where are you going?' I asked.

'Away. It's ruined for me here.'

'Because of what I did in court today?'

'No, but that was the signal to leave.'

'Why don't you stay, get some help?'

'I don't need help,' she said.

'You're a drug addict, Veronica. You need help. You need to check in someplace.'

'I'm going home.'

'Iowa?' I asked.

'Maybe.'

'You need more than a veterinarian.'

'Good-bye, Victor.'

'He's going to let Chester take the rap for what he did.'

'I know,' she said. 'That's too bad. Chet was always sweet to me. We slept together once, did I tell you? The night he said he had a crush on me I let him.'

I tried not to think about it, to imagine it. 'You could save him,' I pressed on. 'You could testify, tell them what happened.'

'No, I can't, Victor. You know I can't do anything against Jimmy.'

'He didn't save you, Veronica. Look at yourself.'

'But what he did he did for me, don't you see? Of all of you, of Zack and you and Norvel and Chet, of all of you only Jimmy loved me. I won't betray that.'

'I love you.'

'You love it,' she said sharply.

'More than that.'

'Really, Victor? Consider it carefully. From the first I've lied to you. We've never spent a full night together, never shared breakfast, the first coffee of the morning, the first cigarette. You know nothing about me, Victor, so what about me could you possibly love other than our sex?'

'It's not so easily calculable, it's not like a ledger.'

'Oh, yes it is,' she said. 'Just like you told me the first night we met.'

'You can't know what I feel.'

'I don't think you know either.'

There was a pause and I started thinking about what she was saying and then I stopped, because I didn't want to think about it, I didn't want to look into it.

'You're the only one who can stop Chester from losing his freedom,' I said. 'Stop him from losing his life for something he didn't do. You have the duty to save him.'

'No, Victor. You're his lawyer. You save him.' She looked up at me with moist eyes and a tear rolled down her cheek. 'Please.'

I couldn't tell if she was asking me to save Chester or asking me to save her, but it didn't really matter. I leaned over and brushed one of her tears away with my lips and then kissed her and her lips opened and my lips opened and I felt her tongue once again and the electricity and the wanting and the unquenchable thirst. I reached a hand to her hair and grabbed and kissed her again and she kissed me back and I wished desperately that it could have been different. She sighed into my mouth. I rubbed my hand in her hair and kissed her again.

'You brushed your teeth, at least,' she said.

I smiled at her and we kissed once more and my hand dropped from her hair to her back to the little hollow at the bottom of her spine and I pressed her to me there and her arms slung themselves around my neck and we squeezed ourselves together and the alcohol in my blood burned itself off with that kiss. And as she pulled me closer toward her, melting herself to the contours of my body, I knew what I had to do. With my free hand I reached into my raincoat and grappled around and pulled out the envelope.

'This is for you,' I said.

She gave me a curious look and then ripped open the envelope with the excitement of a little girl opening a valentine. But it wasn't a valentine.

Inside was a piece of paper with great Gothic letters across the top spelling out 'The United States District Court for the Eastern District of Pennsylvania' and ordering the said Veronica Ashland of 225 Church Street in the City of Philadelphia, the County of Philadelphia, the Commonwealth of Pennsylvania, to appear in the United States District Court on the date specified, at 10:00 a.m., as a witness for defendant Chester Concannon in the trial of *United States v. Moore and Concannon*. The document was signed by the clerk of the court and accompanied by a check for thirty-six dollars, which included the witness fee and travel reimbursement for the four-block walk from her apartment to the courthouse.

'You bastard,' she said when she realized what it was. 'You subpoenaed me.'

'Yes, I did.'

'How could you? How dare you?'

'You told me that I should save Chet's butt. That's exactly what I'm going to do.'

'I won't go. I'm not going.'

'If you don't go, sweetheart, you're going to end up in jail.'

'Fuck you.'

I leaned over again to kiss her on the cheek, but she backed away from me as if I were about to rip her flesh with my teeth. So instead I gave her a light chuck on the arm and left her apartment for good.

From the huge window in her elevator, as it dropped slowly, I could see the empty plaza and the cobbled street beyond. It was still raining, pouring. Across the city old men, dazed by too much alcohol and life, were snoring. I turned up the collar of my raincoat and dashed out into the plaza. When I reached the street I looked first right, then left. I saw the car, an old gray Honda Accord, a short way down the street, parked in front of a little coffee store. I ran to it. The door opened and I ducked inside.

'An umbrella, Victor,' said Sheldon Kapustin. 'It's a relatively new invention, but very handy on nights like tonight.'

'Where's Morris?'

'My father hasn't spent all night on a stakeout since the Rosenbluth jewelry heist of 'seventy-eight. Did he ever tell you about that one?'

'No.'

'He will. It's his favorite story.'

'She's in there. Pretty, shoulder-length brown hair, about five six, thin. She's wearing a navy blue overcoat. She'll be carrying a black suitcase. She didn't pack much, and practically no cosmetics, so I don't expect she'll be going far.'

'Is there a back entrance?'

'Only an emergency exit with an alarm. No, if she comes out she'll come out here. I just want to know where she is. If she's about to get on a train or a plane stop her and then let me know immediately. I'll get a US marshal on her.'

'Sure thing.'

'What about Corpus Christi?'

'Just so happens, Victor, the number I spotted is a pay phone next to a marina. We sent a picture down to someone we trust to check it out.'

'Let me know.'

He nodded. 'You want a ride home?'

'I'll find a cab,' I said. 'You just keep your eye on her.'

'If she's as pretty as you say, Victor, that won't be a problem.'

The rain was falling into my collar and down my back as I walked along Market Street looking for a cab. By the time I found one I was so wet it didn't matter. I sat in the rear, rain-water puddling on the vinyl seat, and leaned my head back. I wanted to sleep is what I wanted to do. I was tired, too tired to even lift my head. I thought about stripping off my soaking clothes and standing in a hot shower and collapsing onto my pillow and sleeping. But I didn't have the time. What I had to do was strip off my clothes and take a cold shower and spend the night with my trial notes and my law books and prepare myself to devastate the inevitably self-serving and perjured testimony of James Douglas Moore.

48

I was working at my red Formica dining table, preparing for Moore's examination, when my doorbell rang. The table was covered with documents and yellow pads and books, Mauet's *Fundamentals of Trial Technique*, Wellman's *The Art of Cross-Examination*, Appleman's *Successful Jury Trials*, my copy of the *Federal Criminal Code and Rules*, but even with all that help I was getting nowhere. And then my doorbell rang. It was after 10:00 p.m. and no one should have been ringing my bell after 10:00 p.m. I remembered that the last time my bell had been rung late at night I had found Veronica on my doorstep. That would be serious trouble, I thought, but I couldn't help but also remember the feel of that last kiss and know that I still wanted more.

In a T-shirt and jeans I slipped cautiously down the steps and peered into the vestibule. Outside, it was still raining. I could see a woman in a raincoat standing in the vestibule, staring back out to the street. My throat closed down on me for a moment and then she turned around.

'Beth,' I said as I ripped open the door. 'God, come in, Beth.'

She stepped into the hallway, her hair flat against her head, her raincoat dripping. She looked closely at my face as if in doubt as to what she would find there. 'I heard about what happened in court today,' she said. 'How you went after that witness.'

I nodded. 'The good reverend. Well, my client seems to have discovered that he was being betrayed.'

'How did he discover that?'

'Somehow, and I'm not saying how, but somehow I got

hold of a document from Prescott's office that spelled it out.'

'And you gave it to him?'

'He's my client.'

She smiled cautiously. 'So I assume then, Victor, your future will not be taken care of by William Prescott III. What about those horrible Bishop brothers?'

'I've been fired,' I said. 'And the *Saltz* settlement's been pulled.'

Her smile widened. 'My oh my. How are we ever going to make ends meet now?'

'We?'

'The news said that Moore would be on the stand tomorrow. I thought you might want help preparing your cross.'

'What about Community Legal Services?' I asked. 'What about aiding the poor and disadvantaged?'

She shook her head at me and then reached around my waist, giving a crushing hug. The wet of her raincoat soaked cold through my T-shirt. 'That's what I'm doing, Victor,' she said. 'And frankly, sweetheart, you can use all the aid you can get.'

She disentangled herself from me and headed up the stairs. I looked after her for a moment. So it wasn't all bad, I thought as I watched her climb to my apartment. Even if everything else turned out wrong, it wasn't all bad.

We worked. Beth's mind was more analytical than mine and she helped me organize my disparate thoughts and far-flung tactics. Together we began to map out a strategy for going after the councilman, a thrust here, a trap there, questions emphasizing two facts that when brought together were blatantly inconsistent. We outlined generally the approaches I would take and then practiced on each other, framing our questions with great care to avoid the inevitable evasiveness of his answers. And where before Beth arrived I had been at a total loss, as we worked together the examination began to form itself into something more than a series of unconnected questions, to form itself into a coherent and effective assault on his credibility.

I was stretching from weariness, shaking my head at how much more we had to do, when the phone rang.

'So how do you think the old lady looked?' said Chuckie Lamb from the other end of the connection. His voice was subdued, not a bark anymore, but the sound of it still sent a shiver through me.

'I didn't mean to bother her,' I said.

'How do you think she looked?' he said again, more insistent.

'Pretty good, Chuckie.'

'Yeah, but you should have seen her when. She was a beauty when. A real beauty.'

'I'm sorry if . . .'

'She was the queen of the neighborhood,' he said, cutting me off before I could finish apologizing for my visit. 'And classy too. The windows in our house, they came from up and down the street to see her curtains, from blocks around. She was artistic, she loved the opera. That's what we listened to, after my father left, all the time. It was great after my father left because he was a fuck and after he left then it was just Mommy and me. She was a beauty, I'm telling you.'

'I believe it,' I lied. I couldn't imagine that toad-faced woman with her working gums as a bathing beauty. Beth was staring up at me, wondering what was going on. I shrugged like I had no idea, which I didn't.

'Once in the fourth grade,' said Chuckie, 'there was some kid beating the hell out of me. A Jewish kid, Levi, the school bully. Just whaling on me.'

Good for Levi, I thought.

'When Mommy finds out she comes to the playground after school and lifts this Levi by his collar, this big kid hanging in the air, and she tells him he touches me again she'd bite his nose off. He pissed himself, he was that

451

scared. Levi never bothered me again. On her way out of the park she slugs me with the back of her hand, knocks me down, gives me a beautiful shiner. I never got razzed as a momma's boy because of the way she hit me. How could they after that, and she knew it, too. That was her way, always taking care of me. She's getting better every day, I can tell. She'll be home soon. Making me her shepherd's pie, putting Wagner or Berlioz on the record player. How do you think she looks?'

'She looks great,' I said.

'She does, doesn't she. That was right of you to visit. Eight years with the councilman and never once did he visit.'

'What's going on, Chuckie?' I asked.

'Not one fucking visit. He never cared, treated me like cat piss the whole time. Chet visited, but he's like that. Brought flowers. She likes flowers.'

'What's going on?'

'You surprised me today,' he said. 'I thought you'd keep bending over for them, I was certain of it, though when I found out you visited Mommy I began to wonder. Why would he do something like that? Except maybe if he's not going to stay bent over. But it was still a surprise. I saw you talking with Prescott.'

'A friendly chat,' I said.

'And you subpoenaed the girl.'

'Yes, I did.'

'What you did in court was bad enough,' he said. 'They are very upset at you, furious. But you shouldn't have subpoenaed the girl. It was a mistake. They have their plans. You are in far greater danger than you realize.'

'Is this another threat? Is that what this is all about?'

'You're misunderstanding again, like you did before. All I wanted was to help Chet. I knew from the first that Jimmy would turn on him. I was certain you knew too and were going along with it. But then you surprised me. Listen, you can't realize the depths of the councilman's betrayal. It goes way beyond Chet, which is bad enough. It goes beyond anything imaginable.'

Suddenly it dawned on me that Chuckie Lamb was trying to help. 'What happened to the missing money?' I asked.

'I have a story for you.'

'Like Jack and the beanstalk?'

'More like Faust,' he said. 'But not over the phone.'

'Okay. Let's meet. Anywhere.'

'I'm close to the Tomb of the Unknown Soldier, do you know it?'

'Yes,' I said.

'Ten minutes.'

'Sure,' I said and then I thought for a moment and let a wave of paranoia float over me. 'I can trust you, can't I, Chuckie? This isn't a setup, is it?'

'You'll understand when we talk,' he said. 'It will all be enough to make you sick. Ten minutes.'

When I hung up Beth was still staring at me. 'I have to go,' I told her.

'Was that Chuckie Lamb?'

'I think so,' I said. 'But he was mellower than usual, like Chuckie Lamb on Quaaludes.'

'What does he want?'

'He wants to tell me a story,' I said. 'I have to go. Don't wait up for me.'

I found my sneakers, put on a white shirt over my T-shirt, grabbed my raincoat out of the closet. I had already opened the door when I turned around and asked her, 'Do you know where the Tomb of the Unknown Soldier is?'

'Arlington?' she said.

'No, here.'

'Is there one?'

'Dammit,' I said, realizing I had told Chuckie I'd be there without knowing where it was. 'Who can I ask?' I said. 'Is the tourist bureau open?'

453

'It's after midnight,' she said. 'How about the phone book?'

'What, under tombs?'

'The yellow pages have maps in the front,' she said and she was right.

I searched through a map of Center City historical sights and there it was, in Washington Square, off Locust between 6th and 7th, the Tomb of the Unknown Soldier of the American Revolution, a soldier so unknown I hadn't even known he had a tomb. As soon as I found it on the map I headed for the door, late already, hoping Chuckie wouldn't leave before I got there.

Through the heavy rain I ran to my car. I soaked the seat when I sat down. I drove east on Locust, past DiLullo's and the Academy of Music, over Broad Street, straight through the rain until the road detoured at 7th Street, routing around Washington Square. I spun around the park and snapped to a stop at an illegal spot on 7th and rushed out.

The park was larger than a city block in size, ringed with a low brick wall. I ran through a gate and toward the center. The square was black with shadow, trees hanging low, blocking out whatever light the sky was dropping down. A few of the colonial-style street lamps let out a thin, lethargic light, the majority were dark. At the fountain in the center, its spout dead on this wet night, I spun around. From there I could see, on the west side of the park, twin rows of flagpoles, like a guard of honor, leading to a large wall of stone fronted by a statue.

I walked through a well of darkness between the flagpoles and came upon the tomb, lighted by two thin beams of white halogen. On a raised stone platform, behind a chain held aloft by bronze balusters, was a sarcophagus and behind that, atop a granite pedestal, a bronze of Washington leaning on his sword. I looked around. Nothing. I read the inscription on the wall of stone behind Washington: FREEDOM IS A LIGHT FOR WHICH MANY MEN HAVE DIED

IN DARKNESS. I looked around again. Nothing. I had missed him. 'Dammit,' I said out loud as the rain spilled from my bare head down the collar of my coat, drenching my shirt. 'Dammit to hell,' I said.

Then I heard something from behind that great wall of stone.

'Chuckie?' I said.

No answer.

But then came the shadow. From behind the wall of stone. It staggered through the low bushes, stumbling around the wall, toward me. I stepped back. It still came at me, stumbling again, reeling, barely maintaining its balance. And then it lurched into that thin halogen beam and the weak white light fell on its face.

It was Chuckie.

He came closer, it looked like he was wearing a beard, a disguise, and then he stumbled again and fell into my arms and slid through them and fell upon the raised chain, his shoulders slipping down until his head rested beside the foot of the sarcophagus.

I bent over him. My God, it wasn't a beard.

He was making a sound, a soft gurgle of a sound, blood pouring onto the stone platform from his mouth, from his slit throat, blood mixing with the rain, pooling into a puddle, growing lighter, weaker, until it was washed clean. Another gurgle, soft, horrifying, and then no more gurgles. Just Chuckie Lamb and the blood falling from his throat being washed to clear by the rain and no sound but the drops falling onto the park, onto the great stone wall, onto Washington's sword, onto the sarcophagus, onto his lifeless body, onto an envelope peeking out from his jacket, onto his neck, onto his face, no sound but the cleansing voice of the rain.

I took the envelope and ran like hell.

455

49

It was big news the next morning. The police had been summoned by a mysterious 911 call and had found him lying in the rain, his throat slashed. The official statement was that Charles Lamb, 43, unmarried, of Northeast Philadelphia, press secretary to City Councilman Jimmy Moore, had been found murdered at Washington Square. No motive for the killing was yet known and there were no suspects. He was survived by only his mother, Connie Lamb, residing at the St Vincent's Home for the Aged. The funeral was scheduled for Thursday afternoon at the Galzerano Funeral Home on Torresdale Avenue. That was the official statement, but there were rumors of late-night liaisons in public places with young boys and an editorial in the *Daily News* suggested that the police kiosk in the park be manned all night to ensure that Washington Square not turn into still another location for shadowy rendezvous as had turned so many of the public parks in the city.

Chester was mute with suffering, his pain marked only in a redness about his eyes, a tightness in his lips. I told him I was sorry and he shrugged me away, but I could see the hurt. I hadn't known before that they had been so close. Jimmy chose to vocalize his feelings, telling the press how valued a member of his team Chuckie had been. 'This crime,' he said on the steps of the courthouse, the start of his speech timed with precision so as to be captured live by the television cameras, 'will only increase my determination to continue my crusade. I have experienced many tragedies in my life, and this is still one more. But whoever thinks they can deter me from my cause, whoever thinks they can halt my progress, whoever thinks they can threaten or bully or kill my good work is deeply mistaken. We go on, we keep fighting, the dealers of death will be beaten and we will be victorious, and those like Chuckie Lamb, who were martyred in the struggle, will for always be remembered as heroes.'

Jimmy Moore, I figured, had wasted no time in grabbing himself another speechwriter.

Chuckie Lamb had neither been indicted nor intended to be called as a witness for either side, so his murder had no real impact on the trial. Judge Gimbel suggested, in light of the death of someone so close to the councilman, that we adjourn until tomorrow and Eggert readily agreed, but Jimmy Moore stood up in the courtroom and stated that he was ready to testify that very day.

'You want to testify today?' asked the judge.

'Yes, sir,' said Jimmy Moore. 'Mr Lamb would have wanted the trial to continue so that I can get this shoddy affair over with as soon as possible and direct my full attention once again to the business of the people.'

'That's fine, Councilman Moore,' said the judge.

And so the jury was brought in and Prescott stood. 'The defense,' he said, 'calls Councilman James Douglas Moore to the stand.'

Jimmy Moore had not spent a career riling up constituents and making impromptu political speeches without learning a thing or two about how to work a crowd, whether it be a thousand supporters on an election-eve rally or twelve jurors and two alternates with his future under their thumbs. I knew what his story would be, that he was the unwitting victim of the fiendish Chester Concannon's extortion plans, and such was the story he told, but the way he told it was something else again. He wasn't the chagrined and sorry defendant, he wasn't the humble man pleading his innocence, he wasn't quiet and reserved, confident to leave his fate in the hands of a jury of his peers. What he was instead was an angry man who had been betrayed by his aide, victimized by his government, subjected to political vendetta, and forced to defend what needed no defending. I would have thought before his testimony that such a demeanor would inspire enemies and turn off the sympathy of the jurors, but I would have been wrong. It was clearly playing in the Peoria that was the jury box.

Under Prescott's gentle questioning Moore spelled out his defense in clear and angry sentences. No, he did not illegally extort money from Michael Ruffing. Yes, he had helped with Ruffing's development plan in City Council because it was a good plan, and yes, he expected campaign contributions for such help, but that was the way the world worked in politics. 'It's the American system,' said Jimmy Moore, 'and God bless the American system. God bless America.' No, he had not known of the $250,000 given to Concannon in cash and had he known he would have forbidden it. No, he had not talked about money with Ruffing, that was not his style, he would have accepted whatever support Ruffing chose to give and he had thought the five fifty-thousand-dollar checks actually received by CUP to be extremely generous. Yes, he was angry when Ruffing told him he would stop payments, it smacked of betrayal. 'We were fighting for something side by side,' he testified. 'Ruffing knew I was counting on him to help with the agenda of healing. And then he had simply walked away.' But no, of course he had not killed Zack Bissonette. He had already raised over two million dollars for a run at higher office, why would he risk everything over a few thousand here or there? No, he had not burned down Bissonette's, it had been one of his favorite clubs. Yes, he lived an extravagant lifestyle, and why not? His wife had money, he had money from outside investments, why not live high if he could afford it? 'If the prosecutor wants to indict me for drinking champagne and having a limousine, then fine, indict me for that and let's try it on those grounds. But not on the fabricated charges they are leveling against me here. Not on the basis of nothing but political vendetta.'

He told them about Veronica in a quiet voice, dripping with abashment. Yes, he'd had a mistress. Her name was Veronica Ashland. She had been a college student hooked on crack. He had pulled her out of a crack house he had been closing down in West Philadelphia and had personally brought her to a drug rehabilitation center. After saving her life he felt some responsibility to her and visited her in the treatment center. She was getting healthier, learning to live without drugs, and between them a friendship blossomed that turned into something more. He was sorry for the pain it had caused his wife, his family, it had happened and he was sorry and now it was over. 'But I am truly bitter,' he said, 'toward my deceitful aide who has sought to use my painful relationship with this poor girl against me.'

He saved his bitterest vitriol, of course, for Chet Concannon. A lying, ungrateful cur, he called him. Chet was a nothing when Jimmy found him, a steak slinger who dreamed of getting involved in politics. He had given Chet a job as an intern and promoted him through the ranks until he had become his chief aide. He had trusted Chet Concannon, he had loved Chet Concannon, and in the end, Chet Concannon had betrayed him. Chet was a thief, a liar, he had peddled Moore's good name for a quarter of a million dollars. For all Jimmy knew Chet was a murderer, an arsonist, he didn't know exactly what Chet had done to keep his scam going, but he had learned the painful lesson that Chet Concannon was capable of almost any heinousness to achieve his self-interested ends. 'Just the other day, in this very courthouse,' said Jimmy, 'Concannon attacked me physically. He is seeking my ruin. He is my Brutus, plotting my fall. He is my Judas.'

When his direct examination was finished, there was an emotional silence in the courtroom. Prescott stood at the podium, eyes down, letting the silence hang there and intensify. I looked at the jury and they were split. Half were looking at Jimmy with sympathy and affection and admiration. The other half were staring at Chet Concannon with a violent contempt. When the silence hung just long enough for maximum effect, Prescott smiled at Jimmy as one smiles to a friend and said, 'We have no further questions.'

'Mr Carl,' said the judge, 'do you wish to cross?' He peered down at me over his half-glasses and waited for my response.

I had not yet recovered from the sight of Chuckie Lamb dying in my arms, I had not yet been able to erase the amazement of it, the sense of awe, the overwhelming rush of fear. This man who had been alive just a few moments ago was now dead, his life had flowed out the gash in his throat, past my shoes, into the sodden ground beneath the Tomb of the Unknown Soldier of the American Revolution. The sight of it was something I would haul along with me the rest of my days. I came home from the park after driving around for hours to find Beth asleep on the couch. What I did was strip off my clothes and dump them in the washer, raincoat and sneakers included, and I washed them with three cups of detergent while I stayed under the shower until the water turned cold. And then I slept, or tried to, shaking myself awake whenever I dreamed of Chuckie with the beard that wasn't a beard. I hadn't yet had the time I needed to deal with my first encounter with a dead man.

But this I knew. Chuckie Lamb wasn't killed by some young hustler out to rob his trick, like the papers made it seem, and Chuckie Lamb wasn't killed by a drug dealer out to scare off the councilman, like Jimmy Moore made it seem. No sir. He was killed because he was going to tell me all he knew about the councilman and the missing money. He was killed by Jimmy Moore, who had killed Bissonette before him and who would kill others if need be, Jimmy Moore, who had lied to Chester, to me, who had lied under oath on the stand, Jimmy Moore, with his cheap sanctimony and elephantine prick, Jimmy Moore. He had done it, dammit, and I would make him pay, I would, I would hurt him, I would. If I achieved nothing else in this life what I would achieve was to hurt Jimmy Moore.

He sat there on the stand, his chest thrown out, his eyes hard with determination, he sat there waiting for me. Well, he would get me, all right.

'Mr Carl,' said Judge Gimbel. 'Do you or do you not want to cross-examine this witness?'

'Oh, I want to, Your Honor,' I said, rising and walking with great purpose to the podium. I stared at Jimmy Moore and he stared back and for a moment we were locked together in some violent rush of antagonism. And then I saw it, what I had been looking for, what I had been hoping to see: fear. He knew what he was facing, did Jimmy Moore. The bastard knew what I knew, knew what I felt, and he was right to be afraid.

I tapped the podium softly with my fist once, twice. And then I began.

50

After it was over, after all the shouting, after all the sustained objections, after all the lies and the questions repeated with emphasis and the repeated lies, after all the pounding on the podium and the admonitions of the court and the requests for citations of contempt by Prescott and Eggert both, after all the sidebar conferences, after all the portentous questions asked and withdrawn before an answer could be given, after all the shouting, I was back in my apartment, hugging my chest as I lay curled on my couch, my shoes still on, my head in Beth's lap as she caressed my scalp and promised me it wasn't, it wasn't, it wasn't as bad as all that.

'Oh, yes it was,' I said, and yes it had been.

I had charged at Jimmy Moore's story like a bull, my horns aimed straight at its heart, but when I picked up my head I realized I had charged past him and he was still sitting in that witness chair, calm, smooth, waiting to deflect my next pass with his cape of lies. He was the matador, controlling me with his pace, with his responses, and he made a fool of me more than once in the course of the interrogation.

'You did all you could do,' said Beth.

'He ate me for lunch, and spit out the bones.'

'Now you're feeling sorry for yourself,' she said.

'The bastard was lying, Beth. All I wanted to do was to show him up to be a liar.'

'That's not so easy a thing to do with a practiced liar. You didn't get everything you wanted out of him, but you got all that you needed.'

'You think?' I asked.

'Yes.'

'Well, maybe,' I said, and maybe I had because I never for a moment thought I could win the case on Jimmy Moore's testimony alone. My idea was that the truth would save Chester Concannon, a quaint idea in this age where obfuscation and spin are the key to success in all realms, but there it was, and I could never have expected anything approaching the truth to come from Jimmy Moore's lips. No, the most I could have expected from Jimmy Moore was to create a pedestal on which the truth could later stand and that was maybe what I had done.

I had asked him about his daughter and he told again how she had died. I had asked about the rush of emotions that overcame him upon her death and, practiced as he was in exposing his inner feelings when they could do him the most good, he spoke of the pain, the agony, the anger. And out of it all, I had asked, had grown a hatred for those who sold drugs to children, hadn't it, Councilman?

'They are murderers, killers of children.'

'And you hate them all, with all the power of your powerful passion.'

'That's right, Mr Carl.'

'You have rededicated your life to fighting the scourge.'

'That is correct. They are murderers and they must be destroyed, each and every one.'

'No matter the means, no matter the cost?'

'They must be beaten.'

'Because they killed your daughter?'

'Yes, and thousands of others like her.'

'And you will see them all dead?'

'It is my mission.'

'Single-handedly?'

'If I must.'

'Vengeance shall be mine, sayeth the councilman, is that it?' I had asked, expecting not an answer but an objection, which was exactly what I got, sustained by the judge.

'That was a nice touch, I thought,' said Beth as she

463

stroked my head. Whenever my mind drifted back to those moments in court I could feel my adrenals kick into action and I began to shiver. It was her soothing touch that would calm me once again, would bring me back to the ease of the evening encampment when the battle was over for the day. 'Quoting the Bible was very Darrowish,' she said.

'Nothing gets them angrier than a Jew shoving the New Testament in their faces,' I said.

'It wasn't the only time you got him angry.'

'I thought he was pretty calm throughout,' I said.

'No, Victor. He especially didn't like when you started talking about his mistress.'

'Who would?' I said.

There was not much I could do but press his buttons and see which ones blew him up. The eruptions hadn't come as colorfully as I had hoped, but they had come and the jury had seen the anger seething within him. Like when I had asked about his high living, his club-hopping, his taste for the finest, most expensive champagnes.

'Life is to be lived, Mr Carl.'

'And you have a personal limousine and a driver?'

'For protection primarily.'

'And you support a mistress?'

'She supported herself, but there were certain expenses involved, yes. But that was the least of the costs to me of that tragic affair. The least.'

'And all that required money?'

'Yes. But I work.'

'A city councilman doesn't earn enough to slosh champagne in his limousine, does he?'

'I'm glad you brought that up, Mr Carl. No, we don't. And I donate much of my salary to charity in any event. But I was in business before politics and sold my company for a substantial amount. And in the last few years our personal investments have flourished.'

'Who controls the money in your family?'

'My wife, Leslie.'

464

'And so to finance your evenings with your mistress you asked your wife for money.'

'We have joint accounts.'

'And she never asked about your expenditures?'

'She trusts me, Mr Carl.'

'As you would have the jury trust you, is that right?'

The laughter from the jury box was answer enough and the councilman had turned bright red. 'That's something I found,' I told Beth when we were on that couch, reviewing the day, trying to find whatever victories we could dig out of the mess that was my cross-examination. 'Defendants don't like it when the jury laughs at them.'

'He didn't like it when you asked him about the anonymous cash donations to his youth centers, either,' said Beth.

'I didn't expect him to,' I said. 'But for all the bluster, it didn't do much good.'

Those questions came from the envelope I took off the dead Chuckie Lamb. I had hoped for revelations, a litany of answers, a solution to the puzzles that had been bedeviling me, but what I got instead were numbers. A monthly breakdown of donations to the Nadine Moore Youth Centers, showing receipt of anonymous cash donations that had been increasing steadily. But even the steady increase couldn't account for the jump that had happened about five months or so back, an extra fifty thousand a month of cash donations flowing into his projects. Fifty thousand a month with no indication where it was coming from. So I asked him.

'From concerned citizenry,' said the councilman.

I asked him about the jump in the amount of cash donations and he grew red for a moment and calmed.

'We've been reaching out to the community for funds,' he said, 'and those efforts have finally borne fruit.'

I asked him why the additional funding was in cash, why given anonymously.

'We don't ask who gives or why they give, we take the

465

money and work our healing magic and we are making a difference.'

For every question I asked him he had an answer and the judge refused to let the jury examine a piece of paper that came out of nowhere and signified nothing. And so, when there were no more questions to ask, I moved on, failing to have learned what the numbers were meant to show. Without Chuckie's explanation they were useless and Jimmy Moore had made certain Chuckie wasn't around to give his explanation.

'You didn't mention to anyone that I had gone to meet Chuckie last night, did you?' I asked Beth.

'Of course not,' she said.

'No one should know,' I said.

'Why not tell Slocum what happened?'

'Chuckie was dead when I got there,' I lied, 'and I ran when I saw him. I've watched enough bad movies to know what happens to the guy who finds the corpse.'

'Be serious, Victor. Slocum won't think you killed him.'

'I'm not gambling my life on what he'll think,' I said, but it wasn't just about Slocum I was worried. I had run with a blind terror from the dead Chuckie Lamb because his mortal wound was only seconds old, which meant that whoever had killed him was right there, behind that stone wall, ready for me. I don't know if he knew who Chuckie was planning to meet, or how much Chuckie had told before the meeting, but if he didn't know already I didn't want to tell him who to ask, now or ever.

'After the trial,' I said, 'I'll make sure Slocum gets the donation list. But I don't want you to be involved.'

She thought on that a while. 'Morris was there today,' she said finally, mercifully changing the subject. 'For a little while at least, talking with one of the court buffs, an old man with what looked like a hole in his head.'

'Herm Finklebaum,' I said. 'He sold toys on Forty-fourth Street.'

'Morris told me to tell you your friend Veronica is at the Society Hill Sheraton,' said Beth.

'She didn't get too far, did she.' The Society Hill Sheraton was about three blocks from her apartment building.

'Is she going to give you what you need?' asked Beth.

'No,' I said. 'She is incapable of giving me that. But she'll testify, and what she has to say will bury Jimmy.'

And it would, too, I thought, if Jimmy didn't kill her first. He had killed Bissonette and had caused the killing of Chuckie Lamb, I was sure, but I didn't believe he could kill Veronica. He had lost one daughter, how could he kill her surrogate, what kind of monster would do that. And suddenly I grew frightened for Veronica Ashland, and rightly so, for if there was any success in that day in court it was my success in showing all of which Jimmy Moore was capable. I had asked him about his temper, asked him if he grew angry when he saw something that shouldn't be, a wrong to be righted. I asked him if his temper ever got the best of him, whether he ever turned violent, and he denied it. But then I asked if he knew a drug dealer named Norvel Goodwin and he sat a little straighter in the witness box. The judge overruled the objection and I asked it again.

'If you step out into the community, Mr Carl, you learn of all the snakes in the grass waiting for the children.'

'Now, Mr Goodwin was operating his drug enterprise out of a house in West Philadelphia, wasn't he?'

'Yes. That was two or three years ago.'

'And one night you stormed that house with a gang from the neighborhood.'

'A group of citizens alarmed about the drugs in their community.'

'And that was the night you found your mistress, Veronica Ashland?'

'That's right. She was in that house being murdered with his drugs.'

467

'And that same night you also beat Mr Goodwin to near death?'

No answer.

'With a chair, isn't that right?'

Still no answer.

'Well, yes or no, Councilman?'

'It was self-defense.'

'Was it self-defense when you burned that crack house down?'

'I don't know how it burned.'

'Was it self-defense that killed the two boys hiding in the attic of that house?'

'I don't know how it burned.'

'Was it self-defense when you broke the jaw of the school-boy who was courting your wife thirty years ago?'

The judge never let him answer that one, too much time had passed for it to remain a relevant incident, he said, but the question had done its work, all those questions had done their work, I hoped. So maybe Beth was right, maybe I had done what I needed to do. Because Jimmy Moore wasn't my star witness and no matter how many times I asked if he had killed Bissonette only to have him deny it I had gotten from him what I really needed. He had shown himself to be a man whose passionate hatred for illegal drugs and their peddlers could cause him to fly into violent rages, a man who had beaten drug dealers with chairs, who had burned out crack houses no matter who was still inside, who had broken the jaw of a rival suitor while still in high school, in short a man who, with the right prodding, in the right situation, for the right reason, was capable of murder. All I had needed from Jimmy Moore was to set up the testimony of Veronica Ashland. It was up to Veronica to do the rest.

'You miss her,' said Beth, her fingers gently stroking my forehead, easing the surge of fear and anger at my own impotence that arose whenever I thought about what was happening at the trial. The smooth brush of her fingertips was drowsing and I didn't hear what she said at first, so she repeated it. 'You miss her.'

'Yes,' I said, and I did. It felt like there was a gap in my life, like something marvelous and strange had just up and disappeared. I wondered if this was what a dog felt after being fixed.

'How bad does it hurt?' she asked.

'Bad,' I said. 'I don't want to talk about it. How about you? Tell me about Alberto.' I rolled the 'r' as I said the name.

'Alberto. Sweet Alberto. He is very handsome and very kind and his accent is wonderfully sexy. A prize, really.'

'And that is why you dumped him?'

'You've been listening to gossip,' she said. And then, after a pause, 'I guess he was too happy, too contented. He accepted the world for what it was and accepted his place in it.'

'Suddenly I'm jealous,' I said. 'That might just be the very recipe for happiness.'

'I've been with you too long, Victor, with your cynicism, your bitterness, your dissatisfaction. After my years with you, how could I ever bear the cheerful acceptance and bland optimism of the Albertos of the world?'

'Alone again, just the two of us,' I said, and then I joked, 'It looks like we're stuck with each other.'

She just stroked my hair and said nothing for a long while, so long a while that if it had been anyone other than my best friend Beth it would have been awkward. But it wasn't awkward. She stroked my brow and eased me into a state just above sleep and the two of us remained like that for quite a while.

'It's never going to happen, is it?' she said finally.

'I don't think so,' I said.

'Why not, Victor?'

'It's just not there. No matter how much we wish it were, it just isn't. It would be too perfect anyway, too easy.'

'I could live with easy,' she said.

'Shhh. I am so tired.'

'I could damn well live with easy.'

'Shhh.' I closed my eyes and felt the softness of her fingers through my hair. 'I need to sleep. Just a little nap. Shhh. We'll talk later, later, I promise, but just let me sleep a little first.'

When I woke on my couch the next morning she was gone.

51

I arrived at the courthouse late to find Judge Gimbel beet-red in anger at me. With the jury waiting in their stuffy little room he gave me a ten-minute lecture on the need for punctuality in the legal system, explaining in wildly mixed metaphors how any delay, like a falling domino, can upset the entire applecart of justice. He was going to hold me in contempt, he said, fine me for each minute I was late, and if it happened again, did I understand, I would land myself in jail, did I understand, as sure as I was standing there, did I understand.

I told him I understood.

And then, after pronouncing my sentence and the terms of my probation, he demanded an explanation for my inexcusable tardiness. Well, he told me, well, Mr Carl, well, he told me, he was waiting.

'I was shot at this morning by an unknown assailant,' I told the judge.

That shut the gape in his great prune face.

'It was not the first time I had been shot at during the span of this trial, Your Honor. The police detained me for questioning, which is why I was delayed.'

So much for my contempt citation.

It again had happened outside my apartment. Two shots. One had spattered the edge of a concrete windowsill just by my head, sending shards spraying in a violent cloud of tiny, incising projectiles that cut a delicate red blossom into the skin around my left eye. The second shot had powered into my briefcase, reflexively jerked chest high after the first spray of cement. They had found the bullet lodged two-thirds of the way through my copy of the *Federal Criminal Code and Rules*.

Yes, the law had indeed saved my life.

After the second shot I dropped prone, more out of paralytic shock than any well-trained defensive instinct, and scooted, on forearms and shins, like a soldier scoots beneath barbed wire, scooted to the side of a parked car and rolled into the gutter between the car's tires. I lay there, waiting, hoping that somebody had called the police, thinking of Chuckie Lamb bleeding to death in the rain in Washington Square.

Five minutes of waiting, five minutes that seemed like five years, five minutes until the police car came. Two officers picked me off the street and led me to the back seat of their car. I sat there, dazed and bleeding, behind the thick wire division, like a criminal, telling my story to the same young officer who had handled the shattered car window just a few weeks before. Whatever had happened, I knew it was beyond him.

'I want to talk to ADA Slocum,' I said.

'On a crime like this,' said the cop with an annoying condescension, 'we don't bring in the DA until we have a perpetrator.'

'I'm involved in a case he is investigating, Officer,' I leaned forward to read his badge. 'Officer 3207. He'll be very upset if you don't get hold of him immediately.'

'We'll see, sir.'

'I don't want you to see, Officer 3207. I want you to do it this instant. Now. Or the commissioner will hear about it, I promise you.'

Slocum showed up ten minutes later.

'Oh man,' he said, opening the door and sitting beside me in the car. He was in his uniform, navy suit, red tie, rumpled tan raincoat with streaks of black newsprint on his sleeve, where his paper rubbed each morning. 'How did I know that trouble was coming to you?'

'This is the second time,' I said.

472

'So I heard. Why didn't you let me know about the first?'

'I thought it might have been just an accident.'

'Oh man, you are something,' said Slocum. 'Whoever the shooter was, he got away again. Nothing left but two casings from a thirty-eight found across the street. We bagged them and we'll check for prints, but don't expect much.'

'What are you going to do?' I asked.

'Me, I'm going back to the office, do some work, maybe grab some lunch later, nothing special. But then nobody's been shooting at me. The question, Carl, is what are you going to do?'

'I've got to get to court.'

'Slow down. You hate to keep Gimbel waiting, sure. But nothing will screw his calendar like the automatic mistrial because you turn up dead. So tell me who might possibly want to kill Victor Carl.'

'They should be taking tickets. Now serving number twenty-six.'

'What about your pal Raffaello?'

I shook my head. 'The one guy with no reason, yet,' I said, though he might just decide there was reason enough if I didn't find out where his money went. 'Besides,' I continued, 'I asked him about the first shot. He said if he wanted me dead I would have been dead. But Jimmy Moore, I think, would like me to disappear.'

'I don't doubt it, with the way you went after him yesterday.'

I lit up for a second. 'You liked that?'

'Not bad.'

'And then there's Norvel Goodwin.'

Slocum let out a low whistle. 'See, I knew something was up when you started asking about him.'

'He took me for a ride, told me he had an interest in this case and to back off. When I didn't he left a dachshund with his neck snapped and his belly split on my doorstep.'

473

'He seems to have a thing for dead animals. Something from his childhood, I guess. But what interest could he have in this case?'

I shrugged.

'Anyone else might want to take a shot at you?' he asked.

'Well, my ex-partner and I are feuding. He's a murderous fuck.'

'Ex-partners are like that.'

'And of course I owe some money to MasterCard.'

'They can be brutal, I know.'

'I have to get to court.'

'Sure you do,' he said. 'I'll tell the unit to stick around while you put on a clean suit. You have a clean suit, I hope.'

'I never needed more than one before.'

'They'll escort you to the courthouse. If you need them again on your way home, let me know. I'll take care of it.'

I nodded at him.

'But before you go,' he said. 'I've been assigned to the Chuckie Lamb killing. You know anything about that?'

'No,' I said, 'not a thing.'

'Because there's something peculiar. I was listening to the 911 tape and the guy who called the murder in, he sounded a lot like you.'

'Strange coincidence,' I said.

'And a witness spotted a man in a raincoat, about your height and build, running out of Washington Square just before the call.'

'Looks like you got your work cut out for you.'

'You'd tell me if you knew anything, wouldn't you, Victor?'

'If I knew anything you'd be the first I'd tell,' I said. 'After the trial.'

He sat in the car next to me, shaking his head. 'And I'm supposed to wait and see if you live that long.' He shook his head some more and then ducked out of the car. He leaned back into the open doorway. 'So, Carl, you've called a city councilman a liar in court, you've made an enemy of the biggest drug kingpin in the city and a friend of the biggest mobster, you've had your picture in all the papers, you've been interviewed like a sports star on the evening news, you are hiding information about a homicide, and now you've been shot at twice. How does it feel to hit the big time?'

He didn't wait for an answer. He just laughed and shut the door and strolled over to the cops, who were doing what cops do best, standing in a group and talking about where to eat lunch. But I had an answer for him, I could have told him how it felt. Just then, with blood on my shirt and a chilling nausea riding up my throat, just then it felt surprisingly good. The closest I had ever been to the big time before was watching the parade go by when the Phillies won it all in 1980. Well, I wasn't watching it all go by this time, I was right in the middle of it, maybe getting run over by it, true, but in the middle of it nonetheless, and what I was discovering was that that was just the way I liked it.

When the trial resumed, after gratuitous and insincere inquiries into my well-being, and after I had pulled my notebook and my legal pads and my *Federal Criminal Code and Rules* from my briefcase, each with a neat round hole through it, Eggert took his turn going after Jimmy. Eggert was very careful in his cross-examination, very deliberate. Bit by bit he went over the story, trying to mold it as much as possible to be consistent with his theory that the extortion and arson and murder were all linked together. It was a very precise, very workmanlike cross. And it was excruciatingly boring.

During one of the many breaks called by the judge to let the yawning jury walk off its drowsiness, I took a stroll down the long courthouse hallway. On my way back I was stopped by Leslie Moore. She was standing with her sister, Renee, but when she saw me she put a hand on Renee's shoulder and came over. Renee stayed about ten feet away, thick arms crossed over her chest, eyeing us suspiciously.

'Oh, Mr Carl,' said Leslie. Her voice was sad and soft, the breathless voice of condolence as one passes through the line greeting the family at a funeral. She was wearing a fine tweed suit, her silk shirt buttoned at the collar, and in the way her arms were held tight to her side and her hands clutched at each other there was something of the shackled prisoner about her. 'I was so sorry to hear about what happened this morning.'

'Thank you,' I said.

'Do you think you are in danger, for real?'

'I'm being careful where I step,' I said.

'After what happened to Charles we are all very shaken.'

I looked at her carefully, wondering how much she knew. Was there guilt in her eyes? It was Chuckie himself who had told me her problem was that she knew too much, that she knew everything. 'It was a tragedy,' I said.

She leaned forward slightly and lifted her arm, placing two fingers very close to the array of bandages around my eye, as close as she could come without touching. There was something so genuine about her concern it was startling, as if she herself had sliced my flesh with a fine-bladed knife.

'Be very careful, Mr Carl. Please,' she said. 'There's been enough tragedy in too short a time.' Was that a warning or a threat? I couldn't tell. 'And how is your eye?' she asked.

'It's all right,' I said. 'Don't worry about it, Mrs Moore.'

'I am a nurse, you know. I don't practice with patients anymore, but I used to. Maybe I should look at the wound.'

'No, that won't be necessary,' I said quickly. 'Why did you stop practicing?'

476

'There is enough money now,' she said, smiling tightly. 'Besides, after Nadine I lost the heart for it. I lost the heart for everything.'

'I'm sorry,' I said, and immediately felt silly for saying it, as if my offhand words could in any way fill the void.

She looked at her sister, creased her brow, and, without turning back to me, she said, 'I want you to know that I don't resent the way you brought out in the courtroom my husband's relationship with that woman.'

'I'm only doing what I believe I have to do, Mrs Moore.'

'I know. And I don't resent what Chester is doing, either. Tell him, please.'

'He'll be glad to know,' I said.

'We've all been protecting Jimmy for so long that it has become a habit. Like brushing our teeth or going to church. That's why I can even admire Chester fighting back like he is.' She breathed a deep, sad breath. 'Though I am paying part of the cost. My husband is a remarkable man, Mr Carl, but he is not without flaws. And it is impossible to know how hard these last few years have been on both of us. Nadine was a very bright and lively child. She wrote poetry for her high school literary magazine. She was very special.'

I stopped myself from apologizing again and stayed quiet. There was something she wanted to say and I could see her struggling with it.

She turned to me and took a step forward and put her hand on my forearm. 'You do believe him, don't you, when he says it is over with her?'

'I hope it is so,' I said.

'I believe him, I believe in him. That might be my great flaw, Mr Carl, but what is there to be done? I don't have the strength I used to have. But I was a good nurse once.' She smiled at me, leaned even closer, placed her lips very close to my ear. In the whisper of a conspirator she said, 'Be very careful, Mr Carl. Please. It would be horrible if something happened to you. And Chester, too. I've heard

477

the voices on the wind. But tell Chester I won't let them kill him. That he can trust I won't let them.'

She once again reached her fingers to my bandages and this time touched them gently before walking away, back to her sister. I watched her go, all that sadness go. She deserved better, I thought, and I realized quite suddenly that she thought so too. But I couldn't help but wonder at those voices in the wind. Time for more lithium, I figured.

Back in the courtroom, as we waited for the jury to reappear, I leaned over to Chester and whispered, 'Leslie Moore said something to me over the break about you being in danger. Do you think there is anything to it?'

His head turned quickly and his eyes startled. 'From who?'

I shrugged. 'She didn't say. Something about voices on the wind.'

'Probably voices from a bottle.' The way the trial had turned had brought forth from Chet a sarcasm I hadn't seen before. It was quite becoming on him.

'I'm not taking any chances after this morning,' I said. I had packed all the clothes I would need for a week and loaded them into my car. For the rest of the trial, I decided, I would live like a terrorist on the lam, never two nights in the same place. 'And after what happened to Chuckie,' I said to Chester, 'you should be careful too.'

He pressed his lips together and nodded.

'Leslie also said she would protect you,' I added as the door to the back hall opened and we stood as the jury filed in.

He turned around to find her sitting directly behind Jimmy. I turned too. Her hands were on her lap, clasping tightly one the other, and her face held the deep cast of a painful concern as she stared back at Chester.

'You can't know how relieved I am,' he said after turning around again, his face calmly looking forward, 'to have her on my side.'

* * *

Early in the afternoon, when Eggert finished his cross and the whole courtroom stretched with relief, Prescott rested Jimmy Moore's defense case.

'We have a few hours before we break for Mr Lamb's funeral,' said the judge. 'So you can begin to call your witnesses, Mr Carl.'

The only witness I planned to put on the stand was Veronica. With Chet's two forgery convictions, Eggert and Prescott both would easily make him out to be a liar if he testified, so everything would depend on her, which was fine by me, except she wasn't in the courtroom. I had expected I wouldn't need her until tomorrow.

'Your Honor,' I said. 'We will have one witness, but if the court will allow, in light of what occurred to me this morning,' I was milking it but so what, 'in light of the events of this morning, and in deference to the Lamb family, we ask that the court be recessed until tomorrow.'

The judge wasn't happy about it, I could see that, being that it was only two o'clock and he could squeeze in another hour and a half of testimony before the scheduled quitting time, but he seemed willing to go along with my request until the disturbance broke out.

'If you could be giving me just a minute,' shouted Morris from the back of the courtroom, standing in the aisle with his hand up. He was wearing his shabby hat and a crumpled blue suit dusted heavily with dandruff and his *tzitzis* were hanging down from beneath his too tight jacket. 'Just a minute is all I am needing to talk here with Victor.'

One of the marshals, blue blazered, his ear stuffed with ominous plastic, immediately rushed to Morris's side and took hold of his arm. Prescott ducked and the judge cringed. Now that the community of our courtroom knew I was a marked man a noticeable nervousness had set in.

'What is happening here?' said a surprised Morris, trying to pull his arm away from the marshal. 'What? Am I now a criminal?'

'Your Honor,' I said. 'Can I have a minute?'

'You know that man?' asked the judge.

'Yes, sir. He is my investigator.'

There was a sudden laugh from the group of young lawyers behind Prescott, from Brett with two t's and the others, a laugh at just how ludicrous it was that someone like Morris could be an investigator. People in the audience joined in, it spread gaily.

Without thinking I turned on the laughing young lawyers and said, loudly and angrily, 'Is something funny, you little pissants?'

It stopped just that fast. There was a peculiar silence, like the whole court had been caught at something, and in the silence I remembered that just three weeks before, when Morris first appeared in court and there had been a snicker, I had turned away in embarrassment.

'Take your minute, Mr Carl,' said the judge.

I motioned for Morris to come forward, and he did. I leaned over and he stood on his tiptoes and whispered in my ear, 'I have for you a witness.'

'Who?' I asked.

'Your friend, Miss Beth, she gave me a paper and I showed it to the man.'

'A subpoena?'

'Because of such paper he agreed to come with me, but I fear, Victor, that if you don't use him now he won't be back tomorrow.'

'Who is it?'

'Mr Gardner, a very nice man, actually, though he pretends to be not so nice. You should maybe, Victor, I'm no lawyer, but maybe you should call this man before he decides he doesn't want to be here anymore.'

'What is this about?'

'You ask this Mr Gardner some questions, Victor.'

He handed me four pieces of paper, a yellow original and three copies.

'Miss Beth said you would be needing more than one. I'll be charging, of course, for the copies. A quarter they

cost in this building. *Gonifs*, and our own government too.'
Then he turned and went to the back of the courtroom
and sat down again.

I looked over the original document briefly. Still puzzled,
I said, 'Your Honor, on behalf of Chester Concannon I call
Mr Leonard Gardner to the stand.'

He was a tall, middle-aged man with a fine suit and
shiny black loafers. His hair was curly and very tightly
trimmed. There was something hard about him, something
defiant and angry. He had been put upon for too long and
was not going to take it anymore, dammit. But even so he
was walking up the courtroom aisle and slipping into the
witness stand.

He answered the usual questions, checking his nails, letting out the arrogant sigh of a man whose time was being
wasted. He was Leonard Gardner, G-A-R-D-N-E-R, he
lived at 408 3rd Street, he was a businessman, primarily
in fashion, importing certain fabrics from Pakistan.

'Now, Mr Gardner, on the night of May ninth of
this year, did you by chance rent a limousine from the
Cherry Hill Limousine Company in Cherry Hill, New
Jersey?'

'I don't know specific dates,' he said. His voice was a
near sneer. 'How am I supposed to know what night May
ninth was?'

'It was the night Bissonette's nightclub burned down.
Does that help?'

'No.' His shoulders hiccuped in a snort and his gaze rose,
as if he were required to inspect the ceiling for cracks.

'Well, maybe this will refresh your recollection.'

I marked the original document into evidence and tossed
a copy each to Prescott and Eggert. Then I handed the
marked document to the witness. 'Do you know what that
is, Mr Gardner?'

'It looks like an invoice for the rental of a limousine.'

'On May ninth of this year, is that right?'

'Yes.'

'Have you ever seen this invoice before?'

'This afternoon. The man in the back with the funny hat showed it to me.'

'You mean Mr Kapustin.'

'That's his name, right. Kapustin.'

'Does this document refresh your recollection as to whether or not you rented a limousine on May ninth of this year?'

'Well, my signature's on it, so I guess I did.'

'And you signed for the limousine.'

'That's what I said.'

'And though you live in Philadelphia, you went all the way to New Jersey for a limousine?'

'That's where I went, yeah. What about it?'

'Where did you go that night, Mr Gardner?'

'We went out to dinner and then drove around. I had just closed a large deal for a shipment from Karachi and we were celebrating. That against the law?'

'Where did you have dinner?'

'I don't remember. The Garden maybe, or someplace. I do remember that the veal was overdone and the wine a little too impertinent, if that's what you want to know. A definite two forks only, no more than that.'

'And after dinner where did you go?'

'I don't know. I possibly celebrated a bit too hard that night. I seem to recollect I fell asleep in the car. I spilled champagne on my suit, too. A nasty stain. Ruined it. Twelve hundred dollars.'

At that moment Eggert stood up. 'Your Honor, I object. There is testimony of a limousine rental on the night of the fire. I will stipulate that limousines were rented on the night of the fire. Beyond that, however, I don't see how Mr Gardner's testimony is relevant.'

'Mr Carl,' said the judge, 'are you going to link this up any further?'

'I hope so,' I said.

'The law doesn't traffic in hopes, Mr Carl,' said the judge.

'Either tell me you can link it up or the testimony will be stricken.'

I turned around and gave a shrug to Morris.

From his seat, he shook his head with sadness. Slowly he stood up and started the long walk toward me. The whole courtroom was watching him now. He had planned it this way, I thought, and I didn't know whether to hug him or wring his neck. When he reached me I leaned over to him and he again stood on his tiptoes.

'Don't be a *goyishe kopf*, Victor. Ask him who the person he was with that night was.'

Morris shook his head some more, shook it at all the *goyishe kopfs* in the world, turned around, and slowly walked again to the back of the courtroom.

'I'll link up the testimony with just a few more questions, Your Honor.'

'Get to it, Mr Carl.'

'Who were you with that night in your limousine, Mr Gardner?'

'I had a date.'

'Who?'

'None of your business,' he said.

'I'm afraid it is, Mr Gardner.'

He turned to the judge and in an aggrieved voice said, 'Must I go into personal matters? Is that necessary?'

'Is it necessary, Mr Carl?' asked the judge.

I turned to find Morris sitting in the back of the courtroom. His eyes rose in exasperation and with a series of flicks from his hand he urged me on.

'I'm afraid so,' I said.

'You must answer the question, Mr Gardner,' said the judge.

'And it doesn't matter who it hurts? It doesn't matter if my date has been happily married to another for twenty years, that doesn't matter, I am still required to tell it all to the tabloids?'

'Answer the question, Mr Gardner,' said the judge.

'So tell us, Mr Gardner,' I said as he turned back to me and dared me with his eyes to ask the question again. 'Who were you with in the limousine that night?'

'This is personal,' he said. 'I don't believe in all this so-called outing going on, angry young men invading other people's lives. I don't care, really, but others do and it's not right. The Constitution applies to us, too. We might as well be living in Colorado.'

'I'm sorry, Mr Gardner,' I said. 'But please answer the question. Who was with you in the limousine that night?'

There was a long pause and a sigh and a shake of the head. He laughed to himself and then shrugged. 'All right, then.'

'Who, Mr Gardner?'

'Michael,' he said. 'I was with Michael that night.'

'Michael who?'

'Michael Ruffing.'

There was a gasp just then. It wasn't loud, it didn't last long, but I heard it in all its sharpness and pain. And I didn't have to look to see who it came from. It hadn't come from any member of the jury, or from Prescott, or from Jimmy or Chester or the judge. It had come from the long pale throat of Marshall Eggert, who had just seen his arson claims against Concannon and Moore disappear and had just seen the credibility of Michael Ruffing, his star witness, who on the night of the fire at Bissonette's had been in a limousine much like the one seen leaving after the arson and who had used the insurance proceeds to pay his tax bill and stay out of jail, the credibility of that Michael Ruffing be crushed to scrap by the aggrieved voice of Leonard Gardner.

52

On my way out of the courtroom Prescott stopped me by grabbing hold of my arm. I looked down at his hand reaching around my biceps, but he held it steady there with a tight grip despite the force of my gaze. I could have said something sharp and clever just then if I had thought of it as he gripped my arm, but nothing sprang to mind, so I stayed quiet.

'Nice bit of investigation, pulling out that Gardner fellow,' he said finally. 'You're a constant source of surprise.'

'I'm just shocked that with all the resources of Talbott, Kittredge and Chase you didn't find it yourself.'

'Maybe we did.'

'But why blame Ruffing when it was so much more convenient to put the arson off on Chester?'

'You subpoenaed Veronica Ashland,' he said in a low, dangerous voice.

'That's right.'

'My advice, for what it's worth . . .'

'Not much anymore,' I said.

'My advice, Victor, is not to call her. You know, of course, if you do call her to testify I'll have no option but to bring out your sordid affair with her.' I had figured they had known, but I looked away from him anyway. On the other side of the courtroom, through a watery blur, I could see Jimmy Moore talking with a small group of supporters but staring at me as hard as a hypnotist. 'The jury will think that rather strange,' Prescott continued, 'calling your lover as a witness.'

'Our relationship is in the past. It ended the instant I realized she had information relevant to this case. But

485

whatever the jury thinks, they'll think she's telling the truth.'

'Her testimony is not going to be all you expect.'

'I think we'll give her a shot.'

'She doesn't want to testify.'

'That's why God invented the subpoena.'

'Jimmy doesn't want her to testify.'

'I'm sure of that,' I said.

'We seem to have the damnedest time communicating, Victor. I apologize if I'm not being clear. Jimmy has told me that he is worried about the pressure of testifying on her fragile physical condition. He believes that forcing her to testify at this most difficult time in her life could be dangerous to her health.'

'That sounds like a threat.'

'Don't be silly. But Jimmy wanted you to be aware of all the possible consequences of putting that girl on the stand.'

'Because if that's a threat,' I went on, 'that would be obstruction of justice.'

'I was just voicing a concern that had been explained to me by my client.'

'Maybe I should call Eggert over here, and Special Agent Stemkowski. Maybe you could voice Jimmy's concern to them.'

He smiled at me. 'That won't be necessary,' he said, then he turned around and walked over to his client. It would have been a small moment of triumph for me, except for that smile. It wasn't a nervous smile, there was no tension in it, no worry. It was a chess player's smile, as if he had opened with P-Q4, I had countered with P-Q4 and he had replied with P-QB4, offering his queenside bishop's pawn for capture. I had played enough chess in the geekdom of my youth to know the price of accepting that pawn. His smile was the smile that invariably accompanies a gambit and I didn't like it one bit.

*   *   *

Morris was waiting for me outside the courtroom. He had agreed to drive with me to the office, my protector now that I was under attack. The thought of Morris protecting me was oddly comforting. I was going straight to the office because I had decided to skip Chuckie's funeral, decided for the best of all possible reasons: naked fear. Together Morris and I walked down the hall to the elevator.

'You could have told me what Gardner's testimony would be at the first,' I said

'So where would be such fun in that?'

'This isn't fun. I'm dying here and you're talking about fun.'

'Such *kvetching*. You drew it out of him in the end. A lawyer as grand as yourself, Victor, I knew you would be getting to the bottom of what he had for the telling.'

I looked around the hallway. 'Where's Beth? Have you seen her?'

'I sent her off on a little errand,' said Morris.

'To pick up your dry cleaning?'

'That too needs doing,' he said. 'Now quiet please, I have news for you from Corpus Christi.'

'You found Stocker?' I asked.

Morris stopped walking, took out his glasses and little notebook, and searched through the notebook's pages and the scraps stuck inside those pages for his notes. 'Aaah, yes. Here it is.' He pulled out a piece of envelope with a tight scrawling over it and began walking again, squinting through his glasses all the while at the tiny print. 'It seems there is a Mr Cavanaugh at the Downtown Marina on a Bay Shore Drive in Corpus Christi that bears a striking resemblance to our Mr Stocker. This Mr Cavanaugh is in a thirty-six-foot sailboat. He sailed over from the west coast of Florida. He is renting his berth at the marina by the week. He has no visitors, no friends, he drinks like a carp, and talks of sailing to South America. And this Mr Cavanaugh makes calls from the marina's pay phone, which just happens to be the same number that has placed calls to that Mr Prescott whose office you burgled like a cat.'

'And you think Cavanaugh is Stocker?'

'Of course I think that, such a *dorfying* you are sometimes, Victor. Why else am I telling all this to you?' We reached the elevators and Morris pushed the down button. 'But whether it is so or not, we can only know by going down and finding out.'

'So go,' I said.

'No, thank you,' said Morris. 'Where would I eat in Corpus Christi? You think they got a kosher deli in Corpus Christi? You think they got pastrami in Corpus Christi?'

'You're not going down?'

'After this trial, maybe, you and Miss Beth can make the trip.'

'Why not now?' I said. 'It doesn't do us any good if you find out that it's him and then he sails away to Paraguay.'

'From what we know it doesn't look like he is going anywhere too fast,' said Morris. 'Besides, he can't be sailing off to Paraguay.'

'And why not?' I asked.

'There is no seaport in Paraguay,' said Morris. 'It is in the mountains.'

'So now you're the geography wizard?'

'I had reason to be searching once for criminals in Paraguay.'

'What, Morris, you were a Nazi hunter?' I asked through my laughter. 'You were searching the mountains of Paraguay for wayward German colonels?'

'Yes,' said Morris in a cold voice that shut me up quick. We stood there in an awkward silence while Morris stared at me until I began looking down at the scuffs on my shoes. The elevator came, breaking the moment, but before I could enter it Eggert grabbed hold of my arm and yanked me aside.

'Are you still interested in a deal?' he asked.

'What are you offering?'

488

'Plead guilty to extortion only, testify against the councilman, we'll recommend minimum jail time. I'll even talk to the US Attorney about probation.'

'Gardner's testimony shook you up a little, hey, Marshall?'

'Not at all,' he said, but his hand was in his pocket and his change was jingling out a very different tune. 'It's inconclusive at best.'

'Maybe. But your taxi driver witness said the limo he saw flashed his brights, like a signal, as if it were hoping to be noticed. And now we know that Ruffing, who collected the insurance on the property, was tooling around that night in a black limousine. It doesn't take a brain surgeon to see the connection. Your arson just disappeared from the case, and so, probably, did the racketeering charge. Now you want my client to plead to the only real charge left.'

He sniffed twice. 'It's a good deal, Carl.'

'This trial has come down to either or. It's either Moore or Concannon. The only way for you to get both is for one to plead and rat out the other. Sit tight, Marshall. We'll talk after my witness tomorrow. If she is all I expect, tomorrow you'll be offering immunity and be damn glad to give it.'

I walked away, not waiting for a response. A week before I would have jumped at his offer, leaped at it like Charles Barkley leaping for a rebound, but it wasn't a week before anymore. I was back in the game, I was on a roll, and tomorrow I was going up for the winning score.

53

It was a cold gray morning, a winter morning at the tail end of the fall. My breath fled in wispy clouds as I walked from the underground parking garage beside the courthouse to the Society Hill Sheraton, where Veronica was hiding out. It was a peculiar place to hide, a large but not tall brick building with a wide and active lobby, from which guests in tracksuits flowed out through the glass doors and around the courtyard to run along the Delaware River. Morris told me he would be in the gray Honda, waiting for me. I spotted it resting at the end of a long line of cars parked across the wide cobblestone street from the front of the hotel. All the cars but Morris's faced the curb; Morris had backed the Honda in so he could see the front of the lobby without twisting.

'Anything?' I asked.

'You didn't bring mine coffee?' said Morris.

'I forgot, I'm sorry.'

'The first rule in surveillance, Victor, the very first rule. Never forget the coffee.'

'I'll get you some coffee.'

'Stop, don't be worrying yourself. It is the first rule, but it is maybe not such a very good rule, because once it goes in it has to go out, which is very inconvenient, believe you me, in the middle of a following. When are you wanting her in the courtroom?'

'This morning, ten o'clock.'

'Does she want to go?'

'I'll talk to her, she'll come. All right, let's go get her.'

'Hold your horses,' said Morris.

'Hold your horses?'

'Yes, hold your horses. That's a very fine expression, I think. What, I couldn't have been a cowboy.'

'Have you ever ridden a horse, Morris?'

'What's to riding a horse, you tell me? I can sit, I can hold onto the straps, I can say go and stop, I can ride. Look over there, by the front driveway.'

'The silver BMW?'

'Such a car I should own. Beautiful, no? Except for that it is German it is a wonderful car.'

'Why are we admiring a car?'

'Because it has been parked there all morning. Just sitting there, but for when one of the men left for a few minutes and came back with coffee.'

'You think they're watching the lobby entrance?'

'The coffee was what gave it away to me,' said Morris. 'Already you're forgetting the first rule of surveillance.'

'They could be waiting for anyone,' I said.

'They could, yes.'

'But they might also be Jimmy's people.'

'That too.'

'No one but Jimmy and us should know she's there. Maybe we should go in from the back.'

'I think it's important that we know who's in that car, don't you?'

'Why?'

'You told me there's a valise full of money missing, floating free, is such a fact?'

'A quarter of a million dollars.'

'Well, Victor, I may be wrong, I'm often wrong, just ask Rosalie and she'll tell you, just bump into her in the street and . . .'

'What are you thinking, Morris?' I said.

'I would bet that whoever has that money is the one who sent those people in that fancy car to sit there watching.'

I took a closer look at the silver BMW. 'You think so?'

'I just said it, didn't I? So what I am thinking is that you should walk into the front of the hotel so that who is in that car can see you. Then maybe we will know who is so interested.'

'I've been shot at twice already, don't you think that twice is enough?'

'Don't you worry about a thing. I am here, Morris Kapustin, and I will be covering you.'

'You're going to cover me? With what, Morris, with a kosher dill?'

I expected one of his witty retorts about Jews and pickles, but that's not what I got. Instead, Morris gave me a cold look and from his great black coat pulled out an automatic pistol. Its blued barrel gave off a dull, oily shine. With one quick and practiced motion he ejected the clip and snapped it back into the handle.

'Jesus, Morris, what are you doing with that?'

'You maybe never heard of Jabotinsky?'

'No.'

'There are many things you must learn, Victor. One shouting in court is not enough to prove you have learned all you need to learn. You still must learn about what it means to be a Jew and what it does not mean. You have much thinking to do about your life and yourself and your heritage, but not today. Today you will walk into the front of the lobby, slowly, as if you had not a care in the world. Don't be looking at the car, just walk in and we'll see what happens. If nothing happens, I will meet you outside her room, number 4016. Now go.'

I hesitated, but Morris literally pushed me out of the car and I was on my way, headed across the wide cobblestone street for the hotel. It was still cold, my breath still steamed in the frigid morning air, but I was sweating. I opened my lined raincoat as I walked to the round courtyard and tried not to stare at the silver BMW, sitting by the front, ominous, as frightening as a shark in shallow water. My neck twitched as I approached. Look straight ahead, Morris had told me, and that was what I did even as I passed the dangerous chrome grill. And then I was beyond it, fighting the urge to look back, heading straight for the entrance. But before I could reach for the long bronze handle to get me inside a car door slammed shut to my right and I heard the shout.

'Yo Vi'tor Carl, the man with two first names.'

The voice was familiar, slippery, and thick, it eased its way around the consonants, approaching then veering off just before it would have grabbed hold of them. I stopped in dread and turned. It was Wayman, Norvel Goodwin's henchman, who had driven me around in the councilman's limo and then smacked me in the face with the back of his hand. Which meant, if Morris was right, that Norvel Goodwin had the missing quarter of a million. How the hell had he gotten his talons on all that money?

Wayman was wearing a black and purple tracksuit, hightop leather sneakers, a sweatshirt draped over his right arm, hiding his hand and whatever his hand was holding. He was hustling toward me in a kind of a skipping step. By the time my frozen nerves thawed enough for me to even think of dashing into the lobby he was by my side.

'How's that eye, Vi'tor? It looks like it's all healed. Maybe you tougher than you look.'

'What do you want, Wayman?'

'Now that's nice. That's very very nice. You 'member my name. Where you headed, Vi'tor Carl? You got some fine looking female stashed in the Society Hill Sher'ton? You up for some early morning twist?'

'I have a meeting.'

'I just bet you do. Yes I do. We'd figured you'd be coming to visit Ronnie girl. Couldn't listen now, could you, couldn't say no. Even after I dropped that dog on your lap. Well, now, I can't blame you, she's not butt-ugly. But Mr Goodwin, you 'member Mr Goodwin, he aks'd me to kick it back and wait right here for you, so's to tell you that he don't want Ronnie to be testifying in court. He don't want Ronnie screwing up his plans with our councilman or mentioning his name to the *federales*. There are things you are

493

interfering with that you shouldn't be interfering with. You still not getting the least idea of what's going on here.'

'You're right,' I said. 'I'm not.'

''Course not, or else you wouldn't been so stupid as trying and make her testify. But now you know, and Mr Goodwin, he 'xpects you're going to be a thorough person.'

'I have to go inside, I'm sorry.'

'Now, see man, that's what I'm talking about, hey? You deaf, Vi'tor Carl, or are you just dissing me right here? I hope not, because if that be it I'm a-gonna kill you, just like I killed your little pigeon buddy Chuckie.'

I stepped back at that, my spine suddenly crawling with so many earthworms they could have dug my back for bait. I glanced behind me, looking for Morris's cover, but I didn't see him. Wayman caught my glance and misinterpreted it.

'You can run, Vi'tor Carl, oh yes,' he said, stepping toward me. 'If I was you I'd be booking too. Be my guest and run, run away, run, Vi'tor Carl, run as fast as you can. Run anywhere you want, just as so you not be running inside the Society Hill Sher'ton. What's inside the Society Hill Sher'ton is for us to worry about. You take my advice, Vi'tor Carl, and you start running.'

I stepped back again, stepped out of his reach, and decided I would indeed take his advice. Oh, I hated the idea of turning tail and letting Wayman see me kicking my butt with my heels as I ran away from the front of that hotel, but I hated the idea of Wayman doing to me what he did to Chuckie a whole lot more. I believe I've mentioned before that I am not, by nature, a brave man, but even the least cowardly would have run in the same situation. There was Wayman, with his anger and his tracksuit and his hand curled around who knows what wrapped in the sweatshirt draped over his arm, and there sat a confederate in the silver BMW, a white lug with ferocious eyes and hands tapping on the steering wheel like a drummer, just waiting to come to Wayman's aid if any aid was needed, and there was my memory of the way Chuckie had died, the way his blood had puddled on the stone before being washed clean by the rain. And there I stood, defenseless, depending on Morris to cover me, Morris, who had apparently disappeared. This Jabotinsky of his must not have been much of a fighter, I figured, if all Morris had learned from him was when to retreat. So I was about to take Wayman's advice and run from him and the drummer when I heard one of the hotel's doors opening behind me and a familiar voice.

'Excuse me, sirs, but I was wondering if you might could help me as I am looking for the house belonging once to Miss Betsy Ross?'

Wayman looked over my shoulder and I turned. There was Morris waddling toward us, his great black coat open and flapping, his fedora pushed to the back of his head, a small map, which he was struggling to open, in his hands.

'Mine granddaughter she told me I must take her to this Miss Betsy Ross's house,' continued Morris. 'But this *meshuggeneh* map, which I can't even begin to open for all the flaps and sections and pages, this map it tells me nothing except that Morris you are a *schlemiel* who never learned to read a map like an ordinary person.'

He was giving me an opening and I took it. 'It's north of here, on Arch Street,' I said.

'North, south, what do I know from directions,' said Morris. 'Thank you, sir, but north might as well be up for all I can tell.' He continued fumbling with his map.

'Come along inside,' I said. 'I'll draw it on the map for you.'

'That won't be necessary,' said Wayman, his voice deep and precise now, the voice of a college lecturer. 'It's very simple. Go out this little street. Take a right, that's north, and go down four blocks, until you hit Arch Street. Then take a left. It is a little brick house with a small courtyard on the far side of Arch Street, between Second and Third. There is a colonial flag out front, you can't miss it.'

I looked at Wayman, flabbergasted by his new voice. He smiled a dangerous smile at me and suddenly, with Wayman having fled from even the shallowest pretense of my comprehension, I was absolutely terrified.

'Aah, thank you, sir, thank you,' continued Morris. 'I should write that down but already it is gone from mine head. Mine memory is like a sieve with a hole in the middle, that bad. If you could just show me on the map, if you could just . . .'

He continued to fumble with the map, struggling to open it, and then, with a sudden, frustrated jerk, his elbows flared and the paper ripped with a quick rasping tear and there were now two confused and jumbled pieces of map where before there had been only one.

'Accht, this is just like me,' said Morris, staring forlornly at the pieces in his hand. 'Now I must to get another one inside. And then, if it is not asking too much to help a visitor, then if one of you gentlemen can draw the way on the map, that would maybe let me get there without going first through Pittsburgh.'

'Sure,' I said, grabbing hold of his arm. 'Let's go.'

'That would be just peaches, yes,' said Morris.

'We're not finished here, Victor Carl,' said Wayman.

'I'll be right back, Wayman,' I said as I headed for the entrance. 'Just wait.'

Morris maneuvered so that he was between Wayman and me as we headed for the doors. In the glass's reflection I could see Wayman reaching over Morris's shoulder for me, and then I could feel his hand grabbing the collar of my shirt, could feel the cloth tighten around my neck. My throat let out a surprised little squeak.

Just then a doorman passed us on his way out from the lobby and seemed to accidentally knock Wayman's arm away. The doorman had huge shoulders, he was dressed in green, he stepped in front of Wayman and said, 'Can I help you, sir?' The doorman's voice was startlingly familiar and even as Morris pushed me inside ahead of him I turned and saw the broad back of the doorman and the yarmulke on his head. The doorman placed his hand on Wayman's chest. 'Is there anything I can do for you, sir?' said Sheldon Kapustin to Wayman as Wayman jerked his head in frustration while Morris and I escaped to inside the lobby.

'Don't run now,' said Morris. 'Like a hawk he is watching.'

'It would have been nice if you had told me Sheldon was inside,' I said. 'Sweat stains are so hard to clean. And even so you took your time.'

'Was there a rush?' Morris pointed to the right, where the front desk sat, out of the view of the doors. We scooted around the lobby furniture, wrought-iron tables and thick couches, and headed straight for the desk. 'I will be feeling in mine pocket for a pen until we are out of sight from the door,' said Morris as we walked. 'And when we are where he can't see us anymore, then we will run.'

Which is exactly what we did.

'Who was he?' asked Morris on the elevator to the fourth floor.

'He's an enforcer for a drug dealer.'

'So this drug dealer then has the missing money?'

'Evidently, and he killed a man already to keep me from finding out about it.'

'Ahhh, now this is worse than your original telling.'

'But he shouldn't know Veronica was here.'

'So how did he learn?' asked Morris as the elevator doors slid open at the fourth floor.

'I don't know,' I said.

'Careful now,' said Morris, and I followed him down the empty carpeted hallway. At Room 4016 he pointed at me. I shook my head. He knocked lightly on the door.

'Yes?' said the voice from inside.

'I'm sorry, miss,' said Morris, 'but I need to be checking on the heat inside your room.'

'One minute,' she said and one minute later the door opened and a loosely draped Veronica, still wet from the shower, peered out. Before she could slam the door in my face I stuck one Florsheim wing tip in the opening. What they don't tell you in vacuum cleaner salesman school is that sticking your foot in the door can hurt like hell, but pain or no pain it worked.

'You've been subpoenaed to appear in court today to testify,' I said when Morris and I were inside her room, the door locked and chained behind us.

'Who's he?' she said, motioning with her head at Morris. She was wrapped in a light silk robe, her arms were crossed on her chest. Her hair fell flat and clean against her beautiful shoulders. I could barely stop myself from dropping to my knees before her, she was that beautiful.

'He's a friend who is here to protect you,' I said.

'How comforting,' she said.

'Thank you, miss,' said Morris, ignoring her sarcasm.

'Who is he protecting me from, Victor? From you?'

'From Goodwin. His men are outside. He doesn't want you to testify.'

'Fuck,' she said in a desperate voice. 'Dammit, Victor. See what you're doing to me.' She walked back into the room and sat on the far bed.

I followed her, like I seemed always to be following her, and stood beside the bed. Morris stayed by the door, listening to the outside, so we were talking in private. 'He is probably going to kill you whether you testify or not,' I said quietly. 'At least that is what it sounded like. How much do you owe him, Veronica?'

She shrugged her shoulders even as she hugged her chest and wouldn't look at me. 'Not too much,' she said unconvincingly.

'Is there ever too much for you?' I said.

She said nothing, her gaze still on the floor.

'Tell me something else, Veronica. How did Goodwin end up with the missing quarter of a million?'

'Is that who has it?'

'You didn't know?'

She shook her head. 'I was just holding it for Jimmy in the account.'

'The one with Chester's name on it?'

'Right, but then he asked for it back, said he needed it all.'

'But first he wanted it in an account with Chester's name on it. Setting Concannon up for the fall from the start, just in case.'

'I never knew what Jimmy did with the money,' she said.

'How would Goodwin have gotten it?'

'He must have stolen it somehow,' she said with a shrug.

'No,' I said. 'I don't think so.' I looked around her fancy hotel room: two king-size beds, color TV, easy chairs, and velour curtains, and began wondering. 'You've been here a couple days now. Have you been buying any crap from Goodwin?'

'No, not from him, Jesus. One of the reasons I decided to leave was to get away from him and his damn dead animals.'

'So only Jimmy knows you're here.'

'And you.'

'Yes, and me. But I wasn't the guy who told Goodwin.'

She looked up at me questioningly. I shrugged. Her eyes opened wide and she shook her head. I nodded my head sadly. She screwed up her face in incomprehension, but then it started working, like the surface of an old computer, lights flashing, tapes winding, as the logic of it all unfolded for her, one syllogism after another, leading ultimately to a look of shock. Jimmy Moore had set her up, her face said, the bastard had put her in this hotel so that Goodwin could take care of both their troubles. Her head shook no, it couldn't be. But she knew it could be, she knew it was. She turned from me quickly and began to cry. It was that moment, for the first time really, that I knew Veronica Ashland would tell the truth, the whole truth, and nothing but the truth on the witness stand.

I bent over to pick up some of her clothes off the floor and took them to the suitcase laying open on the top of the bureau.

'*Nu*?' said Morris from the door. 'Is she coming?'

'No,' said Veronica weakly.

'She's coming,' I said.

'If she is coming then she must come now,' said Morris. 'Because I think that maybe our nice friend from outside might decide to force his way past Sheldon and come up here himself to find out what is happening.'

'Who exactly is outside?' she asked.

'Wayman,' I said. 'And he's the one who killed Chuckie.'

That ended all hesitation; in ninety seconds her bag was packed, she was in a pair of jeans, a shirt, her overcoat, and we were out of the room, running down the hallway, following Morris.

'Where are we going?' she asked me.

'Damned if I know,' I said.

As we ran, we heard an elevator opening. We ran away from the elevator, around a corner and another. By the time we turned the last corner and reached the stairs we could hear a door banging and Wayman's thick and slippery voice yelling, 'Open up, bitch. Open the fuck up.'

We rushed down the stairs, Morris leading as quickly as he could, which was quicker than I would have thought, down two flights. The sign said no reentry from stairwell, but Morris pulled open the door to the second floor, snapping tape off the lock as he went by, and we stumbled through the doorway after him, into the hallway, and a quick left to the room beside the stairwell, Room 2082, where Morris, without knocking, pushed open the door and rushed inside. We fell in after him, as if sucked in by a vacuum. The door closed quietly but quickly behind us.

The room was the same as Veronica's, same size, same furnishings, same two huge beds, same color TV. The door to the bathroom was closed, the window curtains drawn. Morris locked and bolted the door behind us.

'Okay now, Miss Veronica,' said Morris. 'You must give to me your fine coat.'

'My overcoat?' she said.

'Yes, of course. By now they have people watching the front and the back, there is no way out. So what we need is what is called in the profession the *holtzene kochka*. A wooden duck.'

'A decoy?'

'That's it, yes. The *holtzene kochka*.'

'Who?' I asked.

'Why, you, of course, Victor,' he said. 'And someone else to look like Miss Veronica, and for that we need the overcoat.'

'With all due respect, Morris, I don't think you'll pass.'

'Don't be so much the *cham*, Victor. You think I would let myself be the *holtzene kochka*? You don't live as long as I have lived in this business setting up yourself as the *holtzene kochka*. No, rule number two is that the detective is never the *holtzene kochka*. Maybe that should be rule number one and the coffee rule number two. The numbering, sometimes, it gets so confusing.'

'Then who?' I asked.

Just then the bathroom door opened and out she walked in jeans and a wig, a brown wig with soft shoulder-length hair, hair that was styled exactly to match Veronica's. Beth. It was more than strange, my best friend styled to look like the lover of my dreams, a disorienting blend of comfort and kink. In a way, standing there, framed by the bathroom door, was my ideal woman, a fusion of all I could ever want or love. So I stared for a bit and then a bit longer, stared until Beth started to giggle, which broke the mood and let my fantasies slip away until I realized why she was there.

'No,' I said. 'Not Beth. Absolutely not.'

54

Wayman spotted us as we ran out the hotel's front door. I held tight to the suitcase. Veronica's unbuttoned overcoat swung like a cape behind us. Before Wayman could catch us we were in the Honda, windows closed, engine straining in rhythmic moans to life. He had just reached the car, his huge gun waving in our general direction, when I popped it into gear and shot out.

I took a quick turn left on Walnut and another left up 4th Street. I raced past Spruce Street, past Lombard, ran a red at South Street, and kept going. I hadn't gone but two blocks past South before the silver BMW was cruising behind us and gaining.

At Washington I spun into a right turn and headed west, BMW tight behind. It rammed me once as I tore along Washington, then once more. I ran another red and the Beemer followed and I wondered where the cops were, wondered where the closest donut shop was, and then with a screech of tire I turned down 7th and slammed on my brakes smack in front of the Sons of Garibaldi Men's Club.

The silver BMW came to a turning stop right behind us and Wayman jumped out as if his seat was afire. I barely had the time to open my door before he stuck his arm in, jabbing the point of a huge switchblade knife into my throat. The drummer was guarding the passenger door, grinning into the window.

'Run from me again, Vi'tor Carl, you just try and run from me again without I say so and I'll slice another smile into your motherfucking neck.'

I tried to say something but with the knife sticking into

502

my larynx and me shaking like a stripper nothing came out.

'But don't you worry yourself, it's all cool now. Ronnie, sweetie, let's you and I take a little drive, what you say?'

Beth turned from the drummer to face Wayman and Wayman's jaw dropped and when he spoke his voice was deep and precise with shock.

'Who are you, lady?'

'She's my partner,' I managed to get out between shakes.

'Get the fuck out of here,' he said, and then he added, 'Shit,' drawing out the word until the T just disappeared. 'Where is she, Vi'tor Carl? Tell me now or your neck be history. Tell me, Vi'tor Carl.' He twisted the knifepoint into my neck, almost lifting me from the car seat. I could feel a line of blood run down my throat. 'Tell me quick, tell me now, tell me, tell me, tell me. Tell me, Vi'tor Carl, my knife here it is thirsty once again and it don't got much more patience.'

I was about to tell him something when a thick, hairy hand landed on Wayman's shoulder. Beth gasped, or maybe it was me, I couldn't tell. There was something obscene about that hand landing there, like a bony spider. The pressure of the knifepoint slipped from my neck and when Wayman turned to see what it was the hand slid over and grabbed hold of his neck. Before Wayman could say a word of complaint, the hand's owner slammed a brick into Wayman's head. Blood burst from Wayman's forehead. The blow sent him spinning away from the car, his knife sliding with a sweet scrabble across the asphalt. The man with the brick was Dominic and for the first time ever I saw him smile.

It was not a pleasant sight.

I swiveled to check the drummer on the other side of the car, but he was no longer leering inside the window. Instead he was being lifted in a great bear hug, his arms struggling futilely against the pin of some giant whose waist only I could see through the passenger window.

'Step on out, Victor,' I heard Dominic say and when I got out I saw him sitting on top of Wayman, his knees holding Wayman's arms to the ground, his bony hands tight around Wayman's throat.

'Hey, Dominic, where do you want this package?' asked the man bear-hugging the drummer. From behind the thug's shoulders I could see it was Giovanni, his hard face illuminated now with a wide grin.

'Throw it in the garbage,' said Dominic, hands still around Wayman's throat.

Jasper leaned over Wayman, still held down by Dominic, and started searching him. He reached into Wayman's sweatpants and pulled out the huge revolver I had seen Wayman brandishing before I had kicked the Honda into gear and fled from the hotel. 'Whoa, what do you know?' said Jasper. 'What a nasty piece of work this little shit is.'

Jasper checked the gun, unloaded it shell by shell, and then took hold of the barrel. He raised the gun about a foot and a half and dropped the butt end onto Wayman's shoulder blade. Wayman shouted out something wild and started struggling, cursing even as Dominic's hands tightened around his neck. Jasper lifted the gun again, just a foot and a half, and let it drop. He hammered at the shoulder blade again, and again, raising the gun a foot and a half and dropping it, over and over and over.

There was a loud crack, Wayman let out a howl and his right arm went dead.

Calmly, methodically, raising the gun the same height of a foot and a half and then dropping it over and over, Jasper went to work on the other shoulder. There was a practiced air about his movements, the fulfillment of a familiar and somewhat pleasant chore.

'Jesus, this feels good,' said Dominic, still atop the struggling Wayman. He couldn't help but smile again, a smile filled with satisfied blood lust.

I rubbed at my neck, my hand came away slick with my own blood.

'It's not too often us old *goombahs* get a chance to work out,' said Dominic.

'What we need,' said Jasper as he kept hammering at the collarbone, 'is a gym, you know, a few weights, a ring to spar in, a punching bag.'

'You got the punching bag right there,' said Dominic.

'I need something tougher, something with heft,' said Jasper over Wayman's shouts. 'Something to give me a real workout.'

Across the street Giovanni was slamming the drummer's head into the side of a construction dumpster once, twice, thrice for good effect. Then he lifted him like a sack of lime and threw him in.

'What is going on, Victor?' said Beth, who was also out of the car. 'What just happened?'

'We've been saved by the cavalry,' I said. 'Beth, I want you to meet some friends. The young kid is Giovanni, the fellow banging on our friend Wayman is Jasper.'

Just then there was another sickening crack and Wayman let out a desperate wild howl.

Wayman had killed Chuckie, had stuck the point of his knife far enough into my neck to draw blood, had promised to kill me, but even still I couldn't help but wince.

'And this here is Dominic,' I continued. 'Don't play poker with Dominic, Beth, he's a shark.'

'A weekend player,' said Dominic as he rose from the helpless Wayman, slapping his hands clean. 'Here you go, pal,' he said, reaching into his pocket and handing me a handkerchief.

I wiped my hand and neck clean. So I had become Dominic's pal. We had fought the common enemy and come through as blood brothers.

'He's bawling like a goddamn baby,' said Jasper. 'What's this scumbag's name, Sport?'

'Wayman,' I said. And then on the spur of the moment, like some all-powerful don, I added, 'Don't kill him.'

'What are you, an idiot? I wouldn't have gone to the

505

trouble of hurting him if I was going to kill him,' said Jasper over Wayman's moans. 'Now – Wayman,' he shouted, loud and slow as if he were talking to a Frenchman. 'I – don't – want – you – should – bother – Victor – no – more – do – you – understand?'

Wayman let out a little shriek of assent.

'I – don't – want – I – should – hear – that – he – is – troubled – or – that – he – is – dead – because – then – I – will – be – angry – do – you – understand?'

Another shriek of assent.

'That's – good – Wayman,' said Jasper, patting his cheek. 'You're – in – no – condition – to – drive. – We're – going – to – let – your – friend – drive – you – home.'

Giovanni shrugged and reached into the dumpster, pulling out the dazed and bleeding drummer by his collar and his crotch. The drummer collapsed to the ground and tried to half crawl away. Giovanni kicked him in the ribs so hard the drummer shook uncontrollably for a moment before letting out a breathless cry. Then Giovanni lifted him to his feet by his neck and kicked him in the rear, sending him lurching for the car. He fell on its hood like a drunken beggar at an intersection offering to clean the windshield. Dominic opened the front door for him. He took hold of the drummer, pulled him around the front of the car, and shoved him inside. Jasper lifted Wayman by his belt. Wayman, bent and bowed, cradling both arms into his chest, hunched his way over to the car. I opened the passenger door. Without looking at me, he dropped onto the seat.

'Stay the fuck out of South Philly,' said Dominic. When there was no movement from the battered occupants, he shouted, 'Get out of here. Now.'

The car didn't speed away from the scene, it sort of staggered. First it swerved to the right, then stopped suddenly, then drifted to the left, sideswiping a maroon meat van parked in front of a store. There was the loud crinkle of metal bending and plastic cracking. The car dipped back

506

to the right before it shot forward and stopped and moved slowly forward again.

'Where did they come from?' asked Beth as she stood beside me, watching the silver BMW painfully make its way down 7th Street. 'And how are they your friends?'

I shrugged. 'Poker buddies. Remember the phone call I made just before we left the hotel?'

'Yes.'

'That's who I called.'

Just then a great white Cadillac, rear windows tinted so dark it was impossible to see inside, slid to a stop right in front of us. Lenny was driving. He waved at me. With a hum, the rear window opened and the ugly pitted face of Enrico Raffaello appeared.

'Everything is all right, I see,' he said.

'Thank you very much, Mr Raffaello,' I said. 'He would have killed me if you hadn't stepped in.'

'You're welcome, Victor. Protection is what we do, but generally we don't do it for free.'

'I'm very grateful.'

'Well, grateful is something, yes, but it doesn't pay for the ricotta. Consider this a favor, Victor. We take pride in doing favors for the citizens of this city. We expect, of course, that the favor will be reciprocated when the time comes.'

'I understand, sir.'

'Now about that project you were to do for me. I hope you haven't disappointed.'

I gestured at the silver BMW slowly making its way down 7th. 'If you follow that car it will take you right to the money, Mr Raffaello. A man named Norvel Goodwin ended up with it.'

'Now that's almost too ironic, Jimmy's money ending up with a drug kingpin. There must be quite a story in this. You will tell it to me sometime, Victor, but not now. Now I think we'll follow that car. Come here, son, I have something for you.'

Sheepishly I stepped forward. Raffaello lifted a white bag out of the window. I took it from him and stepped back.

'We'll be in touch, Victor, you can be sure.'

He nodded his head and the window rose, concealing his face. Dominic, Jasper, and Giovanni slipped into the car and slowly, carefully, it drove off.

Beth stepped to my side. She was staring at the car. 'Was that who I think it was?' she managed to say.

'Yes,' I said. I opened the bag and looked inside. 'What kind of custard do you like in your cannoli, Beth, chocolate or vanilla?'

'Vanilla,' she said.

I reached into the bag and took out the vanilla cannoli and gave it to her and then reached in and gave her the chocolate one too. 'Hold this for me a moment, will you?'

With the bag in hand, I walked a bit down 7th, scanning the street, searching. Finally I found it. It had slid up against the curb and was resting there, its blade pointing due north like a compass. I took one of the paper napkins graciously supplied by my new liege Enrico Raffaello and, with the napkin between my fingers, took hold of the blade, lifting it carefully before dropping it into the bag. I figured Slocum would be delighted to get hold of the knife that had killed Chuckie Lamb, complete with a clean set of prints. I just wanted to be sure that the prints on the knife weren't mine.

55

The moment when a lawyer stands in court and calls the next witness is a moment fraught with expectation. As the witness walks the long distance down the aisle, the jury, the judge, the opponents, the gawkers, the entire community of that courtroom wonder what evidence will be disclosed, what devastating story will be told, in what way will this witness's testimony be decisive. It is a glorious moment for the trial lawyer, full of drama, full of mystery. No matter how many trials, no matter how many witnesses, no matter how pedestrian the matter at issue, standing in the courtroom and calling the next witness never becomes routine. And the key to that moment is logistics. In every courtroom across this country there is a lawyer with neck craned, examining the benches and the door in the back, wondering if the next witness is waiting to respond to the call. It is not enough to prepare the questions, to practice the testimony, to hone the arguments to razor sharpness. Logistics are all. Standing in the courtroom, calling the next witness and having nothing happen, you might just as well be standing there naked.

'Do you have your witness yet, Mr Carl?' asked Judge Gimbel, and none too kindly. The judge had a docket of 478 cases, and waiting for a witness to magically appear was doing nothing to reduce that number.

'If I can just have another minute, Your Honor,' I said.

'Sixty seconds,' said Judge Gimbel. I was hoping he would leave the bench, tell his clerk to get him when I was ready, take me off the hook, but the judge had brought his paperwork with him and as he sat up on high and scrawled in big letters across some important legal

509

document I sweated like a thief. Like a naked thief.

From the defense table I dashed up the courtroom aisle, suffering the smirks of Jimmy and Prescott and Prescott's coterie, and burst into the cool, cruelly empty hallway. I looked left and then right and then left again. Nothing. The plan had been that I would flee the Society Hill Sheraton with Beth, in brown wig and overcoat, drawing the chase while Morris and Veronica, in blonde wig and jacket, simply strolled out the front door past Sheldon, acting as lookout, and stay on their way straight to the courthouse. Then Morris would bring her here, to the courtroom, to await my call. It was the awaiting my call part that was causing the problem. Beth was outside the courthouse, waiting for their arrival at the main entrance on Market Street. I was rushing crazily about inside, hoping they would magically appear.

Beside the courtroom doors there was a bank of pay phones and quickly I called Morris's office.

'Kapustin and Son, Investigations,' said Morris.

'Morris, you bastard, where are you?'

'There is no one here to take your call, but we are checking in with this machine like crazy. Just leave a message and we'll be with you so quick your head will do a somersault, that quick.'

I cursed into the phone in loud, precise language before the machine beeped me shut.

I called my office, to see if Morris had left me a message, but Rita only sneered. 'Any calls? My, here's a shocker, Mr Carl. No calls this morning. Maybe I'll ring up the *Inquirer* about this breaking story. No calls for Mr Carl.'

I hung up on her and spun out of the phone alcove in frustration, whirling into the frail figure of Herm Finklebaum, the toy king of 44th Street, sending him sprawling backwards on the cold white floor of the courthouse. I leaned over him. He wore his regular plaid shirt, ragged houndstooth jacket, limegreen slacks. He lay there, unconscious, the blood throbbing only faintly beneath the skin stretching over the hole in his head.

'Jesus, Herm. I'm sorry. Are you all right? Herm? Herm?'

He lay there quite still. He was a small, frail man. The skin clung tightly to his cadaverous skull. My already fraying nerves writhed into a panic.

'Herm? Oh, God, Herm? Are you all right, Herm? Herm? Jesus, Herm. Wake up.'

One eye popped open.

'Next time, buddy boy, you watch where you're going or it will end in a lawsuit.'

I helped him up. He turned his neck carefully from side to side.

'It feels a little stiff,' he said.

'Do you need a doctor?'

'Not really, it's been stiff since 'seventy-two.' His laugh was an annoying, rhythmic wheeze, like an asthma attack.

'Look, I'm sorry, Herm, but I have to go. I have to find someone.'

I was already past him, hustling off in my vain search for Morris when he said, 'You maybe looking for that pretty little Miss Ashland?'

I slid to a stop on the waxed floors and spun around. 'You know where she is?'

'Maybe I do and maybe I don't.'

'Oh, come on, Herm.'

'Okay, I do. Morris has her down on the sixth floor. He told me to find you to ask when you wanted her.'

'Now,' I said. 'I want her right now.'

'Morris thought it better to keep her hidden until she was really needed.'

'I need her right this instant.'

'It's going to be interesting?'

'It's going to be dynamite.'

'All right, buddy boy. One dishy little number coming up. Save me a seat.'

Logistics are all until they're solved, then they disappear

511

like a dream upon waking. I had my questions ready, I had prepared the testimony, I had my arguments honed, and now, best of all, I had my witness. I took a moment to slow myself down. I took three deep breaths and gave myself a slight oxygen buzz. When it wore off I straightened my jacket, shot my cuffs, and walked with as much confidence as I could muster into the courtroom.

All gazes were upon me as I strode down the aisle. The judge asked me if I was now ready to proceed and I said I was. The jury sat straighter in their seats. The court reporter wriggled his fingers in preparation. Prescott sat with pen poised over his pad. Much had been paid for this moment and I meant to enjoy it. I scanned the jury, I looked at Jimmy Moore, the wild expectation grew. Before the judge could break the mood with one of his admonitions to get moving, I spoke in a loud and clear voice,

'On behalf of Chester Concannon, I call to the stand Veronica Ashland.'

Right on cue she opened the courtroom door, peered in, and then pensively, awkwardly, with just the right amount of hesitation and awe, she walked down the aisle, her head held nervously forward. She was wearing a white blouse, a black pleated skirt, she looked more like a Catholic schoolgirl than a councilman's mistress. Without glancing at either Chester or Jimmy she took the stand. With hand raised and voice low she said, 'I do,' to the clerk's swearing-in and then sat demurely in the witness chair, hands on her lap, waiting for me to draw out her story.

56

'Did you want to come to testify today, Ms Ashland?' I asked.

'No,' she said.

'Then why are you here?'

'Because you subpoenaed me,' she said.

From the start, I wanted to let the jury know where this witness stood. Here was not Chester Concannon's mother testifying to save her son, here was a potentially hostile witness, sitting up there only because she had a truth that we were insisting she tell. I had her identify the subpoena that I had served upon her and put it into evidence. I would wave it at the jury in my closing as I argued for her credibility.

'Now, Miss Ashland, do you know Councilman Moore?'

She glanced at him warily. 'Yes,' she said.

'How do you know him?'

'We're friends,' she said.

'How did you meet him?'

She let out a deep breath and said nothing.

'How did you meet Councilman Moore, Miss Ashland?'

'He had come with a group to raid a crack house on Sixty-first Street.'

She had given the wrong address. 'Was that Sixty-first Street or Fifty-first Street?'

She sighed. 'You're right, Fifty-first Street. I was inside when he came.'

'Why were you inside?'

'I was using at the time.'

'Using what?'

'Cocaine.'

513

'Crack cocaine?'

'Yes.'

'And the councilman found you inside?'

'Yes. And he took me to a drug rehabilitation center and got me off of drugs.'

'Do you know the councilman's attitude toward drugs?'

'He hates them with a passion. He hates the dealers, the profiteers. He hates those who killed his daughter.'

'They incense him?'

'Yes.'

'Make him angry?'

'Yes.'

'Violently angry?'

Prescott stood up quickly. 'Objection, calls for speculation.'

'Answer if you can,' said the judge.

'Yes,' she said. 'Violently angry.'

'Have you seen the violence?'

'Yes. At the raid he was swinging a chair wildly, knocking down everything he could find. He was almost crazy.'

'Did you see him hit anyone with the chair?'

'Yes.'

'Who?'

'I saw him hit Norvel Goodwin.'

'And who is Norvel Goodwin?'

Her lips quivered in hesitation and her eyes pleaded at me not to force her to say anything against Goodwin, but I looked down at my papers, waiting for her answer.

'The man who was selling in that house.'

'Were you involved with Norvel Goodwin at the time?'

'Romantically, you mean?'

'Yes,' I said.

'I was on drugs. Romance and drugs do not go hand in hand, Mr Carl.'

'Were you sexually involved with Norvel Goodwin?'

'Yes.'

'How did you feel when you saw the councilman swing the chair and hit Mr Goodwin?'

'I was scared. But he didn't hurt me, he helped me.'

'And after he helped you get off drugs, did your relationship change?'

'Yes.'

'How did it change, Miss Ashland?'

She looked at me hard and then glanced at Jimmy and then cast her gaze down to her hands twisting together on her lap. 'We became lovers,' she said.

'You began to have an affair, is that right?'

'That's what I said, yes.'

'And did the affair continue throughout this trial?'

'No, not the whole time. Jimmy told me it was over the day you mentioned my name in court.'

'How did he tell you this?'

'Over the phone.'

'Isn't he putting you up in a hotel room now?'

'I told him I was afraid to stay at home. He found me a room.'

'Did he visit you there?'

'No,' she said. 'You're not listening. It's over.'

'How do you feel about that?'

'Angry,' she said.

'At him?'

'No,' she said. 'At you.'

And so my foundation was laid. I had brought out her relationship with Jimmy, her drug use, Jimmy's propensity to violence when faced with drugs and their dealers, and the end of their affair, leaving her bitter toward me, not Jimmy, so she would have no reason to lie about what Jimmy had done. My difficulty, of course, was that now I had a drug user for a witness. What I had to do, in effect, was to try her in front of the jury for being a drug addict, a slut, a homewrecker, try her and acquit her before Prescott was able to get his hands on her in cross-examination.

515

I had to bring out everything that might be used against her, bring it out as carefully as if it were an armed pipe bomb, and then diffuse it before the jury so that when Prescott tried to impugn her on cross with it the jury would think they were being told an old story and wonder why Prescott was going over it still again.

So what I did was gently lead her through her entire life story, from Iowa to London to her trip around the world with Saffron Hyde. I had her linger as she talked about the bus accident, about how Saffron needed the drugs for his pain, and how she too became addicted. And then, in detail, I had her tell the jury about his swim in the Ganges and his death in Varanasi and the burning of his body. Both Eggert and Prescott objected to the story but the judge gave me the latitude I requested, agreeing with me that I was entitled to give evidence to mitigate any loss of credibility of the witness due to her drug use. So back we went to New York and the University of Pennsylvania and that crack house on 51st Street where Jimmy Moore found her, and the drug rehabilitation center and the apartment in Olde City that the councilman leased for her at a bargain rate in exchange for a street. It was a good story, well told, with tears and hesitations and true emotion and by the end of it there was no doubt that the jury felt for her, shared her tears. The jury had gone through her life story and come out at the other end on her side. I was ready now to get to the meat of her testimony, except for one more disclosure.

'During the time of your relationship with Jimmy Moore, did you have affairs with other men?'

'Yes.'

'Why, Miss Ashland?' It was a question not strictly relevant, but I couldn't help myself from asking it.

'I don't know. I was lonely, I guess. Bored. Jimmy had a wife. I had nothing but a part-time him.'

'Did you have an affair with Zack Bissonette?'

'Yes,' she said and that brought a little 'Aaah' from one

516

of the jurors who had finally begun to see what she was doing in this trial in the first place.

I hesitated for a moment, looked down at my papers. I shuffled one over the other and back again as I screwed up my courage to ask the next question. 'And did you also have an affair with me?' The question itself was enough to silence any murmurs in the courtroom.

'Yes,' she said. 'Unfortunately.'

I could have stopped there, I guess. I had tossed out the worst of it with that simple question and her simple answer. I could have left it to Eggert and Prescott to pick over the carcass of our dead relationship. Chester Concannon was glaring at me with a strange look of doubt that I had never seen from him before, a doubt that would only grow deeper the further I delved into what had happened between Veronica and me, and there was really no reason to delve any further. But when the judge called me to the bench and reamed me out for a good five minutes over getting involved with a witness, forcing me to explain to him that I didn't know she was a witness when I started my involvement with her, I thought I should explain that very thing to the jury, since they too may have been suffering from a misapprehension. So instead of stopping like I could have, I continued on.

'How did you meet me, Miss Ashland?'

She gaped at me, and then said, 'At a restaurant. You tried to pick me up with some of Jimmy's champagne.'

'For how long did we see each other?'

'For as long as it was convenient.'

She was staring hard at me and I stared back at her and for a moment it was only her and me in the courtroom and I had the power to ask her anything I wanted. I was tempted to ask her about her feelings for me, did they ever exist, did I ever satisfy her, was our sex as incredible for her as it was for me, did she ever love me, did she ever dream, like I did, that it could go on forever. And could she forgive me for what I was putting her through now and, if so, was there any possibility that after this was all over, after the trial was finished, after she had cleaned herself up and our lives had resumed their unbearable stasis, after everything, could she ever consider coming back to me? That was what I wanted to ask her, all that and more. But what I asked instead was, 'When did you tell me you had been sleeping with Zack Bissonette?'

'When you asked.'

'That was after we had become involved, is that right?'

'Yes.'

'And did we continue our affair after I learned about your relationship with Bissonette?'

'Well, you kissed me after that,' she said. 'When you gave me the subpoena.' That got a chuckle from the crowd.

'But now our relationship is over, is that right?'

'It was over before it started,' she said.

'And we're not seeing each other anymore?'

'No,' she said and then she let out a sly smile. 'Not even if you begged.'

I stepped back and winced. My reaction was noticed, there was a titter from the jury, a few slight laughs from the audience behind me. And somehow, with the laughter it all seemed all right now. It was the banter that did it, the clichéd angry girlfriend bit that did it. It was as if my relationship with Veronica now fell neatly into that whole boy-girl thing, absolving me of anything dark and sinister. I glanced over to the jury and there were some admiring glances, that someone like me could have played around with someone like her. I had been raised a few notches in their esteem. It was incredible, I thought, that a woman with whom I was obsessed could mash a grapefruit in my face in the middle of a crowded courtroom and it only served to build up my standing. Sure, let it happen just like that. I had a job to do, a story to tell, and now it was time to tell it.

'All right, Miss Ashland,' I said. 'You have a checking account, is that right?'

'Yes.'

'Is there another name on that account?'

'Chet's name is also on the account.'

'Why?'

'I was getting some money from Jimmy every now and then through Chet. Putting Chet's name on it made it easier for him to give me the money.'

'Did there come a time when certain large amounts were deposited in that account?'

'Yes,' she said. 'Chet asked me to put in certain amounts of cash.'

'Chet asked?' She had made another mistake. 'You mean the councilman.'

'No, Chet. I assumed he was asking on behalf of Jimmy. Everything before with that account had always been on behalf of Jimmy.' So that's what she had meant when she said Jimmy had asked her to deposit the money. But why had Concannon gone along with it? I looked at Chester. He had the same look of doubt his face had held before.

'How much was deposited?' I continued.

'I don't know the total, but each deposit was always just under ten thousand dollars.'

'How many deposits?'

'Ten or fifteen.'

'And what happened to the money?'

'I don't know firsthand,' she said.

'Tell us what you know,' I said.

'Objection, hearsay,' said Prescott.

'Sustained,' said the judge.

'Well, what had you heard?' I asked.

'Objection,' said Prescott.

'Sustained,' said Judge Gimbel. 'Move on, Mr Carl.'

That line wasn't working. She didn't know enough to get out what I had wanted to get out about Norvel Goodwin and the money. Her knowledge was secondhand, her answers too indistinct. I looked over at the jury box. I saw a yawn. The sight of it cut me. I was losing them. I needed something big, now.

'All right, Miss Ashland, let's move on to Zack Bissonette.' There was a pause, which sucked back the jury's attention. 'Where did you meet him?'

'At this club. Jimmy, Chet, Chuckie, and I used to go there. That's how we met.'

'How did you start dating?'

'Dating?' She tossed me a little smirk, just to let everyone know she was no cheerleader in a ponytail. 'He asked me out one night at the club.'

'While you were there with Jimmy?'

'Yes. Whatever his shortcomings, lack of gall was not one of them.'

'And what did you say?'

'I gave him my phone number.'

'You wrote it down for him?'

'I just told it to him. I figured if he was interested enough he would remember.'

'And he remembered?'

'Yes. He called me the next day.'

'And you went out together.'

'Yes.'

'Why, Miss Ashland? Why did you go out with Mr Bissonette?'

'He was handsome, he had played baseball, poorly maybe, but he had played, he dressed in black, I don't know, I guess I couldn't think of a reason not to.'

'Now when you started going out with Mr Bissonette, were you using drugs?'

'No. Absolutely not.'

'How long had you been drug-free?'

'Over two years.'

'Did you see Mr Bissonette many times?'

'A few.'

'Did you sleep with him?'

'Yes, I slept with him.'

'Did there come a time when you stopped seeing him?'

'Yes.'

'Why?'

'I grew bored. I grow bored easily, Mr Carl, as you know. He was boring, that's all.'

'So you told him it was over.'

'Yes.'

'How did Mr Bissonette take it?'

'Not very well. He wanted to keep seeing me. He insisted we keep going out.'

'What happened?'

'I said no, that it was over.'

'Did there come a time when you started seeing him again?'

'Yes.'

'Why?'

'Well, he was begging, he was a pest. One night when I was bored, with nothing to do, I called and told him he could come over.'

'Did he bring anything with him?'

'Yes.'

'What?'

'He brought me cocaine.'

I stepped back from the podium for a moment to let the last answer sink in. The points were being laid out and I wanted the connections to be drawn by the jurors before being made explicit by Veronica. I wanted them to expect to hear what Veronica would say, that Jimmy, who was violently opposed to drugs, had reacted violently once he found out that Bissonette had been first sleeping with and then supplying drugs to his mistress, a woman who had filled the gap in his life left from the drug death of his daughter. I wanted to set it up so that when Veronica gave voice to the obvious suspicions her response would be that much more believable. I turned around to look at the rest of the courtroom. There was Morris nodding at me, sitting next to Herm and Beth. Slocum was also in the audience,

521

taking notes as he prepared for the murder trial. Behind Jimmy, where his wife usually sat, was an empty place in the benches. The courtroom artists were busily sketching the scene. Everything was perfectly in place. When whatever murmurs that had arisen from the cocaine response faded, I stepped back to the podium to continue.

'Did you take the cocaine that Mr Bissonette offered?' I asked.

'Yes.'

'Why, Miss Ashland, if you had been drug-free for over two years?'

'Because I missed it, and I was lonely, and I was disgusted that I had allowed a stiff like Zack back into my bedroom. Because I am not as strong a woman as I would like, Mr Carl.'

'Did you become addicted again?'

'Yes.'

'Did you only get cocaine from Mr Bissonette?'

'No.'

'Where else?'

'Anywhere I could.'

'Did you have another primary source?'

'Yes.'

'Who, Ms Ashland?'

'Norvel Goodwin,' she said.

'The same man who had been selling out of that crack house on Fifty-first Street, the same man who Jimmy Moore had beaten with a chair?'

'Yes.'

'Now, did there come a time that someone else found out about your renewed drug use?'

'Yes.'

'And who was that?'

'Chet Concannon found out,' she said.

She had made still another mistake that I had to correct. 'You mean the councilman, don't you?'

'No,' she said: 'It was Chet who found out.'

'And then Chester told the councilman?'

'No,' she said. 'Chet came right to me.'

I gave her another chance. 'So when did the councilman come over?'

'He never did. Chet had the limousine that night, he often used it, and he came over to my apartment after he found out.'

'And you spoke?'

'Yes.'

'And then he told the councilman?'

'No, that's not what happened. When he came over he was very upset, agitated. He demanded to know how I had started up again with drugs and when I told him that it was Bissonette he flew into a rage.'

'It was the councilman in the rage, wasn't it?'

'No,' she said, shaking her head. 'No. You're not listening. It was Chet. He was often my beard on evenings when Jimmy wanted to bring his wife to a reception and then see me afterwards, and he began to fall in love with me. We had sex once, one lonely evening, and it seemed to be important to him. I used to tease him about it, but it was real, I could see that. So when he found out about Bissonette he was furious, as angry as if I had been cheating on him. And the drugs, that made him even angrier. I pleaded with him not to tell the councilman, because I knew how angry he would get, how violent. He promised me he wouldn't, that he would take care of it himself. He said he would take care of it, that he had been stiffed out of another quarter of a million, that they had dropped him like a sucker and that by dealing with Bissonette he could take care of two birds with one bullet. That's what he said. I begged him not to do anything stupid but he told me not to worry about it, that he would take care of everything. And then he left. That's the last I saw of him that night. The next day I heard that Zack had been beaten into a coma. I was terrified.'

I stared at her, shocked into silence, shocked enough to

let her talk on and on, and talk on and on she did. While her other answers were short, two or three sentences at the most, this response seemed to last forever, and I felt helpless to stop her. I was so stunned I didn't even try. And when she had finished she sat on the stand looking straight at me, without even a breath of malice on her face.

In a weak voice I asked the judge for a moment, which he granted, and I walked unsteadily to Chester at the defense table. The doubt in his face had been replaced with anger. I leaned over him and whispered.

'Is any of this true?' I asked.

'No,' he hissed.

'You fucked her, didn't you?'

'You did too,' said Chester viciously. 'So what? The rest of that is crap. What are you doing to me? What are you letting them do to me? You've sold me out.'

Still leaning over Concannon, I glanced at Prescott, who was watching Chester and me with amusement on his thin lips. He looked at me and then through those thin fucking lips there arose the hint of a smile, the merest hint, but there it was. Where before I had seen his smile and read it as 'Welcome to the club,' this time I knew exactly what it meant, and what all the smiles before it had meant too. He smiled that slight smile at me and what that smile was saying, was shouting, was shrieking for the whole court to hear was, 'Got you, you little small-time Jew bastard.'

The feeling I had in that instant was like falling down a pit, falling without a parachute, without hope, fall falling. My stomach collapsed, my knees buckled, my eyes teared wildly, and spots appeared before me as my consciousness dipped. All I wanted to do at that moment was to heave and if I had anything in my stomach, if I had eaten Raffaello's damned cannoli, drunk a cup of coffee, anything, I'm sure I would have, right there in the middle of the courtroom, right there on the defense table, right there in front of the judge, the jury, right there in front of my

524

client, Chester Concannon, my client, who had put his freedom in my hands and who now, I was certain, was going straight and irrevocably to jail.

PART FIVE

A Peel

57

Once again I was riding the marble-lined elevator to the fifty-fourth floor of One Liberty Place, rising to the offices of Talbott, Kittredge and Chase, coming as a visitor, not a member of the caste, coming as a supplicant, as one of the unworthy. But on this ride, at least, I was no longer lugging along a deep-seated resentment. I had been resentful of my exclusion from the hallways of the rich and powerful when I believed I belonged by right of merit, of talent, by right of my innate inner quality. But that belief had fled before the reality of my failure in *United States v. Moore and Concannon*. Not only was I not going to be offered a place at the glorious head table of the law, but the only thing I had proven at that trial was that I was inadequate to take it on my own. The jury had come back after only six hours of deliberations. Jimmy Moore acquitted of all counts; Chester Concannon guilty of Hobbs Act extortion, guilty of Hobbs Act assault, guilty of racketeering. Guilty, guilty, guilty. The words from the jury foreman were like the tolling of some unwholesome melancholy bell. Guilty, guilty, guilty. Six hours of deliberations and Chester Concannon was gone.

There was nothing I could do to salvage the trial after Veronica, my star witness, buried Chester with her testimony. I finally snapped out of my self-pitying stupor and had her declared a hostile witness, so that I could cross-examine her, and then went at her tooth and tong, attacking her credibility, attacking her story, attacking her lies. And they were lies, yes. She had told me the truth in her apartment the black night I subpoenaed her. I had no doubt but that it was Jimmy Moore who had taken that quarter of a million, cash, and handed it over to Norvel Goodwin, resurrecting with fresh capital Goodwin's moribund grip on the crack cocaine market in Philadelphia. I had no doubt but that Jimmy Moore had killed Zack Bissonette with the Mike Schmidt autographed baseball bat, that it was Jimmy Moore who had battered him into a coma and left him sucking air through the blood oozing out of his mangled face. But with all of my hammering, all of my badgering, all of my bombast, I was not able to shake her story. My only hope was to put myself on the stand and contradict her. I was the only one who could impeach her with what she had told me that night in her apartment and so I passionately requested that Judge Gimbel let me testify.

'Mr Carl,' he said, with all the indignation his high position allowed him, 'I'm not going to let a lawyer testify in my courtroom at a trial that he is conducting. That is a clear violation of the Rules of Professional Conduct. You're experienced enough to know you need an investigator or another third party to question a witness if you intend to impeach that witness's testimony with the interrogation. They still teach that in law school, I believe, and I'm not about to start changing the rules now. Was there anyone else in the room when she made her statement to you?'

'No, sir,' I said.

'Did she sign a written statement?'

'No, sir.'

'Is there any tape recording or video of what she said?'

'No, sir.'

'Well then, Mr Carl, you can ask her what she said to you that night, but you will not be able to personally contradict, do you understand?'

'I object, Your Honor.'

'Exception noted for the record,' said the judge. 'Any more questions for this witness?'

'Yes, Your Honor.'

'Then go to it, Mr Carl. You've got work to do.'

And go to it I did, but to no avail. There had always been something slippery about Veronica, she was soft and silky but I could never really get a hold of her, could never pin her down. Even when I had her tied to those bedposts I could never really pin her down. That was the way she was in bed and that was the way she was on the stand too, smooth, clear, but slippery when pressed. And in the end I failed. There was really no way to succeed once she blurted out her lies. If only I had forced her to sign a statement. If only I had placed Sheldon at the doorway with his stethoscope to listen to our conversation. If only I had recognized early on in her testimony the prepared evasiveness with which she answered questions about the bank account and quickly stopped my examination before the real damage was done. If only I hadn't been such a fuckup.

Even before she was finished testifying I had asked the court for a recess and, along with Beth, ran to the clerk's office for a fresh subpoena, filling it out on the ride down the courthouse elevator. There was one other person, I knew, who could contradict her story, the person who had been the liaison between Jimmy Moore and Norvel Goodwin, who had set up the deal for the quarter of a million and had told Goodwin where Veronica had been hiding out the day she was to testify. The same person who had been with Jimmy Moore the night of the murder, the man whose footprints had been encased in Bissonette's vomit and Bissonette's blood. I filled in Henry's name hastily as I rode down to the ground floor and Beth fished in her pocketbook for a check for the witness fee. The murder had happened on Henry's night off and he had flashed an alibi to the cops, who had been all too willing to believe the driver so as to put the blame on Concannon, but I was sure now that Henry's alibi was a lie. In a desperate trot I ran to the Market Street exit of the courthouse, where I was sure the councilman's limo would be waiting with Henry sitting calmly inside. He was my last chance.

I spotted that black cat of a car at the corner of the building and rushed to it, tapping on the window, thrusting the papers inside as soon as there was a gap big enough to fit my arm. But the face underneath the chauffeur's cap was white, not black, and he looked at me uncomprehendingly as the papers waved before him.

'Where's Henry?' I asked.

'Kingston.'

'New York?'

'Jamaica. He went back to his family. Something about it being too damn cold up here, and I don't blame him one bit.'

Six hours of deliberations and then the solemn tolling of the bell. Guilty, guilty, guilty.

Eggert proved willing to settle for a councilman's aide if he couldn't get a councilman. He saw that he had a sure conviction in Chester Concannon, and a now shaky chance against Jimmy, and so in his closing he went after Chester with a fury. In detail he listed his crimes, the extortion, the murder, the taking for his own purposes of the quarter of a million dollars in cash, proven incontrovertibly by the records of cash deposits into and withdrawals from the checking account with Chester Concannon's name on it, all calmly put into evidence by Prescott when he took his turn with Veronica. In Eggert's forty-minute closing he spent thirty minutes on Chet Concannon. He tried, of course, to link Councilman Moore to his aide, but even that attempt only further highlighted his argument that Chester was the real culprit here.

Prescott didn't have to say much when his turn to close arrived. He gave his public servant speech, blamed Moore's indictment on politics. Concannon was guilty, he told them, that was no longer in doubt. The only question remaining was what vile motives led the United States Attorney to indict the councilman too. 'When you acquit Jimmy Moore,' he argued, 'you are not only acquitting an innocent man. You are also sending a message to the

532

powers in this city that you will not tolerate the persecution of a man who is fighting for the poor, the downtrodden, who is fighting the scourge of drugs on our streets, who is fighting for you. Ladies and gentlemen, politics has its time and place, during campaigns, during elections, even in the legislative process, but it has no place before the grand jury. Mr Eggert forgot exactly who he works for when he indicted Councilman Moore. Before the grand jury and before this court he was working for the councilman's political opponents, acting for their and his political gain. Tell him that he works not for the powerful, not for himself, but for you. Tell him the clearest way you can, tell him with an acquittal. Send Jimmy Moore back to his good work.'

I closed too, of course. I stood before that jury and spoke about Chester Concannon and reasonable doubt and how Jimmy Moore had conspired to have his aide take the fall. Oh, I let it rip, I did. But it was a lost cause and I knew it and the jury knew it and when the eyes started rolling and the yawns came, first from Mr Thompkins, who ran his own printing business and who I knew would be a tough sell, and then from the cynical Mrs Simpson, whom I was counting on if I had any chance, it was as good as over. I kept pounding away, repeating 'reasonable doubt,' 'reasonable doubt,' 'reasonable doubt,' as if I were a hypnotist trying to induce some posttrial daze in the jurors. I gave it the college try for dear old Chet, yes I did, but it mattered not a whit. Six hours of deliberations and the groaning moan of the great iron bell of justice: guilty, guilty, guilty.

There was a gay tinkling ring as the elevator stopped at the fifty-fourth floor and the doors slid open. Talbott, Kittredge and Chase. That huge expanse of lobby, beautiful and sterile; that blonde receptionist, beautiful and cold. Maybe there was another reason my resentment had vanished. Maybe the brass ring had been tarnished for me. If deceit and betrayal were the price of admission, I'd just as soon sit it out. That was something I had learned about myself, something good. I had learned enough bad about myself, my incompetence, my capacity for self-delusion, my steep leanings toward venality, but I had learned good things, too. I looked around at the riches of Talbott, Kittredge and Chase and decided that maybe I just didn't want it anymore. Well, the receptionist I wanted still, let's be honest, she was something, sure, but the rest could all go to hell for all I cared. And maybe, just maybe, I would do my part to send it there.

'William Prescott, please,' I said to the receptionist.

'Who can I say is here?'

'You don't remember me?'

She gave one of those patented tosses of her mousse-swept hair and said, 'No. I don't.'

'Victor Carl.'

Her eyes opened wide for just an instant, just long enough so I knew that the story had spread through the whole of the firm, from partners to associates to secretaries to the receptionist. Even the cleaning crew, I bet, had a good laugh at my expense.

'Take a seat please, Mr Carl, and I'll tell his secretary you're here.'

'Don't bother,' I said as I headed toward the stairs. 'I know the way.'

She stood up. 'You can't go unescorted, Mr Carl. That's policy.'

'I'm sure it is,' I said without stopping. 'But it's your policy and I don't work here.'

By the time I reached the stairs on my way to Prescott's office she was already barking about me on the phone.

Up the wide circling stairs with the burnished rail, along the lucratively noisy hallways with secretaries typing vigorously and lawyers bustling in and out of their offices as they hurried to fill up their time sheets with billable hours, around the corners and past the richly furnished conference rooms, generously outfitted with legal pads and embossed pens and soft drinks. I had just reached the custodian's closet, where I had spent desperate hours with Sheldon waiting for the hall to empty, when a flustered Janice rushed to meet me. She wasn't as efficiently pretty as I remembered her to be on our first meeting, though the difference might have been mine.

'Oh, Mr Carl,' she said. 'You can't just wander around the office alone.'

I lifted my hands. 'No staplers in my pockets, honest.'

'It's policy,' she said. 'Mr Prescott is on a conference call. I'll take you to a meeting room to wait for him if you'd like.'

'That's all right, Janice,' I said as I started again toward Prescott's office, brushing past her. 'But I'll just wait with Billy. I'm sure he won't mind.'

She sort of chugged after me saying something or other, but I ignored her. Why I was being so obstreperous is clear to me now. One result of my experience at the trial was to loose some shackle from my neck. I had always felt that there was a right way to behave, a right way to dress, a right manner to affect, as if all these rights would add up to something tangible, and add up to something tangible they did. What they added up to was a slavery of the soul. I had so wanted to be them I pretended to be like them, which only made it easier for them to kick me in the groin and step on my face whenever they liked. I was playing a losing game because I was playing on their turf, by their rules, number one of which stated that they always won and I always lost. But I guess I had lost one too many times. My long bitter period of obeisance had passed. I was reveling in my freedom to be whatever I chose, even if what I chose to be was rude.

The door to his office was open a crack. With Janice just behind, I skirted her work station, pushed open the door, walked into his office, plopped down onto one of the tapestry chairs across from his desk. Prescott was sitting straight-backed in his suit jacket, talking into the phone.

When he saw me his face startled but quickly composed itself again.

Janice, in the doorway, said, 'I tried to stop him, Mr Prescott,' but Prescott waved her off and she backed out, closing the door behind her.

'Sam, Sam, Sam,' said Prescott into the phone while he smiled at me. 'We will get you everything you've asked for, I promise, but we need that opinion letter by tomorrow afternoon at the latest. We're going to the printer tomorrow night and it has to be ready by then.' He spun his finger in the air, indicating that this Sam on the other end was going on and on. He winked at me. 'Listen, Sam. I have to go, I have someone in my office. Simon and Jack, stay on the line and talk with Sam about getting him all that he needs. We'll satisfy you, Sam, but we need you to move on this, all right? Let me know before the end of the day of your progress.'

When he hung up he shook his head. 'Some lawyers are so timid about opinion letters it's amazing that any deal ever gets done. Valley Hunt Estates. We have the interim financing and we're ready to go. It's going to be a killer deal. Too bad you're not a part of it anymore.'

I shrugged.

'But you'll be gratified to know that we gave the business to your friend Sam Guthrie over at Blaine, Cox,' said Prescott. 'He, at least, seems grateful for the opportunity. So, Victor, what brings you unbidden once again to our offices?'

I reached into my briefcase and pulled out a manila envelope, which I tossed onto his desk. 'I wanted to personally serve our motion for a new trial that we're filing today with Judge Gimbel. In it I lay out in detail everything that happened from the moment I was hired to defend Chester Concannon.'

'I see,' said Prescott as he opened the envelope and scanned the lengthy motion inside. 'I expected as much. And frankly, Victor, I wish you luck. Jimmy's been acquitted in the federal trial and the murder charges against him have been dropped. Nothing would please me more than for Chester to get off also.'

'I don't think the judge will see it so benignly.'

He shrugged his shoulders as he continued leafing through the motion.

'You set me up,' I said.

'Yes,' said Prescott. 'It wasn't so hard to do.'

'You figured the only way to really clear Jimmy of the charges was to put them off on Chet, and the surest way to get the jury to believe it all was to get Chet's lawyer to do the dirty work for you. If you had called Veronica to lie on the stand it would have looked obvious and no one would have bought it. But for Chet's lawyer to put her on and to have her bury him, well, that clinched it.'

'Effective, wouldn't you say?'

'And totally improper.'

'No, Victor, that is where you're wrong. We were doing everything in our power to defend our client. The Sixth Amendment requires no less. Were you following the same high standard, hmmm?'

'It's patently improper to have a witness perjure herself, even if you don't call her.'

'But who's to say it was perjury?'

'She told me the truth when I subpoenaed her.'

'Maybe that was the lie.'

'I don't think so.'

'What you think and what you can prove are two very different things. I must say, Victor, you surprised me. The whole Veronica thing was very risky. I thought all our inducements for you to cooperate would stop you from going after Jimmy. I assumed that was our surest way to win, to just have Chester sit there and eat whatever we handed him. I hired you because I thought you'd come cheap, but Jimmy suspected you'd turn into a crusader. I guess he's a better judge of character than I. So to be safe he dangled Veronica before you just in case you decided to play it noble. It worked out better than we could have hoped. You snapped at her like a trout at a perfectly tied fly. We actually expected that she'd have to tell you everything, but your investigation was amazingly thorough. The more you found out, the easier it was for us. But then when you put her on the stand, that was the riskiest part of all. You see, Victor, you seemed to have a great influence on that poor girl, greater than you know. We weren't sure what she was going to say until she said it. Her actual testimony was a great relief to all of us.'

'You planned it all from the day you hired me.'

'From the day Pete McCrae died, yes. Pete we knew we could trust but with his inconvenient death, well, then we needed you, or someone like you. It was too big a case to count on luck. We had all kinds of strategies and contingency plans but in the end we needed something dramatic to win it, and you certainly gave us that, Victor.'

'In fact, you had been setting up Concannon even before the indictment. It was you who told Jimmy to open the bank account with Chester's name on it.'

'Now you're guessing,' said Prescott.

'It was the amount of the deposits and withdrawals that clued me. Federal regulations require cash transactions of over ten grand to be reported to the Treasury Department. Which means you knew all along that Jimmy was giving the money to Goodwin, capitalizing a drug dealer to set up a steady stream of funds for his rehabilitation projects. That's why Goodwin killed Chuckie, to keep him from telling me about it, and why Goodwin tried to stop Veronica from testifying. It must have been Henry who told Goodwin where Veronica was hiding. Goodwin sent his henchmen after her, fearing she would disclose the arrangement, not knowing all the time that she was in your pocket.'

'I'm certainly not going to confirm such scurrilous accusations,' said Prescott. 'One never knows who is taping what, hmmm? But if it all were true, think of the beauty

538

of it. Drug consumers are going to buy drugs no matter what. It is an inelastic demand. But with just a little venture capital, effectively applied, a piece of the profits of the sales would go to helping victims and to drying up the market. The more successful the marketing venture, the more active it would be in sowing the seeds of its own destruction. Pure pragmatism, Victor, a free-market solution to a previously intractable problem.'

'And the kids dying from stray bullets as Goodwin battles to expand his turf?'

'Collateral damage,' said Prescott. 'Unavoidable.'

'Jimmy is preying on the weak, profiting from murder to salve the wound of his daughter's death,' I said. 'It's immoral.'

'Morality is a mere luxury in this world, Victor,' said Prescott. 'It is the enemy of achievement, the last bastion of the failed. Learn that and someday you might learn what it is to be a lawyer.'

'If that's what it takes I'd sooner cut lawns.'

'As you wish. But I'm actually glad you're here, Victor. I've been trying to reach you.'

'I've been out of town.'

'I can understand. The embarrassment. I've talked it over with CUP and, with the trial finished, they've decided that they won't sue you for the retainer so long as you give up your claim to any additional fees.'

'That doesn't even cover half of what I'm owed.'

'Some is better than none, Victor, any day of the week.'

'I think I'll hold out for it all.'

'That's fine. I understand Sam Guthrie has already drafted the complaint.'

'So I'll counterclaim, then. Save me the filing fees.'

'You shouldn't take it all so personally, Victor. It was only business. Actually, you were better in court than I expected. It's too bad it had to conclude like it did. I'm sure we could have worked very profitably together.'

'I don't think so,' I said. 'By the way, I'll be shortly filing a motion to amend the complaint in *Saltz v. Metropolitan Investors*.'

'A little late, Victor. Trial's in less than two weeks.'

'Oh, I think the judge will let me amend the complaint to add two new defendants.'

'New defendants?' he asked, the crow's-feet around his eyes deepening. 'Who?'

'Well, Billy, I told you I was out of town. Where I was, actually, was in Corpus Christi, Texas, with my partner, visiting the Downtown Marina. Maybe you've heard of it?'

By the frozen expression on his face I could tell that he had.

'Well, it seems that our mutual accountant friend Frederick Stocker was docking his pretty new sailboat at that very marina. We showed up there just yesterday, Billy, and, in an amazing coincidence, we arrived at the marina pretty much at the same time as the FBI. And somehow in all the fuss of his arrest and my dropping a subpoena in his lap Mr Stocker seemed to think that you were somehow mixed up in the Feds finding out where he was, though I haven't a clue, really, as to how he got that idea, unless it was something I said. Do you think that might have been it?'

His whole face seemed to harden and contract, every muscle tensing one against the other. His blue eyes turned cold and steely but still he didn't move.

'Well, anyway,' I continued, 'he told a strange story about how the lawyer for the general partners in the *Saltz* partnership had an undisclosed interest in the deal and how, with the market turning against the project, he convinced the accountant to doctor up the numbers in the prospectus, promising him that no one would ever know. It was this lawyer who he says induced him to defraud my clients and then helped him hide away after he ran off with stolen money. And the funny thing, Billy, is he says that this lawyer fellow is you. Imagine that. Which is why, Billy, we're adding you and your partners as defendants.

Now I'm a realist and I figure a smart fellow like you will have shielded most of his assets, so you're probably judgment-proof. I figure the best we can do with you is to pull your ticket to practice, send you to that lucrative hell for ex-lawyers where you'll become a lobbyist or some other lowlife scavenger. But Talbott, Kittredge and Chase, why I'm betting that's a damn deep pocket.'

His face had turned a whitish gray. 'It's too late to amend,' he said. 'The statute of limitations has run.'

'Not technically. It stops running if information is denied to a party due to fraud, which your hiding of Stocker would constitute.'

'I'll beat you in court. Any day of the week.'

I stood up. 'Maybe so, but this Stocker is a very articulate man. I'm certain he'll make a fine witness.'

I turned to walk out of his office, but just before I reached the door he said with a bravado as pale as the coloring of his face, 'Victor, wait. Maybe we should talk some more.'

58

The faded blue Chevette, liberally sprinkled with rust, was parked on Chestnut Street, waiting for me as I came out of One Liberty Place after my meeting with Prescott. Chestnut Street was closed to normal street traffic at that point and a uniformed policeman was leaning in the window of the car.

'You going to ticket this wreck?' I asked the cop.

The officer leaned back and grinned at me. 'There's not enough solid metal left to pin the citation to.'

'You pull back one of those windshield wipers,' I said, 'and the rear bumper falls off.'

'Oh man,' said Slocum from inside. 'You guys should be in vaudeville. Get in, Carl, you're twenty minutes late.'

I ducked in the passenger door and the Chevette groaned forward. At 15th Street it turned right and then took another right onto Walnut, going west. 'How did your meeting with Prescott go?'

'Just fine,' I said. 'Six hundred thousand to settle a case that wasn't worth a dime two days ago.'

'You going to take it?'

'Nope. I'm going to see him and raise him,' I said. 'I appreciate you coming.'

'We'll see what she has to tell us. I have my doubts.'

'Frankly, I was surprised to see you waiting for me.'

'Yeah, well, I'm surprised I came. By the way, don't try to roll down your window. The thingamajig is broken and it collapses if you try.'

We drove past the University of Pennsylvania and then into West Philly, sagging old row houses with decaying porches, small grocery stores, a mattress outlet, seafood stores, a pool hall on the second floor of a crumbling tenement. We were in the middle of a stream of fine automobiles flowing through the synchronized lights on the one-way roadway, heading out of the city to the suburbs, where the taxes were low and the schools safe and the grass in the public parks cut biweekly.

'There are guys in the office,' volunteered Slocum, his voice soft and surprisingly serious, 'who say that anyone can convict the guilty, but only a real prosecutor can convict the innocent. I'm not one of them. Last thing I ever want to do is fry someone who didn't do it. If something smells I won't cover it up and hope nobody notices as some poor fool rots in jail; it is up to me to find out what exactly is smelling and what I need to do about it.'

'What smells in your murder case against Concannon?'

'I had no choice but to drop the indictment against Councilman Moore,' said Slocum. 'After the testimony of your brilliant witness the DA herself ordered the case dismissed. But I heard your little friend testify and if you ask me she was lying. The DA wants me to put her on the stand to hammer the last nail in your boy's coffin. The thought of it makes me sick.'

'You should go into private practice,' I said with a bitter laugh, 'where anything goes and there's nothing to trouble your conscience except where to cash your checks. Maybe then you could buy yourself a car with a window that actually goes up and down.'

'Wouldn't know how to handle all that luxury. Besides, the knife you gave me seems actually to have been the one that sliced Chuckie Lamb's throat. There was blood on the spring. What tests we could do showed it matched his type. We're holding Wayman right now. Someone sure did a number on him before we got there.'

'So you're maybe starting to believe the stories I've been spinning?'

'I'm starting to listen. That's as much as you're going to get.'

'That's all I want,' I said.

When Walnut Street ended he turned right onto 63rd Street, dipped under the tracks of the Market Street elevated, and headed north, alongside trolley tracks, past dark decrepit houses into the dark fall night.

'So what I'm saying,' he went on, 'is that I'm willing to go this far with you because I think it's my job to find the truth. But no further. I'm going to catch hell for this as it is when word gets out, which it will, and it might even cost me my job. My boss was an obscure common pleas judge before Moore put her up for DA. Now she thinks she's going to be a senator.'

'I appreciate it,' I said.

'I'm not doing it for you. I'm not even doing it for Concannon. But I'm not going in front of a jury to ask for death if I'm not sure.'

We were in Wynnefield now, still the city but there were no longer row houses along the dark wide streets, instead large stone homes with wide porches and peaked roofs. There were lawns and nice cars and, though it was all just a little shabby from age, even the shabbiness was a nice touch. Slocum pulled up in front of a large stone colonial with stained-glass windows across the front door. There were bright lights gleaming from the top of the house, illuminating the broad front lawn, and the windows were lit as if a party was roaring inside.

'You been here before?' I asked.

'Fund-raisers,' he said. 'It's better to shell out now and then to the boys in power than to be ringing up headhunters.'

He slipped out of his car and I followed, carrying my briefcase with the bullet hole in one flank. At the door with the stained-glass windows Slocum stepped aside so that I could do the knocking. 'It's your show,' he said.

I lifted the large brass knocker with the head of a lion and let it drop.

There was nothing for a few minutes and I dropped the

knocker twice more before the door opened slowly. It was Renee, Leslie Moore's sister, dressed in jeans and a sweat-shirt, her face heavy with liquor. No late night on the town for her tonight. 'Well, lookee here, it's that thief Chester Concannon's lawyer,' she said, swinging slightly as she leaned on the door. 'Sorry, Mr Carl, but Jimmy's not here right now. Maybe you should come back in your next life.'

'I'm not here to see Jimmy, Renee. I'm here to see Leslie.'

'She's not here either,' she said in thickened syllables, but her glance back and to the left gave her away.

'Why don't you ask her if she'll talk to me,' I said.

'No, I won't,' said Renee, but even as she said it the slight figure of Leslie Moore, in print dress and low heels, her arms crossed tightly across her chest, appeared behind her.

'I thought you'd come,' said Leslie softly. 'I just didn't know when.'

I looked up at Renee and she shrugged in resignation and swung with the door as it opened, letting Slocum and me inside.

Leslie took our coats and led us to a formal living room with red walls and fancy couches. The fabrics were striped and elegant, with maroons and hunter greens and golds, and underneath everything was a rich oriental carpet in a deep navy blue. Everything was in place in this room, the prints of hummingbirds in the gold-leaf frames, the formal photographs on the end tables. There were no bottles or half-drunken glasses or any signs of recent habitation. This was the room where Jimmy hit up the wealthy for contri-butions, where the show was put on. There was another room somewhere in that large stone house, I was sure, where Renee and Leslie did their drinking when the coun-cilman was out on the town without them, and that room was undoubtedly not so tidy.

Slocum and I sat side by side on a couch. Leslie sat across from us on a thin upholstered chair, Louis the Something

I figured. Renee stood alongside the now cold fireplace like the lord of the manor. There was a long moment of silence.

'Can I get you something to drink?' asked Leslie finally.

'No, thank you,' said Slocum.

'Coffee would be great,' I said. I was in no hurry to leave.

Leslie looked up at Renee, who widened her eyes and then gave her a little snort.

'Excuse me,' said Leslie, and she left to make the coffee.

'The councilman's in Chicago,' said Renee.

'I know,' I said.

'Of course you know. You wouldn't have the guts to show up here if he was in town.'

I shrugged.

'He's at the National Urban Conference. He's a featured speaker. He's going to be on the dais with the President.'

'Imagine that,' I said. 'The same President whose administration indicted him for extortion and racketeering just six months ago.'

'Well, now that that little misunderstanding is cleared up, thanks to you,' said Renee with a drunken sneer, 'I guess the President is starting to think about the twenty-three electoral votes that might just hinge on the half-million voters that CUP can deliver.'

'I didn't know you were so politically keen, Renee.'

'Someone has to watch his back from the vipers out to bring him down. That's why you're here, isn't it? But you're too late. They're together again, like lovebirds. She's moved back into his room, so your little scheme's not going to work.'

'We're just here to ask some questions,' said Slocum.

'Oh, I know who you are, Mr District Attorney. You should be ashamed, all that Jimmy's done for your people and now you plotting with this shyster.'

Slocum slowly took off his glasses and lifted the end of his tie to wipe off the lenses. Very carefully he cleaned, first one side, then the other, then the first again. He put his glasses back on. In the time it took to clean his glasses the jumble of quivering muscle at the edge of his jaw subsided. With his glasses back on he said calmly, 'I don't plot. And the only shameful thing in this room, ma'am, is you.'

'I made some for you, too, Mr Slocum,' said Leslie, bringing in a tray with a porcelain teapot and four matching cups.

'Thank you,' he said.

She poured three cups. We both leaned forward to pick up a cup and saucer and then leaned back into the couch. Renee stayed by the fireplace, now seeming to inspect the mantelshelf for cracks with her fingertips.

'I'm here to take you up on your promise, Mrs Moore,' I said before taking a sip of the coffee.

'She didn't make any promise to you,' said Renee sharply.

'No, Renee,' I said. 'I'm sorry but you're mistaken. I know you saw us talking in the courtroom hallway, and I assume you spread the word to the councilman, which may explain certain things, but you did not hear what we said to each other. Only Leslie and I know what was said and what she promised.'

'Would you like some sugar with that, Mr Slocum?' asked Leslie.

'No, thank you,' he said.

'I must admit,' I continued, 'I was confused for a while. It was Chuckie's murder and my being shot at that confused me. You see, when you told me that you had heard the voices on the wind and that you wouldn't let them kill Chester, I had assumed you were referring to the same people who had killed Chuckie and were maybe trying to kill me too. At that time I had thought that maybe your husband was in some way responsible for Chuckie's death and for the attempts on my life and that somehow you had stumbled on that information. I have since learned that I was mistaken. Chuckie was killed by a drug dealer whose operation is being financed by your husband.'

'Lies,' hissed Renee. 'All lies.'

547

'He joined with the devil,' I said, 'to build his monument to Nadine.'

Mrs Moore didn't seem flustered in the least by the accusation. 'Some cream, Mr Slocum?' she said. 'Or would you prefer tea?'

'No, thank you,' said Slocum. 'This is fine.'

'And at the trial,' I continued, 'to my chagrin, I learned I was being set up as a dupe by your husband and his lawyer. No one ever tries to kill their dupe. Dead I was of no use to them, alive I could set him free, which I eventually did. So, while I was on a recent trip down South I began to wonder who it was you were promising to protect Chester from.'

'What kind of nonsense are you talking to us about, Mr Carl?' asked Renee.

'Oh, Leslie understands exactly what I'm saying, Renee.'

'How about some cookies, Mr Slocum?' said Leslie. 'I have some fine cookies in the pantry. Let me get them for you.'

'No, thank you, ma'am,' said Slocum. 'Really, I'm fine.'

'Chet's in jail now,' I said. 'His bail has been revoked. He is awaiting sentencing on the federal charges, preparing for his trial in state court on the murder charge. I visited him just yesterday. He is not adjusting well. He is a little too thin, a little too handsome, which is a very bad combination in prison. During our conversation he almost broke down into tears. You know Chet, you know his self-control. He is cracking. He is of no consequence anymore in the larger scheme of things, a threat to no one. There is only one man who is trying to kill him now.'

I took another sip of my coffee, staring at Leslie even as I tilted my head down to the cup. Her eyes were moist, cast downward, and her hands nervously clutched one the other.

'In another month,' I said, 'Chet is going to stand trial for murder. Mr Slocum is going to prosecute the case. He is going to ask the jury to sentence Chet to death. And I believe, Mrs Moore, you can stop Mr Slocum from killing Chet Concannon, just like you promised.'

After a long pause, Leslie said, 'Renee, please, why don't you get yourself another drink.'

'I think I should stay right here,' she said, 'and keep my eye on Mr Carl, make sure he doesn't steal the ashtrays.'

'Get the drink, Renee,' Leslie said, her voice suddenly filled with an authority I didn't know she could muster.

Renee shrugged and headed out to that other, less tidy room.

When she had left Leslie said, 'I can't tell you what you want to know, Mr Carl.'

'You mean you won't.'

'We have had difficult times in our marriage, I won't deny that. And after Nadine's death, for the longest time there was nothing left for either of us. I can understand now how he could seek comfort with that girl. But the ordeal of this trial has resurrected our commitment to each other. We have gone to counseling, we have opened our hearts to one another. It has changed both our lives, I am sure. It is as it was when we were first starting out together. In fact, it is better.'

'Chester Concannon is going to be put to death with a lethal injection, Mrs Moore,' I said.

'We have both learned again what it means to give, to cherish one another, to trust.'

'They're going to strap him to a gurney, tightly binding his arms and legs with leather straps,' I said, 'and stick a needle in his arm. And attached to that needle will be an intravenous sack filled with a deadly barbiturate, the fluid laced with a chemical paralytic agent to make sure he doesn't jerk the needle out of his arm as they kill him.'

'We have both learned again what it is to love.'

'They're going to empty that sack into his arm,' I said, 'and his muscles will freeze and his brain will slow from the drugs and Chester Concannon will fall into unconsciousness and die from barbiturates just like Nadine fell into unconsciousness and died from barbiturates.'

'Stop it, stop it now,' she said and then, still without looking at me, in a whisper, 'You don't understand. We have renewed our vows to each other, we have reaffirmed our commitments. He will no longer cheat on me, he has promised, and I will love him again, as I had loved him before I stopped loving him. We are together again, I can't turn against him now.'

'You mean you won't.'

Her head lifted and she stared squarely at me. 'That's right, Mr Carl, I won't. I can't be forced to testify against my husband, is that right, Mr Slocum?'

'That is correct, Mrs Moore,' said Slocum. 'We cannot force you to testify against your husband. But what we are talking about here is testifying in favor of Mr Concannon.'

'And you would want me to testify?'

'I don't want to kill an innocent man,' said Slocum.

'Then let him go.'

'I can't, Mrs Moore, without evidence. Right now, as it stands, I believe I'm going to convict him of first degree murder.'

'I'm sorry, Mr Carl. I am so sorry.'

'So am I,' I said, reaching for my briefcase. 'Sorrier than you can know.'

I placed the briefcase on my lap, bullet hole side up. It was a brown leather number, with thick strips binding the edges, a Hartmann, one of the finest cases made. It was a gift, from my uncle Sammy, a message of his faith in my future. It was a solid briefcase, the briefcase of a successful lawyer. I used to like heaving it around, as if the accoutrements could define the man. Now it embarrassed me. All the more for what it contained. I freed the leather straps guarding the latches and opened the case. From inside I pulled out a manila envelope. Carefully I closed the case and placed it on the rug beside the couch and unfastened the metal clasp holding the envelope shut. Then I brought out the photographs.

Morris had had them taken for me. He had complained about the assignment. 'I don't do such stuff, prowling with a camera in the dead of night,' he said. 'I am an investigator, not a piece of dreck.' But when I told him what it was all about and how a man's life might depend on those photographs, and how I was out of town in Corpus Christi and couldn't do it myself, he relented. 'There might be nothing, you know that, Victor, nothing at all.' I told him I knew that, but that I had a hunch. 'You and your hunches, where have your hunches gotten you, mine *freint*. Take my advice, and keep your hunches away from the racetrack and maybe you won't die a beggar.' Of course he had not taken the photographs himself, as he might have been recognized, but he gave the assignment to Sheldon. 'All the stuff he has,' said Morris. 'These fancy-schmancy cameras, lenses like telescopes, special meters like from NASA, special filters, special film, a regular Eisenstadt. So tell me, Victor, why when it's time for a picture of me and mine wife, the heads he cuts off like an executioner.' But in these photographs, Sheldon had not cut off the heads.

I placed the first on the coffee table, facing Leslie.

It was a high-resolution black-and-white photograph from inside one of the terminals still under renovation at the Philadelphia International Airport. Gate D5, a United Airlines gate, where two attendants were taking tickets at the counter and handing out seat assignments. On the board was listed Flight 595 to Chicago, leaving 4:55 p.m. In front of the counter, posing for the photographer, was a man holding up a copy of the *Daily News*. The headline running the entire length of the page read, EAGLES SACK PACK, touting the Eagles' great surge to .500 on the preceding Sunday.

'This was taken Monday at the airport,' I said.

'And?' asked Leslie.

Slocum too was looking at me, wondering what I was doing.

The next picture was of the same counter, with the same

551

attendants. To the side of the counter was a barrel-chested man in a belted raincoat, a garment bag hanging by a long strap from his shoulder. The man was Jimmy Moore.

'This is the flight he took Monday,' I said, 'to get him to Chicago for the first day of the conference.'

'That's right,' said Leslie. 'He called me from the airport to say good-bye. To say he loved me and missed me already.'

'Yes, I'm not surprised,' I said, showing her the next photograph.

It was a wide-angle shot of the same terminal, the counter now on the right and Jimmy sitting on a chair in the waiting lounge, talking on his cellular phone.

'I don't understand your point, Mr Carl,' she said.

'I want you to look at the counter, Mrs Moore. Do you see the woman there, in the heavy overcoat, with her back to us, getting ticketed?'

'And?'

I showed her the next picture. An announcement had been made and the first-class passengers had been asked to board. Jimmy was handing his ticket to an attendant at the mouth of the ramp. The woman in the overcoat was still getting ticketed at the counter.

Without saying anything I placed the next photograph before her. The corners of the prior photographs peeked out from the edges of the latest. Jimmy Moore had boarded, he was no longer in the photograph. The woman at the counter had received her seat assignment and boarding pass and had turned to leave the counter. Just as she was leaving the counter she had taken a glance behind her, looking left over her shoulder and the moment of that glance was when Sheldon had snapped the shutter. Her face was clearly visible in the photograph. It was Veronica Ashland.

I couldn't bear to look at Mrs Moore as she examined that photograph. I heard her breathing, soft and steady, and the scrape of teeth.

I took out the last photograph and placed it atop the picture with Veronica's face. In this final photograph Veronica, her back again turned to us, was handing her boarding pass to the attendant at the mouth of the gate.

'It could be a coincidence,' said Leslie, her voice as weak as a whisper.

'Yes, it could,' I said.

I reached for the photographs to place them back in the envelope, but she tapped my wrist and I let my hand drop. She pulled out the next to last photograph and stared at it, stared at the beautiful face glancing over her left shoulder, soft hair, rounded, gentle nose, limpid eyes wide and scared, as if their owner could feel the camera capturing her image.

'You are despicable, Mr Carl,' said Leslie Moore, and she was absolutely right.

When I had pulled this selfsame trick on Winston Osbourne at that deposition of his wife I had thought myself a very clever young man. In those heady days of my still aspiring youth I viewed myself incapable of the fatal folly and thus felt morally justified to present the bill to others. But I could feel no such justification now. How could I accuse Jimmy Moore of moral failure in continuing on with Veronica Ashland when I had hung my coat and my ethics on a post outside that very same door? And how could I blithely ever sit across the table and inflict the pain I was inflicting when I now knew exactly what that pain felt like? To see that photograph of Veronica, with whom, in my seemingly infinite capacity for self-delusion, I had still hoped for some future, to see Veronica checking onto that plane to continue her affair with the murderous Jimmy Moore was almost more than I could bear. And finally, how could I ever again muster the self-righteousness needed to present the fruits of another's folly when I had been guilty of a folly so grand as to send a man to prison and possibly to death? I was despicable and the photographs I had brought would have stained my hands with their sordidness if I hadn't felt so sordid already.

But there was a difference between my exposure of Tiffany LeGrand to Mrs Osbourne and the exposure of the continuing relationship between Jimmy and Veronica to Mrs Moore. I had exposed the exotic existence of Ms LeGrand, destroyed a marriage, destroyed a man, spread pain and disillusionment, for money. I wouldn't do that again, I swore, not for mere riches, I swore, though all the time I was swearing I knew that mammon has its power over all of us. The photographs I had brought to Mrs Moore were not about money, they were about a man's life, an innocent man in jail facing death, a man whom I had failed, and so, though I knew I was stooping, I would stoop as low as I was able. I had no more pride left, no more false notions of self-importance. I would crawl on my belly like a reptile if it would save Chester Concannon, and crawling I was.

By the time Renee had returned Leslie had fled the room, her thin writhing hands clutched around her neck.

'Where's Leslie gone off to now?' said a slurring Renee, with a half-empty highball glass in her hand.

'I don't know exactly,' I said. 'She told us to wait.'

Renee looked at me and then at Slocum and then she spied the photographs still piled on the coffee table. She stepped over and sat down and went through them one by one, in reverse order, like watching a horror movie backwards.

'You bastards,' she said. 'You goddamn bastards.' She stood up. 'I won't let you get away with it.'

As she was leaving the room Slocum said in his calm voice, 'You know what obstruction of justice is, ma'am?'

She stopped and turned to stare at him.

'About five years is what it is,' he said.

Before she could respond Leslie had come back into the room, clutching a crumpled brown paper bag. Her eyes were red, her face puffy from her tears so that her sharp cheekbones had softened. She threw the bag into my chest.

'Take it and go,' she said.

I looked inside. It was a white shirt, crusted and torn, splattered with the dark maroon of dried blood. On the sleeve was embroidered JDM.

We took it and went.

'We'll send the shirt over to the lab,' said Slocum as he let me out of the car outside my apartment. 'Check out the blood. I'll let you know in a few days whether there's a match with Bissonette.'

'It will match,' I said. 'Down to the last guanine rung of the DNA ladder.'

'Even so, Concannon will still end up serving most of his federal time.'

'I know,' I said. 'And between you and me, his fund-raising was more extortion than anything else, so it's not totally undeserved. But he shouldn't die for killing a man he didn't kill.'

We looked at each other for a moment. 'You did good tonight, Carl,' said Slocum.

'Then how come I don't feel good?'

'You didn't tell that lady anything she didn't already know.'

I shrugged sadly and headed up the steps to my building. Slocum was waiting for me to go inside, as if he were dropping off a baby-sitter. I opened the door to my vestibule and waved him away. The Chevette ground its gears and pulled off into the night.

When I turned to enter the vestibule Winston Osbourne was standing there before me, like the ghost of all my past transgressions.

'Victor. I've been waiting so long for you.'

He was shaking with a ferocious chill, his hands jammed into his raincoat, his sallow, hollowed face staring at me, cocked at a crazed angle.

'Victor,' he said in his shaky, lockjawed Brahmin voice. 'I've come for my car. Give me back my car.'

'Mr Osbourne, Winston,' I said once my nerves had settled from the surprise. 'I'm glad to see you, actually. I have good news for you.'

'Give me back my car.'

I closed my eyes in sadness. 'I'm sorry, Mr Osbourne. It's been sold already. But the good news is that I've talked everything over with Mr Sussman and he's willing to forgive the rest of your debt. I have to sign a few papers and satisfy the judgments on you, but then you'll be perfectly free to start over again.'

'But where am I to go, Victor? How can I get from point A to point B without my father's car? It is a straight line, yes, a direct route, but I need my car to get there. What would you have me do, Victor?'

'There's always the subway.'

'Don't mock me.'

'I'm sorry, Mr Osbourne. I truly am, more than you know. You look cold, not well. Come on upstairs and I'll make you some tea if you want. But with regard to your finances, there is nothing more I can do for you.'

'You can give me back my car.'

'I can't do that, it's been sold already and the new owners have good title under the law.'

'Then you can waltz with me, Victor,' he said and he pulled out a small, shiny automatic pistol from the pocket of his raincoat.

I stared at the pistol for a moment, the gun shaking wildly in his palsied hand, his opaque, striated fingernails grown even longer than I remembered. I was transfixed by the pistol until all the fear seemed to bleed out of me. I raised my head and looked into his eyes. They were sallow, shot through with lightning streaks of blood. They darted back and forth, as uncontrolled as his hand. Then I couldn't help myself. I started laughing.

While I had been feeling sorry for him he had been

shooting at me. No wonder he missed, his hand shaking like that, uncontrollable, wild. It was too pathetic for me to even have considered before. But at the same time I realized there was a purer justice at work here than I could have fathomed. I should have realized long before that if I were to be killed it would not be the Jimmy Moores or the Enrico Raffaellos or even the Norvel Goodwins who would do the killing. It would be the scion of the Osbournes, the grandly Protestant, socially registered Osbournes, who would do me in. With a silver bullet, no doubt, for how else do you kill a Jew? And I deserved it, too, for the temerity to even consider joining their club. Here was Winston Osbourne, with his little pistol and his silver bullet, out to finish that dream forever, as if it could have survived my failures, as if I even wanted it anymore, as if it ever had worth. So I laughed, hard and loud. I threw my head back and laughed at everything I had ever wished for, ever wanted, all my deepest, shallowest desires. I stepped back and leaned against the wall of mailboxes and laughed.

It felt good, too, until he shot me.

59

The good news, I suppose, is that it didn't kill me.

The bad news is that it really hurt a lot.

The bullet went into my chest just below my right shoulder and smashed through a few underdeveloped muscles, including the pectoralis minor, the name of which I considered an insult and tried to convince the doctor to change to something like pectoralis mucho grande, though she didn't seem amused. After it ripped through my pectoralis mucho grande the bullet hit a rib, bounced around a bit, and clipped off a piece of my right lung. That would explain the sucking sound I heard as I slid down the wall of the vestibule; it was air seeping out of my lung, causing a condition called pneumothorax. What happened then is that my lung filled with blood. That was like drowning in ten feet of water without needing goggles to see the world slipping away.

Winston Osbourne could have finished me off right there. I was not one of those heroes who, with a chest full of lead, was ready to fight his way out of a jam. One little .38 slug and I was slumped on the floor of the vestibule in shock, bleeding, breathing the sharp smell of saltpeter into my remaining operative lung, waiting to be finished off. But for some reason, maybe the tremendous report of the shot ringing in that tiny vestibule or the sight of me sliding down the wall with a bullet in my chest or the blood and urine pooling around me, I never knew, but for some reason after that first shot he ran.

I was found by one of the older divorced women who lived in my building, coming down the stairs, cocked forward at the waist with caution, a broom in her hand held like a baseball bat, investigating the gunshot. It was nice of her to call the ambulance and save my life, but I would have preferred if she hadn't screamed so loudly when she discovered me lying there. I jerked involuntarily at the sound and that hurt as much as the gunshot itself.

Have I mentioned that I don't do well with pain?

The pathetic history of my life didn't pass before my eyes as I lay in that vestibule. That treat waited until I was in Graduate Hospital, out of intensive care, ready to receive a seemingly endless stream of visitors. The shooting was in the paper, front page of the *Daily News*, CONCANNON LAWYER BLASTED AGAIN, and so they came, one after the other, old friends from high school, old lovers, my ex-fiancée Julie, who is now unhappily married to a proctologist, yes there is a God, lawyers with whom I had tangled in court, law school classmates who had achieved a success I couldn't match, Rita, Vimhoff, Ellie, Guthrie that bastard, Lauren, Dominic and Jasper and Virgil, trundling in loudly together like the Three Stooges, Saltz, Lefkowitz, Judge Gimbel, Slocum, even the mayor, with television cameras in tow.

Beth came every day after work and sat by my bed during visiting hours. She was there when my test results for HIV came back negative and we each raised a urine-colored apple juice in gratitude to whatever angel had been looking out for me. We talked about the *Saltz* case, and how much money we'd earn, and then we talked about how, after my debacle in the *Concannon* case, I'd never get another client. I had a rich dim future ahead of me, which, as I lay in that bed, fighting off an infection in my chest, pus draining like curdled milk from a tube running out of the side, didn't seem so bad. She visited as regularly as a relative, Beth did, which was nice of her since my mother decided not to come in from Arizona, seeing that I survived and all, though she assured me in the letter that she would have dropped everything for my funeral. My father visited only now and then to grumble.

'What's that you got there?' he said, pointing to a large book that lay on my bed table.

'A get-well gift from a friend,' I said. 'Someone who knew Grandpop. It's the first book of the Talmud.'

'Who the hell would give you something like that?'

'He's a private investigator. He thought it would be good for me. The start of my education. I might like it, who knows? It's mostly translated into English, though there's still some Hebrew, and your favorite language, Aramaic.'

'My father wasted his time on that crap.'

'Really?'

'I remember he read it every Saturday and then, when he was already in his sixties, he finished the last book and threw a party. A lot of smelly old men smoking cigars and farting.'

'What did he do on Saturdays after he finished?'

'He started over again, volume one, page one.'

So that's what I did in the hospital, I read Morris's Talmud, starting, like my grandfather, at volume one, page one. There was a section in Hebrew in the middle and then a translation with commentaries surrounding it, all in English except for those from some guy Rashi, who wrote in his own alphabet that they didn't bother to translate. It was all about property and contracts and torts, like the first year of law school, except it was different in a strange soulful way. The first section was about a piece of cloth claimed by two men. Cut it in half, the book said. Sounded right to me.

In my first week back at Derringer and Carl I had a visitor, a Michael Tombelli from down on Two Street in South Philly. He was a dark young man with a scary smile and thick belly. He sat down across from me with a sneer, leaned back, and put his feet on my desk.

'I got a little problem, Vic.'

'Call me Mr Carl, Michael,' I said. 'And take your feet off my desk.'

'Sure thing,' he said with his smile as his feet dropped loudly. 'A couple days ago I get stopped by the cops on Oregon Avenue.'

'Were you speeding?'

'Sort of.'

'Pay the fine,' I advised.

'Yeah, right, well, I would, sure, but then they tell me the car is stolen.'

'Imagine that.'

'You borrow a car from a friend and look what happens.'

'So you're up for grand theft auto, is that the story?'

'And they find a gun in the trunk.'

'A pistol?'

'A Chinese MAK-90 assault rifle modified for fully automatic performance.'

'You're a deer hunter, I suppose?'

'You'd be surprised how fast those suckers can run.'

'And still, with all these problems, you are walking around, eating cheese steaks, grabbing a beer at the corner tavern?'

'The prison cap.'

'Such a wonderful thing for nice young men like yourself. You're right, Michael, you do have a problem. So what are you doing here?'

'I need a lawyer.'

'Yes, you do, Michael. But I haven't been so successful on the criminal side. I'm sticking to civil law from now on.'

'What, you're not going to take my case?'

'That's right. Now, after you get out of jail, if you want to sue the friend who lent you the stolen car with the automatic rifle inside, give me a call and I'll see what I can do.'

'But I was sent.'

'You were sent?'

'Yeah. I was sent. The man told me to come here and that you should become my lawyer.'

'The man sent you. What man?'

'The big guy.'

'I'm supposed to guess, is that it, Michael? This man who sent you, he was big as in tall or as in fat?'

'Now I know you're putting me on. Mr Raffaello sent me, said you would take care of me, said you owed him a favor.'

'Oh,' I said slowly. 'That man.'

'He told me to give you this.' He reached into his brown leather bomber jacket and pulled out a stack of bills, green and dirty, bound with a rubber band. He tossed the stack onto my desk. I didn't reach for it.

'What's that, Michael?'

'Ten thou. He told me to give it to you, like an up-front fee.'

'My retainer?'

'Yeah. That's it. Your retainer.'

I knew it would come, I just didn't know when or what. I thought maybe I'd get a call in the middle of the night, a soft voice telling me to show up at some deserted corner in South Philly for my instructions. I had already decided I wouldn't kill anybody for him; but I had also decided that I would do anything short of that. The surreptitious delivery, the stashing of stolen goods, the hiding of a fugitive until the heat died down. I owed Enrico Raffaello, yes I did, and even though it hadn't turned out well for me it was a debt I would have to repay. I was almost disappointed that repaying my debt would be so pedestrian – represent Michael Tombelli and I was off the hook.

'Hey,' said Michael. 'You're the guy shot by the wacko they stuck in that loony bin up there in Haverford.'

'That's right,' I said.

He leaned forward. 'What did it feel like, getting shot and all?'

'I figure you'll find out for yourself someday, Michael.'

'Not me. I'm too smart for any of that. But my buddy

562

Peter Cressi, he plays it so far to the edge you never know. You know Peter?'

'I haven't had the pleasure.'

'He's coming in too, today or tomorrow. Nothing serious, just a DUI. But he'll be back. He's the guy what they should put up in the loony bin.'

'Tell me something, Michael,' I said. 'Am I on a list of some sort now? Are your friends going to keep coming in to see me?'

'You bet, Mr Carl. The word's out that you're the guy when we have our little problems.' His smile again. 'You're going to be busier'n shit.'

'Now I understand,' I said, and I did. No more worrying about my future, it was set in Carrara marble. 'All right. Michael, here's the word, and you should tell it to your friend Peter and anyone else who is going to come visiting. The law says I can't accept any money that is the fruit of an illegal transaction, so any money you give me has to be clean. You understand what I just said?'

He scrunched up his eyes and rubbed the back of his hand across his nose and then said, 'Sure, yeah.'

'Is this money from a drug transaction?' I asked.

'Hey, wait, what do you take me for?'

'Is this money stolen?'

'Get out of here. Rest assured, Mr Carl, I work hard for my money.'

'Knowing the law as well as you do, can I, in good conscience, take this money, Michael?'

'Trust me, Mr Carl,' he said with his broad smile.

I looked at him very carefully, weighed everything, and then I took hold of the bundle of bills and placed it in my desk drawer. 'Wait just a second,' I said as I reached into my drawer for some letterhead, 'while I write up a receipt.'

'Receipt?' he said, as if he had never heard of the word before. 'What's with the receipt? I paid you cash.'

'Lawyers who don't give receipts for cash sometimes

have the peculiar problem of forgetting to report the payments to the IRS.'

'Yeah, isn't that funny,' said Michael Tombelli. 'That's what happened to my last lawyer. He just got four years.'

'First I'll write out your receipt, Michael,' I said, 'and then we'll discuss what to tell the District Attorney.'

So that was that. I had once aspired to walk among the paneled corridors of wealth and power with the elite names of the legal world. I had wanted to shed my past and my heritage as a snake sheds its skin and ascend to Olympian heights. Now I would skulk around the City Hall courtrooms, representing baby mobsters and other lowlifes as they tried to minimize their jail time for their petty and not-so-petty crimes, socking away my retainers and advising my dear clients how to stay just to the right side of that narrow and shifting line. I knew what life was like for a lawyer who represented the members of the mob. It was no different than for a lawyer like Tony Baloney, who spent his life defending drug dealing scum. He was scorned by his fellow practitioners, excluded from the finer firms, from the prestigious clubs, from the sober-minded committees of the bar association. Aspersions were cast as to his integrity, his veracity, his fitness to stand before the bar. He was investigated relentlessly by the District Attorney, he was hunted like wild game by federal authorities, his taxes were audited each and every year. He became a pariah.

I had found my calling.

HardScape

Justin Scott

'Some books excite, some delight; this contrives to do both.'
Observer

The first Ben Abbott mystery, a masterful story full of atmosphere and unforgettable characters.

Benjamin Abbott was a Wall Street trader whose high-powered activities got him sent away for a spell. Coming home to the small Connecticut town where he grew up, Ben turns to his family's real estate business. Then a New York City private detective hires him to train a camcorder on a bedroom in the 'castle' built by newcomers Jack and Rita Long, where the ravishing Rita betrays her husband. But a murder wasn't part of the deal. And now Ben Abbott, real estate agent, finds himself as a reluctant private investigator.

'A first-class novel that is far more than a detective story. It is filled with real people, wit and wise observations on post-eighties America. A delicious put-your-feet-up-and-don't-disturb-me weekend read.'   ERIC LUSTBADER

'Scott writes wisely and wittily about post-1980s America and the caste-ridden community of Newbury. The plot is a cracker and in Ben he has the perfect narrating participant, shrewd, compassionate and profoundly engaging.'
Sunday Times

ISBN 0 00 647711 9